THE DAMNABLE LEGACY OF A MINISTER'S WIFE

A Novel

G. Elizabeth Kretchmer

The characters and events in this book are fictitious. Any similarities to any persons, living or dead, are coincidental. Although factual information contained herein is intended to be reliable as it is based on extensive research, the author cannot guarantee absolute accuracy and apologizes for any unintentional errors or omissions.

Cover art by Laura Paslay
Cover design by Visual Quill

THE DAMNABLE LEGACY OF A MINISTER'S WIFE
G. Elizabeth Kretchmer. -- 1st ed.
ISBN 978-0-9961038-0-0

In memory of those loved ones
who left this earthly life
with unfinished hopes, dreams, and plans.

You know who you are.

Those who believe in God would say this was all part of His or Her plan. Those who don't would say this was simply the way life goes: a combination of ambition, choice, good and bad luck. And those in between, my sisters and brothers in agnosticism, would spend eternity never knowing what to think. Maybe it doesn't matter. What happened happened, and there wasn't a damn thing I could have done about it.

~Beth

Out
Of a great need
We are all holding hands
And climbing.
Not loving is a letting go.
Listen,
The terrain around here
Is Far too
Dangerous
For That.

~Hafiz, 14th century poet

1 Chapter One

She faced the lone gray wolf with a cold stare, mirroring the animal's own haunting gaze and confirming what I'd known all along. Lynn Van Swol was comfortable in wild territory, composed in the face of danger, unencumbered by fear. And she wasn't even fifty yet. In other words, she would be the perfect grandmother for a troubled teen like Frankie.

But there was much to be done before that day would come. For now, Lynn needed to get past this gorgeous and terrifying fur-clad adversary. When she first spotted it, she stopped immediately, probably assuming—as I had—that it was someone's dog whose owner would soon appear on the trail as well. But it only took a couple of heartbeats for me to realize this was no average dog.

It was a she-wolf, standing in the middle of Lynn's favorite running trail in the heart of Portland's West Hills, which wasn't exactly wolf territory. Its fur was thick and wet, mottled in shades of silver and gray with a hint of brown at the base of the fur; its legs were long, its paws huge. And the eyes were a piercing, hungry shade of amber. A numbing April rain slanted at both Lynn and the wolf like pinpoint darts as they studied one another, sizing up the situation, neither of them showing a speck of fear. From what I knew, wolves don't want to be seen by humans; they might follow you from the shadows, lurking like cancer cells, but they're unlikely to come right out in the open. And most people will naturally experience a rush of fear in the face of a dangerous beast. But this must not have been your typical wolf, and Lynn was surely not a normal person. This was no doubt just another ho-hum instance of woman versus nature for Lynn. Another day to be patient, logical, calm.

Of course, we climbers are trained to be patient, logical, and calm. And when it comes right down to it, climbers and wolves have a lot in common. Both wait for opportunity. Likewise, it only takes one wrong move to ruin the plans of climber or wolf. I had big plans for Lynn that I'd set into motion before my death, and now that I watched from the safe distance of my empty afterlife, there would be nothing I could do to change those plans if the wolf interfered. All I could do was hope for the best.

A twig snapped somewhere. The animal's nose twitched. I don't know what it detected—I smelled only musky, wet fur. It lifted its nose upward and for a moment I thought it sensed my presence. But of course it couldn't do that; I knew by now I was invisible to the living. The wolf took a few steps forward, so that it stood only a few yards from Lynn.

It was time for Lynn to take charge. She slipped the straps of her cinch bag off her shoulders and pulled out a Clif bar. When she ripped the package open, the scent of peanut butter and chocolate erased the smell of wet fur and tantalized me. The wolf, too, apparently. It sniffed the air again and perked its ears. It licked its lips. What did Lynn think she was doing? For a slick second, I decided she was insane, until she flung the bar into the forest. The wolf startled, and I figured this was the end.

They both watched the food's trajectory, then returned their gazes upon one another. The wolf took another step toward Lynn.

"Okay, then let's try this," she said, her voice strong, steady, and deep, not wavering in the slightest.

After retrieving a polyurethane bottle from her bag, she took a long swig of water—another luxury of the living—while keeping her gaze directly on the wolf's eyes. I wondered if that was the right thing to do. With some animals, you're supposed to avoid any such exchange, even a glance.

"You're probably going to destroy this," she said to the wolf. "But here you go anyway." She turned away from the animal and hurled the bottle into the forest in the same direction as the Clif bar, her pitch athletic and firm. The bottle thwacked against the trunk of a Douglas fir, then ricocheted off. "Now go on," she said. "Go on!"

When the wolf lunged, I nearly fell back in fright. But it headed away from Lynn, into the dense brush to sniff out its prize. Lynn watched for a moment and then, seemingly unfazed, picked up her cinch bag and hung it from her shoulders. She licked the sticky residue of the energy bar off her fingers and began to run again, in the same direction she'd been heading all along. She didn't turn back, not even once, to see if the wolf followed.

2 Chapter Two

Moonlight stole into Frankie's bedroom around the edges of the cracked window shades. She lay on her side, one arm draped over the edge of her bed. The light illuminated several parallel cuts on her forearm like stripes on a tabby's tail, and it pained me to see the damage she'd done to her otherwise beautiful skin. I almost felt nauseated, the way I used to feel after each chemo treatment.

Nearly a year ago, Frankie had told me not to think of them as scars. "They're more like tattoos, or beauty marks," she had said. It was shortly before Ryan and I had moved away, and shortly after my surgery. Just as I envied Lynn's composure in the face of death, I wished I could think of scars the way Frankie did. "They're part of me. You shouldn't worry."

What she didn't understand at her young age was that worrying was not a choice, like whether to wear blue jeans or capris, at least not for me. She was my best friend's adopted granddaughter. Of course I worried.

And now my friend Cece had died, and so had I, and Frankie was left in the care of Raina, an unfortunate woman who was Frankie's mother in the biological sense, but certainly not in the nurturing sense. I found myself checking in on Frankie more and more these days, and noticing more scars each time I did. They looked worse, too. These were no longer little paper clip scrapes. She was into cutting big time now; once, I spotted her using a kitchen paring knife, and another time she used a pair of gardening shears that she took from the neighbor's yard. I worried that time was running out for poor Frankie. If she could just hang on a while longer, everything would work out for her. At least that's what I hoped.

She had been sleeping soundly that night when the front door slammed, and then came the sounds of Raina's stilettos tapping across the fake hardwood floor and the popping of ice as gin or vodka or whatever Raina was drinking sloshed into a glass. After a moment, Frankie sat up. She glanced toward her locked door, then dabbed at the dried blood on her arm with a washcloth. She lay back down, pulled her gray frayed blanket up to her shoulders, placed her pillow over her head, and rolled toward the wall.

The next morning, the fragrance of strong coffee wafted into her room. How I would have loved a big mug of that! Frankie rolled out of bed, and I heard her stomach growl. I knew she'd only had an old apple and two slices of Kraft American cheese for dinner the night before. The aroma of sizzling bacon was probably as enticing for her as it was for me. But something was amiss; Raina never made breakfast. Not for Frankie, not for anyone.

Frankie stepped into her jeans and pulled her only hoodie over her t-shirt. She stuffed her cell phone into her back pocket, glanced at the backpack by her bedroom window, and shuffled out to the kitchen in bare feet. She rubbed her sleepy eyes in the doorway.

The kitchen table and counters were, as usual, cluttered with filthy ashtrays, empty booze bottles, crumpled napkins, and pizza boxes. The trashcan was overflowing, too. What was different was the fresh pot of coffee, the grocery bag on the counter, and the man standing at the two-burner stove. He wore a neat buzz cut and a clean white undershirt, and although his skinny arms were sleeved in colorful tattoos, I began to think Raina had raised her standards. He was actually rather handsome, I thought, with thick dark hair and crystal blue eyes, until I saw the repulsively tight gray boxers, the open can of Coors beside the stove, and the way he stared at Frankie.

She was a girl worthy of staring. She was tall for her age and slim, with thick, black hair and remarkable skin. I could never quite decide what color her skin was. Honey? Caramel? Latte-hued? She looked neither white nor African American nor Mediterranean but some lovely combination of all three. And her eyes were her greatest jewels: slightly slanted up at the outer corners, surrounded by a fringe of black lashes and sparkling with amber irises rippled with copper flecks.

"Is Raina here?" she asked, ignoring his lecherous grin.

She rarely referred to Raina as her mother.

"I guess that's debatable," he said, his voice raspy. "Depends on what you mean by *here*." Now that his mouth was open, with gaps in his teeth where his incisors should have been, he was starting to look like all the other creeps Raina brought home.

Frankie started for Raina's bedroom at the end of the hall.

"I wouldn't bother going down there," he said. "She's pretty wasted. Been passed out for a couple hours. Want some?" He held the pan of eggs toward her. The yolks were still runny.

Frankie ignored his question and cracked open Raina's door. She sighed and shook her head. "Yet again."

There was her mother, stretched out face down on the stripped mattress, her black hair trailing across her bare back and drool dripping from her mouth. Cigarette butts, joint roaches, and ashes were mounded in an ashtray on the floor, alongside a hypodermic needle.

The room stank like old smoke, weed, sex, and sweat. Frankie sat on the mattress and shook her mother. No response. She examined the inside of Raina's elbows. Fresh bruising. She gently gathered Raina's hair into a loose ponytail and swept it to the side, then lay her head on top of her mother's back as though listening for breath. She sat up.

"Got lucky again, Raina. Guess I don't need to call 911 this time."

She picked up Raina's purse and took out a wad of cash and her mother's driver's license, which she had done numerous times before. She also retrieved a tattered Koran from underneath a sweating tumbler, brushed it gently, and cradled it in her arms as though it were an injured creature rescued from its captor's lair. I respected her for that act of kindness. Although I knew little about Islam and was lacking in personal conviction toward any faith, I'd always honored the sacred beliefs of others. In fact, I sometimes found myself bordering on jealousy of those who had strong and certain beliefs.

Back in the kitchen, the bacon was still cooking and the eggs were now burning. The man wasn't there. I wondered where he'd gone, but Frankie didn't seem to pay attention to his absence. I figured she was used to men appearing and disappearing all the time.

She turned off the stove, poured some coffee into a cup, and opened the fridge. The quart-sized carton of low-fat milk had only a splash left, and after taking a whiff of it, Frankie poured it down the drain. She wrapped two slices of bacon in a paper napkin and took them back to her room.

She saw him before I did.

He was standing in her closet lifting a beer to his lips with one hand while the other was shoved down in his boxers. She charged the closet door and slammed it shut, bit off a slice of bacon, and leaned back against the door as casually as if she were waiting for a friend.

"Hey!" he called from inside the closet. He tried to open the door while her weight held the door firm. She stuffed the rest of the bacon into her mouth and took a gulp of coffee. Then, when he started to push harder against the door from inside the closet, she lunged for her backpack, raised the window, and climbed out.

3 Chapter Three

Ryan was passed out on our faded leather sofa with the lights still on from the night before, a recurring event ever since I died. I guess he still couldn't bring himself to sleep in our bed without me. On this day, it was well past noon when his best friend Tom Marquardt blasted through the unlocked door.

"Time to wake up, Pastor!"

Tom was a tall, handsome man, a former athlete with a broad smile and one of those megaphone voices, always sounding upbeat, as though he were bringing cheer to the entire team. Today he had also brought coffee, and he stood at the end of the sofa now with an extra-large Styrofoam cup in each hand. He gently kicked at Ryan's hand, dangling onto the floor.

Ryan squinted one eye open, groaned, and rolled over.

Tom walked around to the backside of the sofa and held

the steaming coffee over Ryan's head.

"Go away," Ryan said.

"Can't make me. Besides, this is for you." He lowered the coffee closer to Ryan.

Ryan grunted.

Tom took a sip from the other cup. "It's good stuff," he said, sounding like a father trying to convince his son to eat arugula.

"What do you want?" Ryan opened one eye again, aiming it this time at Tom like a loaded gun. "And could you please shut those damn blinds?"

The tone in his voice pinched me. This was not my kind, loving, welcoming husband. This was an imposter.

"No can do," Tom said. "Sunlight's good for you. And so am I. Speaking of what's good for you, why didn't you go to church this morning?" Tom knew, of course, that Ryan hadn't been for a long time. Everyone knew that.

"Why did you let yourself into my home without knocking?" Ryan wrestled a throw pillow out from under his shoulder and held it over his head as Tom set Ryan's cup on the end table.

"I did knock. And rang the doorbell twice. And then I realized the door was unlocked— which by the way isn't very smart or safe—but regardless, here I am. This is the day we agreed we'd work together, to get you ready for your big trip. So here I am, at your service." Ryan didn't see his friend's satirical salute.

The big trip Tom referred to was a climbing expedition to Mt. McKinley, otherwise known as Denali. I had asked Ryan to climb it for me, in memory of me. We had climbed so many mountains together when we were younger, but we'd never made it to Alaska. I was confident it would be good for him, and I was sure he could do it if he'd start working out just a little bit more. I'd even picked out the guide service and the date of the trip, and I'd sent away for all the materials. All Ryan had to do was sign some paperwork and send in the check. Which he did. But that was back when I was alive and he was, physically and emotionally, in far better shape.

Tom picked up a twisted blanket from the floor and folded it across Ryan's legs. He shook Ryan's shoulder. "Come on, man."

It took a couple of minutes, but eventually Ryan rolled over again and hoisted himself up into sitting position. He ran one hand over his face. He obviously hadn't shaved in several days, and his face looked chubby beneath the new growth. I couldn't help but glance down at the roll around his middle that never used to be there, and then over at Tom, who was as fit as ever.

Ryan yawned, rubbed the heel of each hand against his eyes, and reached for the coffee cup. "I don't know what makes you think you can help me," he said. "You don't know a goddamn thing about climbing."

If I could have, I would have scolded him then for talking to his friend that way. And for taking his lord's name in vain. But Tom let it all go.

"You've got me on that one, Ryan. I don't know a thing about climbing. But I'm not the one heading to Alaska." He sniffed the air, scowled, and cranked open a window. "And I do know a thing or two about my best friend. And about your promise to Beth. So let's get you up and showered and then go for a run."

At the mention of my name, Ryan's entire expression sagged. He'd had months to grieve for me, and by now I'd hoped his spirits would be lifting. I'd been wrong. Whether it was my death, or my absence, or the promise he'd made to me, something still weighed him down, and it was then that I first wondered whether I'd made a horribly grave mistake.

"You expect me to go on a run?" Ryan said. "Go fuck yourself."

4 Chapter Four

It was last fall when Ryan started to unravel before my eyes, right after I got the dreaded phone call. Under any other circumstances, the voice mail would have been words to curl up against, like a rumpled pile of soft lamb's wool. "I'd like to see you. Right away. Please call me."

But in this case they stung like a thousand scorpions because the message was from my oncologist.

Ryan and I went to see her two days later. I remember the day well. He stood at the window of the doctor's office, his hands in his pockets, his back to me. I studied the coppery shine of his thick hair. His broad, strong shoulders, his shirt stretched tight across his upper back. And that butt. Even in middle age, his belonged in a Levis commercial. Beyond him, the high desert sky was tinged with orange from a distant wild fire, and the barren Cascade Mountains were thirsty for new snow.

"I'm sorry," the doctor said. She started rambling on about test results and using those cancer words: markers, antigens, metastases. But I'd already known the cancer was back.

"How long?" I asked. But I knew that answer too.

When we got home to our little cabin, after a drive through eternal silence, Ryan tossed his keys into the raku bowl I'd made for him years ago and walked directly outside to the back deck. I hung my denim jacket on the hook in the hall and poured us each a tall glass of iced tea.

"I'm worried about you," I said, after I joined him outside.

"You're worried about me? I'm not the one with cancer."

"Exactly. That's why I'm worried about you." I handed him a glass. "You're the one facing an uncertain future. And you're not yourself anymore."

When I'd first been diagnosed, more than a year earlier, he'd started to show some moodiness. He slept a lot. He laughed less often. He hid his Bible in a drawer and came up with excuses about why he couldn't preach.

After a few months, he retired from the clergy. We packed everything up, said good riddance to the Midwest, and moved back to Central Oregon. We thought that maybe, if he took a break from the church, he could cope with the stress better. And also that maybe, if I was back home in the clear mountain air, I'd be able to beat it. But neither of our hopes came true. Instead, he'd pulled farther away from his faith, spiraled deeper into depression, and become angry with everything and everyone. Including me.

Now he ran his hand along the smooth cedar railing. He had spent the last three weeks refinishing the deck, scrubbing every ounce of his energy into the wood grain. The warm sunlight sprinkled down on him through the Ponderosa pines the way it used to filter through the church's stained glass windows. In his white oxford shirt, he still looked saintly to me. I spent a few minutes letting his profile ingrain itself into my memory, watching his Adam's apple bob as he drank while my thoughts darted every which way.

"We need to talk," I finally said.

I set my glass down and hugged him from behind, resting my head on his back, warmed by the sun. When he didn't move or turn or reach for me, I decided maybe now wasn't the time to talk. I released him and walked down the steps, toward the river. Only when I pulled out my cell phone did he say anything.

"Who are you calling?"

I hesitated before turning around. "I need to call Frankie."

I died six weeks later, but, to my surprise, that wasn't the end.

At first, everything was dark, so dark it reminded me of waiting for the power to come back on after a wicked Midwestern thunderstorm. It was quiet, too. Eerily quiet. And painfully boring. After some time I grew sad and deeply depressed. And then I got angry. I cursed the cancer that ripped me out of Ryan's life, like a photograph torn from an old album. I screamed inside my mind. This was unfair! I was so young! There were so many things I had yet to do! And what about Ryan? But these were the very same protests and questions that parishioners had brought to us over the years, and we knew even back then there was no answer. Eventually I became drained. Overcome with fatigue. I gave up; I gave in. I admitted defeat. And that was when things began to change for the better, as though that was all death had wanted of me. A simple surrender.

Scenes began to unfold before me after that. They were colorful, enticingly real, and welcome little tidbits of life. In one, Ryan sat on the railing of our back deck, throwing pine cones toward the river where the water splashed around small boulders. In another, Frankie pressed her schoolbooks against her chest as she crushed through fallen leaves on her way to school. And Lynn Van Swol, a woman I'd never actually met, showed up in all sorts of places I could now see from my new vantage point. It seemed as though a curtain slowly opened and a film reel unwound, image by image, as I sat in the balcony of a grand old theater.

Things appeared randomly until I discovered I could shift the object of my attention through my thoughts. It required serious concentration—nothing like channel surfing with a remote control. But I could check in on anyone I wanted to if I really set my mind to it. Later, I realized I didn't just see the scenes, the way you do when you're watching television or movies. I had all my senses back. I could hear the river's voice. I could smell autumn's damp leaves. I was once again connected to the living world, and it was delicious. I wondered if this was heaven.

I found Ryan again, this time washing a single plate and glass at our sink and setting them side by side in the dish drainer. I reached out to him, where the soapsuds clung to his arm, and squeezed him. I felt his strength and his warmth, and I smelled the citrus scent of the bubbles. I could barely wait for him to discover I was there with him.

But he didn't stop what he was doing. He didn't turn around. He didn't even tilt his head in curiosity. I squeezed his arm again, harder. I brushed my lips against his hair. Still he didn't flinch. I was heartbroken. Was he so despondent that he could no longer respond to me? Or was he angry with me, or afraid to face me because he felt so vulnerable?

Then I had an idea. I blew at the soapsuds, hoping to pique his interest with a playful approach. But the suds didn't waver.

That's when I realized the tragedy of my new existence. I could think, and I had my senses, but I couldn't impact anything in the living world. Yes, Ryan was still in my life—as were Frankie and Lynn and everyone else—but I was no longer in theirs. I had set a plan into place to help them, but it was like a high tech driverless car on the road. I was now relegated to bystander status, and my plan was moving forward without me, completely on autopilot.

There was nobody, and nothing, here with me on the sidelines; wherever I was felt like a universe devoid of all life forms and galaxies and noises and temperatures and time. My only sensory input was from the view on my earthly screen. Worse than that: my story wasn't really mine anymore. It had been assigned to the living, given away like a closetful of clothes. There was no way I'd be able to rest in peace while my story played out through the lives of my loved ones. I would have to sit on the edge of my seat and helplessly watch it unfold, no matter what might happen.

I was certainly not in heaven.

I was in hell.

5 Chapter Five

Oh, what I would give to have just one more cup of coffee, to feel its heat blanketing my tongue and releasing the damp chill from my veins and bones and skin. It was pure torture when Lynn opened the heavy wooden door of The Monastery Coffee and Tea House, with all those aromatic coffees grown by Trappist Andean monks, and bins of jasmine teas, and pastries and yogurts and seasonal fruit salads.

As I lingered amidst the fragrances, she ordered her usual morning blend of decaffeinated green and hibiscus herbal teas. Once served, she walked straight for a corner table by the window. Outside, cars honked in rush-hour gridlock worsened by a sudden downpour, and a few misguided umbrellas lost their battles against the wind. She plopped her wet cinch bag on a wooden chair and hung her dripping running jacket on a nearby coat rack. After she shook out her short pixie cut, Lynn looked as though the weather's assault was as benign as her meeting with the wolf. I liked that about her.

She excavated a hand wipe from her bag, along with a soaked copy of *Time* magazine. On the cover, a gorgeous girl with glacier goggles and sun-kissed skin smiled beneath the headline: *New Generation Climbs Up (and Over the Has-beens).*

Bells chimed near the front door of The Monastery, and a man walked in. When he flipped back the hood of his drenched rain jacket, I saw he had a boyish face with freckles sprinkled across his nose and a crooked smile. I recognized him from a framed photograph in Lynn's bedroom. It was Greg, her ex-lover.

He surveyed the restaurant, panning from right to left. When he spotted Lynn, he smiled and waved the wet magazine he was holding. It, too, was the latest *Time.*

She started to flip her magazine over. But somehow her hand flailed as though possessed, and she bumped her tea. It toppled, spilling over the magazine, the table, and her lap.

"Damn it!"

She scraped her chair back from the disaster, stood abruptly, and suspended her arms and dripping fingers mid-air.

He hurried toward her table, grabbing a dozen or so napkins from the condiment bar on the way. I saw him try to stifle an impish smirk as she took some of the napkins from him. As she dabbed at the magazine, he reached down to blot her running tights with another napkin, and she swatted him away. Although she'd recently described their breakup in her journal as an "inevitable chasm on an already-cracked glacier," the heat waves emanating from her body—I could feel them from where I stood—made it obvious she still had feelings for him.

"Here, you can have mine." He set his soggy *Time* down on top of hers. Their eyes met briefly, and he took the wad of soaked napkins from her hand and tossed them into a nearby trashcan. Then he spun a chair around and sat on it backwards, not so much like a cowboy straddling a horse as a lover straddling his mate. Open, vulnerable, anticipating.

"So, have you read it yet?" he said, picking up the damp magazine and waving it in front of her face. It smelled like wet pulp. "By the way, you look spectacular."

Everything about Lynn spoke of natural beauty and strength. Her complexion was fresh without a hint of makeup. Her jaw was chiseled and her arms carved, without looking too masculine. Her breasts were small but appeared firm, and her abdomen taut, in her skinny black tank top. I was never in such good shape as that.

He didn't wait for a reply. "So, about this," he said, pointing to the magazine, "no time like the present. Get it? *Time*?"

She ignored his pun and gave him a blank stare.

"Here, let me help you," he said. He pried the wet pages of his magazine from one another, passing stories about the economy and the latest discovery of political corruption. Meanwhile, Lynn leaned back in her chair and crossed her arms.

When he finally got to the article he was looking for, he pointed to a gray sidebar next to a colorful image of the

Alaska Range. "Read this part first," he said, tapping on the gray box. "Out loud."

She hesitated.

"What?" he said with feigned innocence.

"I was planning to look this over by myself."

Now it was his turn to ignore her. He pulled a pair of tortoise-shell reading glasses from his pocket and offered them to her.

Lynn started reading aloud.

> "DENALI NATIONAL PARK, Alaska – The frozen body of an unidentified climber was found late last week by fellow mountaineers alongside the West Buttress, a popular route to the summit of North America's tallest peak. The climber was found lying in the snow, with her goggles and boots placed neatly beside her. 'It looks as if she simply laid [sic] down to die,' National Park Ranger Hugh Denton said. Further details have been withheld pending identification and a complete investigation."

She peered over his reading glasses at him. "And your point is?"

"My point is obvious. It's hell up there. Dangerous as hell."

She rolled her eyes and shook her head. "You haven't changed a bit, have you?"

He leaned toward her and dabbed a few drops of splashed tea from her bare shoulder with a clean napkin. "Keep reading."

> "First responders estimated the woman was in her late fifties. 'I know they do it all the time, the geezers I mean,' a twenty-year-old bush pilot based in Talkeetna said on the condition of anonymity. 'But it's crazy. They shouldn't be up here.' This latest tragedy further ignites an ongoing debate about the safety of unqualified adventure-seekers in mountain-wilderness conditions where search and rescue resources are limited."

Lynn stiffened. "And now your point is, what, that I'm too *old*? Do you actually agree with that snot-nosed bush pilot? Obviously she doesn't know what she's talking about. Yes, there are plenty of unqualified climbers on Denali, but age has little to do with it. There are also plenty of older climbers who succeed every year. I think the record right now for oldest climber on Denali is seventy-something. The ones that don't make it are the ones who are physically and mentally unprepared."

I felt a twinge when she said that. Lynn was right; those who don't succeed are often less careful or out of shape. I would not have chosen her as Ryan's guide, or Denali as their meeting place, if I weren't completely confident in her skills. I wouldn't have chosen her for Frankie, either, if I didn't trust her implicitly. Her age didn't worry me in the slightest. But when she made that comment about other climbers being unprepared, I couldn't help but think about Ryan, who should have been prepared by now but wasn't.

"So thanks for your concern, but you can stop railing on me about Denali, Greg. You know how important this is to me. I'm going to do it. I've got to." She reached up to the agate necklace that hung around her neck; the rock was a quarter-sized stone adorned with swirls of browns, rusts, and blues. "Besides, all you know about climbing is huffing and puffing up the hill to the eighteenth tee. I know what I'm doing. I'm experienced." She smoothed her hand across the page. When she lifted it, her fingers were stained with black ink. It reminded me, eerily, of frostbite.

Greg took her stained hand and held it in both of his. "Yeah, I know you're experienced." He raised one eyebrow, looked her up and down, and smirked.

"That's not what I meant." She pulled her hand from his and wiped her fingers with a damp napkin.

"But seriously, Lynn," Greg said. "That's exactly why you know how dangerous this is. Because you *are* so experienced. You've seen it all." He reached again for her hand.

"You act as if you still care."

Greg stood, and Lynn rifled through her cinch bag for something, perhaps an excuse not to look at him.

"I do."

All the other sounds in The Monastery—the rain spitting on the window, the coffee grinding, the conversations around them—muffled into an indistinguishable hum the moment he spoke that duet of words. I wished I could hit the rewind button so that Lynn could hear them again, savor them, let them echo over and over in her mind. Those are two words that, when spoken together, you just don't want to miss.

When a long minute had passed and she didn't reply, he walked toward the counter and ordered a drink.

"Damn you," she whispered aloud. Looking down at his magazine, still lying on top of hers, she skimmed the pages. There were three more sidebars at the end of the article. One was devoted to several great twentieth-century climbers. Another listed some of the sport's rising stars. And the final one, a small box in the lower corner of the last page, was entitled "*Last Seen,*" but the title was faux-scratched out, and in a font resembling handwriting, the words "*Has Been*" had been inserted. Lynn's name was the fourth of the five names listed.

> "Lynn Van Swol: Last seen on Denali in 2000, when tragedy struck and a member of her team fell to his death."

She gathered her belongings and headed for the door. Greg called to her as he waited for his drink.

"By the way," he said. "Did you hear the morning news?"

She shook her head.

"Thought you should know. A Mexican gray wolf just escaped from the Portland Zoo. They haven't found it. Be careful out there."

"Thanks. Thanks a lot."

Lynn set her cinch bag on the kitchen counter of her little house. She hung up her jacket, scrubbed her hands in the kitchen sink, and went straight into her home library. It was a dark room, lined with floor-to-ceiling bookshelves. The books were carefully arranged by author or subject; spines lined up precisely. She had the usual classics, a few books devoted to religion and philosophy, and a shelf of self-help books ranging from journaling to guilt to fitness. Unsurprisingly, the vast majority of books related to her lifelong passion: climbing mountains.

But there were also dozens of three-ring binders on the top shelves, with dates spanning nearly three decades printed along the spines, and these were the most fascinating items in her collection. Arranged neatly and chronologically, they were filled with unsent letters to Sunny, the daughter she'd given up for adoption thirty years ago: the same girl, I suspected, that Cece and Jack had adopted and renamed Raina.

I first discovered the letters when she pulled one of the binders down a couple of months ago. She opened to a letter dated several years earlier, and I tried to refrain from reading it. Honestly, it didn't seem right. I was watching something that should be private. I was not a snoop.

But I was also not a saint, and as she sat pouring over this one letter in particular, I gave in to temptation.

There was nothing especially enlightening about that letter. But as the days and weeks went by and I read other letters over her shoulder, I became increasingly more convinced who Sunny was.

It touched me that she had written to this unknown daughter all those years. But then, when I thought about the sheer volume of letters, I wondered if this was more of an obsession. Were the letters cathartic? Was she clinging to the past, as Greg had suggested several times? Or was she engaged in an imaginary relationship with her daughter because she'd been unsuccessful in other relationships, as though she'd attached herself to a ghost and refused to let go? It was easy to wonder, and at times to even be judgmental, but who was I to say how a birthmother should feel a day or a lifetime after giving up a child for adoption? I certainly would never know.

Now Lynn sat down at her writing table, a rickety old antique, and pulled several sheets of lined paper from the drawer. She tapped them against the desk, set them down, and then picked up the pile and tapped it again, checking that the pages were aligned perfectly. By now I knew this routine of hers. She removed a pen from a blue felt-lined box, clicked it open, and waited.

On the wall, above her desk, was a circular arrangement of six photos. In each a younger Lynn stood at the top of a mountain. A round sticker had been placed in the lower right-hand corner of each frame: Vinson Massif, 40; Everest, 36; Aconcagua, 31; Mt. Elbrus, 28; Carstensz Pyramid, 24; Kilimanjaro, 21. Smack dab in the middle of the arrangement was a vacant space. I knew what it was for: Denali. Known as The High One by the Athabaskans, it was her nemesis, having sent her home twice before like a jilted lover. She stared at the white space on the wall, or maybe through it, and fingered her pendant until she pointed the tip of the pen to the page.

Dear Sunny~

Today the world is conspiring against me. First a wolf in my path, which had to be a bad omen. Then the new issue of

Time *magazine, calling me a has-been. Can you believe that? And then Greg, who has accused me repeatedly of being stuck in the past, practically begging me not to climb Denali. I'm too old, he said. Which of course is pure rubbish.*

But still, something feels off all of a sudden. Have you ever felt there was someone staring at you from behind? Or have you ever thought that maybe you should take the stairs instead of the elevator, or reschedule a flight? I had that sort of feeling today, that odd notion that maybe, for some reason, I'm not meant to go to Denali.

The thought had never crossed my mind that Lynn might back out! I had finished my research last September, learned she would be leading this Denali climb the following spring, and laid the rest of the tracks for Ryan to follow, unwittingly, of course. She could not change her mind now. I had no backup plan for Ryan and Frankie. She had to go.

Lynn went into the kitchen and poured a glass of filtered water, squeezing a slice of lemon into the glass. I thought about Ryan and Frankie, but then caught myself and stopped. If I thought about them too long, I might lose my focus on Lynn, and I needed to know what she was thinking, what she was planning to do. She came back and set the glass of water on a cork coaster beside her paper.

Why do I let these naysayers bother me? I really don't believe the age thing is an issue. If I lived all alone on a deserted tropical island, would I be too old to climb its mountains or dive its seas? Too old to swing naked from tree to tree on a vine? No, because there'd be nobody there to see, to question, to judge.

So what is it? What's this feeling I'm having? Could it be fear?

They say as you grow older your fears grow right alongside you. I don't know if that's true, and I've never been afraid of climbing before, but it's like my memories are trying to sabotage me, like demons creeping into my mind.

There's no place for fear on Denali. And no place for tragic memories of the past. You have to keep moving forward on that mountain. She knew that; she had to.

All I know is that something's gnawing at me, rebelling against my dreams, threatening the promise I made to you all those years ago when I dedicated my Seven Summits quest to you. I swore I'd climb every one in your honor, and now, like a disease, something is threatening to pull me further away from you. But maybe that's the way it should be. Maybe it's time for me to let you go. Thirty years is an awfully long time.

Lynn Van Swol had spent thirty years grieving for her daughter. I'd spent almost thirty years longing for one of my own. At this point, neither of us would ever have the chance for another child, which was probably why I'd been so determined to make sure that Frankie, the one child I loved, even if she wasn't my own, would find someone to whom she could really belong.

Lynn put her pen back in the box and went into her bedroom, where she lay down on the bed and rested her forearm over her eyes. I stared at her, willing her to get up and finish the letter. To get up and tell Sunny she would climb Denali after all. She did sit up, but she merely opened her nightstand drawer. Beneath a box of tissues and a tube of menthol foot cream, a faded picture rested in a tarnished silver frame: a picture of her, thirty years ago, in a hospital gown, wearing a black cord around her neck with several colorful stones hanging from it. Beside her stood a dark-skinned, handsome man. She held a beautiful, black-haired baby in her arms.

I don't know if Greg was right about Lynn being stuck in the past. But I do know there's a difference between getting stuck in the past and going back there for a reason. Sometimes you don't even know what that reason is. But if you go to the right part of your past, I wanted to tell her, it can be your springboard to a new place, a place you wouldn't otherwise find if you just moved through normal space and time.

Oh, hell. She had to go back to Denali. For her sake and mine.

6 Chapter Six

Tom was successful, after all, in getting Ryan out for a run. They followed the Deschutes River, uphill and down again on a trail cushioned by pine needles and fragranced with sage and juniper. Ryan, once a great runner, panted more than usual, and had to stop a few times to catch his breath. This worried me; by this point in the training regimen for Denali, he should have been able to run those six miles without breaking a sweat.

When they got to Farewell Bend Park, they slowed down to a walk. A couple of women passed by them on the way to a small beach, and a Jack Russell terrier chased down a Frisbee.

"So, Ryan," Tom said.

Ryan stopped beside him and rested his hands on his knees, trying to steady his breath.

"Tell me the truth. You ever going to church again?"

Ryan started walking. "Nope."

"Wanna talk about it?"

"Nope." They walked toward an old footbridge. Ryan stopped in the middle of the bridge, set his hands on the railing, and looked upstream.

"I've never asked you this before, but I was just wondering: was Beth okay that you...quit?"

Ryan shot a dagger-look at Tom.

"Sorry. I shouldn't have mentioned her."

Ryan moved farther across the bridge, and Tom followed a few steps behind.

"No, it's okay," Ryan said. "It's not that I don't want to talk about her. I mean, I don't. But then again I do." He kicked at a mound of fine dust. "To answer your question, she encouraged me to stay with the church at first. But then she told me it was okay to take a break. She knew my struggle."

They walked on toward the Old Mill. Tom wiped his brow on his arm. "God, I loved Beth. I really miss her."

Ryan nodded and kept walking.

"I remember the wine," Tom said.

Ryan looked up at him; their eyes met, and they laughed. Tom and his wife Rhonda were the only ones to whom Ryan had revealed my love affair with wine. All those years as the minister's wife I felt like I had to be pure, and I'd drive for miles to find a store where I could be sure I wouldn't run into any parishioners. I'd buy a case or two at a time and hide it in the closet behind all my boring long skirts and dresses. I hadn't had much taste for it during all my cancer treatments, but near the end, when the treatments were over, I had Ryan go out and buy a case of Napa Chardonnay for me. I barely had a chance to taste it, but what I did have was divine.

"Believe it or not, I still have some of it," Ryan said.

"Beth's wine? You still have some?"

They made eye contact again, and Ryan smirked. "Race?"

They went back to our little cabin and opened a bottle. Ryan, who never drank any alcohol for as long as we were together, got out two stained coffee cups and splashed some wine into each one. He took a swig and puckered his lips as the acid coursed over his tongue, reminding me that wine, like many things, is an acquired taste. I certainly had acquired a taste for Chardonnay, and I could almost sense the zing of the acid on my own tongue as he drank.

After another sip, he and Tom began to haul dusty cardboard boxes of climbing and camping gear from the detached garage into the cabin. Tom scooped up some papers and brochures scattered on the coffee table and put them in one of my Longaberger baskets. Ryan switched on one of his recordings from March Madness, when Duke had played Baylor.

"Did you see this one?" he asked Tom. Tom shook his head.

"You've gotta see it."

At first, Ryan inspected all of his gear closely, as though he were the surgeon instead of Tom. He checked the stitching on his harness, tested each carabiner to be sure it opened easily and closed securely, and inspected every square inch of the tent. He had not climbed for years, but I could tell it was all coming back to him. Meanwhile, Tom began to unpack the ice axes, trekking poles, and backpacks.

At the same time, the game was heating up on the TV. Before long, they were each keeping one eye on the television and one hand on their wine cups, and the mountain climbing preparation slowed down. If I'd still been alive, I would have stood in front of the television and told them to get back to work. Time was short. But I obviously couldn't do a damn thing.

The din of the stadium crowd was constant, like wind that rushes through a canyon, and the guys yelled at the TV as though they were in that stadium too. They watched, they drank, they stood up and hollered. They cheered and drank some more, and frankly I was getting bored and impatient. I was also beginning to worry about how much alcohol Ryan was consuming.

By halftime they were already into another of my bottles, which I sorely wished I could share with them. Tom had arranged the cooking gear on our floor like a little girl sets out a tea party, with a packet of stale freeze-dried stroganoff on each of four tin plates, camp utensils set neatly at each place. When he dragged in an old box containing crampons and a tangle of climbing rope, he wrapped the rope around his body in tight coils, like mummy cloth around a corpse. He snatched a headlamp from Ryan, donned the crampons over his socks, and sat cross-legged at one of the place settings. With a metal camp cup in his hand and pinky raised high, he asked Ryan how he looked.

Ryan, who had been flicking a knife open and shut and

absently watching the half-time free-throw competition, tossed the knife back into a pile of camping tools and pressed his hands together and against his lips. This was his thinking pose. Then he tossed a sidelong glance at his old friend, a glance nearly as sharp as that knife. "Like an idiot."

Tom threw a packet of freeze-dried stroganoff at Ryan, without realizing there was a rip in the packet's seam I'm sure, and powdery flakes scattered all over the tent, my red Persian rug, and Ryan's hair.

"You asshole," Ryan said. The look he shot at Tom, and the tone in his voice, were as sharp as that knife he'd been flicking. "Who in God's name do you think has to clean this up?" I was startled by his severe reaction. I wanted to ask him who in God's name gave him the right to treat his friend that way.

"Sorry, I was just goofing around. Jesus, take it easy."

Ryan started flicking the knife again, and Tom slowly began uncoiling the rope from around his body.

"Everything okay?" he asked Ryan.

Ryan poured more wine into his cup without offering any to Tom.

"Ryan, buddy?"

He flicked the knife shut. "Yeah?"

"Seems like something's gotten into you lately. I thought maybe the run would do you some good. But you're still..."

"What?"

"Well, you're still a dick. Maybe you should hold off on any more wine."

Ryan took a deep breath while staring at the television.

"Ryan? Talk to me, man."

Ryan ran his fingers through his hair and looked at the wine in the cup. "I got a phone call from Frankie yesterday."

"Tell me again who Frankie is?"

"It's complicated, but here goes. Beth's best friend back in Chicago was Cece. Cece had an adopted daughter named Raina. Then Raina had a daughter—that's Frankie. In other words, Frankie is Beth's best friend's granddaughter."

"That's the girl whose mother is a prostitute?"

"Yeah. Raina's turning tricks nearly every night these days and Frankie's scared."

"Not much you can do about it way out here, I guess."

"I know. But Beth told me she had a plan for Frankie, and I didn't want to hear about it. Now I wish I had."

"Maybe after the climb you can have Frankie out for a visit."

"Maybe. I don't know."

"There's something else bothering you, isn't there?"

Ryan shrugged.

"You stressed about the climb?"

He shrugged again, then nodded. "I haven't been on the mountain for a long time. Years."

He got up, headed into the kitchen, and reemerged a few minutes later with a bowl of peanuts and some microwaved macaroni and cheese. The sports announcers were reviewing highlights from the first half, and Ryan turned up the volume as he handed the peanuts to Tom. Tom grabbed the remote and turned the volume back down.

"Hey!" Ryan said. He tossed a peanut in the air and tried

to catch it on his tongue. He missed. He tried again, missed again. He picked up a handful and threw them across the room.

"Hey," Tom said. "You need to chill."

"Chill? How the hell am I supposed to do that? Look at me. I can't even catch a fucking peanut. How in God's name am I supposed to climb Denali?"

Tom's grimace told me he'd been thinking the same thing. But the game started up again, and the two turned their attention to the TV. After Duke missed a shot, Tom turned down the volume again and asked Ryan why he was doing this.

"Doing what?"

"Climbing. Why *are* you climbing Denali? That's a major mountain, man. I'm no climber but..."

Ryan looked up at him, his expression once again reminding me more of an angry animal than of a loving husband or a retired pastor or a best friend. That wolf Lynn encountered looked friendlier than Ryan.

"You know damn well why. Because Beth asked me to. That's why. And after I shut her down on the whole Frankie conversation, I had to give her something."

Ouch.

I hadn't realized his agreement to go to Denali was out of pity, or maybe even guilt, and not ambition. I figured he'd be gung ho to get back into climbing once I was gone. He used to say there was no better way to clear your head than from a mountaintop. I had no idea he said yes because he was afraid to say no.

Tom replaced the batteries in the headlamp, strapped it on his head, and shone the light onto Ryan's face. Ryan looked tired.

"So it's not something you want to do," Tom said.

"Shut up, will you?"

"And," Tom said, walking on his knees toward Ryan and blinding him with the headlamp, "it's something you don't think you even *can* do. But you're still going anyway."

Ryan held his hand up against Tom's advance. "You're a real asshole, did you know that? It doesn't matter whether or not I can. I promised her I'd do it, and that's that."

I felt ill. Promises aren't supposed to make you sick.

I thought back to those final days, as Ryan sat beside me, waiting for death to free us both. He asked if there was anything he could do for me. I told him that, as a matter of fact, there was one thing. I squeezed his hand and asked him to climb Denali, to take my ponytail up to the summit and send it into the Athabaskan winds. I showed him the materials I'd sent for, but I didn't tell him why I chose that guide service or that particular climb. I didn't tell him about Lynn—the climber I'd admired for most of my life who was scheduled to be the assistant guide on that climb and who, I was pretty sure, was also Frankie's biological grandmother. I didn't tell him about my plans for Frankie meeting up with Lynn or how I thought he could facilitate the introduction. He hadn't wanted to hear anything about Frankie, so I kept it simple for him. I told him that, if he'd just agree to go on the climb, I could rest in peace.

Maybe I was wrong to withhold the whole truth, but when

you're on your deathbed those rules about what's right and wrong start to look pretty hazy.

Now he was staring over the top of the TV and out the window. I wondered if he was remembering the same miserable day.

"Okay," Tom said. "So she asked you to climb Denali, and I get that you said yes and that now you feel like you have to. But Beth was a smart cookie and more of a climber than you, really, right? Obviously she figured you'd train hard for the climb." He glanced at the game. Duke scored a three-pointer against Baylor. "I'm sure she'd understand if you changed your mind, or waited until you were ready."

"I can't do that to her. She was pretty adamant I go now, on this one."

Tom looked puzzled. "You think she had some other *ulterior* motive?" His tone suggested a sinister plot.

Ryan shot Tom a hard look. "What do you mean by that?" He shook his head. "Of course, she had a motive. She wanted me to keep busy, meet people, all that. She knew I loved climbing. And she sure as hell didn't want me to sit around all lonely and feeling sorry for myself."

Tom stood up, picked up a ski pole, and swung it as though he were teeing off. "Which is exactly what you've been doing, if you ask me. The sitting around feeling sorry part. So she was probably right about that. And now it's too late to join a fitness club or whatever. I mean, I know it's probably like riding a bicycle, but you haven't exactly been getting any younger."

"Haven't you heard? Forty-four is the new twenty-four.

I'll be fine."

"You'd better be fine. Rhonda would never forgive me if something happened to you."

"Not like you're in charge of me. But tell her, just in case, that I'm making you executor of my will, and beneficiary of my vast estate, weeds and all. Just be sure to keep the scrawny little lawn mowed this summer and the pine needles raked in the fall."

Tom put the ski pole down and tried to figure out how to put on a harness as Ryan wadded up the tent and threw it onto the couch. He left the room and came back with yet another bowl of peanuts.

"Jesus, Tom."

I cringed every single time he took his lord's name in vain. This was such a radical change in behavior that I wondered if something was more seriously wrong with him than simple grief.

"What do you want me to say?" Ryan said. "That I don't think I'm up to it, so that means not keeping my promise to Beth? That you're right, I've let myself go? That I'm putting myself in harm's way? What?" He broke open some peanuts and dropped the shells back into the bowl. "I mean who cares? Not me. All I know is that she wanted to have her ponytail scattered to the wind."

"Her ponytail?"

"Yeah, her ponytail. We cut it off before the chemo, you know, and I still have it in one of her drawers. What she said is that she wanted me to climb Denali, throw her ponytail to the wind at the summit. And then climb down and get good and drunk." He tried on his old glacier goggles.

"Did she say that? The last part I mean?"

"What do you think, asshole?" Ryan looked at the wine in his cup, but then set it back down without drinking any.

Tom had the harness on crooked, with straps dangling all wrong. He still wore the crampons over his socks and the headlamp on his head. Ryan stood at the other side of the room with glacier goggles covering his eyes and the wine cup in his hand. They looked like ridiculous adversaries. They should have been having fun, best friends sharing a few laughs. But this discussion was obviously weighing heavily on Ryan, more than I would have thought, and the tension was heavier in our cabin than on the NCAA basketball court. Ryan *was* a good climber, a strong athlete, a devoted husband. I had no misconceptions about the dangers of climbing, having done it for a good chunk of my life. But I also had been confident he'd make it just fine, with good gear, a strong will, and a team that included Lynn—as well as his God. But that was last September, when he was still in good shape, before he'd really started spiraling downhill physically, emotionally, and spiritually. Before he completely gave up on his faith.

And now I had a sinking feeling, too. If being torn away from your loved ones is hell, then I was now dropping fast into a deeper, second level as I realized the mistake I'd made. Putting burdens on your loved ones before you die, and then watching them suffer beneath the load, is a lot worse than just watching them go on living without you.

"Can't you climb something else?" Tom said, taking a step toward Ryan. "Something easier, like South Sister? Or even

Mt. Hood, which I know isn't a cake walk—hell, I sure couldn't do it—but it's a whole lot easier than Denali."

"That's cheating." Ryan said. He was starting to slur.

"It's not like she'd know."

Ryan ripped the headlamp off Tom's head. "Get out."

"What?"

"Didn't you hear me? I said get out." His mood had shifted more abruptly than alpine weather. It felt like the air had stopped moving and the clocks had stopped ticking. Here were a couple of guys in a room together with a lot of toys and a lot of alcohol, a neck-and-neck playoff game on TV—even if it was a rerun—an argument flaring up, a knife, and no women to referee. I was worried where this would lead. Apparently Tom was, too.

"Ryan, I'm worried about you, man. You're not yourself." Exactly what I'd said to Ryan months ago.

"Thanks for your worry. Now, like I said at least twice already, get the fuck out."

"This isn't a good way to go off to climb some beast of a mountain. You're not in the right mindset. I don't know what's going on, but it's not a good thing." Tom was right. A bad mood is not on the recommended gear list. You can always acquire one on the mountain; in fact, it's almost guaranteed you will, but starting out with one? No.

Baylor scored against Duke, and Ryan's face reddened. "Goddamn it, Tom. I just don't like you second-guessing me. Or Beth either. I made a promise to my wife and my mind's made up."

"Seems to me you don't care much about what might

happen to *you.*"

"Yeah, well." He raised his cup as if in a toast. "Maybe I don't."

"Okay, now we're getting somewhere. So how do you feel about that?"

"Great, now you think you're my goddamn shrink?" Ryan jerked his head to the door. "Now you can go for sure."

Tom looked hurt. It was my fault they got into this rift, but there was nothing I could do to get them out of it. They were tangled up in it the same way Tom was trapped in the harness. He tried to step out of it, but he may as well have been trying to step out of silly string. In another time and place, this would have been grounds for backslapping laughter, but not now.

Tom eventually freed himself and sat down on the couch to take off the crampons, with one eye still on the game, and then he glanced at my basket. There was the brochure from Alpine Aspirations—the climbing outfit for whom Lynn Van Swol would be co-leading the trip to Denali. He lifted it from the pile of stuff in the basket and folded it into his back pocket.

"What do you think you're doing with that?" Ryan asked.

Tom stood, kicked the crampons out of his way, and moved for the door. "Just taking it home to show to Rhonda."

"I don't believe you."

"So what."

"Tell me why you're taking it."

Little beads of sweat started to form along Tom's hairline and he glanced to the left, away from the TV. Ryan moved to block the door. "Tell me."

"Okay. I assume this is the group you're going with?" He waved the brochure at Ryan.

"Yeah, what's it to you?"

Tom looked at the TV again but I don't think he saw the free throw.

"You're going to call them, aren't you?" Ryan said. "You're going to tell them your friend is signed up but shouldn't be going 'cause he's loony tunes, right? Lost his mind? Give it back." He reached for the brochure, but the crowd roared and Ryan was distracted by Duke's next breakaway, layup, and basket.

Tom never took his eyes off the TV. When the play was over and the crowd quieted, he said, "You're not loony tunes. But you have changed. You're not yourself. I'm just looking out for my best friend." He moved to step around Ryan, but Ryan still blocked his path. Now the two locked eyes like a couple of rutting caribou locking horns.

And then Ryan swung.

This was Ryan, my gentle former pastor husband who preached about the Lamb of God to all the little children of the church, who held my hair away from my eyes when I threw up, who held my hand as I lay dying. This was Ryan who worked diligently in our community to raise awareness on domestic violence. Who never raised his voice. Who always voted for gun control and against the war. This was Ryan, now about to pummel his best friend.

At first, Tom didn't fight back, but finally he got his fists in front of his face and then got a hold of Ryan's arm and held it tight. They shifted and Tom had Ryan's arm behind his back. He wrapped a leg around one of Ryan's, and the two went down, landing on top of the sleeping bag and just inches from the crampons and ice axe. They punched and wrestled, their feet kicking the sofa, until Ryan reached out and picked up the knife.

The TV crowd's roar intensified then, and both Tom and Ryan instinctively stopped what they were doing to watch the game for a moment—as men are prone to do, no matter what's happening right around them. Wouldn't you know there was a fight right there on the shiny hardwood court between Duke and Baylor, with four or five players tangled up and two referees trying to pull them apart? Tom and Ryan watched the outcome of the TV brawl, and when that was over they went back to their own wrestling match but with a little less gusto than before.

Ryan eventually let Tom take the knife from his hand, but when Tom flung it across the floor, the knife knocked over Ryan's cup of wine, which had been sitting at a tilted angle on the edge of my Persian rug. I held my breath, waiting for Ryan to explode again as they both stared at the spilled wine, now blending with the beef stroganoff powder Tom had also spilled on the rug.

"Might add to the flavor," Tom said, with a quick smile.

Ryan's face remained angry for a few seconds, his fist still clenched. But then I saw his jaw relax as though the steam had been let out of the pot. Tom got up, wiped blood from his nose, and pulled the brochure from his pocket. He tossed it back toward the basket, missing the shot by a couple of inches.

“Here, keep it,” he said. “I’ll see you later. Hopefully before you leave. Assuming you’re still going.”

Ryan, still breathing heavily, stood up too, and nodded. They faced off, and I wasn’t sure if they’d go in for a man-hug or another slug. When Ryan turned and bent over to pick up the brochure, Tom went into the kitchen. He took a bag of peas from the freezer, pressed it against his brow, and let himself out the back door.

Neither one said goodbye.

7 Chapter Seven

Frankie was six the first time she ran away. It was a Sunday morning after the late church service. I was serving blackberry pie in the narthex when Cece Irving cried, "Stop that girl!" A scrawny little thing with a head full of braids and piercing amber eyes raced toward me, and I threw my arm out to the side, spatula in hand. She stopped, licked the spatula clean while I stood frozen in surprise, and then kept on running right out the door. Cece and I took off together to catch her. That's when we became friends, and it's also when I fell in love with poor little Frankie.

Lord knows how many times she's run since then, probably at least as many times as she and Raina have moved. The last time she ran, that I knew about, was last fall. She stole a rowboat and paddled her way down the Mississippi River until the first lock and a swarm of mosquitoes forced her back to the riverbank. Now here she was at it again. She shushed the neighbors' barking dogs as she ran down Rosemary Street, past the corner fire hydrant, and then turned left toward the main highway, where she stuck out her right thumb.

A rusted blue Chevy sedan slowed down, four teenaged boys hanging out the windows. They whistled and cat-called, and one of them called her a vulgar name when she showed them her middle finger. Later, a grizzled truck driver offered her a ride, but she turned him down too. Several other cars and trucks honked, and a few more slowed as they drove past. She turned down every offer for a ride as she walked along the road's shoulder, and I was glad she did. It was too easy to imagine what could happen to a hitchhiking teen. But after she'd walked nearly three miles, a shiny red Jeep Wrangler stopped on the gravel shoulder for her. She jogged up to the passenger door, and the driver opened the door from inside.

"Need a ride, miss?"

Frankie bent down to look at the driver. He was a white man, around my age. He had a ponytail but was clean-shaven and wore a button-down shirt. His smile seemed sincere, and his eyes were the same shade of jade as Ryan's. Frankie glanced around the car: a McDonald's bag on the front seat, a leather messenger bag on the floor behind the driver, a pin-striped suit coat hanging at the rear side window. He seemed safe enough.

Still smiling, he pointed to her backpack and dirty feet. "Looks like you've been on the road for some time, I'd say. I'd be happy to give you a lift." There was a lilting rhythm in his voice, reminiscent of peaks and valleys in a pastoral countryside. Irish, I guessed.

"Where you headed?" she asked, smiling. Ryan had once said that seeing Frankie's smile was like spending a day in heaven. Her teeth were white and straight. Her lips were marshmallow-soft. And something about the shape of her smile seduced you, not in a sensual way but magnetically. It was hard to believe she was still only thirteen.

"Chicago," the driver said. "I'm heading toward Chicago." Yes, definitely Irish.

When she said she, too, was heading to Chicago, I breathed a sigh of relief. She was going to her grandfather's. In a few hours she'd be in safe hands again. She pulled the passenger seat forward and tossed her backpack into the back seat.

"You can ride up front with me if you'd like."

"No thanks. Like it back here." He watched her climb in after her backpack, and I wondered if he noticed her unusual speaking style. It was a long-term habit: short sentences and an apparent refusal to start any sentence with the *I* pronoun. It started the same time she started cutting, and I didn't quite understand why; my best guess was that it was her way to draw as little attention to herself as possible. The driver didn't seem to find it odd, however. He still had a friendly look on his face, and as concerned as I was about her, this seemed the best possible situation right then.

After pulling onto the road, he held up the McDonald's bag and asked if she was hungry. When she said she was, he offered her the bag. "My eyes were bigger than my stomach. There's a breakfast burrito and some hash browns I haven't touched. Help yourself."

Frankie devoured the food, then curled herself on the back

seat and fell asleep. He drove in silence over the Mississippi and past the exit for the trailer park where Frankie and Raina used to live. He occasionally turned around to take a peek at her, as a father might check on his child. It was a quiet two hours until traffic came to a sudden stop and he hit the brakes.

Frankie sat up. "Where are we?" She squinted out into the bright light.

"Looks like the western suburbs of Chicago. Major traffic from here on, I'd suppose."

Frankie looked out the side window nonchalantly as she slyly unzipped the driver's messenger bag. She reached in and explored with her fingers.

"Mind if I ask what are you doing, miss?" He adjusted the mirror.

She sat up, combed her fingers through her hair. "Nothing."

"Unless you live in a vacuum there's no such thing as nothing. We're all of us always doing something, so why don't you join me up here for the rest of the drive? That way you can avoid temptation."

She glanced at the laptop and iPad in the bag, then climbed up to the front seat.

"Really appreciate this ride," she said. She pulled down the sun visor, where there was a clip-on mirror, and wiped sleep from her eyes. Then she reached for her backpack and pulled out the Koran and a zippered Sponge Bob pouch. She retrieved a tube of lip-gloss from the pouch, which she applied in slow, deliberate motion. She smacked her lips together, and he watched as she did. I was becoming a little worried.

"Said thanks for the ride."

He nodded. "No problem. It's a good thing when a fella can help out a young lady." He had both hands on the steering wheel and his right thumb kept tapping as if it had its own agenda, its own music. She pulled her feet up on the seat, wrapped her lanky arms around her knees, and looked out at a construction crew in orange vests.

"Except I'm worried that what I'm doing might be wrong," he said. "You're not running away, are you? I'd hate to be accused of harboring a runaway."

She concentrated on the workers, still, as she began to chew her fingernails. "No," she said. "I'm not." She continued to chew, and when one of the cuticles started to bleed, she sucked at the blood. I wondered why couldn't this be enough blood for her to know she was alive. Why she had to cut too.

He asked her about the Koran in her lap, and she merely shrugged, never taking her eyes away from the view out the window. "Okay, I get it," he said. "You don't want to tell me anything about yourself. That's chill. My daughter never wanted to talk to me either." He stepped on the accelerator.

She pulled her fingertip from her mouth and looked over at him. "You have a daughter?"

He drove for a full minute without answering. "Had. I had a daughter. She was lovely."

"Oh," Frankie said. She looked at his ponytail. "You don't much look like a dad."

"And you don't look like someone who's *not* running away. Especially with those bare feet."

She curled her toes under.

After a few minutes of silence, he asked her where exactly she wanted him to take her, and she bit her fingernails again. "Wherever you're going."

He laughed. "I'm sorry, but I don't suppose that will work very well."

"Why not?"

His jaw shifted as he shifted gears. "It wouldn't be right, that's why. Besides, I'm on a business trip. I'm only staying one night here in Chicago, and then I'm going on to New England. From there, it's home to Ireland."

"Home. I wish."

He tapped his fingers against the steering wheel. "What I meant was where, in Chicago, should I drop you?"

She shrugged and checked her mother's cell phone. There were no voice mails or text messages, no one trying to find her. "Can you take me to the airport?"

The airport? Her grandfather lived in the heart of downtown. I couldn't imagine why she wanted to go to the airport.

A short while later, the driver pulled into the O'Hare Oasis on I-294 for gas. He pulled his wallet from the messenger bag, took out a $50 bill, and tossed the wallet back into the bag. When he went inside to pay, Frankie opened the wallet, thumbed through the bills, and pulled two twenties out. She slipped them into her bra.

When they arrived at the terminal a short while later, he got out of the car and walked around to open her door. She just sat there. He held out his hand to her, but still she didn't move.

"Miss?"

At last she took his hand and climbed out. He pulled out her backpack and set it curbside.

"Well, Miss, I would say this has been my pleasure. Those were a quick three hours, they were."

She looked down at the ground and shoved her hands in her pockets.

"Miss?" He took her chin between his thumb and forefinger and lifted her face. With the back of his other hand, he brushed her cheek. It was an intimate gesture from a stranger and yet somehow it seemed just right.

"Give you some money for gas?" she said, fingering the neckline of her sweatshirt.

He laughed. "No, thanks. You need that money more than I do." If ever I thought I saw a look of guilt on her face, it was now.

"We hardly even talked," she said.

"Yes, it's true. But we talked some. And sometimes just a little talk is the right amount."

"Don't even know your name."

"Nor do I know yours. And maybe that's for the best as well." He took her right hand into his and forced a handshake from her. "You take care, Miss."

"Thought you'd..." she said.

They stood still in frozen handshake as he waited for her to finish her sentence.

"I thought you'd be like all the others."

"Excuse me? I'm not sure what you mean by that."

"Like all the other men."

He tilted his head to the side, and the bright sun lightened his green irises. He reached for her other hand and clasped her two hands inside his.

"Look at me," he said. "I don't know about these other men. But I do know this. You're a beautiful young lady and a strong one at that, I can tell. You'll be fine, Miss. Just fine."

"Frankie." She blurted it out. "Name's Frankie."

As she stood with him, immobile, it occurred to me how young and small and lonely she really was. With all she'd faced over the years, I sometimes forgot she was still a child. And now here she stood vulnerable but also desperate for someone to tell her she'd be okay, for someone to believe in her. Ryan and I had left her by moving West, and Cece left her through death, and Raina...was Raina. There was her grandfather, but he had his own life and grief and simply wasn't fit to raise Frankie no matter how much he loved her. It came down to a perfect stranger giving her what she needed.

"So where will you be heading, Miss Frankie?"

"Don't know for sure. Out West somewhere. Oregon."

Of course. It made sense now. She was trying to get to Ryan.

He walked around the car, got back into the driver's seat, and leaned over toward the open passenger door.

"You're a good man, aren't you," she said, a statement rather than a question.

He rubbed his chin for a moment. "That's difficult to say, Miss Frankie. Is anyone all good? Is anyone all bad? We're all human, you know. We do the best we can as long as we have something to believe in."

I made a mental note of what he said: *something to believe in.* I had been so focused on this plan I had for Frankie that I'd lost track of my own fate. Like Frankie, I didn't know exactly where I was or where I was headed. I, too, needed something to believe in—even if it was just the possibility of resting in peace.

The man shifted into first gear and adjusted his rearview mirror. "And Miss Frankie," he said. "My name's Seamus."

He nodded at her and she shut the door gently. She stood at the curb watching the back of his Jeep, waving until the car was lost amidst the limos and shuttle buses and all the other airport traffic. Brakes squealed, cars honked, skycaps called out to travelers, and Frankie hoisted her backpack onto her shoulder. She wiped her eyes with the back of her hand, and entered the terminal, still barefoot.

8 Chapter Eight

Frankie found the nearest women's restroom, went into the furthest stall, and locked the door. She waved her hand in front of a motion detector, and a fresh plastic cover slid over the seat. She waved her hand two more times, and two more fresh covers slid out. She smiled. Then she pulled down her jeans and panties and sat down. Before I thought to look away, she took a razor blade from her Sponge Bob pouch, and then I couldn't leave her. Instead, I watched as she drew it down the inside of her left thigh and adjusted her position so the blood—that one sign that she was really alive—drained into the toilet bowl.

When the blood dried, she switched into the clothes in her backpack: one of her grandmother's black silk dresses and a pair of Raina's four-inch stilettos. Outside the stall, she positioned herself in front of a mirror, swept her black hair up in a chignon, and put on a silver locket once given to her by a boy in middle school. She traced black liner along her eyelids, winging it at the edges of her eyes, and applied a fresh coat of reddish-brown lip-gloss. When she left the restroom and walked through the terminal, she looked like an exotic runway model, other than the scars on her arms and the tired backpack slung over her shoulder.

She did not look back when a woman ran out of the restroom screeching for the police about a stolen wallet.

At the security gate, Frankie held out Raina's driver's license for the TSA agent as though she'd done it a thousand times before. The plump old woman asked for her boarding pass.

"Oh dear," Frankie said, her voice lower than usual, mature, sultry. "My younger sister has it, and she's already gone through here." Frankie looked out beyond the security area into the terminal and pointed to a young girl in braids, skipping along.

"See there she is! Lecia! Lecia, come back here!" I don't know where she got the name Lecia, but her act was entirely believable until the agent suggested she have the girl paged. Frankie declined, explaining her sister was deaf, and the agent eyed her and laughed.

"Really? You just called her name, so she can't be that deaf. I'm sorry; you'll have to go back." The line of travelers behind Frankie had grown. Some of the passengers were starting to grumble. The TSA agent pointed to the exit. "That way," the agent said. "That's the way out."

Frankie kicked off Raina's heels and walked all the way to the next terminal in her bare feet, swinging the shoes from her hand as she went.

Soon she spotted a bedraggled-looking woman sitting in a row of black vinyl seats and watching over three small children, two boys, around five and three, and an adorable toddler in a pink stroller. This was the kind of family I had wanted, and I would have given anything just then to be in Frankie's shoes, even if they were Raina's stilettos, to be able to sit with those children for a few minutes. Which is exactly what Frankie did.

She sat at the end of the row and ignored the family at first, pretending to talk on her mother's cell phone. Then she started up a conversation with the young mother, telling her how cute her kids were and so on. One of the boys—the smaller one with a devilish grin—started to run toward an airport door, and Frankie jumped up to stop him. She grabbed him and swung him up in the air and tickled him all the way back to his mother. At that point, the girl asked to sit in Frankie's lap.

"No," the mother said. "You leave this nice lady alone." It was odd to hear Frankie referred to as a lady, but in that black dress, with her hair and makeup as they were, it made perfect sense. She didn't look like a young teen anymore.

"It's all right," Frankie said. "I'm in no hurry."

"You sure?"

"Absolutely."

The girl snuggled eagerly into Frankie's lap, and as she settled in, Frankie started to relax. She closed her eyes, hugged the girl tight, rocking and humming a little. My heart ached to be there with her.

The two boys, however, were as unsettled as possible and ran around whooping and shooting imaginary guns at one another and ignoring their mother's commands to stop until the younger one froze abruptly, his eyes widened. He grabbed his wet crotch with one hand. The poor mother, whose hair was already slipping down from a comb, looked like she couldn't take one more thing.

"Go on," Frankie said. "I'll stay here with the others."

"No, that's okay," the mother said. "Come on everyone, time to go to the bathroom."

"No, me stay here," the little girl said. "Right here." She tapped at Frankie's nose.

"Go on," Frankie said again. "How 'bout you take the boys and I'll watch this little pumpkin. And leave your bags. I'll watch them too."

The mother didn't move.

"Here ," Frankie said. She handed the mother a wallet. "You can keep this as collateral. That way you'll know I'm good for my word." The master manipulator had offered the woman the wallet she'd stolen in the restroom.

"You are too kind," the mother said. "And no, that's all right. I trust you." She reached into one of the boy's backpacks for a fresh pair of overalls and Spiderman underpants. Taking the boys' hands, she marched off to the nearest women's restroom. Frankie set the little girl beside her.

"Let's see if your Mommy has any treats for you in here."

She dug around in a cluttered diaper bag and found a bag of dry cereal. Once the child was busy smashing Cheerios into her mouth, Frankie rooted through the outer pockets, where she found four boarding passes and the woman's wallet. She flipped through the passes and took the one that said Danielle Clifton. From the wallet, she took some cash, along with a Visa card and a library card featuring the same name, and she slipped all the stolen goods into a zippered pocket on her backpack. Then she asked the girl if she'd share some of her cereal. Which naturally the child did.

I was impressed by her cleverness and anxious for her to escape her miserable life, but I was disheartened to see that she was following in Raina's path, using crime as a crutch. Frankie and I had spent a lot of time talking about honesty and integrity and doing the right thing. We talked about Raina's choices: drugs, shoplifting, prostitution. We talked about how it may have seemed that was the only way Raina could provide for her family, the only way they could get what they wanted or needed. But we also talked about right from wrong, and I thought Frankie understood that. Deep down, I think she did. I'd bet she felt at least a tinge of guilt over what she was doing. I'd also bet she found a way to justify it all, too. Maybe she figured when she was older she'd redeem herself. What she wouldn't know yet, at her young age, was that redemption is something you can chase all your life but never quite capture.

The mother approached, followed by two whining boys. Frankie stood up.

"I'm glad you're back," she said when the mother was still ten paces away. "I totally lost track of time. I've got to run or I'm going to miss my flight. Your daughter was just perfect."

The mother blew her bangs out of her face. "Thank you so much. I couldn't have done it without you."

"No problem," Frankie said. "By the way, where are you all heading?"

"Disneyland!" the two boys shouted in unison.

"Go see Mickey Mouse!" the little girl said.

Frankie's smile twitched. She had just stolen Disneyland from these kids.

"We need to get moving, too," the mother said. "Let's all go to security together." She looked at Frankie as she strapped the girl into the stroller. "Maybe you can help us. Looks like you're traveling light. Where are you going, anyway?"

Frankie scanned the nearby monitors with a look of panic. "Oh my gosh. I just realized I'm in the wrong terminal."

"You're not flying Delta?"

"No, United. Oh my gosh, I've got to run. Goodbye, everyone!" Frankie grabbed her pack, blew a kiss to the little girl, and ran toward yet another terminal, shoes swinging from her hand once again.

She had to wait twenty minutes in that security line, and she grasped Danielle's boarding pass so tightly I thought the ink would bleed onto the palms of her sweaty hands. She kept looking over her shoulder. Finally she made it to the front of the line. This TSA agent was a tall, handsome black man.

Frankie flashed her smile and leaned in toward him as she handed over the boarding pass, the way Raina leaned into her clients. For some reason, the more you lean into another person, the more sincere you seem.

The agent told her she was in the wrong terminal. Without even blinking, she said she was meeting a friend in this terminal before going to hers.

"You have a driver's license or passport, Miss Clifton?" he asked.

"No, sir," she said, standing tall. "I live in the city, don't need to drive. And I've got no plans to leave this fine country, ever. So I don't need a passport. This is all I've got." She was quite the actress, that girl. No problem with pronouns this time. She handed him the credit card and library card, along with a small piece of paper with a phone number. "When I called the airline," she said, "they said this would suffice." She emphasized the word suffice. He looked at her, then the scrap of paper, and then back at her quizzically. She responded with a coy smile. "I'll be back in town in a week or so."

He told her she really should get a government-issued identification card, but he handed the documents back to her and wished her a good trip. She flashed him another flirtatious smile as he waved her toward the metal detector, and I wasn't sure whether to be pleased for her or disturbed by what just happened. In today's world of security and terrorism, I would have thought she wouldn't make it through. But apparently loopholes are still alive and well, at least for beautiful young women. Living women.

Some of the concourses at O'Hare are like miniature shopping malls. After changing back into her jeans and sweatshirt, and washing off the makeup, Frankie browsed in stores that sold sunglasses, books, men's ties, body lotion, electronics, jewelry, and even Harley Davidson souvenirs. She picked out a pair of red flip-flops with little brass tacks around the edges, a Snickers bar, and a big white comb, and she used Danielle's Visa to pay for everything. She also stole a Toni Morrison paperback and some sugar-free gum. Then she walked down the B concourse, scanning departure display monitors along the way. San Francisco, Washington D.C., New York. Tokyo, Frankfurt, Houston, Minneapolis, Omaha, Los Angeles.

In a restroom, Frankie leaned over a woman's tote bag to reach for a paper towel. While the woman applied her lipstick, Frankie stole a boarding pass from the outer pocket of the tote. She visited every other restroom in the B concourse, too, and found something to steal in each: a wallet, a cell phone, an iPod. In less than a half-hour, she'd ripped off more than a dozen passengers, and as she headed for the escalator to the C concourse, some of those befuddled passengers were already lining up at the United customer-service desk.

In the C concourse, she came upon a gate where a plane was boarding for nonstop service to Portland, Oregon. She approached a college-aged young man, blonde and muscular, who was leaning back in his seat and listening to his iPod with his eyes closed. His backpack was on the ground next to his feet; the boarding pass was sticking out of the front pocket like a flag. She pretended to be deeply engrossed in her new book and tripped over his outstretched legs. When he sat up startled, she fumbled forward and slyly slipped his boarding pass from his pack into the pages of her book.

"I'm so sorry," he said. "My big feet."

"No, my fault. Sorry."

He blushed, and she held his gaze as though studying her prey. "My mother says it's amazing I find my way anywhere because I always have my nose stuck in a book. Mind if I sit here?" She pointed to the seat next to him.

He shook his head. After glancing toward the line of passengers, he began to gather up his belongings. She touched his arm gently.

"Hey," she said. "Going to get a drink. Want something?"

He blushed. "Sure, but let me get it, and yours too. What would you like?"

"Just a Coke. Thanks, I'll watch your stuff."

When he was gone, she flipped the book open and took a look at his boarding pass. His name was Harrison. She looked toward the gate's doorway; the line to board was thinning. He returned and handed her the soda, but she frowned.

"Sorry, I said Diet Coke."

"You did? My bad. Can you make do with this? I need to get on that flight."

She shook her head. "Diabetic. Can't have sugar. Forget it, that's all right."

"No, no. I'll get you the right thing. Just hold the plane for me okay?" He ran back into the concourse, and she checked the overhead monitor. There were still twelve minutes until departure.

She abandoned his bag and ran down the concourse to another gate. The sign said Vancouver B.C. That flight wasn't scheduled to leave for two more hours, and the waiting area was relatively empty, but Frankie immediately found her mark—an old woman dozing in a wheelchair. Once again, she stole this woman's travel documents and wallet like a seasoned criminal.

As she jogged back toward the Portland gate, I searched for a hint of remorse in her expression. I saw none. Rather, it seemed that what she did was simply natural, a part of who she was, almost instinctual. Was there something in her blood that made it impossible for Frankie, like Raina, to live with integrity, to follow society's rules? Cece and Jack had been hard-working, honest, church-going people who I doubt had ever stolen so much as a Tootsie Roll, and they'd tried their best to teach their adopted daughter and granddaughter right from wrong. I would never have guessed this sort of selfish, cunning behavior could be inherited. And if it could, I wondered, who would have been the genetic source for Raina's actions? Lynn?

Frankie slipped into another restroom. I checked the monitor. The gate's door would be closing in seven minutes. She quickly reinvented herself again, switching into the black dress and heels, scooping her hair back, reapplying Raina's makeup. When she re-emerged, she stood in line at a Vienna hot-dog stand across from the Portland gate.

The vendor moved in slow motion as he filled the orders of customers ahead of her. When it was finally Frankie's turn, he held up his finger. He added more hot dogs to the steamer, changed the roll of receipt tape on the cash register, and added some bottles of fruit juice to the refrigerated case.

"A Polish, just with mustard, please. And a Pepsi," she said, when he was finally ready.

"Coke, no Pepsi."

"Okay, Coke, whatever. Please hurry."

"Diet?"

"No, no Diet."

He set the hot dog in a bun so carefully you'd think he was putting a baby in a crib, squirted the mustard in a curlicue design, and handed it to her along with the plastic bottle of soda pop. Two minutes to go.

Frankie gave him a five-dollar bill.

"Eight-fifty," he said.

"For a lousy hot dog and a drink?"

"That's right."

She pulled out a ten-dollar bill. "Here, keep the change. Just give me back my five."

"Thank you," he said, and then he looked up at the man behind her. "Next?"

"Hey," she said. "I want my five back."

He gave her a blank stare, but then pushed some buttons on his cash drawer and slowly pulled out a five-dollar bill. She took it and ran for the gate in her mother's heels, with her backpack slipping off one shoulder. The gate area was empty and the attendant was closing the door.

"Wait, please!" She was slightly out of breath.

"I'm scheduled to fly to Vancouver later today, but I just got a phone call that my grandmother is very sick in Portland. She has cancer. I wondered if I could fly stand-by to Portland now, and then I'll figure out how to get to Vancouver later." She pulled the wheelchair woman's boarding pass out. Dolores Ahern, seat 15E. How Frankie even knew about standby status, or came up with this idea, completely baffled me, and her entire charade at O'Hare illuminated for me what sort of actress she could be when necessary.

The attendant shook his head. "I don't know. It might be too late. I'll see what I can do."

As he typed on the keyboard, Frankie glanced around. Harrison was nowhere to be seen. She set the hot dog and drink on the counter, reached into her pack, and swung a flamboyant scarf over her head, deftly wrapping it like a hijab. I recognized it as a scarf Cece had given to Raina; it was ablaze with citrus yellows and fiery oranges.

"You're in luck," the attendant said. He hurried to the jet way door, scanned her boarding pass, and handed it back to her. "15E on this flight too. Have a good flight, Miss Ahern."

Frankie climbed over an old man in the aisle seat and shoved her backpack under the seat in front of her. Before the plane even took off, she wolfed down her hot dog and fell asleep.

Four hours later, the pilot's voice came through the speaker system.

"Folks, this is your captain. We're in our final descent. And I'd like to be the first to welcome you to Portland, Oregon, where the local temperature is 51 degrees and visibility is good. We'll have you on the ground shortly, but before we let you deplane, it seems we have a little official business to take care of. So we'll kindly ask you, on behalf of the Port of Portland authorities, to stay in your seats when we land. And as for your cell phones, we must ask you to keep them stowed and in the off position until we give you the all-clear."

The other passengers looked around at one another. The man in 12C, however—a middle-aged slim man in an outdated jogging suit—leered back at Frankie and it gave me the creeps.

When the plane landed, he stood up and walked down the aisle to her row, even though the passengers had been instructed to remain seated with their seatbelts fastened.

"Miss, you'll need to come with me," he said sternly. He flashed a badge: U.S. Marshal.

Everyone stared at Frankie, still wearing the black dress but now back in her red flip-flops. She climbed over the old man again and moved toward the front doorway as directed. She acted neither surprised nor embarrassed.

Once in the terminal, she saw three officials waiting for her: a white male police officer, a TSA woman in a blue shirt that barely stretched across her breasts, and a young black man in jeans.

The police officer nodded at the U.S. Marshal, then took Frankie by the arm. The other two who greeted her followed. The entourage hurried through the airport to a secure elevator that delivered them directly to the Port of Portland Police Department office.

They led her past several holding cells, and after the TSA official patted her down, she was told to sit in a chair that was cracked and looked barely able to hold Frankie's minimal weight. She looked at her surroundings. The table in front of her was scratched with initials and graffiti symbols; the worn blue carpet was stained and pocked with cigarette burns; a pile of filthy jackets and other orphaned items cluttered a corner of the room. In nearby cubicles, police officers worked on computers or talked on telephones, only paying nominal attention to her. She leaned back, kicked off her flip-flops, and set her bare feet up on an adjacent chair.

The police officer who had met her at the gate, Officer Tracy, began to search her backpack.

"Hey. What are you doing?" she said.

"Just looking. You've got quite a collection of gadgets and boarding passes, don't you?" He inspected each item and fanned the passes out like a deck of cards. "So which one are you? Dolores? Danielle? Miriam?"

"Frankie."

"Your name is Frankie?" He studied the documents. "I don't see anything in here that says Frankie." He rifled through the wallets and pulled out some drivers' licenses, tossing them one by one onto the table until he found Raina's. He studied the photo on that one and then Frankie's face. "Sure your name isn't Raina? Raina Lynette Irving?"

"No, that's my mother. I'm Frankie. Françesca Cecilia Rizzoni.

"All right, here's the deal, Ms. Rizzoni. Or whoever you say you are."

"Whomever," she said. I loved her spunk, although I wasn't sure she was correct.

He took hold of her arm and squeezed it tightly.

"Ow!" She twisted free from his grip as the other man who'd met her at the gate approached. He introduced himself to Frankie as a social worker with the Department of Human Services, and he told the officer to go easy on her.

"I'll let go of you now, but don't think you're getting away with anything else, young lady," the officer said. He began to stuff everything back into her pack, hesitating to sneer at the Koran. Then he started to walk away with all of it.

"Hey, some of those things are really mine," she said. "It's not all stolen. Give that back to me."

"Well, that's nice to hear," he said. "But difficult to prove."

"You doing okay?" the social worker said once the police officer was out of earshot. He had neat cornrow braids, gray eyes, and gentle hands that matched his voice.

"Yeah, I guess. What's going to happen to me? Am I going to be arrested?"

"We're waiting to find out," he said. "Has anyone read you your rights?"

She shook her head. "Why? Am I going to jail?"

He smiled and shook his head. "I doubt it. Not at your age. That cop just has a bug up his ass, don't worry about him. But don't get me wrong, I'm not saying what you did was okay. In fact, it was very wrong."

He brought her a bottle of water and then, and then waited for the police officer to return, he asked her about school, friends, music—the things you try to talk about with teenagers. Her answers, like those of many teens, were mostly monosyllabic.

The police officer finally came back an hour later and tossed the backpack to her. "Looks like this is your lucky day," he said. "You must have one helluva grandfather. He's agreed to meet you at O'Hare first thing tomorrow morning, along with Chicago PD and whichever other authorities decide to come to the party. And then we'll see what happens to you next. Capisce?"

Frankie looked to the social worker, who nodded in confirmation, and then turned her attention to her backpack.

"Don't bother looking for your stolen items," the officer said as he handed a large sealed envelope to the social worker.

"What about my money? And my mother's driver's license? Had some money of my own to start. You can't take that away from me."

"We're going to leave that up to Chicago PD to sort out. Right now, you've got a plane to catch."

With the sealed envelope in hand, the social worker whisked Frankie off to the red-eye flight to O'Hare. He rushed her to the front of the passenger boarding line, flashed a boarding pass and his identification card, and escorted Frankie onto the plane to a first class seat. He handed the sealed envelope to a flight attendant and told Frankie she'd best behave from here on out.

"You're not coming?"

He shook his head and laughed. "Wish I could. Good luck."

9 Chapter Nine

A few hours after Frankie left on the return flight to Chicago, Lynn was on her way to the Portland airport to take off for Anchorage. Like Frankie's flight, this would also be a three-and-a-half hour journey. But while Frankie was given a leisurely seat in first class, Lynn was stuck in a middle seat in the back of the economy cabin, squashed between a guy with refrigerator-wide shoulders and a young woman who stank of stale onions. Poor Lynn perspired for almost the entire flight.

As they approached Anchorage, she looked past the large man in the window seat to the pristine sea of snow-capped mountains and enormous blue-white glaciers. I wondered how she felt. For me, the vista was so mesmerizing that I felt an antsy patter where my heart would be. I had always experienced an unstoppable exhilaration whenever I set out for a big climb, and this would be the greatest climb ever for me, even if I wouldn't be doing the hard work myself. I was finally going to see Alaska, where I'd always wanted to go. And best of all I'd be with Ryan and the great Lynn Van Swol, a female pioneer in mountaineering and a long-time idol of mine. Even if she was now puking a medley of dried apricots and raw almonds into a little paper bag.

As the other passengers turned toward her, I studied them. They were mostly a young set, dressed in blue jeans and Patagonia shirts and hiking boots. One young woman had tattoos up and down her arms. Several passengers had boarded with sleeping bags and guitars. These were my kind of people, the people who called a landscape like this home. How I longed to be with them.

"We are now beginning our final descent into Ted Stevens Anchorage International Airport," a flight attendant announced.

Final descent.

Final is such an irrevocable, definitive word, implying that much had come before, and now it's over. In college, finals are your last exams. Our move back to Oregon was our final relocation. At my own funeral service, the pastor said I had reached my final resting place, suggesting there had been other rest stops along the way. Little did he know I have yet to really rest.

The word *final* seemed to have been Lynn's favorite word lately. She'd assured Greg over the past several months that this would be her final climb. She'd sworn the same thing to her boss, as well. The same to anyone else who asked, in fact. "This is it, my final attempt on Denali."

Which would have been fine with me except for what she

often tagged on afterward: "Or I'll die trying." This, of course, wouldn't work for me, or more precisely, for Ryan and Frankie.

As the airplane descended through a band of clouds, Lynn started to sweat again. I hoped it was just a hot flash, and not something more ominous. You can't start a high-altitude climb sick; that could be suicide. I doubted she was ill though. Lynn was more careful about germs than the staff at my cancer clinic.

The Anchorage airport was light and airy, with glass sculptures resembling ice seracs and wrought-iron scenes of salmon leaping ladders. The taxidermy was impressive too: a golden eagle swooped down on a ptarmigan; a polar bear showed off its fangs; a pack of gray wolves feasted on a slain caribou. The atmosphere was both welcoming and foreboding, with the terminal and its artwork reflecting the competing forces that are bitter realities in Alaska. Enjoy the beauty but do not trust it, they seemed to say. This is not a land to be taken lightly.

After scrubbing her face and hands in the women's restroom—and brushing and flossing her teeth—Lynn headed for baggage claim. She untangled a luggage cart from the rack and carefully swiped the handle with a hand wipe.

Three of her pieces came out quickly: the monstrous blue duffel stuffed with a fleece jacket, parka, snow pants, and other mountain clothes; a smaller blue duffel containing her sleeping bag and tent; and her big red backpack full of ropes and harnesses, carabiners, a mess kit, and all her other climbing and camping gear. Every time she tried to heave the largest duffel onto the lower rack of the luggage cart, the cart rolled away a few inches. She eventually got the duffel on, but then the rest of the luggage fell off. It reminded me of trying to keep preschoolers in a straight line at Sunday school. By the time Lynn managed to stabilize the tower, she was sweating again. And when she turned for her fourth piece of luggage, the conveyer belt whined to a stop.

"Shit," she said, to no one.

She maneuvered the unwieldy cart, with a front wheel that insisted on going the opposite direction, to the customer service desk, only to find it deserted. She looked around for help, and it was then she noticed a young raven-haired woman near the door carrying a baby in a backpack. The woman held a sign that read:

Lynn Swoll
William

Lynn steered the cart toward the woman.

"Hi, I'm Lynn. Van Swol. With one l."

The woman stared blankly at Lynn, who then pointed to the sign, raised the volume of her voice as though speaking to someone hard of hearing or mentally challenged.

"On-your-sign. That's-me. Are-you-my-driver?" Lynn brushed her bangs back from her sweaty forehead; the hairs settled in an unattractive clump on top of her head.

The woman, so small she didn't reach Lynn's chin, shrugged. "I guess so."

"Okay, then. I'm still waiting for one more piece. It's my

suitcase with all my street clothes."

The woman looked over the gear in the cart. "Is all this stuff yours, too?"

"Yes, it is."

The woman laughed. "Okay, I guess." Her tone was snide and doubtful. "That's a lot for a climber."

"I think I know what I'm doing," Lynn said under her breath. She headed for the customer service desk again, and this time a handsome man intercepted her. He was well over six feet tall with dark, espresso skin and a deliciously strong physique. He wore a starched black shirt, brown leather jacket, and black reptilian boots. His hair was trimmed short, his skin unblemished, and his teeth nearly fluorescent white. I'd seen him on the plane. I figured he was around my age—fortyish—but nowadays I find it hard to tell how old people are. As long as they're living, they look young to me.

He was trailing a black roller bag behind him. "I believe this is yours," he said. His voice was like rich chocolate.

Even at 5'7", Lynn looked small next to him. Her pale cheeks and the tip of her nose reddened as her damp bangs dropped back to her face.

"I'm Will," he said, extending his hand to her. She took it, nodded, and said nothing. He turned and introduced himself to the driver, who now brightened like a southern belle.

"Hello, I'm Marisa," the driver said cheerfully, holding her petite hand out to his strong, large one. "Nice to meet you. No bags, sir?"

"Oh no, no bags. I had them shipped FedEx," he replied, as though everyone did this. "They should already be at the hotel."

"Oh, very smart of you," Marisa said. "Okay, well then, let's go." She held his gaze for another moment, and then he gently took her baby's little fingers in his, the way you would hold the fragile handle of an antique china teacup. What better way to melt a mother's heart than by fawning over her baby? I felt a twinge of self-pity.

"That's Aashka," Marisa said, beaming even more brightly.

"A pleasure to meet you, young lady," he said. Even Aashka cooed.

Lynn struggled to keep her things on the cart, steer it in a straight line with one hand, and pull her big suitcase with the other. Will stepped aside, watching as she jabbed her left elbow out and attempted to veer the cart to the right. When the cart missed the doorway and bumped into the wall, he gripped the handlebar of the cart and smiled down at her. His eyes skimmed her body, stopping at breast level and then again at her hips.

"Allow me."

For a moment they both gripped the cart's handle, two strangers locked in an unexpected and spontaneous power struggle. Finally Lynn, studying his eyes and his face, let go and wiped her brow with her forearm. Will grinned down at her and pushed the cart outside as easily as if it were an empty baby stroller. Lynn followed, pulling her suitcase like a child pulling a toy on a rope.

Cold wind whipped at her face as she walked through the door, a frigid assault expected on the mountain but not at the airport on the first of May. I felt its sting, too. Normally the temperatures should have been much warmer, but an unseasonal foot of snow had fallen a few days earlier, and the wind chill was in the teens. Lynn was dressed in only a thin t-shirt and jeans, and the cold air made her nipples harden. A fact that did not escape Will's notice.

"Normally, I can make this drive under three hours, easy," Marisa said, leading them to a dilapidated red minivan with more rust than paint on its exterior and an interior cluttered with sippy cups, paper coffee cups, and muddy footprints. Marisa strapped Aashka into her infant seat. "But the roads are slick today, so we'll be going a little more slowly. And I need to make a couple of stops. Hope you're not in any hurry."

Lynn hoisted her bags into the back of the van by herself, retrieved a sweatshirt from her suitcase, and slammed the rear door shut. Perspiration drenched the armpits of her t-shirt and spotted the front of her shirt between her small breasts.

As she climbed through the side door, she took stock of the van's layout. There were three rows behind the front seat. The baby was in the first row. Lynn chose the second row, and Will climbed in next to her, ignoring the empty passenger seat and open third row. Lynn leaned her head against the cold window and pulled her sweatshirt over her chest like a blanket.

"No time like the present to get to know one another," he said, scooting closer and stretching his arm along the back of the seat behind her. She fanned her face with her hand.

Marisa asked if anyone needed a bathroom break or food and explained more about the stops she'd be making. First would be Antelope Joe's house to pick up some frozen halibut for her Auntie. Next a quick stop at Costco. And, closer to Talkeetna, she'd need to pick up some birch sap.

Lynn groaned. "Let's just make them quick stops, all right? It's already been a long day."

Will tried in vain to make small talk as they drove. Lynn was the quiet type; some even called her a loner. Regardless of how you'd categorize her, I knew what she needed then wasn't superficial conversation but some time and space to center herself, to empty her mind of distractions, to prepare for the big climb. Eventually she leaned back and closed her eyes.

The road out of Anchorage aimed first for the snow-draped Chugach Range and then toward the Talkeetnas. But once it veered north, the land became flat, barren, and unforgiving. Lynn slept until the van swerved; a pick-up had practically sideswiped them.

The truck had Washington plates, which triggered an important memory for me. It was in Washington that I did my first major climb. My father took me there when I was a teen, to Mt. Shuksan in the North Cascades. It was that trip that changed everything for me.

My father had crawled into our tent right after we summited and made it back to camp. But I couldn't rest; I was so wired up with the thrill of conquering nature. I also loved the camaraderie with other climbers—and the campfire gossip. I wandered to a neighboring campsite, where three guys sat around a campfire drinking cheap wine from bota bags and dreaming out loud about massifs like K2 and

Kangchenjunga. As they drank more, they started arguing and bragging about who'd crossed the worst glaciers or who'd climbed the highest peaks. And later, after offering me a sip or two, or three, of wine—I'd acquired a taste for wine by then even though I was well under age—they shared stories about some of the female climbers they knew, or knew of. There weren't that many women on the climbing circuit back then, but these guys seemed to know them all. And one of them was Lynn Van Swol.

Having already bagged Kilimanjaro and the Carstensz Pyramid, she was making a name for herself by the time she was in her mid-twenties. Articles had been written about her in the climbing magazines. *Life* magazine had even run a photo montage of her. One of the guys said she was too skinny and another thought her body looked too hard. The third guy said it was her eyes that bothered him. They were too cold and cunning, like a wolf's. How ironic. At that time, I had not heard of her or seen her photo, but just as I was becoming addicted to the mountains, I became obsessed with her. I needed to find out more about this woman, wanted to grow up to be like her. But that was before the Internet had as much to offer as it now does, and Lynn, they said, was notoriously private. I would have to rely on stories like theirs.

"I heard she's a lesbian," one of them said.

"I heard she's running from her past," another said as he lit up a joint.

"Did you hear she got knocked up?" the third said. The fire's light brightened his face. This woman was pregnant! Now that caught my attention. I was still a virgin when I heard this, although not for much longer.

"Yeah, and the father was Arabian or Iranian or some other –ian dude. Some Aladdin sort of guy. What was his name?" This was getting better and better. I didn't know anyone who dated what we called *ethnic* boys back then.

"Abdul, or Famool, or something like that. Ali Ababa, maybe."

One of the climbers stirred the fire's embers with a stick. "Farid. His name was Farid, I think." The others shrugged and nodded in unison.

"So did she marry him?" I said. "This guy, Farid?"

The group looked at me and laughed in unison. "What planet did you come from?" one of them asked. "No, she didn't marry him. She didn't even keep the baby."

"She didn't? What happened to the baby?" I asked.

"She abandoned it."

"She sold it."

"She ate it." One of them handed me the joint as they all guffawed. I didn't think it was very funny. Not at all. But I took the joint and stashed the image of Lynn and a baby into a protected corner of my memory. "Yeah, she's a black widow," he said. "They kill their mates and eat their young, you know."

Aashka also woke up when the van swerved again and started to wail, which awakened Will. He let out a big yawn and reached over to brush back a tendril of hair drooping down over Lynn's eyes. "How're you doin'?"

She told him she was fine and brushed his hand away. They rode for a while longer, and Will asked Marisa a few questions about Talkeetna.

It was her hometown, she said, and the gateway to Denali. "Was once an old mining town, and then a ghost town until thirty or forty years ago when all the climbers and outdoorsy types moved in. That's when it became legendary, because nearly everyone who climbs Denali starts in Talkeetna. Bradford Washburn, Harry Karstens, Doug Scott. I grew up hearing about them all."

Will asked about the wildlife, and she said there were plenty of sandhill cranes, eagles, and seagulls this spring. The bears—both grizzlies and blacks—were just waking up and would soon be coming down to the river, when the salmon come up. Will asked Lynn if she'd ever been to Alaska before.

"Yes, I have."

He grinned. "So you're not a virgin."

She scowled at him. "Hardly. This is my third trip, as a matter of fact. Third and final."

There was that word again.

After a while, he pulled a picture from his wallet. "That's my wife and my little girl, Savannah. Aren't they beauties?" His wife wore a strapless green gown, and his daughter was dressed in a matching green party dress with bows on each shoulder and short, puffy sleeves. She had the same eyes as her father. I couldn't help but think of Frankie.

"Cute." Lynn handed the picture back and pressed her shoulder against the van wall.

"So now it's your turn," he said to Lynn. "Why don't you tell us about yourself?" He started to reach for her wayward bangs again, but again she blocked his hand.

"I've got a better idea. Why don't you tell us a bit more about yourself. Like who you are and how you knew that suitcase was mine."

He threw his head back and laughed. "I saw your name on the luggage tag."

"Brilliant. But how did you know who I was?" she said.

"I saw your picture on the Internet," he said. "So I'd recognize you at the airport."

"My picture? On the Internet? But why would you be looking at pictures of me?"

"I Googled you."

"Googled?"

"Yeah, Googled. You know, Google, the search engine."

"Yes, I know what Google is for Christ's sake. But why on earth would you do that? I mean, who are you, anyway? And how did you know I was coming to Alaska? And why Google me?"

Marisa looked at Lynn in the rearview mirror.

"What do you know about this?" Lynn asked.

"Nothing."

Lynn still looked perplexed, and Will laughed again.

"What is so goddamn funny?" Lynn asked.

"You really don't know who I am, do you?"

She studied his face.

"No. Just William Somebody. That's all I know. So who the hell are you? I'm getting tired of whatever this annoying game of yours is."

He leaned into her so that his face was only inches from hers, and she drew back as far as she could, her head now pressed against the side window, but that didn't deter him. He placed one of his big, strong hands on her knee and whispered into her ear.

"I'm your new climbing partner."

Her face went blank, solid. Like granite.

They rode in a different type of silence now. The type where one person has taken control of a situation and the other has unwillingly surrendered, the type where the loser is trying to figure out how to get her power back. Like the way my relationships with my endocrinologist, and later my oncologist, evolved. I felt like they took my life away, and I desperately wanted them to give it back.

Marisa pulled off the highway just before the Talkeetna Spur Road, at an old roadside cabin surrounded by rusted cars, scrap metal, and hundreds of barren birch trees. This was where she needed to pick up the birch sap for Auntie. While Lynn waited, she reached into her backpack for a pen and a two-pocket folder. She climbed over Will, retreated to the last row of the van, and began to furiously write.

Notes for Sunny~

- *Heart pounding ...feeling torn...Alaska's unwelcome memories.*
- *Shuttle driver unprofessional...van a mess!*
- *Fellow climber. William. Doesn't look at all like a climber. Handsome. Unsettling.*
- *Farid.*

Farid! The name those climbers had mentioned so long ago, a name I'd never forgotten.

- *Must finally write about him. Tall, strong*

hands...amber eyes...phenomenal climber...wanted to conquer the world.

- *Birthfather.*

There it was, the confirmation of what I'd known all along.

I hadn't revealed my discovery to anyone, not even Ryan, because the coincidence of it all seemed too fantastic and because Ryan always cautioned me about meddling in other people's lives. And because he didn't want to focus on anything but the two of us in my final days. But now there it was, on paper. I wished I could run and tell him. And Frankie. And Cece, too.

Even now, Ryan would probably tell me to sit back and stop meddling.

As for Cece, I'm not sure what she would say if she heard I'd found Raina's birthmother. She had shared very little with Ryan and me about the adoption, which I assumed was because it had been a closed adoption. But maybe it was something else. Was it because Raina's birthfather was Middle Eastern? Thirty years ago, there was a lot of unrest in the Middle East, as there still is today, but it all seemed so foreign to us here in the United States then. We didn't know as much about Muslims or the Islamic culture or Iran. Or was she tightlipped about it not because of Farid but because she was afraid that Raina's birthmother might someday surface and Cece would be replaced, as an adoptive mother and as Frankie's grandmother, too?

I had been conflicted about doing all that research without Cece's approval, but it was too late for regrets or reservations. Ryan would soon be climbing Denali with Lynn, would soon get to know her during their struggle up the mountain, and together, if all went according to my plan, they would discover their mutual connection to Frankie. I was getting exactly what I had hoped for.

But that expression about being careful what you wish for was starting to haunt me. What if, for some reason, Lynn wasn't right for Frankie after all?

10 Chapter Ten

Jack looked old and tired at the gate, hunched over in a beige cardigan sweater and a wrinkled blue shirt. The woman with him was dressed stylishly, however even though the sun hadn't yet risen, in a purple shirtdress and matching shawl. They stood alongside two police officers who were also waiting for Frankie.

When she deplaned, they all escorted her to the Chicago Police Department office at O'Hare. She sat down at an old metal table, scraping her chair across the tile floor. Jack and the others remained standing opposite her. When two more men entered the room, Jack leaned against the wall and crossed his arms. One of the newcomers was Jack's attorney. The other introduced himself as Mr. Wick. He was obviously the person in charge.

"By all rights, young lady," Mr. Wick said, "you should be convicted of a plethora of crimes: suspicious behavior, theft, traveling with fraudulent documents." He paused, and Frankie looked to her grandfather.

"Dear Lord, Frankie," Jack said.

"What?"

"What on earth were you thinking? I don't know what's gotten into you."

"Oh, Papa, it's not that big of a deal."

"Not a big deal?" Mr. Wick said.

"Yes it is, a very big deal," Jack said. "What you've done is illegal. Not to mention immoral. I've been beside myself ever since I got the call from your school yesterday."

The woman in purple reached out for his arm.

"Who the hell is she?" Frankie pointed.

"Frankie, watch your language," he reprimanded. Jack was right; Frankie had no business speaking so rudely to anyone. But I knew her enough to know this was just her tough girl persona, completely opposite of the girl who'd ridden in Seamus's car the day before. She was wearing a mask to hide her fear.

"This is Ms. LaCroix. Ms. Beatrice LaCroix, an old friend of your grandmother's. She's a family therapist, and she's here to help."

Frankie sneered. "Yeah, right. Don't need her help." She reached into her pack for the gum she'd stolen, which somehow hadn't been confiscated, and popped a piece into her mouth. "Why'd the school call you anyway?"

"Because no one had called in to excuse your absence yesterday. And apparently you've got a number of other unexcused absences, so they tried to reach your mother."

"And of course they couldn't reach her 'cause she was passed out like always," Frankie said. I cringed when I heard her say this, recalling the scene in her mother's bedroom the day before, a scene no child should have to witness.

"Well, at any rate," Jack said, "they called me because I'm listed as your emergency contact. They said you'd missed twenty-three days of school since the beginning of the semester. Twenty-three days, Kitten! How could that be?"

Frankie studied her short, ragged fingernails and the cuticle scabs as she chewed dramatically.

"Oh, yes," Jack continued. "This was interesting. The principal also mentioned you were failing every class except English. Even PE. How the hell do you fail PE?" The room shook as an airplane thundered overhead.

"And now this. What were you doing, running away? Where on God's green earth did you think you were going? And then all this I've heard about you stealing boarding passes and wallets." He set both of his hands on the back of an empty chair, facing Frankie. "My God, Kitten. It's like I'm living the nightmare all over again. The nightmare of raising your mother. I had expected more from you." He began to scratch each temple—short, slow strokes to claw the stress from his skull. "What do you have to say for yourself?"

She nibbled on a fingernail and shrugged. "Jeez, Papa. Chill. It's not that bad. It's not like I killed someone." She leaned back lackadaisically in the folding chair, hiked the dress higher up her legs, and clasped her hands behind her headscarf.

Mr. Wick spoke up then. "You don't seem to think you've

got a problem, young lady, but let me assure you, this could turn out very badly for you if you don't show a little more respect and cooperation. Very badly. Any questions?"

She shrugged again, then smirked. "So how did you find me anyway, Papa? And how did you find out it was me who stole the wallets and boarding passes?"

Mr. Wick slapped a grainy photograph on the table showing Frankie outside the airport next to a Jeep Wrangler. "This is from one of our airport security cameras," he said. "It was taken shortly before all the thefts were reported." He spread a few more pictures out on the table, taken from various locations within O'Hare. Some showed Frankie dressed up with her hair pulled back; in some, she wore her jeans and hoodie. "The time-stamps on these photos correspond to the times of the thefts."

Frankie stared at the pictures. "O-M-G."

"Also," Mr. Wick said, "a man called the airport police yesterday afternoon. Said he'd given you a ride all the way from Iowa. Reported you as a runaway." She shut her eyes and jerked her head away as though she'd been slapped.

"Who was that man, Frankie?" Jack said. There was a hint of panic in his voice, understandably given the lifestyle her mother was living.

"That can't be," she said as though thinking aloud. "He was so nice. Thought I could trust him. What a dick."

"Frankie! Watch your mouth! And tell me who the hell he was!"

"Jack," Beatrice stepped forward. "Let's all try to remain calm. I know it's hard, but shouting isn't going to get us anywhere."

"Just a friend," Frankie said. "Nobody really." She tipped her head toward Beatrice. "Like her."

Jack glanced at the woman. She nodded, then Mr. Wick continued. "Anyway, when we got that call, we contacted the authorities in Iowa. It must have been shortly after your grandfather reported you missing."

"And when I got a call from someone here at O'Hare," Jack said, "and they told me about all these thefts, I knew right away you were the culprit."

She looked at him quizzically, and his face softened. "It was the same kind of mischief your mother used to get into."

Frankie shone with pride, the way most children would beam over a straight-A report card.

Jack's attorney, who'd been mute until then, asked the police officers and Mr. Wick to give them all a few minutes of privacy. When they left, he sat down opposite Frankie, and Beatrice walked around the table to sit beside her. Jack began to pace.

"Let's start at the beginning, Frankie," Beatrice said. "Tell us what happened, starting yesterday morning when you left your home."

"Home? Yeah, right. Bet you wouldn't call that a home if you saw it." She sneered at Beatrice's clothes and the rings on her fingers. "If you came out of your rich neighborhood and designer clothes and saw where we lived, you'd realize I don't really have a home."

"Frankie," Jack said.

"It's all right," Beatrice said. "I'm sorry, Frankie. But I

think you know what I mean." She stood up, whispered to the attorney, and they both left the room.

Frankie picked at her cuticles for another minute and then began to recount everything for Jack—Raina's condition, the creep in the closet, her ride with the Irish man. She said she didn't know what her plan was until halfway to Chicago, and then she got the idea to try to fly out to Oregon. To see Ryan.

"And why did you create all that chaos with the stolen boarding passes and other stuff?" Jack asked.

"Don't know. Just something to do."

"So you just did it for kicks?"

"Yeah, I guess so."

That might have been what Frankie honestly thought, and her response sounded typical for a teenager. But I knew there was more to it than that. Subconsciously, all those shenanigans gave her a sense of power in a world where otherwise she felt she had none. For an underdog like Frankie, power meant hope.

Frankie asked if Ryan knew about her brief trip to Oregon, sounding hopeful, as though he would have been proud of her for what she'd done. In an odd sort of way, I think he would have been.

"I doubt it," Jack said. "Ryan doesn't even live in Portland. He's in Central Oregon, over the mountains and hours away from Portland."

I imagined Frankie in Bend, sitting on the back deck of our cabin in the bright sunlight. It was a marvelous image.

They waited for a while, and finally the attorney and Beatrice came back in with some paperwork. The attorney said Frankie would be released to her grandfather's custody because of her age and Jack's good citizenship. "But only under certain conditions." He handed a one-page document to Frankie.

She skimmed the page, then crumpled it up and tossed it into the corner. "No f-ing way."

Jack sighed. He picked up the paper, flattened it out, and read it for himself. The attorney handed Jack a pen.

"You have to sign this," Jack told Frankie.

"No."

"It's a pretty good deal," the attorney said. "Lots better than going to juvi."

Beatrice, leaning back against the wall, nodded.

Frankie looked from one adult to the other and groaned. She flopped her hand on the table, palm up, and Jack placed the pen in her hand. She signed her name with a small flower dotting the i in her name. Despite her tough outer shell, she was still a little girl inside.

When Frankie walked into her grandfather's plush condominium overlooking Lake Michigan, Raina was lying on the white sofa, mascara smeared beneath her eyes. With her disheveled microbraids splayed out on the sofa, and her complexion now more gray than olive, she reminded me of Medusa. Frankie ignored her mother and went straight upstairs where she found clean flannel pajamas in the guest-room dresser, as well as her grandmother's sewing scissors. She went into the bathroom, washed her hands and face, changed her clothes, and then sliced a thin red line around each ankle.

Jack, Beatrice, and Raina—now awake and up-right—were sitting around the glass-top dining room table when Frankie came back downstairs.

"We're all stressed and tired," Jack said, "but we need to talk about some things here. Have a seat, Kitten."

She sat down opposite him.

"As I told Frankie in the car," he said, looking at Raina, "Beatrice and our attorney had to jump through some pretty dicey hoops to keep your daughter out of Chicago's juvenile system for now, although there are no guarantees about the future. And we had to agree to certain things. I need the two of you to commit to me that you'll abide by these rules."

Raina rested her head on one hand and yawned.

"Number one, Frankie is going home with you tomorrow, Raina." Oh, Lord, I thought.

"Yes!" Raina said, pumping a fist. "Back home with your Mama, baby girl."

"No. Not going home, Papa. Let me stay here."

He glanced from Frankie to Raina to Beatrice, then back to his granddaughter. "I'm sorry, Kitten. I know it's not the ideal thing right now. But I have some important meetings coming up at work." Damn his work, I wanted to interject. It shouldn't have mattered whether those upcoming meetings were with God himself, as far as I was concerned. There was no reason in the world that Frankie should go back to Raina. I couldn't understand how he would send her back to Iowa again, or how this therapist friend of Cece's would support that. But the only other choice, I surmised, would have been foster care.

"Number two," he said, "you have to finish school. There are only a few more weeks till summer vacation, and if you do a good job then we'll see about you coming back here for the summer. For now you need to follow what you signed on that document."

Frankie slouched, not in boredom like Raina, but in defeat. That was almost more heartbreaking for me than the thought of her returning home. Her spirit was beginning to break, like a thin fracture in the ice. If only she could hold out for a few more weeks, things would get better for her. I hoped.

"Number three, Raina, you must stay clean. No hooking, no drugs."

Raina rolled her eyes. "I didn't sign no contract." You would never know, by the way she spoke, that her adoptive parents had sent her to private school.

"She can't do it," Frankie said. "She can't stay clean."

"I'm serious, Raina." Jack ignored Frankie. "It's either that or you lose Frankie. But we're getting you some help. And that's number four. We're going to find you an outpatient program to sign up for this week, and you—both of you—have to see a family therapist at least once a week. Beatrice here has some connections and is going to find you a good one in Davenport."

"I ain't goin' to no rehab, and I ain't goin' to no therapist," Raina said, crossing her arms. She could have been so beautiful.

"Me neither." Frankie mimicked her mother with crossed arms, too.

Jack and Beatrice looked at each other, and Beatrice nodded.

"Okay, fine then." Jack stood. "I'll call the police right now. They'll be here in less than five minutes and you'll be off to juvenile detention."

Frankie set her elbows on the table and dropped her face into her hands. She was facing her own private hell. If only she'd made it to Oregon without getting caught. If only I'd brought her to Oregon with me.

"You wouldn't do that to your own granddaughter," Raina said.

"Try me. What you don't realize is how worn out I am. How terribly worn out. You've pushed me to the edge for years, Raina. Sadly, I don't have much energy left for your daughter." He picked up the phone.

"You bitches are asking for an awful lot," Raina said. The creases in Jack's forehead thickened. Poor, poor man.

"I have no choice," he said. "And, by the way, I suspect you'll be facing a whole lot of investigation, Raina. Pretty soon all your little secrets will be out."

Raina sat up straight then. I wondered what secrets she had that we didn't even know about. I figured we'd never know; Raina was a mystery from the day she was born.

"And when Frankie's released from juvenile detention," Beatrice said, "she will most likely wind up in foster care."

Frankie bit her lip and squinted at Jack. "You used to love me, Papa. And now, look at you. You're a mean sonofabitch, now that Grandmother isn't here."

Jack's face reddened. He opened the top button on his shirt

and loosened the collar.

Beatrice held up her hands. "This isn't productive. We just need you two to agree to the terms."

"We don't have a choice," Raina said. "Do we? You're blackmailing us." She reached her hand across the table, palm up. Frankie placed her hand in her mother's, a lovely image in an otherwise sour moment.

"The bottom line is this," Beatrice said. "Raina, you are on the verge of losing your daughter, possibly forever. And Frankie, you are on the verge of going into the system. And the sad truth is this: you both need help."

11 Chapter Eleven

My heart quickened as we approached the legendary town of Talkeetna. I was finally here. And it looked...dead.

The deciduous trees were barren. The roads were deserted. The small homes we passed—log cabins, A-frames, a few old trailers—were dark and quiet. The town was buried under several inches of snow, and the train tracks running parallel to the spur road, also covered with snow, looked as though they hadn't been used in decades. The wrought iron gates to the cemetery appeared to be frozen shut.

I felt a lump in my throat. Maybe Talkeetna wasn't the gold mine I'd always imagined it to be.

But when Marisa turned onto Main Street, my spirits lifted. Lynn straightened, too. There was Nagley's General Store; I'd seen so many pictures of that old place. And the West Rib Pub, and the world-famous Roadhouse. There was the Fairview Inn, where the climbers let loose at night. And most importantly, there were the people. They were milling outside all these places, wearing t-shirts despite the cold, leaning against railings and sweeping porches and waving at Marisa's van as though it carried a load of dignitaries.

At the end of Main Street sat the old Antlers Hotel, overlooking the confluence of the Talkeetna, Susitna, and Chulitna Rivers. It was a simple, modest structure with a matching reputation—you wouldn't find any king-sized beds, marble bathrooms, or fancy Pendleton blankets there. It was a haven for climbers.

When Lynn stepped out of the shuttle van, the fresh, resinous scent of spruce was everywhere, and even I felt it permeating my sinuses and skin, penetrating deep into my marrow. She hauled her gear into the hotel lobby, where she found a group of men huddled in front of the woodstove, laughing.

"Here she is! The great Lynn Van Swol." Will announced her like a celebrity, then put his arm around her shoulders and squeezed her toward him the way old friends, or lovers, show their solidarity. She shifted her weight away.

Brad introduced himself, shook her hand, and gave her a red plastic-coated pocket folder. The label on the front read:

Alpine Aspirations, Inc.
"Where Your Dreams Reach Their Summits"

I knew that Brad's new company had recently been selected as one of the few guide services authorized by the National Park Service to lead Denali climbs. Like Lynn, he had climbed dozens of major mountains, including two of the Himalaya's 8,000-meter peaks. Brad and Lynn would be a perfect team to guide the adventure.

"Come on," Brad said. "Let's do some proper introductions." He motioned toward Marisa, who was just coming in with the baby.

"First, everyone," Brad said, "I'm guessing you've all met Marisa by now. She's our driver, of course. But she's also our pilot, and our lifeline."

Lynn glanced quizzically at Will. I noticed everyone else looked surprised, too. She was the pilot?

"Wait a minute," Lynn said. "You're not by any chance the pilot they quoted in that *Time* magazine article, are you? About the recent tragedy on the mountain?"

Marisa shrugged. "I don't know. Could be. I get interviewed now and then."

The women glared at each other icily.

"Anyway, she'll be our key contact from the mountain," Brad said.

Will asked Marisa if she was also a climber.

"Hell, no," she replied. "I'm not that stupid."

Brad laughed and then introduced Mark, a muscular man dressed in a tight, black Mickey Mouse t-shirt that showed off his pecs and biceps. He had a short, scruffy beard, and his thick, black hair was slightly tousled and curled at the base of his neck so that he looked both elegant and disheveled, like a movie star. His eyes, the color of stonewashed denim, were penetrating.

"Mark's by far the strongest climber on the team...aside

from the guides, I mean," Brad said. "He'll be a real asset. And, next to Mark, there's Nick." Nick wore retro Ray Ban eyeglasses, a Metallica t-shirt, ripped jeans, and skateboard shoes. His hair was dishwater blonde like Lynn's, but much longer. He had adorable big, brown eyes. "Nick's our youngest climber, just twenty-one last January, so the good news is he can drink with the best of us, after the climb." Nick laughed. "And full disclosure, Nick's my nephew, too."

I was a bit taken aback by this news, and I suspected the other climbers were as well. While the family relationship didn't necessarily guarantee problems would arise, I had seen on more than one occasion a situation where a family member, especially a young one, got special attention to the dismay and frustration, and even threatened survival, of the others. It even happened once with my dad. I was the one who got special treatment.

He introduced Will next. "Will's relatively new on the climbing circuit, but he's bagged a few impressive peaks already. Mt. Kenya and Kilimanjaro in Africa; Whitney, Shasta, and Thunderbolt Peak in California." Lynn and Mark both looked at Will as though searching for something, and I found myself doing the same thing. He just didn't look like a climber; I could see him traveling through Africa and the Sierra Nevada, and countless other places, in fancy trekking clothes with well-paid guides. But I couldn't see him hauling gear up those mountains. Brad had obviously believed the information in Will's application, or else he wouldn't have accepted Will on the climb. Of course the application process depends upon integrity and full disclosure; Brad also didn't know Ryan was suffering from severe depression.

Finally he turned to Lynn. "And this, my friends, is the great Lynn Van Swol, who's been climbing since I had a binky in my mouth, maybe even before that." Brad waited for the laughter to stop, which it did long before the flush on her face paled. "Lynn has summited six of the big seven, and we're all going to help her get to the top of Denali, so she can finally retire. So I want you all to be nice and give her a hand whenever you can." She scowled at him, and I would have too. There was no reason for that attitude. That condescension.

"I'm not that old, Brad. And I doubt anyone's going to need to give me a hand. More likely the other way around. But thanks anyway for the sentiment."

The desk clerk set a bowl of oranges on a small table in the lobby as the door opened and a gust of wind raced into the room. "Ah, here's our final team member," Brad announced. "Just in time. It's Father Ryan Mahoney."

There he was, my Ryan, strolling in, with his hair blown every whichway and his deep jade eyes smiling with those little crinkles at the corners. He was clean-shaven, his skin was pink, his step light. He wore that old army jacket he'd always loved, and the wrinkled, baggy cargo pants. He looked so good you'd have thought he'd been in the clear northern air for months. It may have been a miracle, but he looked totally pulled together. Unless it was an act.

Brad introduced Ryan to everyone. With each handshake, Ryan exuded that sincere warmth—the prolonged eye contact and the way he took everyone's hand in both of his—just as he'd done as a pastor every Sunday morning for twenty years.

"Hello, Father," Lynn said, when it was her turn to greet Ryan.

"Let's get one thing straight," he said gently to the group. "I'm not a Father and never was." Of course he meant he was never a priest, but I felt a stab nonetheless. He was never the other kind of father either, but not for lack of our trying. "I was actually a Lutheran pastor, but I'm not that anymore either."

"Okay, that's everyone," Brad said.

"But who's this?" Ryan asked, reaching his index finger toward Aashka's hand the way you'd reach toward a small bird.

"This is Aashka," Brad said.

Ryan said her name was as beautiful as her face and asked Marisa if it was a traditional Native Alaskan name.

"Yeah, right," she said. "That's what Auntie had led me to believe. But I found out later it's an Indian name, as in India, not Native American Indian. Whatever. I got used to it, even though nobody knows how to spell it or pronounce it. It means blessing, though she wasn't exactly planned." She shot Brad an accusatory look.

"Well, regardless of its origin, it's a lovely name," Ryan said. He continued to let the child grip his finger and I thought I felt an ache in my womb.

"Why don't you all go back to your rooms and get settled," Brad said, "and take a look at some of the information in your folders? Then we'll get together later this evening for our orientation meeting."

"Wait," Lynn said. "I thought there were two more climbers."

"They cancelled," Mark said. "Chickened out because of all the bad weather they've been having up here. And they're predicting more. It's just the six of us now, right Brad?"

Brad nodded. "Yes, unfortunately, that's true."

Mark looked first at Nick, and then Will, and then Ryan. "I sure hope you all know what you're getting yourselves into," he said.

Lynn strapped on her snowshoes and trekked across the Talkeetna River on the old iron bridge toward the Chase Trail, parallel to the Susitna River. There wasn't a human soul in sight, and you could hear the soft swish of snowshoe webbing as she took each step. You could also hear an occasional rustling through barren branches low to the ground, and the steady rippling of the river off to her left. She kept her eyes focused on the trail, but I kept scanning the landscape. It was instinct. This was the land of plenty when it came to fauna, including large predators. Grizzlies and black bears coming for the salmon. Moose cows giving birth; moose calves leaving home. Dall sheep, which have been known to occasionally attack humans. And wolves.

I could have sworn I saw something large and dark on the other side of the railroad tracks. A shadow, maybe, prowling through the trees. What were the odds? I asked myself. The odds of meeting a bear? Or a wolf—again? A golden eagle flapped overhead and landed atop a tree, and the thick branch swayed. I wondered if the bird, too, saw the creature. But

Lynn went on for a couple more miles and then turned and headed back toward town.

As she approached the bridge on her return trip, I saw something again. I was sure of it. A movement in the brush, the sound of a breath. Lynn glanced in the direction of whatever it was, but still she kept going, confident and graceful. Her breath was steady, her focus precise. She was a trained climber, a trained survivor. She was nearly back to the bridge when the train whistled.

It was the late afternoon Denali Star, plowing through new snow as it headed south from Fairbanks toward Anchorage. Lynn waited for it to pass, then stepped onto the bridge. That's when a man jogged out from behind a cluster of boulders. She startled and lost her footing.

"You okay?" It was Will, also dressed in winter running attire, and slightly out of breath. Perspiration trickled down each side of his face.

She recovered from her misstep and kept on going. "I'm fine," she said to him, over her shoulder. "You just startled me."

12 Chapter Twelve

Ryan had showered and was now buck naked, shivering in front of the open windows of his hotel room. I wished I could wrap myself around him, sharing our body warmth, no longer two bodies but one, as we'd done on Hood and Rainier and so many other mountain climbs together in the past, breathing into each other's faces, keeping each other alive. Or at least I wished I could close the damn windows. He didn't need to develop hypothermia now. But all I could do was watch as his body trembled, until he finally came to his senses and got dressed.

He paused outside Lynn's room on the way to the stairwell. Her door was ajar, and it looked as though he was planning to knock. But then he saw her sitting on her bed, still in her jog bra and running pants, next to Will. They sat so close that their thighs and shoulders touched. Ryan kept on going down to the lobby.

Mark and Nick were already there. Will came in just after Ryan, and Lynn flew down the steps five minutes later, her hair wet and a towel draped around her neck and shoulders. She wore a tight tank top and low-rise jeans, and her clothes showed off her strong physique. She looked nowhere near fifty.

Brad hurried through the front door with Aashka in his arms and opened the meeting by saying he was thrilled with the group he'd put together.

"We're small, and you're diverse in age and experience levels. But you're all first-rate." Not surprisingly, he was looking mostly at Lynn and Mark when he said that. "With any luck in the weather, we'll be up and back before you know it, safe and sound with a lifetime's worth of memories."

Ryan noticed how Lynn looked down after Brad said that. She was intently studying her fingers and thumbs.

"I'll make this meeting as brief as possible, and then we can go have some fun. But speaking of safety—and fun—let's talk about that. The first matter of business is safety; it's our number one priority. Sure, gaining the summit is our goal, but never at the expense of safety. And how well we do will be directly correlated to how well we've all trained till now and how we balance risk and safety from here on out."

I realized then that Nick was wearing earbuds and tapping his foot. Ryan must have realized it at the same time, because he elbowed the kid's side and the earbuds came out.

"So when we talk about managing risk, it's important to keep that in mind while we're having fun," Brad said. "Along that line, nobody should be drinking alcohol or using any controlled substances—other than prescription medicines you've already disclosed to me—and certainly no one should be smoking or otherwise using tobacco products from this point on until we make it back down, safely, in about three weeks. Okay, everyone?"

Mark rolled his eyes and groaned.

"Is there a problem?" Brad said.

Mark shook his head but looked exasperated. I knew his type. He was an experienced climber and didn't need the lecture. But those are the types that, sometimes, become the biggest liability.

Aashka, who had been quiet in Brad's arms until now, started to squirm. "I have three quick agenda items for the evening. I want to go over some general ground rules and review our itinerary. I want to go over the gear list and see if anyone has any questions before I inspect everyone's gear tomorrow. And I want us to do a little team building."

Now Mark, Will, and Lynn all grumbled, and then Mark repeated the phrase team building with evident scorn.

"You know, Mark," Brad said, "I accepted your application because of your incredible experience and your physical condition. You could be an important asset here." He set Aashka on the floor and she crawled toward Ryan. "Or you could just be an ass. And that won't work for me. We need to be able to trust each other, you know. Trust is fundamental here on Denali. No trust, no deal. So let's just check that arrogance at the door next time, shall we?"

"Sorry."

"Okay. Good. Now, let's get started." Brad handed out another packet to everyone, a large zip-lock bag with a laminated folder inside. As they opened their folders, he began to read his mountaineering philosophy statement and corporate mission, like a teacher reading to his class. He turned to the next page and began to cover some specifics of climbing Denali.

"I think we all know this shit," Mark said. "We're not a bunch of neophytes."

"That may be true," Brad said, "but I've learned when leading a group it's always a good idea to start from an elementary level and never assume." He went on reading about how Denali differs from other high-altitude climbs, including Mt. Everest. He summarized key hazards to be wary about. Rescue and evacuation procedures. Disposal of trash and human waste. He was in the middle of talking about the role of National Park rangers on the mountain when Mark interrupted again.

"Whoa! This says we're climbing the West Buttress instead of Cassin Ridge."

"Well, you've jumped ahead of me," Brad said. "But you're right. That's a last minute route change I had to make." He turned to the next page.

"You can't do that," Mark said. "The deal from day one was to climb Cassin Ridge. Your website said that, and all the materials you sent out said that. You can't make changes at the last minute."

"I'm the guide," Brad said, "and I can. Read those materials more closely next time."

Mark bristled, and so did I. I wasn't sure which bothered me more: the fact that Brad would make a switch like that, which was completely unorthodox from my experience, or the fact that he'd be so condescending. Although in truth I was, initially, a bit relieved to hear they would be climbing an easier route now that I'd seen how little preparation Ryan had undertaken.

Nick raised his hand like a kid in school. "I told Mom and Dad I'd be on Cassin Ridge. If there's an emergency, will they know how to find me?"

"Of course they'll know where to find you," Lynn said. "We have to check in with the rangers. They'll know where we all are. Besides, didn't you bring a cell phone?"

"My battery's dead and I forgot my charger. Anyway I didn't know it would work up here."

Lynn made a face.

"Actually, Nick's right about the cell phone," Brad said to her. "There isn't any cell service up here anymore. We're relying more on family band radio services and satellite phones these days." Nick scored a tally for himself in the air, and Lynn shrugged.

"But you brought your iPod," Mark said.

"Well, yeah, of course I did."

"And I suppose you remembered that charger? At least you've got your priorities straight."

I didn't like Mark's sarcastic tone, and Lynn was acting a little haughty herself. Team coherence is critical on climbs like these. They both needed to lay off Nick.

"Back to the topic at hand," Mark said, "I am not going to climb the West Buttress. The handicap ramp. The Girl Scout hike. The place for beginners."

"Neither am I, brother," Will said. The two fist-bumped.

"It gets too congested on that route. Especially on The Headwall," Mark said.

"And the Summit Ridge," Lynn said. "Which means this can actually become a more dangerous climb than some of the other routes, even though it's not as technical."

A heated debate broke out. Mark pointed accusations at Brad. Will stood up and began to pace behind Lynn. Nick and Ryan talked with one another on the couch, and Aashka started to screech like an injured ptarmigan. The desk clerk pounded on his desk bell several times until he got the attention of the group. They turned toward him, and a customer he was trying to help glared at them. Aashka's pitch elevated.

Ryan scooped the baby off the floor and started pacing as well. The girl quieted to his soft, gentle voice—his prayer voice—and miraculously the rest of the group quieted too.

"Thank you, Ryan," Brad said. "I can use all the help I can get. The bottom line is this. It's bad this year. The weather sucks, the crevasses are open wide. Even though there's been a lot of snow, it's all being blown off. There's a lot of blue ice up there. The high hasn't even reached -20 °F at Camp 3. Everyone's coming back down with frostbite and hypothermia, at best. And there have already been a couple of deaths."

"I only heard about one," Lynn said.

"There've been two now."

"And the one I read about was on the West Buttress," Lynn said.

"There's another factor I've considered, in deciding which route to climb," Brad said, "and some of you won't like this. I've re-evaluated our collective technical expertise, and I don't think this group can be successful on Cassin Ridge, especially with the weather conditions."

"I knew it," Mark said, pointing at Brad again. "You were full of it when you said a couple of minutes ago we're first rate. First rate what? First rate bunch of clowns? Look at these people." He swept his arm around the room. "Some of us have the experience...and some of us don't. Especially Little Nicky here."

Ouch. But he was absolutely right, and I could see how Brad might have been concerned about taking that group, including his nephew, up the Ridge. Still, Brad and Mark didn't need to be so rude.

Mark stood and flexed his pecs through his tight t-shirt. "I've done the West Butt three times. I'm not doing it again. I'm going up the Ridge. Anyone want to come with me, you're welcome. Otherwise, I'll do it on my own." He looked at Ryan. "And God-willing, I'll meet you all at the top."

Lynn started to say something, but Brad motioned for her to stop.

"If you do," Brad said, "you'll be on your own for gear, food, and all other equipment. You will not be taking any of mine. I won't be responsible for you. And don't expect a refund."

"The climb hasn't even started yet. What do you mean no refund?"

"As far as I'm concerned," Brad said, "this meeting

constitutes the beginning of the climb. You're SOL."

"Sucks for you, brother," Will said.

Mark flexed his pecs again and clenched his jaw. "Fine, for now. I'll get back to you later for breaching your own contract. Meanwhile," he shot a look at Lynn and Will as he made his way for the door, "Anyone want to join me?"

Oh, no, I thought. This wasn't part of the plan. She had to stay with Brad. Or at least Ryan had to stay with her. But if I were her, I'd have thought pretty hard about that offer. As any experienced climber knows, the West Buttress is a highway these days with too many climbers, including the inexperienced ones, just as that Time article had reported. With all the traffic jams on narrow routes, it can definitely be more risky than other routes. I found myself hoping the weather forecast of nasty storms was accurate. Maybe that would keep the beginners away.

"Well," Brad said to Lynn. "Are you with Mark? Or with me?"

Of course an expert like Lynn would want to take the more isolated route. I knew she could leave Brad's team without a second thought—except that she had been hired as his assistant guide. She was obligated to him. "Let me talk to Mark a minute," she said. "Outside."

It was when she followed Mark out the door that I noticed something I still can't shake the image of. It was a tattoo stretched across her upper back, hidden only slightly by the thin straps of her tank top. Six mountain peaks, seemingly true to scale in relation to one another, and remarkably drawn so that you could tell which was which. Everest, the regal pyramid, was in the center. To its left were the double humps of Elbrus; to the right was the flat-top Kilimanjaro. Aconcagua, Carstensz, and Vinson were there too. The miniature mountain range was slightly off center, and there was clearly room for one more peak on the left. I couldn't decide if the tattoo, and her dedication to climbing the Seven Summits, highlighted her eccentricity or just made her über-cool.

When Lynn and Mark returned a couple of minutes later, shivering, Marisa was with them. She had arrived with a basket of feathers and offered the first one to Lynn.

"For you. It's from Auntie. She says Eagle brings good luck when he soars close to Naq'eltani." Lynn's gratitude was unimpressive. She shoved the feather in her back pocket.

"Close to *who*?" Nick said.

"To God. You know, the Great Spirit." Marisa said, handing a feather to him and then to each of the others. "It's also a sacred healing tool, Auntie says. It can keep you alive if you're willing to open your heart to new horizons." Marisa took Aashka from Ryan. "But beware when Eagle flies low over the ground."

After she left, Brad apologized to Ryan. "I know you probably don't believe in that stuff."

"I'm not sure what I believe in anymore to be honest with you. But I do believe Auntie is sincere in her good wishes for us."

"Auntie also says that young eagles who cannot look straight into the sun must be thrown from the nest to die," Brad said. "That shows you how crazy she is. So you can do whatever you want with those feathers as far as I'm concerned. Now, Lynn, what's the verdict? Are you with us?"

"Yeah, what's the verdict, babe?" Will asked. "I want to climb with you."

Lynn's cheeks reddened.

"And my wife talked about you for years," Ryan said. So he had been listening to me. "I want to climb with you, too."

Lynn rubbed her hands over the goose bumps on her arms. "This may sound harsh, but I don't care who wants to climb with whom or what route anyone wants to take. All I care about is getting to the summit."

"Sounds like you're saying you don't care about anyone else," Ryan said.

Brad looked pissed. "What kind of attitude is that for a guide?"

Before she had a chance to respond, Ryan said, "And that tells me that you don't care about yourself, either." It was a distinct echo of what Tom had said to Ryan.

Lynn began to finger the agate pendant at her neck. "How exactly do you make that leap? I mean concluding I don't even care about myself?"

He rubbed his chin where stubble would soon sprout. "It's not a leap. It's what you've said and how you said it. Your tone of voice. Your body language. People don't matter to you. How you accomplish your goals doesn't matter either. You only care about the end result. If you don't care about the process, the relationships along the way, then you must not care about yourself. It sounds cliché, but it's true."

"Just make a decision, Lynn," Brad said, checking the

clock behind the front desk.

Lynn reached for the agate again. It dawned on me where I'd seen it before: at The Monastery and then again in that picture in her nightstand. But there had been seven colorful agates hanging from the cord in the picture. Now there was just one.

"Something's bothering you," Ryan said, examining the way she toyed with her necklace. His voice was calm, his face relaxed. He knew he'd hit a nerve just as I'm sure he'd intended. He held her gaze, the same way he used to do with me, especially when something was wrong, when I was withholding information from him. About my wine stash. About my first cancer diagnosis. About so many other things, too. I was powerless when he did this, as though hypnotized.

"I'm staying with you, Brad," she said.

Right after the meeting, Ryan went to the West Rib. When his bowl of chili, loaded with caribou meat, corn, tomatoes, onions, black beans, and a thick, spicy sauce was served, I wished so badly I could sit on a barstool next to him and dip my spoon into his bowl. I wished I could set my hand on his knee and kiss him, tasting the chili on his tongue. I wished I could just be there with him, listening to the Rolling Stones and Pink Floyd and shooting the breeze with the bartender in his knit cap and Mountain Hardwear jacket. I was nowhere near ready to rest.

Later, Ryan walked across the street to The Fairview, a century-old building with wood paneling, hardwood floors, and the stench of every cigarette that's ever been lit up in there. Although it was in the middle of Alaska, it was world renowned. The rest of the team was already there, mingling with climbers from China, Sweden, and Patagonia. They all seemed to speak the same language when it came to mountains.

"How was your winter?"

"Going up tomorrow?"

"So-and-so's team's bringing up five dozen eggs. Five dozen!"

They traded stories about skiing, played the do-you-know game, and discussed the latest conditions. They rattled off routes, sections of routes, or pitches: *Sultana Ridge. Muldrow Glacier. Dracula. Football Field. Motorcycle Hill. Mini Moonflower. Death Mushroom.*

A local band, The Crazy Fates, was taking requests. Ryan asked if they played any R&B, and they started the next set with their version of Marvin Gaye's "What's Going On?" Brad and Marisa began to slow dance, and Will took Lynn's hand. She shook her head, but he placed his other hand on the small of her back and led her to the dance floor.

His moves were slow and deliberate. His hips swayed sensually to the beat, and he held her close. At first she pulled back, but by the third song she seemed more relaxed in his arms. His smooth chin grazed against the top of her head, and she closed her eyes and rested her forehead against his chest. He tightened his arms around her, reaching low. When the Crazy Fates switched to disco, Lynn told him she was tired. They left the bar, and Ryan followed them out the door and back to The Antlers.

Ryan sat on one of the old rockers on the hotel's rear veranda. It was late, nearing midnight, but this was Alaska, only a few hundred miles from the Arctic Circle, and it was still as bright as day. Murmuring voices drifted out from the windows of the guest rooms, and a dog barked somewhere. A wind chime tinkled in the breeze and music from the Fairview could still be heard, faintly. Something rustled in the branches of a nearby tree, and if you looked through those branches, you could see Denali's silhouette. If only I could have touched Ryan's shoulder, told him to look that way. If only I could have been there with him, living in a place like that, in one of those A-frames or log cabins, with a baby and a couple of dogs.

But that would never happen, and this was now the only way for us to be there together. We looked out at the river; we heard the low who-who of a short-eared owl. We smelled the scent of wood-burning stoves and listened to a Talkeetna baby cry. We drank in the peace of the night. It was, for a brief time, both heaven and hell.

13 Chapter Thirteen

I was waiting for Lynn to wake up, when there was a knock at her door.

"Will?" She pulled her head out from underneath her pillow and patted the other side of the bed, which completely threw me off my guard. I had not followed her back to her room last night, and now I wondered if Will had. She sat up and looked around, squinting at the light and rubbing her neck, still in her tank top and jeans. She shuffled to the bathroom like a stiff old woman, and when she looked in the mirror I, too, noticed her puffy eyes. Despite her strength and figure, she wasn't a spring chicken anymore. That was for sure. As she lathered antibacterial soap on her hands, already raw from all her germ-eliminating soaps and wipes, there was another knock.

"Will?" She opened the door.

"Well, aren't you the epitome of youthful sunshine," Brad

said. "Sorry to disappoint you. It's only me." She stepped aside and he entered the room like he owned the place. He glanced at the sheets and blankets, rumpled on both sides of the bed, as he went to the window.

"Good, it's raining," he said.

"Good?"

"A good omen, according to Auntie. She says rain gets it all out of your system." I wanted to ask what, exactly, the rain gets out of your system. And what was it with all these omens? First Lynn was worried about the wolf and the magazine article, then came Auntie's eagle feathers. And now this.

She yawned. "What time is it, anyway?"

"Time to get going. You and I have shopping to do. Helping me with food and supplies is part of your job description, you know. I'm a little worried you're confused about what exactly your job description is." He looked in the bathroom and behind the shower curtain.

"I'm not sure what you're insinuating."

"I'm not insinuating anything," he said. "I know Will spent the night here. I'm not at all pleased about that."

She combed her fingers through her hair. "It's not what you think. He locked himself out of his room, and the reception clerk was nowhere to be found. So I told him he could sleep on my floor. That's all it was, nothing more."

Then why were the linens disturbed on the entire bed, Lynn?

"Whatever," he said. "Just get yourself ready. Meet me in the lobby in ten."

She splashed water on her face, finger-combed her hair again, put on a clean t-shirt from her suitcase, and grabbed her sweatshirt from the hook on the bathroom door. On her way downstairs, she passed Nick and Will in the hall. Nick coughed.

"You feeling okay?" she asked.

"I'm fine," he said. "It's probably just a morning thing."

Will nodded at Lynn and asked if she slept all right.

She rubbed her temples. "I don't know, I guess so. You?"

"Oh yeah. Slept like a baby. So you want to get some breakfast at The Roadhouse? I hear their cinnamon rolls are mighty fine."

"Can't, I've got things to do with Brad. I'll catch you later."

He pantomimed an angler reeling in a fish. "I hope so."

At the store, Lynn cleaned a shopping cart handle with a sanitary wipe as Brad fished two crumpled pieces of paper from his pocket.

"I've made two separate shopping lists so we can get through this as quickly as possible. You're in charge of the fresh and perishable foods and the meats." Did he not know she was a vegetarian?

She started with oranges, Yukon Golds, and other produce. Then she moved to the meat department, and after staring at the case for several minutes, selected lean ground beef and chicken. She also threw packages of smoked salmon, elk jerky, and tofu in her cart. She gathered a variety of organic yogurts, an assortment of cheeses, and the freshest bagels and English muffins she could find. She grabbed a super-sized package of tortillas, along with a box of herbal tea and a large canister of whey protein powder—even though these most certainly wouldn't qualify as perishable.

When she met up with Brad at checkout, I saw he'd filled his cart with pasta, instant potatoes, crackers, Bisquick, and other processed carbohydrates. There was no other protein, like peanut butter or refried beans, and no granola, oats, or whole grains. There were no cooking oils, spices, or treats, unless you'd consider a two-pound can of coffee a treat.

Lynn questioned him about the same things I'd been thinking. He said the foods she mentioned were extraneous and expensive. She scanned his cart again. "We'll need more nonperishable proteins as we run out of fresh foods, and as we get higher up, Brad. And we'll need condiments and flavorings and some snacks too. And whole grains. Maybe oatmeal packets. I'll go back and grab some more stuff. I'll be quick."

"No. Stop right there."

"Excuse me?" I did a double take. Did he just command her to stop?

"I said stop. We have enough."

"I disagree, especially when you consider we'll need to cache some proteins for the descent. Look, Brad. I'm the last person who wants to eat junk or snacks, trust me. But everyone needs oils for cooking; we need the fat intake up there before we get high up. And the idea of not having any spices or treats is ridiculous. When you're at 13 or 14 in a blizzard?" She was referring to elevation. "And you can't feel your toes? And you hate everyone you're with, and you can't remember what day of the week it is? Believe me, you'll need something to liven up your day. You'll need flavor, and even sugar by then, to keep your brain going in the right direction. If *you* don't want that stuff, that's fine with me. But I'll need it and I'd bet the others will too."

He pushed the cart into the checkout line. "Sorry, but I said no."

"What? Why? Do we have budget problems or something? I can make some adjustments in my cart, get some lower-priced things."

"Don't worry about the budget," he said. "Just do what I say, that's all I'm asking. Your cart's fine. Let's just check out." He started to unload the food on the conveyor belt.

I did a quick calculation in my head. Five climbers, twenty-one days. Lynn was right. There weren't nearly enough of the right kinds of non-perishables. There weren't enough complex carbohydrates to keep everyone's belly full, and there wasn't enough protein. They needed raw nuts, soup with meat, canned meats. Even Spam would do in a pinch. There was hardly enough for five people for three weeks, and nowhere near enough if the weather held them up along the way, or if they came upon a lost climber and had an extra mouth to feed. Money, or the lack thereof, sure makes people do strange and dangerous things.

Lynn stood frozen in line as customers began to line up behind her.

"This won't work, Brad. I'm sorry if you have budgetary constraints. Really sorry about that. But we can't go on the mountain without enough supplies. It's suicide."

"That's my problem, not yours. Keep in mind, you're my *assistant.* And furthermore it's a matter of opinion. In my opinion, which is the one that counts, we have plenty. Let's go already; stop wasting my time." He finished unloading his cart onto the belt and began unloading hers.

She grabbed some trays of Red Vines and a handful of candy bars from the nearest rack and slipped them under the tortillas on the belt. When it comes to survival, honesty isn't always the best policy.

Will was waiting for her in the hallway when she got back to the hotel. He was wearing only sweatpants, and his chest—dark, bare, and hairless—glistened.

"I've laid everything out for you," he said. "I want to show you what I've got."

She looked tired, even bitter, and proceeded toward her room.

"Come on," he said. "I want to show you my gear." He took her hand and led her into his room. All sorts of climbing gear was spread out on the furniture and floor.

"Some of this is mine and some is Nick's," Will said. "He wanted to show you what he had, too, so I told him to bring it on over for a little two on one." He smirked, then picked up the phone and called Nick's room.

"Usually," Lynn said after Nick arrived, "the lead guide likes to be involved in this. I'm not sure what Brad's plans are, but we can take a peek now if you'd like. Trust me, Brad will want to be the ultimate judge. But of course, in actuality, the mountain will have the final say."

The first time I climbed Mt. Rainier, Dad wasn't there to help with my gear. I borrowed most of it, and it looked like it came straight out of a Salvation Army store. My climbing partner, a stuck-up girl who went on to become a cocaine addict, sneered. Her gear still had price tags attached, which I figured she'd done on purpose to impress me. All of it was clean and brightly colored and neatly folded. "Sorry, I don't mean to laugh," she'd said when she saw my stuff. But when her new goggles cracked and her new tent popped a rip in the seam, she didn't laugh anymore. And after her feet sprouted boulder-sized blisters in her fancy new boots, and she nearly slipped off a cornice because she could barely walk, she swore off climbing forever, which was probably a good thing. Image, it turned out, was her first drug of choice. Too bad she didn't swear off cocaine too.

Nick had the basics covered. As you might expect from a young wannabe rock star, it *was* basic—like straight out of basic training from the Second World War. He had a beat up mess kit, and most of his outer clothes were army khaki, faded to beige. He was a little light on layered underclothes, and I would have figured he'd be better equipped with Brad for an uncle, but he had what he needed to get by, at least in terms of gear. Whether he had the strength, endurance, or mental fortitude to get up and down Denali was another question.

Will, on the other hand, had gone overboard and reminded me of that early climbing partner. He had enough clothes to spend the entire season on Denali, and most of the gear still sported REI price tags. He had multiple sets of socks and boots, an extra set of crampons, and enough gloves and mittens to outfit the entire team. There would be no risk of him blending into the landscape, either, with his bright yellow parka and neon-green climbing pants.

"It looks like you're both in good shape," Lynn said. "At least in terms of gear. In fact, Will, you've got too much. You can leave that snazzy cookware behind; you only need your personal mess kit, utensils, and cup. And water bottles. And make sure you both have plenty of hand sanitizer. Now, on a separate note, I have to ask—after looking over your stuff, Nick—what kind of mountaineering experience you really have."

Nick blew his nose into a tissue and tossed the crumpled paper toward the corner wastebasket. "Oh, I've climbed plenty. I went through all this with Uncle Brad."

"Like what?" Will asked.

"Hood, South Sister, Shasta."

Good mountains. But nothing like Denali.

"Do you know how to tie knots and handle belays? Arrest a fall? Use crampons?" Lynn asked, mildly distracted by the used Kleenex on the floor.

"Yeah, I've done some of that in the field, and I took a course this winter, too."

"Ever clip through running belays?"

He shrugged.

"Ever been involved in a crevasse rescue?"

He shook his head.

"Built a snow cave? Been in a white out? Been over 14,000 feet?"

"Shasta's a little over fourteen."

"Not by much. Well, Nick," Lynn said, "this is going to be the adventure of your life. I just hope it's not the adventure of my life, too. It's going to be tough, I hope you know that."

Will asked why the hell a kid like him was climbing Denali anyway.

Nick laughed. "To win a bet."

"To win a bet?"

"Yeah, got a thousand dollars riding on this. A thousand bucks if I'm successful. So what about you?"

"Hold on," Will said. "You paid like six thousand dollars to climb a mountain so that you could earn a thousand dollars?"

Nick's expression went beyond sheepish and Lynn, now seated on the bed, her legs folded in lotus position, shook her head. "Brad didn't charge you anything. Did he?"

Nick shook his head and blushed.

"Shit," she said. Now those budgetary concerns made a little more sense. "So what about you, Will? Why are *you* climbing Denali?"

He laughed. "I'll have to get back to you on that one."

That afternoon they all attended the mandatory National Park Service orientation. It started with a video about the mountain, the weather, and climbing statistics. The ranger went over climbing requirements and protocol. He warned about the dangers of the slick blue ice and reminded the team to wear their helmets in avalanche zones. He told them to expect disturbed sleep patterns at higher elevations and cautioned them to watch for symptoms of acute mountain sickness, high altitude cerebral edema, and high altitude pulmonary edema. He told them never to pass another team on The Headwall and emphasized the dangers of Denali Pass, the spot on the West Buttress route where the most fatalities occur. Finally he reminded them that the weather is always worse above Denali Pass.

After the orientation, Lynn asked Brad to meet her at the new Twister Creek Restaurant. She ordered a glass of sparkling water, and he got a beer, pouring the ale into an aluminum canister. She didn't comment on the fact that he was breaking his own rule, and covering it up like a politician. Instead she thanked him for meeting her and said she felt like they needed to clear the air.

"I feel like we got off on the wrong foot."

He waited.

"I know I'm not the easiest person to work with," she said. "I'll try to do a better job on that front. But I also wanted to ask you how you're doing. I mean, since the accident and all. Are you sure you're up for this?"

Brad had made headlines several months earlier with a spectacular fall in the Andes. He'd been caught up in an avalanche and buried in snow, and then spent two weeks unconscious in a Bolivian hospital. This was after I'd found his Denali expedition on the web and asked Ryan to go to Alaska for me. I figured my plan was ruined when I first learned the news. But somehow Brad made a full recovery, at least physically speaking, and here he was.

"I'm fine," he said.

Lynn took a sip and smoothed out her cocktail napkin. "I

also wanted to express my appreciation to you for hiring me as your co-guide. It means a lot to me."

He nodded. "I'm happy to have you too. I just wish we had a bigger, and more cohesive, team. It will be critical that you and I are united and do what we can to draw everyone together. But just to set things straight, you're my assistant guide. There's a difference, you know."

Before Lynn could reply, the server came over and set the bill on the table. Brad frowned and pulled his thin wallet from his back pocket.

"I'll get it," Lynn said. She put out a twenty. "But I need to ask you a couple more things. First, when are you planning to do the gear check and talk with the team about load carrying, sled rigging, and such?"

He told her that, since there had been such mayhem at the team's first meeting, this part of the orientation would now have to take place on the glacier, and she said she thought that was too late. They should go over those critical details in a warm, calm environment, she said. But he told her not to worry, he had everything under control, and she met his scowl with a stare cold enough to cause frostbite.

"Why?" he said. "Are you, like Mark, concerned about the experience and technical skill levels of the team? Or are you specifically questioning my abilities?"

"Frankly, both," she said. That took guts. "Other guides require their clients to take specific alpine courses or provide details of where they've climbed and what formal training they've had," she said. "They also require them to be involved in a physical conditioning program in the weeks or months leading up to the climb. I thought your registration process was, well, a little lame, and the Park Service orientation didn't cover the details of avalanche rescue and whatnot because they presume the guides will do that. I look at the people on our team, especially your nephew, and I'm worried. I think we need to find a way to get that orientation done before we head out."

"And your other question?"

"My other question?" Her face went blank, perhaps because she was as floored as I was that he ignored what she'd just said. But I thought there was more to it. I'd suffered from chemo brain, which, from what Cece told me, is a lot like menopause brain. They both produce that same blank expression that accompanies an empty mind. You forget names, you forget where you left your keys, you forget what you were about to say. You lose your ability to focus, to concentrate. Cece and I would laugh about it even though it was no laughing matter. Now there was Lynn, one of Ryan's guides, trying to find her brain for some reason. I wondered what effect altitude would have on her in that regard.

"You said you wanted to ask a couple more things. You asked about the technical part of the orientation. What was your other question?" He sounded irritated. The server came back with Lynn's change and receipt.

"Oh, yes, I remember now. It's about payment of my fee."

"You mean, are you going to get paid?"

"Well, yes, to be honest, that question did cross my mind. You seem to be having some financial difficulties."

"You'll get paid," he said. He stood, facing the television

on the wall. The Cubs were up by one in the sixth inning. "So is that it?"

"No, there's still one more thing."

Brad let out a big, inconvenienced sigh.

I wondered if Lynn was going to say something about Marisa. She looked awfully young to be their pilot and main contact; she barely looked old enough to have landed on the other side of adolescence. In fact, to me, she didn't look much older than Frankie. But it wasn't Marisa she asked about.

"It's about Will. He's been coming on to me, and I think I should be assigned a different climbing partner."

"Really?" Brad said, with a knowing smirk. "It's about time you came to your senses." He tipped his canister back in search of one last drop of beer. "So who would you prefer to climb and sleep with? Nick? Or maybe the grieving widower?"

I felt like I'd been slapped when he called Ryan that. I didn't like his tone, and I also didn't like the way Lynn narrowed her eyes back at him. The animosity between the two of them concerned me; maybe my plan had been a mistake from the get-go. I had placed a heavy burden on Ryan, and I'd entrusted his life to Brad and Lynn, and now they seemed to be sparring with one another constantly, and there was nothing I could do about it. Nothing I could do to help Ryan, nothing I could do to influence the outcome of the climb.

I also felt like I was having one of those dreams where you keep falling. People always said that if you hit bottom in a dream like that, you would die in real life. Well, I wondered, what if you were already dead when you had the dream? That brief reprieve from hell, last night on the veranda, had faded, and now I felt sure I was slipping into a third level of hell—that place where you realize how powerless you are over events you once had a hand in when you were alive. How many levels of hell were there, anyway? How much deeper could I go? How much worse could it get? And why was I there in the first place? There were so many questions building in my mind, and with Nick's inexperience and Will's suspicious behavior and the departure of Mark and the other climbers, I feared this expedition was headed for disaster.

"No," Brad said. "I think we'll stick with what we have. You stay with Will; Ryan can be with Nick. At least Ryan has some bona fide experience. To put Will and Nick together could be deadly."

He stood and slid his wallet back into his pocket. "But you'd better watch yourself. I didn't hire you to get it on with my clients. Right now, I suggest you get back to the hotel and get some rest. By yourself. I'll let you know if I decide to reconvene the orientation tonight. Otherwise, we're heading out at 8:00 sharp tomorrow morning. And trust me; Marisa doesn't like to be kept waiting."

Lynn went back to her room at the hotel and put the do-not-disturb sign on the door. She turned the deadbolt and clicked on the TV. It was tuned to the local weather channel.

She began to unload all her gear from her packs and suitcases, which she'd packed with military precision. Now she took it out as though re-examining, or re-evaluating, it. Her face was set hard; I could practically feel her teeth grinding into each other. It was clear that thoughts were racing through her mind.

She unpacked her outer layer of clothes—the down jacket, snow pants, gaiters: the layer that takes all the beatings—and lay them out on her bed. Then the middle layer—fleece vest, turtlenecks, polypro pants and socks: the layer that protects your heart like bubble wrap around a fragile vase. And finally the inner layer—the sock liners and silk bicycle shorts, the panties and bras: the layer only your tent mate gets to see, the same layer her last climbing partner had seen before he died. The same layer her *first* climbing partner, Farid, had seen. The layer that Will would soon see.

She sat among the piles of clothes and turned her attention back to the TV. Ten inches had fallen at Base Camp, with two more fronts moving in over the next several days.

"Big ones," the meteorologist warned. "I wouldn't be surprised if this winds up becoming the storm of the century. Authorities are recommending you don't go out unless you have to. And no matter what happens, folks, you can be sure this month's records are certainly going to be shattered."

As she stared at the screen, unblinking, her composure seemed to disintegrate systematically. Her shoulders dropped. Frown lines appeared on her forehead. The corners of her mouth sagged. She reminded me of a clown in her dressing room methodically removing her painted mask. Something was bothering Lynn deeply. I wondered if she was having the same serious doubts as me.

Suddenly her eyes filled with tears.

"Damn it!" she shouted. "God damn it!"

She had been holding a folded set of panties and she threw them at the TV, and then she picked up her bras and her camisoles and hurled them in the same direction. Angrily. Crazily. Frenzied. She picked up a jacket and flung it across the room, and then a pair of pants. She picked up socks and scrunched them like a child frantically packing snowballs for a major battle, and she threw them, too. "God damn it! God damn it! God damn it!"

As she hurled things around her room, I became terrified. This was Lynn Van Swol, a woman who could stare down wolves and climb mountains all over the world. A woman who'd given a child up for adoption and kept on pursuing her goals. A woman whom I'd slated to become Frankie's next mentor and caregiver. A woman who was not, after all, the woman I'd thought she was.

While I'd discovered, in the last twenty-four hours, that she was even more self-absorbed than I'd expected, I was now witnessing something far more distressing. I was watching this woman—the one who was supposed to save my loved ones from ruin—collapse on the verge of...what? A nervous breakdown?

She was the one I'd chosen. What a fool I'd been.

When she was done flinging things around the room, she pulled a stack of hole-punched blank pages from her backpack and sat at the little hotel room desk, perspiring. She pressed her pen against the pages so hard they practically tore, and she wrote furiously.

Dear Sunny~

I wish I could say I wish you were here. But I'm glad

you're not right now! Thirty years of climbing gear is scattered around this hotel room now, like littered oxygen canisters on Mt. Everest. Thirty years of gear representing my entire life and it all fits into a few duffel bags. How sad is that?

She threw down the pen and picked up her harness. She seemed to be inspecting it for something of microscopic size, then threw it into the corner.

It all started with that damn harness. Your birthfather, Farid, gave it to me. He said this was only the beginning, that climbing would change my life, forever. He said that harness would save my life. I guess it has. But to what end, I'm not sure. I'm still trying to climb that godforsaken Athabaskan mountain and I'm still trying to figure out what to do with the damn men I encounter, pardon my language. I'm still dangling from the precipice.

Damn it, Sunny. I don't know what I'm doing anymore. The storms are coming, and I'm not just talking about the meteorological ones. They're working against me; I know they are. But I will go out tomorrow to climb Denali and set this last agate on the mountain no matter what, because, thirty years ago when you were born, I promised you I would.

She got up, went to the bathroom, and washed her hands. Then she came back and picked up the pen again, this time writing with more composure.

As I held you in my arms on that long-ago day, I told you, although you couldn't understand, that I was sacrificing you for what I thought was a higher goal. I told you I was giving you up so that you could live a happy, supported life. A better life than I could give you. I promised you, my dear Sunny, that I would honor you with a stone on the highest peak of each continent, my talisman for you, and I will. I will, damn it! I will bury this final stone in the ice at the top of The High One for you, or I will die trying. And that will be that.

That will be the end of all this.

Lynn slouched back in her chair, stretching out her legs and crossing them at the ankles. She stretched her arms overhead and then folded them across her chest. She stared at the page for so long I nearly left to check in on Frankie. But before I did, she picked up the pen one more time.

But I don't expect you to understand.

I don't expect you to ever understand why I'm doing all this. Whether it's for forgiveness or redemption or just because I've gone stark-raving mad, you won't be able to appreciate this force inside me. How could you? You were the one given up. You had no voice in the matter.

You were the casualty.

14 Chapter Fourteen

Frankie did what she'd agreed to do when she signed that contract. She went to school. She spent her lunch hours getting help from her teachers. She did her homework. She picked up around the house. She even cleaned the toilets. She behaved like Cinderella waiting for her miracle.

It was more of a struggle for Raina. She cancelled her tricks for that first week after Frankie returned home from her escapade at O'Hare, but when Ed—Raina's pimp and landlord—came over to collect the rent, they fought. While Frankie tried to concentrate on integers and decimals at the kitchen table, Ed shoved Raina around and shouted that he'd be back in three days. It was less than an hour before a couple of men showed up at the front door. Frankie let them in as Raina prepped herself in her bedroom, and the men sat in the living room, smoking blunts and watching Court TV as they waited their turns. Frankie gathered her schoolwork and retreated to her room, putting on the ear buds she'd stolen at O'Hare from another passenger—one of the prizes the cops hadn't confiscated. But as I didn't have any ear buds, I couldn't drown the sounds coming from Raina's bedroom, and I confirmed she was definitely back in business.

The house was a mess again when Frankie got home from school the next day. Ashtrays overflowed with butts and roaches. Beer and whiskey bottles littered the kitchen counter. Half-eaten crusts of pepperoni pizza were scattered on the coffee table. She picked up a crust and tore a hunk off with her teeth.

I wanted Frankie to charge into her mother's bedroom and confront her about how she was risking everything. Instead, Frankie brought the kitchen wastebasket into the living room and started cleaning up. But as she began to dump trash into it, she spotted a piece of paper at the bottom. She pulled the paper out and shook it off.

It was the one from Beatrice, listing the recommended outpatient rehab programs and some therapists for Raina. Frankie scowled at it, and I thought I saw her chin quiver. But girls in her circumstances don't have time to cry. She shoved it back into the trash.

Later, she spread her books and school supplies out on the kitchen table and took out her English assignment. The assignment was to write a free verse poem about a family member. It was worth fifty points and it could raise her grade to a C if she did well.

The words seemed to flow from her pencil like blood from a wound.

Ode to My Father

Rizzoni.
Just like a pizza,
You drew in my mother with the smell of your meat,
You were something she craved, something to feast on.
You were spicy and saucy, a new sort of treat;
But your sweet, fluffy dough was really a con.

She said that she loved you; her stomach grew big,
She savored the taste of your spices and fruit.
She did not discover you were really a pig
Till the day you gave her the Sicilian boot.

Now look at me here, amidst all this clutter.
It's your fault I'm stuck here on this rotten earth.
Look at the way I live in the gutter.
Living a life without any worth.

Rizzoni.
Just like a pizza,
You are cheesy and greasy; you dine and you dash.
And just like these leftovers, you belong in the trash.

My heart cried for her. And for Raina, too, in a way, who had followed in her birthmother's footsteps, giving birth to a daughter as a single woman all alone.

I reread Frankie's poem over her shoulder as she added

commas and other punctuation marks, and I thought about how I should have pressed Ryan harder to adopt Frankie somehow after Cece died. Or at least we could have tried to gain legal guardianship. If only we'd done that, there's no telling what Frankie might be doing now. She had so much promise, but no one to tell her that anymore.

Once, a couple of years ago, we were invited over to Jack and Cece's for Sunday dinner. Raina and Frankie were there too. The conversation came around to what Frankie wanted to do when she grew up, and she said she wanted to be a writer.

Raina laughed. "You ain't never gonna get a job doing that," Raina said. "You're gonna wind up just like me. It's in our blood."

I remember my mouth going dry at her rebuke.

"But you don't know what's in your blood," Cece said to Raina. "You were adopted. For all you know, your birthparents were smart and successful." Cece held her chin high as she said this, but I knew my friend well, and whenever the subject of Raina's birthparents arose, an expression of fragility took over. She was like a china doll teetering on the edge. "And it doesn't matter where you came from," Cece went on. "We are your parents—and whether or not we adopted you or gave birth to you, we are what matters."

"If you're all that matters, then why do you suppose I turned out the way I did?" Raina asked, punctuating her question with a sassy head shake. We all stopped eating for a moment, and Cece paled. "I guess you're sayin' it's your fault I'm a loser."

"You turned out the way you chose to turn out," Jack said. "I don't know much about the whole nature versus nurture topic, but from what I do know, I can say that how you turned out certainly had nothing to do with the way we raised you." He told Frankie not to listen to Raina's nonsense, and Raina told Frankie he just refused to accept responsibility for his mistakes. Cece, who probably had cancer even back then but didn't know it yet, threw down her cloth napkin and left the table. Frankie stormed off too, in the opposite direction. But later, as we prepared to leave, Ryan went into Frankie's room. He told her to hold on to her dreams.

Now, after rereading her poem, Frankie opened a drawer and pulled out a pizza cutter. It was loose at the hinge and rusted along the edge. She sat back down and began to cut herself with it as I tried to delete the idea of tetanus from my mind. After she scored a fine line along the inside of her forearm, she held her arm over the page, letting her blood drip next to the word *pizza.* Then another drop, carefully positioned, and then a third.

She hadn't even winced when she sliced her arm open; it was as though she couldn't feel the pain. I finally understood how horrible that must be. Although I could still somehow see and smell, and even feel some sensations on my skin or in my soul, I could no longer feel physical pain. I should have celebrated this, maybe taken it as an indication that I was indeed in heaven. Isn't that what we learned in church? In heaven you'd feel no pain? But what I knew deep down was that physical pain is part of life, and without it, you are in hell. Which meant Frankie was in hell—hell on earth. And it meant that I was in an even deeper level of hell than I'd thought. I was in the level where you cannot feel pain.

Holding a paper towel to her arm, Frankie checked in the refrigerator. There was nothing to eat again—the same moldy wedge of cheddar cheese from before she'd run away and a few brown and wilted leaves of lettuce. The freezer offered only a half-tray of ice, orange juice splattered and glued to the inside of the freezer door, a bottle of vodka, and a Cool Whip tub.

"Fuck it, Raina."

She retrieved another piece of crust from the garbage and headed for her room.

15 Chapter Fifteen

At least he was getting out of bed these days. Ryan, the first team member to the lobby the next morning, ran into Mark with his red parka and its reflective striped sleeves.

"You change your mind about going it alone?" Ryan asked.

"Nope. But Marisa's still taking me out to the glacier with the rest of you."

"Same starting point?"

"Yep. Same endpoint too. It's just the guts that are different."

Ryan poured the hotel's complimentary bad coffee into two Styrofoam cups. He added three single-serve containers of half-and-half to each and four packs of sugar, then slowly stirred. As he blew at the steam rising from each cup, he peered at Mark. "You comfortable with going solo?"

Mark shrugged. His eyes looked darker, like stiff new

denim rather than the stonewashed blue I first noticed. "I gave up a lot to move to Alaska. No offense, but I'm not going to spend my time babysitting on the easy route."

"None taken. I'll keep you in my prayers."

I've always wondered if people meant this when they said it, and now I wondered if Ryan was speaking the truth. I hadn't seen him pray for a long time.

It would have been a short drive from the hotel to the airfield, ten minutes at most, but it took two trips with all the people and gear. Marisa stopped on the second trip in front of the cemetery's wrought iron gates.

"Anyone want to visit the memorial?" she asked.

"Absolutely not," Lynn said. "Bad idea. Never before a climb."

But Ryan said he'd like to see it, so Brad scrambled out of the van and led him over to a sign constructed of wooden posts with a shallow protected overhang. Lynn heaved a sigh and followed.

There were dozens of plaques affixed to the sign, dating back to 1932. Each plaque showed a year, the names and ages of climbers who had died that year, their countries of origin, and which of several nearby mountains was the tragic site.

Death, as it turned out, did not discriminate. There were men and women. Americans and Canadians. Asians. Europeans. Two men tied for the oldest; they were both 61 when they died on Denali. The youngest was a boy of only fifteen, barely older than Frankie.

The dead climbers were memorialized by a John Muir

quote.

> *Let children walk with nature, let them see the beautiful blendings and communion of death and life, their joyous inseparable unity, as taught in woods and meadows, plains and mountains and streams of our blessed star, and they will learn that death is stingless indeed, and as beautiful as life.*

I loved the first few words. I had always tried to let Frankie walk with nature whenever we spent time together, and I knew how much she loved the river near her home. But the rest of the quote I found odd, and I couldn't help but wonder whether that fifteen-year-old climber would agree that death is stingless. Or whether his mother would agree. I certainly didn't.

"Know anyone?" Ryan asked Lynn.

She scanned the plaques, narrowing her focus on the one for the year 2000, when she was last on Denali. There were deaths listed for Yentna Glacier and Mt. Johnson, but none on Denali that year.

"No, I don't," she said. She backed away, still fixated on that plaque, then turned and quickly walked back to the van, almost as though being chased. Marisa called out for Brad and Ryan to hurry.

"There's a temporary break in the weather," Marisa said when Ryan climbed back in. "But it can change without notice. And conditions can be different up at the Kahiltna

Glacier from here. I don't want to be stranded up there with Uncle's old Beaver."

The Beaver De Havilland was a single-propeller, single-engine plane that accommodated four climbers at a time, which meant Marisa would need to make two trips out to Base Camp. Ryan asked how old it was.

"Ancient. Nearly fifty years old."

"Hey," Lynn said. "Fifty is not ancient."

Will had just finished loading his gear into the belly of the plane when Marisa threw the van into park. She started yelling at him before she had both feet on the ground.

"Whoa there, Mister! I'm the pilot. I say what goes in, and when, and where."

She marched over to the plane. From what I knew, all the pilots liked to be in charge of loading their own planes because doing it the right way, or the wrong way, could be life or death. Marisa jumped into the plane's cargo hold, retrieved the backpack and duffel Will had stashed there, and threw them back out onto the snowy ground.

"Go inside," she told the group. "Use the john, grab a cup of coffee, or whatever. Just stay out of my way. I'll let you know when I'm ready for you."

Just as pilots decide how to load the gear, they also decide who sits where. When it was time for the first trip to Base Camp, she told Ryan to take the co-pilot seat and Lynn and Nick to climb into the back seats. After she explained where the survival gear was in case of a crash landing—the flares, the sleeping bags, the water, and the fire extinguisher—Ryan looked nervous. He asked Lynn if she wanted the co-pilot seat.

"You sit where I tell you to sit," Marisa said.

Of course I could ride wherever I chose.

The Beaver sputtered as it warmed up, and the seats vibrated on takeoff. I thought I felt the vibration in both my stomach and my head. There was a cold draft seeping in from somewhere and a slight odor of metal and oil. At first, the plane seemed to be flying out of control, the way the tail veered to the right, and I wondered about Marisa's skills. But she was calm, and soon the little plane straightened out, heading directly for the Alaska Range.

It was pure exhilaration as we flew over spruce forests, silty rivers, remote cabins, and stands of charred trees flagging the locations of past wildfires. Ryan pointed out the window and asked if those were bear tracks dotting the snow. Marisa confirmed that they were, but comforted the group by explaining that the bears would be heading down to the rivers, not up to the climbing routes.

"Any wildlife on Denali, where we'll be?" Ryan asked.

She laughed. "Just climbers. They're plenty wild."

She took the Beaver up Ruth Gorge, where the view became impossibly stunning. Imagine an ocean of choppy waves as far as you can see, then replace the waves with peaks of snow and granite, and you can imagine our view. As we flew deeper into the gorge, the sheer walls of granite seemed to grow exponentially. Below us, we saw a couple of tiny climbers dotting the snow. And all around we saw evidence of rock falls, snowy avalanches, and crevasses—which were anything from narrow striated ridges in the snow to wide chasms large enough to swallow our plane. Soon after we flew over the Mountain House on Ruth Glacier, Marisa started pumping the Beaver's skis down for landing. Then, she rounded one last turn, and there it was.

Base Camp! After all those years of wanting to climb Denali, I was finally there.

Red, yellow, and blue half-dome tents dotted the snowfield, and in the center was a cluster of orange cache wands marking the supplies climbers had left behind for their return to camp. At that moment, there were few clouds, and the sky was a brilliant primary blue. With all the colorful tents, the footprints crisscrossing the blanket of white, and the blue sky, it reminded me of a preschool playground, all geometric shapes and bright colors.

We bounced onto the landing site, like a jackrabbit bounding through a field, and the medical tent came into view. It was protected by solid walls of snow. Next to it was another sturdy, protected tent: the temporary home for the Base Camp manager. And in front of everything was a teepee structure of three one-by-fours, at the top of which was the National Park Service sign. There was the government logo confirming that we were, really and finally, here on Denali. But the fact that it was erected on such a flimsy structure reminded me that even a United States government agency is powerless to tame a place like this.

The sky in the west was dark, the color of a fresh bruise, and Marisa left immediately after unloading the gear to retrieve the rest of the team. I watched all the other climbers at camp. Some rushed to finish securing their tents, some were fortifying their snow walls, and still others were practicing rope and rescue techniques. Unlike the relaxed mood of climbers in town, the atmosphere here was now serious, bustling, and businesslike.

The wind gusted, and several yellow windsocks ballooned. Ryan shouted to Lynn for direction on what to do first. She had already scouted the area and found a campsite recently abandoned by another team; partial snow walls were still standing.

"Help me get the tents set up and the snow walls fortified," she said, cupping her hands to her mouth so her voice sailed directly to him. "And then we need to get the cache sorted and buried." She glanced at the sky. "We need to get this done quickly."

Lynn and Nick set up the four tents: the one she'd share with Will, the one for Ryan and Nick, Brad's tent, and a kitchen tent. Ryan got out a shovel and saw and started working on the leftover walls. It was heartening to see him working like that—keeping both his mind and body active. He was beginning to look like my husband again. The snow blocks he cut were perfect. I knew he could do this.

When the rest of Marisa's group arrived, Mark trudged directly past Brad's tent and claimed a site twenty yards away. I wondered if he did that in case he needed help, since he was now going solo, but when Ryan ventured over to help him set up his tent in the uncooperative wind, Mark declined the offer. I figured then that he picked the spot more to be an irritant than anything else. There's a jerk in every crowd.

Soon, clouds darkened the entire area and the wind grew angrier. Climbers retreated to their tents, now illuminated by interior lanterns. Fragments of European, Asian, and East Indian voices drifted out through open flaps, as well as music ranging from Mozart to Mary J. Blige, and the wind carried whiffs of both garlic and urine throughout the late afternoon.

Then snow began to fall hard. Brad called everyone out from their tents and rushed through the glacier orientation lesson, covering only crevasse rescue, sled rigging, and rope management. He frequently had to interrupt himself to clean snow from his goggles or to answer calls from Marisa on the satellite phone. Each time he stopped, Nick and Ryan cubed out a few more snow blocks and Lynn, in charge of the camp stove, refilled their mugs with hot cocoa or tea. Marisa's last call was to tell Brad that all air travel had been suspended for the rest of the day, and probably for the next couple of days too.

"She said the forecasters are now saying the storm will be worse than expected, hitting earlier than expected too. Like now. So that's the end of our lesson for today. Go back to your tents and make yourselves comfortable. Looks like we'll be settling in here for a while."

They spent the next two days dug in at Base Camp rather than carrying supplies to higher camps, which had been the original plan. It was unusual to be held up by weather at only 7,200 feet elevation, but with pummeling winds and snow so thick it made walking tedious, it didn't make sense to do anything else. They holed up in their tents, like all the other climbers at Base Camp, acclimatizing more to the cold and the strains of cabin fever than to the elevation, which would come later. The wind was so loud that, even though the tents were just a few yards from one another, inhabitants couldn't hear their teammates next door. They left their tents only to shovel, reinforce snow walls, visit the makeshift latrine, or eat. They gathered three times a day in the kitchen tent for meals, where Lynn reminded everyone to keep their hands clean for the sake of the entire team's health. On the first day, they discussed little else but the weather and making the summit, but as time slowly passed they started to discuss everything *but* those things. The economy. The wars on terror and drugs. River rafting and scuba diving. Mother's Day. Lynn even encouraged them all to attempt a few yoga stretches.

"Keep those muscles limber, keep the blood flowing. Keep breathing."

The third meal of each day coincided with the 8:00 p.m. weather report on the family radio service. "Just remember," the Base Camp manager said each evening after her announcement, "forecasts tend to be less reliable early in the season. Always keep an eye on Mt. Foraker, too. Usually the weather you see there will be heading your way next."

Ryan and Nick played a lot of cards, and Ryan was ruthless, winning nearly every hand. I spent most of those three days with them, savoring the time with Ryan even if he didn't know I was there. Brad stopped by the tent at one point, ostensibly to check in on them although I think he must have been bored silly by himself in his tent. It was good he did; you have to be almost as careful about cabin fever as frostbite up there.

"Think we'll ever get to climb?" Ryan asked Brad on the

second day.

"You paid for a climb, right?" Brad said.

"Yep."

"Then we'll climb." At least he was a man of his word.

On Wednesday—the third day—the snow stopped but the wind worsened, targeting the southeast fork of the Kahiltna Glacier with a vengeance. Snow rose up from the ground and swirled into twisters, defying both gravity and conventional weather patterns, and creating an otherworldly landscape. Ryan and Nick stayed inside their sleeping bags that morning, kicking their feet almost constantly to keep them from going numb. Nick's nose ran constantly, and he coughed a lot, and I started to worry about his health.

When Brad didn't check in with them by noon that day, Ryan loaded up with a warm jacket, pants, and boots, and tried to unzip the tent door. The zipper was frozen. He tried jiggling it and breathing on it and lighting a butane lighter against it, but all that did was scorch the nylon. Nick sat in his bag watching, slowly eating the salmon jerky that was meant for later in the climb. The tent filled with the stench of fish.

"Hey! Can anyone hear me?" Ryan yelled. "We need some help in here, we're suffocating!" He fiddled with the zipper and yelled out for help again.

The snow crunched outside, the slow beat of deliberate steps, and then came Lynn's voice through the nylon fabric.

"Did you call, Pastor?"

"Yes, I called. We're stuck in here. The zipper's broken. And Nick's eating salmon jerky and I have to go to the john."

He tugged on the zipper tab again.

She laughed. "Happens all the time. I mean the stuck zipper problem. Not to worry." We listened to the crunch of retreating and then returning steps, and then the sound of an aerosol spray. When she zipped the tent open, she handed him a can of WD-40.

"I think you saved my life," Ryan said. He pushed past her and hurried off to the latrine, paying no attention to the abrupt laughter chasing after him. I stepped out for fresh air; the salmon odor was overwhelming even me.

When he came back, Lynn was sitting on his sleeping bag with a binder, three-ringed and a soft polypropylene cover, at her side.

"So I see you've made yourself at home," Ryan said.

"I came in to visit with Nick."

"What's *that*?" he asked, pointing to her notebook. I'd forgotten that I was the only one, besides Lynn, who knew about its contents.

"A journal."

"A journal?"

"Yes, you know, something you write in."

Nick asked what she wrote about.

"Oh, I don't know. Stupid stuff, I guess. Random thoughts, philosophies on life. Whatever. Nothing of interest to either of you I'm quite sure."

"So, let me understand this," Ryan said. "You just happened to bring your notebook to my tent when you heard my call for help. A notebook with nothing we'd be interested in?"

She shrugged the way a child might—trying to pass herself off as nonchalant but secretly hoping for more questions.

"Let me guess," Ryan said, pointing at her notebook. "You're writing your memoir."

"No. Not exactly."

"You're writing about your future?"

She shook her head.

"Recording your goals? Dreams?"

"Getting warmer."

"Warmer? Hmmm." He pressed his finger against his lip. "Are you writing about sex?"

That naughty husband of mine. He was always completely faithful and much purer than me. But his sense of humor sometimes belonged in a pool hall rather than a sanctuary. When the words left his lips, I worried she'd take offense. But thankfully both she and Nick laughed.

"No. Most certainly not."

He shook his head. "I give up. Politics? Religion? Confessions?"

She picked up the journal and hugged it to her chest. "It's not important. I should be going."

"No, no. Please stay. And that's all right. No need to explain about your journal," Ryan said. "We'll be spending plenty of time together in the next few weeks. I'm sure we'll have a chance to talk more, later, if you want to."

Although it was entertaining, I was surprised he had interrogated her that way. I doubted he would have appreciated that treatment in return, especially since these days he certainly had plenty of things he was working on:

grief, loss of faith, depression, fear of the future. Things I suspected he wouldn't want to talk to a complete stranger about. Then again, maybe he was trying to open a door so he could share with her. Sometimes it's easier to share your deepest thoughts with someone you don't know. There's less at stake that way.

"There is one thing I know you could help me with," Lynn said to Ryan. By now it seemed as though Nick were invisible to Ryan and Lynn.

"And that is?" Ryan asked.

"That is that, if something should happen to me on this climb, you'd make sure my notebook got into the right hands."

"What do you mean, if something should happen?" Nick asked.

She ignored him and kept her focus on Ryan.

"All right," Ryan said. "I guess I can help with something like that. To whom shall it be delivered? A secret lover, perhaps?" Again he looked lovably devilish, and the irony of the situation hit me: he had been moping around in sunny Central Oregon for months, and now that he was entrapped by a fierce act of nature, his spirits finally seemed to be lifting. Unless it was because he was entrapped with Lynn. I dismissed that thought immediately.

"No, not a lover. A daughter. It's a long story and I'm sure this all sounds stupid. But anyway, that's my request."

"I didn't know you had a family," Ryan said. I'm not sure why he would have known. "Tell me about her?"

"It's complicated. Just promise me you'll be sure she gets

this journal. Okay?"

Ryan hesitated, then took a breath. "Now, now, let's think positively. Can we agree on that? And then, at some later date, I'd like to hear about this mysterious daughter of yours."

16 Chapter Sixteen

7,200' Elevation

Dear Sunny~

Here I am at Base Camp. Stuck in my tent with a man I barely know, in a blizzard. I'm trying to ignore the wind, the cold, and the looks he shoots over at me. I'm trying to imagine your face, your hair, your smile. Trying to imagine your expression when you get my letters, because one way or the other, when this climb is over, they will be sent to you.

I have no fantasies about what you will think of me. As I've already said, I have no expectations of forgiveness or grandiose reunions although, of course, that would be my nirvana. I only pray that my letters won't upset you but rather that they'll bring you some sense of peace, which—selfishly, I admit—they bring to me.

The sky is gray and filled with swirling snow. I can't see the sun. But I can see you, Sunny.

Have you ever wondered about this name I've given you? Of course I don't know what you call yourself now. But to me you have always been Sunny. Your warmth and energy, in my memory, have kept me going just like that bright orb in the sky.

I will try to write every day on this mountain as the end of my final challenge draws near. I will tell you of the people I meet and the trials I face.

And perhaps I will, finally, tell someone about you. I am done keeping secrets. Silence is lonely. Sometimes, I think, it has made me crazy.

I recalled her outburst in her hotel room, which did seem like a fit of insanity. I hadn't realized then just how lonely of a woman she was. I could relate, especially now. How I wished I could have a miniature temper tantrum too, just to clear my mind. How I wished I could be heard again.

Maybe she was right. Maybe silence, and the loneliness of silence, does drive you insane. You're a hostage to your own thoughts, in solitary confinement, trapped with all your worries and regrets swirling around like spinning snow devils, and no one understands. No one can help.

At least if you're among the living, you can hope someone will come along to save you. But for me there was no hope. I had slipped into a deeper level of hell yet again, entrapped in a loneliness-induced state of insanity, a state of mind I'd never have expected for myself. I was once happy-go-lucky, cater-to-the-church, love-life-every-minute Beth. But not anymore.

Lynn looked over at Will. He lay on top of his sleeping

bag, a book in hand. A musky scent wafted through the tent whenever he shifted position. Neither he nor Lynn had had a shower for three days and wouldn't for many more.

She opened a bottle of hand sanitizer and began rubbing it into her palms, her arms, and beneath her shirt to her armpits. The skin on her hands was cracked and threatening to bleed.

"Those hands look awfully sad," Will said.

She slipped on some gloves.

"You know all that germicide is ruining your lovely skin. And from what I understand, it's not going to heal while we're up here."

"Better to have a little pain than come down with something nasty," she said. "You're right, these wounds won't heal on Denali. But if you get sick up here, your immune system won't fix that either. It's the lesser of two evils." She put the sanitizer back in her pack and nodded at his book. "What's it about?"

"It's a mystery."

"I love mysteries," Lynn said. "Tell me about it."

He dog-eared the page and shut the book. "It's set in winter in the mountains. There's a plane crash with only a few survivors. A woman is murdered, and one of the passengers goes missing. The usual who-done-it, I suppose."

"And then?"

"That's really all I can say for now; I'm not sure how it will turn out. Except the victim sounds a lot like you." He cast a sinister stare and then laughed.

"Old and decrepit?"

"That's not exactly how I'd describe you." He scanned her body with his laser eyes; she threw a sock at him. They both laughed. He went back to reading and she picked up her pen.

More thoughts to elaborate upon later:

- *Denali harder than Everest for me;*
- *Not afraid of climb, exactly. But afraid of rejection by mountain, and*

"Lynn?...Will?"

It was Brad calling. Lynn unzipped her tent flap; angry wind and swirling snow blasted her in the face. Brad was crouched in the midst of the gale.

"Time to start digging again!" He had to shout, even though he was just a foot from her, and still the wind was so strong you could almost see his voice being carried away. She gave him a thumbs-up, zipped the tent closed again, and began the tedious process of putting on more layers of clothes, her boots, a parka, two layers of gloves, a facemask, and goggles. Meanwhile, Will kept on reading.

"Come on, Will. Our turn."

Once outside, she searched for the shovel. The tip of the handle was barely sticking out from a new snowdrift, and she found it only after circling the tent twice. She called one more time for Will, yanked the shovel out of the snow, and started working. She brushed snow off the tent, deepened the trench around it, and sawed more blocks for the snow wall, all before Will crawled out of the tent. I would have given the lazy SOB a tongue lashing, but all she did was throw a snowball at his chest.

They worked together on the snow wall after that. Will

sawed, Lynn positioned the blocks. He frequently stopped to watch her. When she rested, she studied him. Once, she reached up, lifted his goggles, and brushed ice away from his lashes. It seemed the heat between them was re-igniting despite the bitter temperatures all around.

Ryan was also shoveling around his tent. He called Lynn over, and Will followed.

"I need you to check in on Nick," he said. "I don't think he's feeling too well."

"Shit," Lynn said. "I noticed he had a cough and a runny nose earlier." She bent forward to crawl into Ryan's tent, and Will put his hands on each side of her hips and followed her inside.

"Two pair," Nick said as he set five cards down on his sleeping bag. He sat upright, wrapped in his parka with his legs inside the sleeping bag and his hood pulled tightly around his flushed face. His teeth chattered. "I'm playing poker against myself. Wanna join in?"

"Not right now," Lynn said. "But I do want to see what's going on with you." She reached into her pocket and retrieved a Ziploc filled with disposable latex gloves. She touched Nick's forehead, removed his gloves to inspect his fingertips, and then asked him to show her his feet.

"Any burning or tingling? Stinging? Throbbing?"

"A little tingling, I guess." He coughed. It was wet and phlegmy.

"Does your uncle know about this?"

Nick shook his head. Will shuffled the cards and dealt a hand for Nick and himself.

"So what is it?" Ryan said, crowding into the tent next to Lynn. "I wasn't thinking frostbite."

"No, no sign of frostbite...yet. I'm sure it's just a little cold, compounded by the weather here. Just keep those hands dry and protected, Nick. Rest up and drink plenty of fluids. Warm fluids." She looked at Ryan. "Which means you'll have to let us help you with the shoveling. You can't do it all yourself. Especially since we have the saw."

She touched Nick's cheek with the back of her hand one more time, this time without the latex glove. "You do feel feverish to me. How long have you been feeling this way?"

"I don't know."

"Do you have any other symptoms? Headache? Nausea? Have you been with anyone who's had the flu or anything?"

Will winked at Lynn. "I guess you aren't the only one who's been feeling sick."

"You're sick too?" Ryan said.

She shook her head. "I'm fine now. It was before we got started. I was just nervous."

Nick set the cards down. "Maybe that's all it is with me."

Lynn thought it was more and said as much. Nick admitted he'd been on a road trip with some friends, and one of them got pretty sick. But they all figured it was either food poisoning or a bad hangover.

"I bet it was something else. Did your friend have chills, sore throat, headache?"

"Yeah, he did. I guess I sort of feel that way, too."

"He's been coughing. A lot," Ryan said.

"Shit. It sounds like you brought the flu with you," Lynn

said. "Didn't you read the instructions? Brad specifically said not to bother showing up if you're sick."

"I didn't know I was sick. Please don't tell him. I'll be fine."

"Perhaps so," she said. "But it's hard to recover on the mountain. And now you've contaminated the rest of us." She pulled another bottle of hand sanitizer out of her pocket and squirted some into everyone's palms.

I hated to go into worry-wart mode, but it seemed the plans were crumbling faster than rocks in a slide, especially now with Nick being sick. Ryan was dealt into the next hand and I watched the slight tilt of his eyebrows, the curl at the corners of his mouth. He had a good hand. He wasn't worried about anything, it seemed, and I needed that reassurance from him.

"How much longer do you think we'll be stuck here?" Nick asked, rubbing his hands together.

"It's hard to say. Hopefully, not much longer," Lynn replied. "And then we have to decide whether we need to send you back and let a smaller group head for the summit."

All three men looked dejected at the suggestion. Surely none of them wanted to see Nick, or anyone else, sent back. Ryan dealt the next round and they studied their cards in silence. Lynn left.

When she got back to her tent, she stripped off her jacket, boots, and other outer gear and sat in lotus position, eyes closed, chanting a mantra. She kept repeating the same word, louder and louder, her vocal chords competing with the tent's flapping nylon and the wind's freight-train whistle. Her chant sounded like 'me,' and she held the long e for at least a count of thirty, maybe more, without a single waver in her voice. She kept chanting until she heard Brad's voice again and looked out.

A miniature abominable snowman staggered in the wind.

She scrambled back into her jacket and boots, ran out, and looped her arm around Brad's.

"Can't find my tent," he said, trying to pull away from her in the direction where his blue tent had been set up. It should have been about twenty yards away, but you couldn't even see five yards ahead in the late afternoon white-out. "I can't find it, Lynn. I went to check in with the Base Camp manager, and now my tent's gone." His voice was desperate.

She motioned him to the kitchen tent. Two other bulky forms came toward her through a curtain of snow. It was Will and Ryan, and they followed her into the kitchen tent as well. As Brad shivered, Lynn helped him take off his saturated outer and middle layers, and Ryan wrapped a fleece-lined tarpaulin around his shoulders. Lynn stepped out into the tent's vestibule to boil water just as another tarpaulin flew past in the wind.

The three men began to argue as she poured the hot water into tin mugs. Ryan thought they should give up and go back to Talkeetna. Will, however, was adamant that the climb should go as planned. Brad said he couldn't believe they'd had this much trouble, and this type of weather, down here at Base Camp; he'd never heard of such a thing. He certainly couldn't climb without his tent and his gear.

"We'll help you find it," Lynn said. "It's got to be here

somewhere."

"Who was in charge of setting up tents and building walls, anyway?" Brad asked.

"I was." Lynn said.

"And you call yourself an expert? Pathetic." He pointed a fleece glove finger at Lynn. "You'll pay for this."

"Perhaps we should withhold blame and consequences until we know what happened and figure out the extent of the damage," Ryan said.

After finishing their tea, the four roped up. They checked the other tents to make sure they were secure, and then set out, roaming from one campsite to the next, in search of Brad's gear. They found some of the gear, scattered, but no tent until they approached the farthest campsite and Lynn spotted something blue pinned by the wind against a snow wall. It was the tent, and it was still useable, aside from some rips in the seams that Lynn offered to repair.

"I'll do it myself," Brad said. "And I'll let you know the full damage report when I'm done."

I was sure he would.

The wind weakened gradually during the night, gasping intermittently before quieting altogether like a climber exhaling his last ounce of breath. In the morning, the sun shone lavishly, the snow was fabulously blinding, and the temperature was downright warm. It was hard to believe the weather could change its mind so completely. But that's the way it is on Denali.

The skies hummed as bush planes delivered new climbers

and picked up those desperate to leave. Tents zipped open. Jackets were peeled off and coconut-scented sunscreen was slathered on. If you closed your eyes, you could almost imagine you were on a beach in Mexico, especially with sounds of Jimmy Buffet and Bob Marley filling the air.

Lynn was the first of Brad's team to awaken. She came out of her tent wearing only a white, skin-tight silk undershirt, flannel bottoms, and a pair of sunglasses in place of goggles. She started a couple of camp stoves outside the kitchen tent and set to work making breakfast: tofu bacon, hash browns, fried eggs for the omnivores, and hot water for instant coffee or tea. As she waited for the water to boil and the potatoes to cook, she rubbed her fingers around her agate. Then she traipsed back into her tent and came out with Marisa's feather clipped to her sunglasses, so that it hung down like one long earring.

Brad was waiting when she returned. "Ready to start carrying supplies?" he asked.

"You mean we're not turning back?"

He shook his head and smiled weakly. "Most of my stuff's okay, except for my camera and headlamp. One of the satellite phones seems to be on the fritz too. You owe me a few hundred dollars, but we'll talk about that later."

She ignored his comment and poured hot water into her cup.

"Right now," he said, "let's get rolling. He waved his hand toward Denali's peak. "This is why we're here." The view of the mountain rising majestically in the distance stole my breath.

"Did your wife confirm we're clear to go?" Lynn asked.

"My wife? You mean Marisa?" He shook his head. "She's not my wife. She's not even my girlfriend, if that's what you're thinking. She's my daughter's mother, and that's about it, except that she also works for me on these expeditions. Anyway, she doesn't tell me what to do. Ever."

"Sounds like you don't like being told what to do."

He shook his head. "No, I don't."

"That makes two of us." She shook a bit of cayenne pepper into the potatoes, added a couple pats of butter, and stirred.

He sniffed the food in the pan. "She did say we're supposed to be getting a break in the weather right now, other than extreme cold. And more weather's coming in a couple of days, so it's best to get going and then we'll have to take it as it comes."

"What about finishing the orientation?"

"We'll get to it higher up. We've got the basics done at least."

They began the first carry to Camp 1, at the base of Ski Hill, after breakfast. The elevation gain would only be 600 feet, starting first with an icy descent before climbing. It would be a pleasant hike, visually at least—with the bluebird sky, the virgin snow sparkling like diamonds, and the grayish brown granite outcroppings—though not an easy one. They would eventually cover over five miles. They had to get three weeks of supplies to the next camp, in two trips, which made for twenty miles of hiking round trip over the next two days. I had it easy of course, and I felt a little guilty. But it was thrilling to be there. Even though I'd never been on Denali, I had thought about it and dreamed about it so much that it felt like I was coming home.

The team stopped frequently to rest. Lynn reminded everyone to re-apply sunscreen, while Brad urged them all to drink more water. Maybe these two would make a good guiding team after all, I thought. And then the time came for the first route decision. You can go straight up the crevasse field or swing wide. Brad headed for the crevasses.

"It's too late in the day," Lynn said. "Too hot. This might have been fine if we'd left early in the morning, but we dunced around in camp. We need to head farther west."

"We'll be fine, and it's because we left so late that I want to take this route. We need to get to Camp 1 and stake out a spot before every other Tom, Dick, and Harry gets there." He had a good point; a long line of climbers was heading up the western route already. It was always this way on a sunny day, especially this early in the climbing season. Again, it reminded me of Mexico with its crowded beaches. You'd think you'd be all alone on the highest mountain in North America, when in fact Denali is a draw for exactly those types of people who want to avoid the crush of vacationers in Mexico and who end up in their own traffic jam on the mountain.

Brad and Lynn argued, and then he sighed and pulled rank. Then they argued about whether to cross the field in two teams or one. They followed Lynn's recommendation this time and roped together as one team. Brad took the lead and Lynn took the rear. She kept calling ahead to remind everyone to keep probing as they made their way and to call out if they felt any weakness in the snow. After they had passed the last crevasse without incident, they split into two teams.

She was roped to Will.

"Hey Lynn, can I talk to you?" Will said as they approached the camp.

"Yes, of course."

"It's about something you said to me, earlier this morning." They were moving along at a good pace—relatively speaking—and she was in her element. Even though Will was in great shape, ten years younger, and nearly a foot taller than her, he had to work to keep up. "You were talking in your sleep, I think. I suppose you could have had me mixed up with someone else."

"Why? What did I say?" She kept hiking at the same pace.

"Look, don't take this the wrong way. I think you're hot, sexy. I really do. But I'm a happily married man."

She faltered with her next step, then looked around. Brad's team was a few paces back, out of earshot. "What are you talking about?"

"You came on to me. In your sleep. You reached over, touched me, and whispered some pretty intimate things."

She stopped. Sweating, she forcefully stripped off her jacket and stuffed it into the straps of her pack.

"Hey. I'm sorry if this is upsetting you," he said.

"I don't believe you."

"Well, it's true. Like I said, maybe you were asleep, dreaming of someone else. Or maybe you just don't remember."

"I certainly don't remember because I don't believe it

happened. As far as I see it, I think you're the one who has, intermittently, been coming on to me. And that, I confess, is a bit unsettling."

Her pace quickened again and he tried to keep up. "Just tell me one thing. Who's Farid?"

She stopped again. She took a long, deep breath. So did I.

"Mind your own business," she said. "And I'll mind mine."

When they reached camp, Brad and Lynn started arguing again. She thought they should have brought all their gear to Camp 1 on the first trip, rather than leaving some back at Base Camp and having to do a double carry, which is also known as expedition-style climbing. Using that strategy, you shuttle fuel, food, and other supplies higher up the mountain, cache it securely, and retreat down to the original camp to rest. The next day, or maybe the day after that, you break down the rest of your camp and haul it up to the cache. It's a leapfrog procedure that allows each climber to slowly acclimatize to the altitude, but it also means everyone is basically climbing the mountain twice. Brad defended his decision to use the double-carry strategy, saying he hadn't wanted to take any unnecessary risks by pushing the team too hard.

"You didn't want to take any unnecessary risks? What about rushing across the crevasse field?" she said.

"We made it, didn't we?"

She ignored his question. "And what about him?" She pointed at Nick, who was coughing. "He needs to rest."

"He can rest back at Base Camp," Brad said.

On the way down, Lynn kept Will moving at a brisk pace, and they barely spoke to one another. When they finally got to their tent, Lynn crawled inside and immediately slid into her sleeping bag. She switched on her headlamp and began to write in her journal.

Dear Sunny~

Silence isn't the only thing that makes me feel like I'm going crazy. Sometimes I feel like I'm being haunted by my past.

I've told you about Will, my tent mate. I can't figure him out. He flirts, then he ignores. He touches, then he reminds me he's married. I wonder if it's just my imagination, then I wonder if he's got a problem. Maybe he's bipolar.

But what really concerns me is that he said I mentioned Farid in my sleep. Yes, your birthfather. I haven't seen or heard from him for nearly thirty years and can't imagine why he'd show up in my dreams. But there's no way Will could possibly know about him, so maybe he's telling the truth. Maybe Farid is *haunting my dreams.*

She shook cramps from her hand.

A few more thoughts:

- *Will reminds me of Farid, but not necessarily in a good way. He has the same belittling tone in his voice. I resent him for that, especially here. This is my mountain. MY mountain.*
- *I don't trust Will. But I also melt faster than snow in a pot whenever he comes near. Maybe it's menopause. Lord help you when you get to that stage of life. Talk about insanity.*

17 Chapter Seventeen

After Raina went out for the evening, Frankie brought the old Koran and the book she'd stolen at O'Hare into her mother's bedroom. The windows were open, but there was no breeze, and the room was hot and humid. She lay down on Raina's bed and opened up the book. It was *Beloved*, a book I knew well, and it was a book that had troubled me. It was about sacrifice, about the lengths a mother will go to protect her young. In that story, a slave killed her own daughter to save her from a life of slavery. Years ago, I read about the celebration of Muharaam—the spiritual event when some Shiite Muslims self-flagellate—and I learned that some mothers intentionally cut the heads of their owns babies to make them bleed. While many mothers make sacrifices *for* their children—careers, personal interests, relationships, even health—I could never understand how any woman could make a sacrifice *of* her child.

Cece once told me she believed that Raina's birthmother had made the ultimate sacrifice by giving her own baby daughter up for adoption to be raised by a loving, financially secure couple. Even that was hard for me to believe. Was that a sacrifice *for* a child, or *of* a child? After all the years I'd spent trying to have a baby, I couldn't imagine under what circumstance I'd give her up.

Frankie read a few pages, then tossed the book aside and leaned over the mattress. Raina had left an empty can of Bud Light on the floor, along with a plastic bag of white powder and a needle syringe. Frankie opened the bag and sniffed, dipped her fingertip into the powder, and rubbed it on her gums. I had never seen her show any curiosity about her mother's drugs before now; in fact she had been adamant with me that she would never, ever use drugs. But now she picked up the syringe and studied it, testing the sharp point against her index finger. I wanted to shout out to her. Tell her to put it down.

She got up from the bed, carried the needle to the bathroom, and rinsed it under hot water.

I was perplexed, and embarrassed, when she set the needle down and took off her clothes. Her small breasts sprang free from her bra, and after she slipped off her jeans, she stood naked in front of the mirror, except for her Hello Kitty panties. I felt like I was creeping on her, and I wanted to turn away, but I couldn't help admire her perfect body and skin: no trace of fat, no blemishes, and no scars on her torso. I was also curious about her intentions. Until she picked up the needle.

She drew the pointed tip down the inside of her left thigh as though drawing with a pen. Soon blood surfaced, began to stream down her leg, and pooled on the floor beside her left foot. Then she scratched the needle down the inside of her other thigh, and after watching that stripe of blood, she returned to the bed, shoving *Beloved* and her Koran to the side.

I so badly wanted to pull her into my arms.

She traced a finger around each nipple while the blood from her legs stained the sheets. I felt like a voyeur watching and yet I couldn't bring myself to turn away. I was far too worried about her. When she brought the needle to her left breast and began to carve a delicate circle around the dark areola, gasping slightly, I tried again to cry out. Tried to tell her to stop. She made another circle around her right areola. She exhaled, lying still with her eyes closed, as gentle rivulets dripped down onto the sheets.

I had no suspicion that her studying of the Koran had anything to do with her self-mutilation; she was a teen caught up in cutting like many, sadly, are. But I couldn't help but see the coincidence between the two, especially since her biological grandfather was Iranian and therefore probably Muslim, and possibly even Shiite. As I understood it, the act of self-flagellation for that sect is—as it was for Frankie—a symbolic act of sorrow and struggle against oppression. I was no expert in spirituality despite my role as Ryan's wife, but it seemed to me that if only Frankie had a way to find a place she felt she belonged, she might find the peace she so badly needed.

I stayed with her for two hours until the doorbell rang. When she didn't get up and answer, I heard the lock being picked, and a moment later a young police officer came into the room. He paled as he surveyed the bloody scene and quickly called for an ambulance. His voice startled and awakened Frankie.

She clutched the edge of the sheet by her neck. "Hey! Who are you?"

The officer cleared his throat and introduced himself. "Are you Frankie Rizzoni?"

Frankie nodded.

As his eyes darted around the room, he explained that Raina had been picked up for prostitution and possession. He had been dispatched to check on her daughter, and when no one answered the door, he let himself in.

"Can you tell me what happened here?" he asked.

"Cut myself shaving. Now please leave."

He was a young officer and no doubt a bit shaken by the situation. When she refused to say anymore, he went out into the living room and waited for the ambulance. When it arrived, he and I both watched as she was lifted onto a gurney against her protests, strapped to it, and rushed away.

At the hospital, a nurse rushed Frankie through triage and into the emergency room, where she was transferred to a bed surrounded by pink curtains. Once her wounds were cleaned and bandaged, she was admitted to the psychiatric ward and given a sedative. I figured she could use the rest.

The next morning, Jack sat by her bed waiting for her to wake up. Her arms and legs were restrained with padded straps, and the room was dark. There were no windows other than a small, square porthole in the door. It looked more like a prison cell than a hospital room.

"Oh, Kitten," he said when Frankie opened her eyes. "I should have known it was a mistake to send you back with your mother. But I never thought it would come to this, Frankie. I had no idea you'd try to kill yourself."

"Didn't," Frankie said. "Knew exactly what I was doing. Now just get me out of here."

Of course, before she was discharged, she had to be evaluated. First a social worker and then a psychiatrist barraged Jack and Frankie, separately, with questions. In the afternoon, they all met.

The social worker explained that cutting is not necessarily an indication of suicide ideation. "But it's still a cause for concern; it's a symptom of mental health issues," she said. Frankie rolled her eyes. The psychiatrist said Frankie was likely suffering from the loss of her grandmother and could be dealing with some post-traumatic stress disorder too, given the sorts of things she may have witnessed or experienced in Raina's world. She would need intensive therapy and anti-psychotic medication, as well as antidepressants, he said.

"Not insane," Frankie said. "Or depressed. You just don't understand. No one understands."

I did. I totally understood. But that didn't do her a damn bit of good.

After she was discharged, she asked Jack what would happen next.

"I'm taking you back to Chicago. For now, anyway."

"And Raina?"

"She'll be in the hospital for a while."

"Thought she was at the police station."

"Not anymore," he said, finally meeting her eyes. "Looks like your mother overdosed somehow while she was at the station."

They stopped by the house on Rosemary Street to get a few belongings, including Frankie's silver necklace and Koran. From there, they drove in silence, a repeat of her trip to Chicago with Seamus. Jack kept his eyes on the flat, distant horizon. Finally Frankie broke the heavy air.

"You're mad, aren't you?"

Jack pulled over onto the shoulder and sighed deeply. "Kitten, I'm tired. I don't know what I feel anymore. I was worried sick about your grandmother, and then she died. I've been worried sick about your mother for most of her life. And now I'm worried sick about you. But worrying doesn't seem to help anything. I don't know what to do anymore."

They both sat looking out through the windshield as the engine idled.

"Sorry, Papa," she said.

They drove a while longer, and then Frankie said it was butt ugly out there. "Wish I lived out West with Ryan. Beth said it's like no place I've ever seen. Wish I lived in the mountains. Not in this boring old place where all you see is dead trees and empty fields and concrete highways and buildings. Out West, there are lots of tall, green pine trees, Beth told me. And waterfalls and snowcaps on the mountains, making them look like peaks of whipped cream. That's what she said. If I ever move again, that's where I'm going."

Even at her young age, Frankie had probably moved more times than I ever did. She had bounced from one apartment or trailer park to another with Raina since she was a toddler, but none of those places could really be considered homes. They were usually dilapidated, often surrounded by a dangerous environment, and far too temporary for any roots to grow. There was nothing about them that would make you want to connect, to feel like that was where you belonged. And Frankie, even when she was much younger, had always seemed desperate to get away, to explore something beautiful and natural. She often convinced me to take her to a river or a park or a forest preserve, and she loved nothing more than sitting on top of the car's warm hood alongside a country road at night to watch the night sky. The poor girl. She was lacking a cohesive family. She didn't know much about her genetic framework. And she had never felt a sense of place, a perspective of how she fit into the world as a whole. Talk about a lost soul.

She looked over at Jack. He shifted in his seat and pursed his lips.

"Someday going to climb a mountain, like Beth used to do," Frankie said. Again she looked to her grandfather for a reaction. "Missing Beth a lot. And Grandmother too."

"I miss them, too, Kitten. I do, too." He looked weary, and she reached across the seat and touched his arm.

"Not trying to screw up, Papa. Really. Think maybe it's just the way I am because of who Raina is. Like she said, it's in our blood."

"That's nonsense. We've had this discussion before, Kitten. Your mother's actions are her choices, and your actions are yours."

"So why does Raina do these things? You know...why is she always in trouble?"

He tapped his fingers on the steering wheel and sighed. "It's complicated."

"Try."

He checked in the rearview mirror and changed lanes to slow down. "You understand we loved your mother—your grandmother and I—and always will. She was a real blessing for us. But she was a challenge, too, right from the get go."

"Boys and drugs and stuff."

"Well, yes, from the time she was about your age, she was interested in boys—much too early, as far as we were concerned. But even before that, she was just defiant and didn't follow rules. As a toddler, she climbed out of her crib at night, stole from Grandmother's purse, and refused to stay in her time-out chair. Then, when she was a little older, she got in trouble at school, practically weekly. She picked on other kids, talked back to teachers, cheated on tests. Later still, she played hooky from school and started drinking and smoking, before she was even an official teenager. And she was a chronic thief. She stole money, candy, whatever she could get her hands on. She didn't need to; we had plenty of money. It was like a compulsion."

"But why? If you and Grandmother loved her, and gave her things she wanted, why would she be that way?"

The traffic came to a sudden halt as if the whole world waited for Jack's reply. He let out another big sigh.

"You know about her being adopted, right? At first we assumed she must have gotten those rebellious traits from her birthparents. We didn't know much about them. But then, when we consulted with the adoption agency about this, we learned that her birthparents were *both* bright, college-educated kids."

"You mean my grandparents?"

Jack looked startled.

"I mean, my *other* grandparents?"

"Yes, Kitten. Your biological grandparents were upstanding, as far as we knew."

"What else do you know about them?"

"Not much."

She mulled this over, then asked Jack more about Raina.

"We took her to all sorts of specialists who said it had to do more with attachment than genetics."

"Attachment?"

"Yes. We had never heard that term either until a specialist talked to us about it. Simply put, it means that sometimes an adopted child never quite fits into her new world because of the trauma of being taken from her birthmother. Even if the baby never really knew her mother, she at least knew her mother's sounds and so forth from inside her womb, and the baby became attached to her. When you then take the baby away, it's extremely frightening and traumatic. The baby learns, subconsciously, not to become attached again, to avoid that sense of loss a second time. She never really attaches to her new, adoptive parents."

"That's so sad."

"Yes, it is. But there was little we could do about it other than love Raina. Still, she always seemed kind of lost. It's hard to understand, but someone once told us that some adopted kids never feel loved even if it's served up right beneath their noses on a silver platter. They just don't recognize love. It's like sending a ladder down to a child who's trapped at the bottom of a deep pit. Even though you're offering love to them, sometimes they still won't climb the ladder to get out."

Frankie took a sip from a water bottle as I thought about what Jack said. If Raina had never learned to love or trust her adoptive parents, how would that ingrained attitude affect her ability to love her daughter? This was the first time I'd really thought about it this way. Poor Raina. Everyone, including me, had always looked at her as a total screw-up when, to at least some degree, her flaws weren't even her fault.

"And then," he said. The car inched forward in the traffic.

"And then what?"

"Well, we learned that her birthfather was Persian."

"Persian? Like a rug? Or a cat?

He laughed. "Well, yes. But Persia is a place, not a breed. It's in the Middle East. Nowadays it's called Iran."

"You mean...I'm Iranian?"

"Part Iranian, part American." He looked over at her apologetically, as though he told her she had inherited an incurable disorder. She scrunched her eyebrows together when she saw his expression.

"Is that bad?"

"No, of course not. Persia has a rich history, and many smart and beautiful people are Iranian. Raina's heritage didn't make a difference to your Grandmother and me; we loved her, and you of course, no matter what. But your mother was born shortly after the Iranian revolution, and we made the mistake of telling her about her heritage when she was too young to understand. She experienced a lot of unnecessary discrimination when she was younger. We often wondered if that was part of why she became so wild and rebellious and detached. By high school she was studying the Koran on her lunch breaks and wearing a headscarf to school, even though nobody else at her school did, and she was desperate to find other kids from the Middle East. Frankly, here in the Midwest, there just weren't that many Iranian kids back then. She was teased ruthlessly."

I remembered how Frankie had been teased too. Although she dressed like the other kids, her skin was such an exotic hue, far different from the pasty white of her Midwestern peers, and she was ostracized for looking so different. It seemed that, each time she moved, she acquired a new nickname. Once she was called a mutt; at another school the kids called her a host of nut varieties. One boy referred to her as a fungus, and a gang of sixth grade girls called her Honeybutt. The name that upset her the most, shortly before she and Raina moved to Davenport, was Swamp Girl.

But now Frankie didn't seem to be thinking about that

prejudice; she was devouring Jack's story about her mother. I was glad Jack finally told her a little more about her history. Even a little bit of self-understanding can help a lot when you're trying to figure out who you are.

"What about my dad? What can you tell me about him?"

"Not a lot. We sent your mother abroad the summer before her senior year in high school, at her request. She was obsessed with the Middle Eastern culture by then, which was ironic because many of her behaviors would have been frowned upon by Islam. She found a student tour she could join. It didn't go to Iran—that would have been too politically dangerous. But the group visited other parts of the Mediterranean, the Middle East, and even North Africa. We assumed she would be well supervised, and we hoped this would help her calm down and become more comfortable in her own skin—literally. We would have sent her to the moon if we thought it would help."

I'd never really put it all together that way, but all of a sudden I saw the challenge Frankie faced was even greater than lacking sense of family, heritage, or place. How can a child feel secure with herself when her own mother never did? She watched out the side passenger window for several minutes.

"And that's when she got pregnant with me?"

"Yes, as a matter of fact it is."

"So was my father really from Italy?"

He shook his head. "We're not sure. Raina's not even sure. She said he may have been an Italian fisherman. Or he may have been a student protester from Sudan."

Frankie's eyes widened.

"Raina put the Italian man's name on your birth certificate. I'm not sure why. I think she thought it might be better for you to think you were Italian, that maybe you'd fit in better in our own culture. But I don't know if that's even true. Here I am sixty-three years old and I don't know what's true anymore, Kitten."

She crossed her arms and watched the world pass by.

"I'm sorry to be the one laying all this on you. It must sound awfully confusing. I wish Grandmother had had this talk with you. Or Raina. What I'm saying, really, is that Raina's problems, and choices, shouldn't necessarily dictate yours. Everybody's got a different situation. And everyone needs to find a way to live. For you, we need to figure out how to get you a safe, loving, normal life. And you've got to stop all that...cutting."

"So how are you planning to do that? What if I don't want to stop?"

"There will be changes," he said. "But for now let's just go home."

Beatrice met them at the door of Jack's condo in a snazzy velour sweat suit and purple satin wedges.

"Oh you poor thing," she said, holding her arms out for a hug. Frankie walked right past her.

"What's that bitch doing here? She living with you now, Papa?"

Jack started to chastise Frankie, but Beatrice interrupted him. "No, your grandfather asked me to be here when he brought you home. So we could talk together. But if I make you uncomfortable, I'll leave."

"No, stay. Please," Jack said.

Beatrice smiled coldly at Frankie and then went into the kitchen to finish making dinner. Jack led Frankie to the large picture window in the living room. Together they looked out at the streams of headlights and taillights on the streets below and at the eastern sky over Lake Michigan. It was a spectacular canvas of plum, purple, and indigo.

"I'm going up to my room," Frankie said, referring to the guest room where she had always stayed when visiting her grandparents.

"Hold on a minute, Kitten," Jack said. He put his arm around her shoulders. "Let's have dinner first."

The dining room table was set for three, with tossed salad at each place setting and a basket of garlic bread in the middle. Beatrice set a pan of lasagna down and poured red wine into two glasses at one end of the table. A glass of milk was set at the other end.

As she served up the lasagna, Beatrice said the problem was that Frankie needed a lot of personal attention to work through her issues. "More than your grandfather can offer you."

"This isn't your business," Frankie said.

Jack said Beatrice was right, however. "You do need to work on your issues." He gestured toward Frankie's breasts and abdomen, where thick bandages made her t-shirt look lumpy.

"Don't need help with that," Frankie said, casting her eyes

down to her plate.

"We think you do," Beatrice said. "We think you need a specialist."

"A shrink," Frankie said.

"Not a shrink, honey. A therapist."

Frankie said she'd already agreed to see one in Davenport, and it wasn't her fault Raina didn't make the appointments. "Whatever. Fine, I'll see one here in Chicago."

Beatrice said that wasn't going to work. "You need more intensive therapy, more than we can offer here, honey. Something more full time."

Frankie tossed her fork on the table and it slid toward Jack, leaving a trail of tomato sauce. "What do you mean full time?"

Her eyes grew wide in terror. She stood up, threw down the cloth napkin, and stormed upstairs. She ripped off her clothes and bandages and scraped what was left of her fingernails against the wounds. Then she threw herself face down on the guest room bed.

A half-hour later, when there was a knock on the door and she sat up, she saw that her blood had stained the comforter.

"I'd like you to come downstairs, Kitten," Jack said through the closed door. "There are some people I want you to meet."

"Like who?"

"You'll find out. Just come downstairs."

She sat there for a few minutes, looking at a photograph she had tucked into her Koran. It was taken shortly before Ryan and I moved back West. Frankie and I stood together in front of my rose garden, laughing at some joke Ryan had told. I remember it was one of those laughing seizures for both of us, where we laughed so hard that our stomachs ached. She tucked the picture back into the Koran, got dressed, and went downstairs.

A man and woman were standing by the front door. They didn't look like they'd be friends of Jack's; the man had on a windbreaker and jeans, and the woman wore a denim jacket, jeans, and no makeup. Jack and her grandmother's friends were always dressed nicely and had expensive taste.

When Frankie stepped down from the last stair, the man reached for her arms. A set of handcuffs dangled from one of his hands.

"I'm being arrested?"

The woman smiled kindly and shook her head. "No dear, we aren't police officers. We're transporters. We're here to escort you to your new facility. The handcuffs are just part of the process."

"Facility?" Frankie looked from the woman to Jack and back. "Papa, what is she talking about? What's going on?"

Jack's eyes immediately flooded with tears. He couldn't speak. Beatrice walked to Frankie and took her hands.

"This is very difficult for your grandfather. It's breaking his heart. But this is what we think—what he thinks—is best. There's a place in Utah that works with young teens like you, troubled teens. They can help you more than we can, help you with the stealing and cutting and all that."

Frankie's face reddened, and her eyes became watery now, too. "This was your idea wasn't it! You fucking bitch!"

Jack shook his head. "No, Kitten! This was my idea. All mine. Please understand, I'm doing this only because I love you and want the best for you. And I am worried about all that...cutting. And about you living with Raina..."

The man in the windbreaker again reached for her wrists, but Frankie jerked away so he couldn't grab them.

"Don't worry, dear. Once you're down in the car, we'll take the handcuffs off," the woman said. "It's a safe car, like a police car. You won't need them then."

Frankie exploded. "This is bullshit. You're sending me to some nuthouse way out in Utah, wherever the hell that is, and I'll be trapped in a police car all the way there?" She glared at Jack. "You're sending me away, just like that? I thought you loved me Papa, but obviously you don't."

She started to run upstairs, but the man in the windbreaker grabbed one of her arms this time. She tried to wrestle herself free.

"It's only a hundred days, Kitten. It's a short-term program and then they'll evaluate how you're doing, and it will give us a chance to figure out what's next."

"A hundred days? You call that short? That's like my whole summer vacation! And I'll be there for my birthday?" She looked from one adult to the next.

Again, she tried to twist free of the man's grasp. The woman said she'd be better off if she cooperated. Frankie stood frozen on the stair, her knuckles whitened from gripping the railing so hard and her arm red from the twisting.

"Please cooperate," Jack said.

"You don't really have a choice, honey," Beatrice said,

"while your mother is in rehab."

Frankie's eyes bored into Jack's until I thought he would crumble. Finally, through gritted teeth, she acquiesced.

"Fine then. You want to send me away? Fine, have it your fucking way. But just wait. You'll be sorry."

Tears now streamed freely down Jack's face.

"I'll get you for this," Frankie hissed to Beatrice. "Grandmother wouldn't have ever done this to me."

Behind Jack, the sky was clear and nearly black. The lake had an eerie, phosphorescent sheen from the reflection of the city lights. Beatrice hurried up the stairs and returned with a small suitcase, which she handed to the man. The woman gently put a hand on Frankie's arm and led her out the door.

From the hallway, Frankie turned to look at Jack over her shoulder. Her eyes were dry.

18 Chapter Eighteen

7,800' Elevation

My old Ryan was back. No longer waking with a hangover, his eyes were nearly as clear as the sky. He looked ready for just about anything—which was a good thing, since today they'd be carrying supplies toward Camp 2, at 11,200 feet.

Again, they used the double-carry climbing strategy, shuttling gear up and then descending to rest. As they climbed higher, their pace slowed, and each step required more effort than the one before. But with each step, the view became more spectacular. The climbers rested frequently, partly to catch their breath and partly to absorb the setting, which gave me the chance to do the same. New ridgelines appeared. New peaks emerged in the distance. The light shifted throughout the day, rendering an ever-changing palette of whites, blues, and grays. And at sunrise and sunset, which were only a couple hours apart in the Arctic north, the mountains looked a little like candy gumdrops as the rising and setting sun splashed them with vivid pinks, purples, oranges and yellows.

And just as the light shifted, the team members seemed to shift their allegiances. One minute Lynn and Brad would be in harmony, the next they'd be arguing. Brad would be friendly to Ryan for a while and then suddenly snap at him for the slightest thing. Will would intermittently be patient with Nick and condescending toward him. But the most noticeable dance was the one involving Lynn and Will.

"Seems like we're all doing fine when Lynn and Will are separate entities," Brad had commented to Ryan that morning over coffee, "and then they get together again and a rift forms among all of us."

Ryan agreed that he'd noticed a similar pattern, an advance-and-retreat ballroom step, between Lynn and Will. "Frankly, I can't figure either of them out," he said. "So I'm just sticking with you and Nick and staying out of their way."

The three men were on one rope team; Lynn and Will were on the other. Ryan took Nick on as his personal project, cheering him on when the load got too tough, and he chatted with Brad during rest breaks about politics and the economy. When Brad let Ryan break trail for a while, after they made the turn at Kahiltna Pass, I was envious that I wasn't there, right behind him. But I was also concerned; the area is prone to avalanches coming down the northern ridge, and crevasses abound on the Camp 2 approach. But they made it to camp safely, stashed their gear, and retreated to Camp 1 as planned.

Everyone gathered for the mean pasta primavera dinner Ryan made.

The next day, they roped up as two teams again, this time hauling their tents and their sleeping bags. Ryan led his team, and I thought he was keeping a stellar pace, but soon Lynn and Will passed him. There was something about the purposeful way she marched ahead that said, "This is mine, all mine." Ryan breathed out a small laugh when she cut back in front of his team.

They trudged on in the glorious sunshine. The snow, windswept in all directions, was as smooth as frosting on a cake. Ahead, cotton-like clouds hung in the air. It was so calm you might think you were in heaven. Ryan's team stopped frequently to snap pictures and rest.

"I wish she'd wait for us," Brad said when they stopped at one point. "She should know not to leave us behind. We're in the safety-with-numbers zone from here on out. You don't just leave your team behind, especially when you're a guide."

"Want me to talk to her?" Ryan asked. "When we catch up?"

"No, thanks. That's my job. And believe me, I will do my job."

They passed a Swedish group coming down the mountain that had summited via Cassin Ridge. They briefly shared stories about where they were when the last storm hit, and Nick asked if they'd seen a guy climbing alone, a guy wearing a red jacket with silver reflective stripes. They said they hadn't.

"It's much too early for Mark to have been up there," Brad

said, evenly.

By the time Brad, Ryan, and Nick got to Camp 2, Lynn and Will were nowhere to be found. Brad tracked them down using the family radio service. They had continued on to Windy Corner. Brad shouted into the radio to get their asses back to Camp 2, but Lynn said it was glorious up there and she was thinking they should camp higher up. They argued for a couple of minutes and then the radio went dead.

"She turned it off," Brad said. "She hung up on me."

After taking a break, during which Nick was coughing more than ever, the men pushed on to Windy Corner and spotted Lynn and Will, basking in the sun on a slab of rock. From that vantage point, it was a spectacular view. There were those same three colors—the blue so divine it belonged in a stained glass window, the pure white draping over the ridgelines like communion linens covering an altar, and the candle-smoke gray of the boulders and rock faces rising up toward the heavens. I wasn't much of a believer all those years I sat in church, supporting my pastor husband, but a day like this could make a believer out of anyone.

Brad told Lynn she had no business taking off like that.

"What are you talking about? I wasn't *taking off.* For Pete's sake, I had Will with me. And I can't help it if your team is slow. Look, we're having exceptional weather...no blowing snow at Squirrel Point, hardly any wind here for a change...it's like a miracle...so I was simply setting a good pace, leading by example, to get here. Then just enjoying it a little once we did. You know as well as I do that you have to take advantage of these primo conditions."

"I also know, as do you, that there are crevasses everywhere around here. You just strolled across an entire plateau of crevasses. The Windy traverse is not to be taken lightly."

He was right, and Lynn should have known better. It was clear to me that Will was having an influence on her, and not a good one.

"Also," Brad continued, "you know this altitude can really start showing in the climbers. You and I, as guides, need to be on the lookout for AMS and address this together."

Ryan walked up just then, "Sorry, couldn't help overhearing. Just wanted to add my two cents—Nick's still not 100% yet." He paused to catch his breath; unlike Lynn and Brad, he was laboring a bit. "If you're talking about altitude mountain sickness, I think we might be looking at that with him. 'Course I'm not the expert. But seems to me if we push him too hard now, it'll be bad news later."

"It's *acute* mountain sickness, Pastor," Lynn said.

"The proper name of the condition is not what's at issue, Lynn," Brad said. "What is at issue is what Ryan meant by Nick not being 100% *yet.*"

Ryan glanced from Brad to Lynn. "Nick hasn't been feeling well since Base Camp. He's actually feverish."

"Did you know about this?" Brad asked Lynn, raising his voice.

"Yes, and I handled it. As your co-guide, I didn't think I had to trouble you about every little thing. It obviously was just a touch of flu, not AMS. And you seemed to be having such a tough time handling your personal challenges, and the other obstacles we were facing, that I didn't want to burden you any more than necessary. Besides, you can't tell me you didn't notice him coughing."

"Of course I did. But I had no idea he had a fever. And you might say I've been a little distracted by your behavior, taking off with that hot-shot up there." He nodded toward Will. "Who, by the way, seems to be standing alone near the top of the world without being roped to anyone." He turned to Ryan. "You said, Pastor, you were worried that if we push Nick too hard now, it could be bad news for him later. But it's not just Nick it could be bad news for, I'm afraid, with the way things are going."

Brad checked his watch and the sun's position. He looked out at the lower peaks. Nick coughed. "We need to head back down. Now. Back to Motorcycle Hill."

"You're nuts," Lynn said. "We just turned Windy Corner on a calm day. If we go back down, we have to retrace our steps again, and I guarantee it won't be so nice next time. Once you gain the crux, you don't go back and do it again."

"You do if one of your team members isn't well. You do if you want to do the responsible thing."

"Then perhaps you should take Little Nicky all the way back to Base Camp," she said.

I felt sorry for the young man, watching from the sidelines as they argued about him like parents who couldn't quite get on the same page, and I was dismayed by Lynn's attitude.

"No, I don't think we need to do that—at least not yet," Brad said. "We need to watch him closely though, and let him have some more time to acclimatize. It's decided. We go back to Camp 2 and stay there for a day." He fished a small tube of sunscreen out of his pocket and applied the lotion to his already sunburned nose. "You can set up a small cache here. But mark it well, Lynn. We wouldn't want you to forget where our belongings are."

When he walked away, she stuck her tongue out at his back and Ryan shook his index finger at her.

That night, Ryan stopped by Lynn's tent and asked to speak with her alone. Will said he'd go out to use the latrine. Once he was gone, Ryan and Lynn chatted about the great weather, the tough hike, the buttered tortillas at dinner.

"I just want to apologize for what happened today up at Windy Corner," Ryan eventually said. "For getting involved."

"You don't need to apologize. You did nothing wrong. It's Brad that's got the problem, disorganized one minute and then turning into a dictator the next. Sheesh."

He lowered his voice. "You know, Brad's pretty bothered by whatever is going on between you and Will."

"There's nothing going on between us."

Ryan pressed his hands together and bounced them off his lips. "Mm-hmm."

"Really."

"Okay then. Well, anyway, I wanted to be sure we were still on good terms."

Her face softened. "Thanks."

He pointed to her journal on the sleeping bag. "How're you coming along with your writing?"

"All right. I was just scribbling some thoughts down about that scene with Brad today."

"And?"

"And I didn't appreciate that comment he made about not marking the cache and forgetting where it was. Greg—my ex-significant other—teased me about my poor memory all the time. He's a golf pro, doesn't know a damn thing about climbing. But he, too, once brought up the idea that I might forget the cache."

"Golfers are smarter than you think."

"Are you a golfer? I hope I didn't offend you, Pastor."

Ryan laughed. "That's a matter of opinion. My friends would say I wasn't, but my wife would say I was. 'Course she never saw me hit the ball. She just saw me leave on Saturday mornings with a glove on my left hand, a bag of clubs slung over my shoulder, and a smile on my face. So if that made me a golfer, then I guess I was."

That was the first time he mentioned me, and the tent suddenly seemed very small.

"I guess it's time for me to go," he said.

Lynn reached out her hand. "Friends?" The temperature of her voice seemed to have climbed by one or two degrees. It's remarkable how one person's vulnerability can ignite another's warmth.

He took her hand in both of his. "Friends."

19 Chapter Nineteen

Pocked sandstone cliffs and strange rock formations jutted up from the valley floor as Frankie and the transporters drove through southern Utah. The landscape was vivid red and terra cotta, and the sky had turned deep periwinkle. They'd been driving for nearly two days, past cornfields and prairies, alongside twisting rivers, and among snow-capped mountains, and Frankie had slept much of the way. Now her head swiveled from side to side as she studied this new terrain.

"Never seen anything like this," she said. "It's like everything's dead. It's not the way Beth described it at all." True, when I'd given her images of the West, I'd focused more on the Pacific Northwest where conifers rule the mountains. This was a much different landscape, but even this one made me feel more alive than anything back in the Midwest. The road out here was full of suspense; you never knew what you'd see around the next bend, and the climax of this mystery was the hogback—a narrow, knife-edged stretch of road that gave way on either side to thousand-foot drop-offs. It gave me shivers even now, and Frankie must have been spooked by it, too. She scooted to the middle of the back seat and squeezed her eyes shut. But once the car made it safely to solid ground again, scraggly pinion junipers started to appear, and then clumps of wild grass, and finally grazing pastureland.

The car slowed and turned onto a dirt road that meandered through pasture for at least a mile until grass gave way to sagebrush, weeds, and rocks. Finally, they came to an open wrought iron gate affixed to lodgepole pine posts. A grandmotherly woman with a big bosom and wide hips met them as they pulled up in front of a primitive cabin. She introduced herself as Erma Lou.

"Where the hell are we?" Frankie asked.

"Your new home," she said.

Frankie stared at the vast emptiness all around. "You gotta be kidding."

The driver handed Frankie's suitcase to Erma Lou. The woman in the denim jacket wished Frankie good luck. Then the transporters got into their car and sped away, leaving Frankie and the old woman to watch their cloud of dust. When the car disappeared from view, Erma Lou led Frankie into a small cabin and told her to make herself comfortable.

"I'll be back shortly," she said, and when she left, she locked the door from the outside.

Frankie looked around. An empty gun rack hung on one wall; a moth-eaten wool blanket with Native American patterns hung on another. An array of taxidermied animal heads were mounted on a third wall: a longhorn steer, a couple of deer, a cougar, a marmot, and a squirrel with tufted ears. Frankie chewed her fingernails as she studied each animal, gazing into its glass eyes. Then, on the coffee table, she discovered a rattlesnake, coiled and mouth agape as though ready to strike. She skimmed her finger over the stuffed reptile's scales and slipped it into the snake's open mouth. The whole décor was strange for what was meant to be a rehabilitative facility for teens; it seemed to convey defeat rather than renewal.

Frankie yawned, lay down on the sofa, and fell asleep with a throw blanket across her shoulders.

It was dark when she woke to the sound of the door opening and yapping coyotes outside. Erma Lou came in and flicked on a propane lantern.

"How are you feeling, Frankie?" Erma Lou asked.

"Cold."

The woman lit a woodstove in the corner of the room and handed Frankie another blanket.

"It's time we have a little chat now that you've had a rest," she said.

Frankie pulled the blanket tight under her chin.

"Let's start from the beginning." Erma Lou settled into a folding chair, poised with a notebook and pen. "Do you know why you're here, Frankie?"

Frankie rubbed the goose bumps on her arms. "Guess so. Stealing. Cutting. Running away. Guess I'm being locked up for that."

Erma Lou's face softened. "Oh, honey. We're not locking

you up. Hasn't anyone told you about our ranch? What we can do to help you?"

"Didn't even know I was on a ranch. Looks like a shitty old cabin in the middle of nowhere if you ask me."

"Well, you are on a ranch, and there's no need to be frightened here. Or sassy."

Frankie cocked her head to the side. "Who said I was afraid?"

"Okay, good then," the old woman said, her face half covered in shadows. "If you're not afraid, things will work out even better for you. What I mean by that is this: our job is to help you acclimate to the ranch, learn the rules, and explore what's going on in your life that leads you to make poor choices. As long as you get with the program, and you're not afraid to follow our rules, then you'll do just fine."

"What do you mean *our* job? Who else is here? Besides a bunch of other kids held hostage like me."

Erma Lou explained there was an entire staff of counselors there to help Frankie and the other teens.

Frankie started chewing on her fingernails again, her eyes focused on the rattlesnake rather than Erma Lou.

"I see you aren't very communicative," Erma Lou said. "That won't do here. I expect you to respond when I speak to you, thoughtfully and politely."

Frankie inspected the snake's fangs.

"Did you hear what I said?"

"Yeah, whatever."

"That," she said, pointing at Frankie, her face now stern, "is exactly what I'm talking about. Comments like that are a waste of your breath and my time. They're meaningless. If you have something you want to say, please say it in a way that we'll understand."

Frankie got up and walked over to the window. Aside from the thousands of stars in the sky, the only light was a floodlight attached to a telephone pole at the far corner of the property. It illuminated the iron gate as well as the chain link fence that extended in both directions until it disappeared into the dark. Frankie spun back around, jutted one hip out, and pointed back at Erma Lou.

"Okay, you want me to talk? I'll talk. First off, I know damn well why I'm here and why I behave the way I do. My mother's a drug-addicted whore with some kind of adoption attachment shit going on. My father's a disappeared deadbeat on the other side of the world. Grandmother's dead, and my grandfather's too busy to take care of me. I got sent away because nobody understands me. It's not my fault I have such a rotten life. I don't want to be here, and I don't plan on *getting with the program.* In fact, I don't plan on sticking around very long. How's that? Is that *communicative* enough for you?"

I was at least pleased to see her snarky attitude had returned.

"Yes, dear," Erma Lou said. "That was a good start. And I know right now you're probably confused on how we can possibly help you. And angry, too, of course. But over time, you'll see." She then explained that Frankie would undergo more psychological testing, receive intensive counseling, and undoubtedly discover things about herself she didn't already know.

"You'll come to enjoy life on the ranch," Erma Lou said. "Working in the garden, tending to the animals. All the children enjoy that. But, first, you'll spend some time in Retreat. To clear your mind. I'll explain more about that tomorrow. For tonight, you'll sleep here, on a cot in the back room," she pointed toward a doorway with her thumb, "and I'll sleep right here on the sofa. In case you need anything."

"You mean in case I try to run away or cut myself."

Erma Lou smiled.

"What about my stuff? Had a suitcase."

"I have all your belongings," Erma Lou said. "They're locked away safe and sound."

Frankie reached up to her neck. The silver locket was missing, and she started to look around the sofa for it.

"I have your necklace, too. I took it when you fell asleep. And that awful book you had." The Koran. "Out here, we study the Bible."

Frankie did not grace Erma Lou with a reply, and the two stood facing one another, sizing each other up. I was not a student of the Koran or the Bible, and I didn't know what Frankie's spiritual beliefs were, but I knew one thing for sure. No one can take away what you do believe in. Not even Erma Lou.

"In time," Erma Lou said, "you'll get your things back, but not until I have a chance to inspect everything, and not until I know you're safe. You won't be needing your personal things for a while anyway, not until you graduate."

"Graduate? From what grade? Thought I was only going

to be here for three months."

Erma Lou laughed. "Not from a grade, from the program. You're right; it's a hundred-day program. That's all children usually need to turn themselves around. It depends, of course, on how well you develop, and how well you cooperate with my staff. But don't you worry about that now."

Erma Lou handed Frankie a shopping bag that had been placed behind the folding chair.

"What's this?"

"These are your clothes for while you're here with us."

Frankie pulled out a tan t-shirt, red sweatpants, and slip-on canvas shoes.

"This is it? This is all I have to wear for a hundred frickin' days?"

"I'll bring you a couple more sets of clothes tomorrow. And I'll get you some more warm blankets for tonight. But let me suggest, Frankie, that you watch your language. Once you leave this cabin in the morning, you will be in Retreat for three days, and every time you speak without permission, another day of Retreat will be assigned. If you cuss, extra days will be added. Now, do you have any questions?"

"Are you saying I can't talk to anyone for three whole days?"

Erma Lou nodded with a smile plastered on her face.

"What if I need something? What if I'm sick?"

"Someone will tend to your needs, don't worry."

She meant, of course, Frankie's physical needs. Her emotional needs could not possibly be met if she was confined to silence. I, of all people, understood that.

Over the next three days, Frankie met with the program director, a psychologist, two counselors, and a nurse practitioner. She answered hundreds of questions, filled out dozens of questionnaires, took standardized academic tests, and was subjected to medical exams for lice, STDs, and tuberculosis. When she wasn't undergoing one of those procedures, she was required to sit in Retreat: a patch of sand and dust behind the cabin, five feet in diameter, surrounded by a circle of football-sized rocks. There was a primitive lean-to slab of plywood for protection from the baking sun or the occasional downpour, and there was a porta-potty nearby. Prohibited from speaking or even making eye contact with anyone else while in Retreat, unless instructed to do so, Frankie was also not allowed to read or sleep while there. The only privileges granted to those in Retreat, she was told, were three bowls of oatmeal sprinkled with cinnamon each day, a stenographer's tablet, and a pencil.

Frankie filled her first tablet quickly. She wrote to Jack about what a god-awful place he had sent her to: how the dust was so thick it caked her eyes shut in the morning, how the climate was so dry her lips and knuckles were cracked and bleeding. She wrote how cold it was at night and how ugly it was, with cactus and scrubby plants and trees that looked like they were a million years old. She told him the only thing resembling a flower was the bruise on one of her arms, given to her by one of the transporters.

Then she lied to him, saying she was fed stale food, beaten with sticks, and sexually abused by the old woman. Erma Lou *was* a bit on the creepy side, with her roving eyes and a nasty habit of darting her tongue out like a reptile. But Frankie went a little too far with the sexual accusation. She also told Jack she wished she was dead "like Grandmother and Beth," and I wasn't so sure if that was also a lie, or an exaggeration, or if it was the truth. After two days of frantic writing, she ripped the pages out of the tablet, handed them to one of Erma Lou's assistants, and asked her to mail them to her grandfather.

On the third day, she wrote to Ryan, another combination of truths and lies about life in Utah.

"My goodness," the assistant said when Frankie handed this newest letter to her. "You certainly have a lot to say."

"Just mail the letter," Frankie said.

"I need the address."

I felt a heavy lump in my stomach. I had spoken to Frankie daily after moving out West, but I didn't think I ever gave her our address. Ryan would never get her letter.

"Can't remember it for sure. His name's Ryan Mahoney and he lives in Central Oregon. If I heard it, I'd recognize it. Can you just try to find him online? I'll know it when I hear it."

The assistant came back in a few minutes with a pink post-it in her hand, and I had to laugh. Frankie was even more clever than I'd realized.

"I think I've found it," the assistant said.

"Let's see." Frankie reached out for the paper, and there it was.

Ryan and Beth Mahoney
21725 Volcano View Road
Bend, Oregon 97702.

20 Chapter Twenty

11,200' Elevation

The team spent the next day resting at Camp 2. Early on Wednesday morning, before the sun had a chance to heat the ground and any other teams headed out, they abandoned their skis and snowshoes, donned their crampons, and retraced their path toward Windy Corner, where they would retrieve the small cache. From there they would climb to the next camp at 14,200 feet.

Although they followed the same path as two days earlier, there were no footprints or sled tracks left. The wind had rearranged the snow, and now it was a barren surface, blinding in its emptiness. The pre-dawn light was almost luminescent, a ghostly purple gray, and the entire landscape had become eerie with howling wind and no evidence that any other humans had ever been there before, or would ever be there again, except for a scrap of red nylon caught under a boulder, slapping at the air and trying to break free.

The trail was knee-deep in some spots, and I could almost feel my own legs aching. Brad had it the worst as the leader in the thick, pristine snow. It was arduous work, one of the downsides of being the first team out. The wind had picked up too; by the time they reached the top of Motorcycle Hill this time, it was an incorrigible fifty miles per hour with bits of ice, and even rock, whipping through the air. When something hit Brad's goggles, he held up his hand and said it was time for everyone to take a break. They stepped off the trail and sat on a slab of rock that had been swept clean of snow since the last time they'd been there.

I watched Ryan nibble on a peanut butter and chocolate energy bar that looked teeth-shatteringly hard. Nick sat with his head in his hands, and when Ryan asked how he felt, Nick admitted he had a headache again.

"This one's a lot worse," he said. He was breathing hard, and when he ripped the goggles from his face, you could see he was flushed and sweating.

"He needs to go back," Ryan called to the group. "I don't think this is the flu."

"Since when are you the expert?" Will shouted back into the wind. He, like Nick, was breathing more heavily.

"Calm down, Will," Lynn said. "Maybe we can let Nick rest here a while, and the rest of us could carry some of his gear for him." She motioned for Will to get Nick's pack.

"It's definitely the altitude now," Brad said. "Maybe we should all turn back." He had also been panting hard before they stopped.

"Oh please," Lynn said. "We're not even at 13,000 yet. Nick's young. He'll be fine. Let's just help him with his gear."

Nick coughed. "I wish you'd all stop talking about me as if I wasn't even here."

The climbers gathered around Nick but continued to argue.

"Good thing we didn't stay at Windy, like you wanted to," Brad said.

"How could you say that?" Lynn said. "If we'd camped there then perhaps we'd be less stressed now. We could be resting there now, closer to the summit."

"This is nobody's fault. We just need to solve the problem."

"Sorry I've become a problem."

"That's not what I meant, Nick. It could happen to anyone."

"All I've got to say is that we're wasting a lot of time and money on this kid," Will chimed in. "A kid who went and got himself sick right before we left."

"Oh, be quiet."

"You be quiet, too."

It didn't matter who said what; what mattered was that they were becoming less cohesive by the second. Finally Brad reclaimed control.

"Hold on, everyone. I'm your leader, so I'll tell you how we're going to solve the problem. Lynn, you're to stay right here with Nick. The rest of us will do the double-carry. We'll finish taking the gear as far as Windy Camp. Then we'll come back for the two of you, and we'll all move on to Camp 3."

"Why me?" Lynn asked. "What am I, the old den mother now? You know damn well that I can make it to Windy and back faster than anyone here. Yourself included."

"It's not a demotion," Brad said. "And it has nothing to do with age, so get over yourself. You have more experience with altitude sickness than the rest of us put together."

"Which is why you should listen to me. I don't think altitude sickness is the problem."

"Yeah, listen to her," Will said, stepping closer.

"No, I will not," Brad said. "Lynn, you are to stay here with Nick. That's an order."

I half expected Lynn to go storming off, but instead she took a long, deep breath and then tried to coax Nick to use some hand sanitizer and eat an energy bar.

He shook his head. "I'm not hungry. And if I don't have to carry anything, I think I can keep going." He started to stand, swayed, and sat back down. He tried to stand again, despite Lynn's appeals. Ryan came over and told him to sit back down too. But Nick convinced Ryan he could keep hiking.

"Maybe Lynn's right," Nick said. "I can do this."

It was slow going, and they were all roped together as one team. Brad was in the lead, followed by Will, who was carrying most of Nick's load. Then came Nick, coughing almost nonstop, and then Ryan. Lynn was at the end. As they started the traverse toward Windy Corner, a thunderous boom filled the air, followed by sounds of cracking and breaking.

Ryan pointed to a shelf of snow slipping away from a nearby slope. "Run!"

At the sound of his voice, the others on the team turned toward him to see what he was shouting about. As they did, massive chunks of snow and rock began to crash toward them.

"Avalanche!" Brad called. "Run!"

They had not rehearsed avalanche protocol, as they should have. Brad tried to run uphill, with his sled and gear, to escape the run-out zone, while Lynn, at the other end of the rope, released her sled and pack and tried to retreat downhill. Will started to dig in for self-arrest. The effect, since they were all roped together, was pandemonian inertia.

"Down!" Lynn shouted. "Down!" Nick apparently thought this meant to get down, so he dropped to his knees. But everyone else, including Brad, understood her order meant to turn around and head downhill. In the confusion, they lost precious seconds, and even as they finally began running in unison, the weight of the snow and their gear hindered any attempt at speed. Nick wound up being dragged on the ground until Ryan could snatch him back upright. Lynn, unencumbered by gear, and now in the lead, was held back by the others who couldn't keep up. Ryan began to move his arms in a swimming motion, which is what you do if you think you'll be buried, even though the powder cloud hadn't caught up to them yet. Will, who was trying to release his sled, was fast approaching Ryan, with Brad on his heels.

The avalanche rumbled ominously behind them: monstrous boulders, slabs of ice, human-sized snowballs, and an asphyxiating spray of snow. The ground shook so violently it threw them off balance, causing them to stumble as though invisible demons had pushed them from behind. When Nick lurched to the ground, Ryan again grabbed him and pulled him back up. They could not, of course, out-run the slide, as Brad would have known all too well from his episode in the Andes. If an avalanche wants to bury you, it will. But they ran anyway. From my perspective, it looked like a brightly colored, slow motion stampede, and there was nothing I could do but watch in terror.

The avalanche had come from the side and crossed over the trail rather than speed downhill. A few rogue boulders tumbled past the team, and a few small ice rocks hit their packs, but it turned out to be a small avalanche, relatively speaking. Still, they kept running even after the slide had finished its assault, even after the wild spray settled, until they could run no more. When they finally stopped to catch their breath, each of them was panting and gasping, including Lynn.

Nick's face was flushed to crimson as he collapsed, and Will—for once—looked both humble and afraid as he looked back over his shoulder at the debris. Brad wrapped his arms above his head and hunched over, his shoulders shaking, until he thought to call out to his nephew to see if he was all right. Ryan was the only one who didn't throw himself to the ground in exhaustion. He remained standing, threw back his hood, and tore his hat from his head. It was the Peruvian cable knit I gave him years ago, with the tassels hanging from each side. He stood there, sweating and wheezing, and then he began to laugh like a maniac, completely out of control, until tears streamed down his face.

When he regained his composure, he found everyone staring at him. "I suppose you're not all just looking at me for my good looks?"

"No, we think you've gone berserk," Will replied.

"No, that's not exactly it," Lynn said. "At least not for me. There's something, a feeling I suddenly had while you were laughing like that. I'm not the religious type, and I can't speak for anyone else, but I can't help wondering if you've got some pull with the guy upstairs. We were a pathetic circus act. Look, none of us was even wearing a helmet or a beacon. We should be dead."

"I don't think I can take credit for our survival," Ryan said. "Fact is, I don't think God's been too happy with me lately."

After they had rested and ate a snack, Lynn said she was heading out to find her pack and sled.

"You lost your gear?" Brad asked.

"I didn't lose it. I dropped it on purpose. That's what you're supposed to do in an avalanche, Brad." Her snide tone mirrored his. "We could have run faster if everyone had dropped the gear, which makes our luck, or the Pastor's divine connections, even more remarkable."

"We also could have run faster if we'd left our sleds back at Camp 2, like most of the other climbers do these days," Brad said. "And which I told you we should do."

Not this again, I thought. Not another volley of insults and blame.

"Either way, we should have all dropped our gear," she said.

"And run the risk of starving to death?" Brad asked.

"Well, there's no sense in arguing," Ryan said. "Let's just find the damn stuff."

"Right," Lynn said. "Everyone get your helmets and beacons on, loosen your packs a bit, and have your axes at the ready. And stay alert."

Picking their way through the avalanche debris, they eventually found Lynn's belongings. As she was reorganizing and clipping into her gear, Lynn asked Ryan if he'd be willing to say a little prayer for the group.

"I'm not even religious," she said. "But somehow it feels like it would be good if you did. That is, if nobody objects."

Ryan cinched his hood tighter, slowly applied some ChapStick, and tugged on his gloves as the others gathered around. I was curious what he'd say. As far as I knew, he hadn't prayed in months.

"Truth be told, I'd rather go out for a stiff drink than stand here and hold a chapel service. But the way you're each standing there looking at me makes me feel like some sort of monkey in the middle. I suppose if I refused then Auntie would say it was a bad omen."

Right about then I wanted to get down on my own knees and pray. Lord knows it's not because I was devout; it's because Ryan *was* once devout, and you never want to see somebody lose something that defines them so, something that gives them such a sense of peace and purpose. Not even if it feels like they're closer to you when they do give it up.

They wrapped their arms around one another's shoulders like soccer players before a big game. Ryan stood in the center of the circle and lifted his arms and face toward the sky. But no words came. It was Will who finally broke the silence with a simple hallelujah, and then everyone said hallelujah, and Ryan pressed his hands together and lowered his head and whispered amen.

The snow was much less stable than two days earlier as they plugged along, and Windy Corner was unrecognizable. The wind was blowing at a steady fifty miles per hour, with even stronger intermittent gusts. The sleds tried to swing away in the merciless wind, dangling from waist harnesses perpendicular to the path and threatening to pull the climbers off balance. Carved bits of ice blasted at their faces and stuck in the men's thickening beards, and they all retaliated by thrusting their axes forcefully into the ice with each step in an attempt to stay tethered to the mountain. When they finally came around the corner, gusts pushed back at them so hard they each dropped to the ground and dug in, the air viciously biting at them. From my point of view, it looked like they were trudging in place in fresh white cement. They finally reached their cache, huddled together for a lunch break and a brief rest, and then trekked on to the edge of another crevasse field—the last real obstacle on the Camp 3 approach.

Brad checked knots and carabiners; Lynn scraped ice from goggles and handed out wipes. Ryan made Nick drink water and felt his forehead, and then he pulled Lynn aside. They could not step too far from the group, however, as they were all roped together.

"What do you want me to do, apologize?" Lynn asked. "Admit I was wrong about Nick? There's nothing we can do right now."

"There's always something we can do," he said. "We can turn back at any time."

"Not in this weather, we can't. We're lucky we didn't sail right out into space back at Windy." She bit her lip. "What? Why are you looking at me like that, Ryan? You think I don't care about him? You think I don't have a conscience?"

"Well, to be honest, you've made it perfectly clear to everyone that you won't let anyone or anything get in your way of summiting. So I can't help but wonder, at what expense, Lynn?" Ryan pulled a bag of elk jerky from his pack and offered it to her. She refused, instead pulling a bag of dried fruits from her pack. She poured some into her mouth without touching the bag to her lips. She didn't offer any to him in return.

"I think I need to appeal this to Brad."

Ryan motioned to their leader and told him he thought Nick's AMS symptoms were worsening: blue lips, dizziness, nausea.

"You should have stayed with him when I asked you to, Lynn," Brad said. "I hate to say this, but you're seriously letting me down as my assistant guide."

"As if."

"As if what?"

"As if you're even worthy to be—"

Ryan stepped between them to referee before she could

even complete her sentence. I knew where she was going. The Park Service maintains strict standards for authorized climbing guide services, and Brad wasn't measuring up. He wasn't measuring up to mine exactly, either. But it wasn't like she was infallible, having completely misdiagnosed Nick's health condition. For a moment a voice inside me asked whether she would be good for Frankie after all, but right then I couldn't listen to the voice. There were more pressing matters.

"That's enough," Ryan said. "Let's get to Camp 3 and be done with this till tomorrow. In the meantime, isn't there something you could give Nick right now just to help him get by?"

"Yes," she said. "There are some things you can give, but you have to be careful. They have side effects. We should wait till camp."

"I actually agree with you, Lynn," Brad said. "Water's the best thing for now." Brad pointed to Nick. "Let's pull out that water bottle of yours. Climbing 101. Get drinking."

"But not too much," Lynn added. "Too much water can work in reverse."

Nick sipped from his bottle and then asked what medicine they could give him.

"I've got Dex," Brad replied, slipping his pack off his back.

"Dexamethasone is the proper name," Lynn said. "But that's not for you Nick. Not yet. How about some Diamox?"

"Yes, I have that too." Brad pulled out a red first-aid pouch.

"You're not allergic to any medicine, are you?" Brad

asked, as he dug through the pouch.

"I'm allergic to penicillin, sulfa, and Ceclor," Nick said.

"Shit, no Diamox for you then." Brad zipped the first aid kit closed.

Brad and Lynn debated what to do for Nick, as the rest of the team waited in frustration.

"Never mind. Can we just go?" Nick said. "Sitting here arguing isn't going to help."

Brad finally agreed with Lynn. They would wait until they got to the next camp and consult with the Park ranger stationed there.

It started to snow again as they approached Genet Basin. The visibility was still good enough to spot some of the narrow crevasses, with the telltale wiggly cracks emanating from the edges like snakes trying to slither away, and the deep blue color that rose up from beneath the surface. There were countless other crevasses, though, hiding in wait for the hurried or unsuspecting climber. Brad wanted to take the northern route, circumventing most of the field, but Lynn didn't want to risk being in the path of more avalanches. Especially in light of Nick's condition, she wanted to take the most direct route through the field. They were taking exactly the opposite position from when they crossed the first crevasse field, like two boxers dancing around one another in the ring.

Visibility worsened as they progressed, and ice pellets dropped from overhead like little bombs. The team was roped together single file once again. Brad was at the lead, probing for crevasses with the basket at the tip of his ski pole, and

Ryan, behind him now, held his ice axe ready. Then came Nick, who seemed petrified with each weak step, and then Will, and finally Lynn.

I don't know why, but Ryan began to drift out from the path, and Nick called up to him. When Ryan didn't respond, Nick shouted a little louder, and Lynn did too. This time Ryan stopped and turned. He was a good four feet off the line that Brad had probed. As Nick and the rest of the team came nearer, Ryan began to walk backwards.

"What did you say?" he shouted back. But before Nick could answer, the crust gave way beneath Ryan's boot. I heard something crack, then saw the ground open. One second my husband was there; the next he was gone. The mountain had swallowed him.

21 CHAPTER TWENTY-ONE

13,800' Elevation

"Falling!"

Lynn dropped into self-arrest. She anchored herself to the ground with her axe as though it were part of her body. She arched her back, locked her legs, and dug the toes of her boots in. Brad mirrored her movements, like a mime, on the opposite side of the crevasse. Will and Nick dug in, too. The team members lay there with ice pellets pounding down on them, frozen in fear and wondering who could, or should, move. It was an apocalyptic scene where one wrong move could spell the end.

Ryan, meanwhile, was dangling on a rope, out of sight over a weakening ledge, and a horrifying thought came to me, like an evil creature worming its way into my mind—a terrible, disgusting, selfish thought. A horrible what-if that I couldn't shake. What if he wasn't alive? *What if Ryan were here with me?*

It was one of those times when you have a horrid thought, one you'd never admit to, one that makes you question who you really are.

"Shit!" Lynn said. Nick, closest to the crevasse, was not holding his position. He had thrust his ice axe into the ground wrong, straight down rather than at the appropriate angle, and was now clinging to it like a child clinging to his mother's leg. "Hang on, Nick! We need to anchor you."

"Will!" Brad shouted from across the crevasse. "Will, set an anchor!"

"Brad, I've got this," Lynn called, although the wind was sending her voice in the wrong direction. "Just hold your position over there. Trust me, okay?"

She then turned her attention to Ryan. "Pastor, can you hear me?"

He didn't answer.

"Shit," she said again, then shouted into the wind toward Will. "Okay, Will, it's on you. You've got to hold the pastor's load. And Nick's too, for now."

Will groaned, and Nick trembled, as Lynn self-belayed toward Will, keeping her ice axe ready. She unclipped to get around him, then clipped herself back onto the rope to proceed forward to Nick. By the time she reached him, his legs were shaking, and he was whimpering.

"Nick, get a hold of yourself. You're fine. I'm here." The wind battered her from behind. "Nothing's going to happen to you. I promise." She drove a picket into the snow between

Nick and the crevasse and set up a complicated system of rope loops and knots that would allow Nick to get out of self-arrest while keeping Ryan's weight anchored in place. She shouted to Brad to do whatever he could to anchor himself in place too.

"Hang on, Pastor!" Lynn shouted. The wind stole her voice once again, and there was no answer from Ryan. But that's the way crevasses work. Unless you can make your voice go directly up and out, the sound gets absorbed by the ice. You have to just wait and hope your team works fast, before you suffocate. And your team just has to hope and assume you're still alive until they can check on you, which isn't necessarily the first order of business. She glanced across the crevasse at Brad, who was slightly uphill from where she knelt.

His goggles had been knocked askew. "I suppose you're going to say this is my fault?" he called over to her.

"Shut the fuck up," Will called out from behind Lynn.

"Brad. Will," Lynn shouted. "Calm down, everyone. Both of you be quiet. Just do what I tell you to." For no experience as a mother, she sure had the authoritative tone of one just then, and whatever doubts I had were now gone. "I've got this." She switched her gaze back and forth from Brad uphill to Will downhill.

Brad nodded. Will did too.

"Okay, good. Now Will, I'm coming back to you to set a backup anchor to give you a little break. Then we'll set up the rescue pulley." After she set up the backup anchor for Will, he started to pull his ice axe out.

"Stop!" she shouted at him even though he was only two

feet away. "You need to move slowly. No jerky movements. Nice and smooth." This time he carefully released from self-arrest. As she was reminding him, and Nick too, to be ready to self-arrest again if necessary, Brad again called to her.

"What kind of main anchor are you using? Use a deadman!"

A gust of wind nearly knocked her over then, and she ignored Brad. She went about setting up a rescue pulley system, then she set up Will to belay her as she moved closer to the crevasse.

"What the hell are you doing now?" Brad called.

"Setting an axe under the rope," she shouted back, cupping one gloved hand at her mouth. "At the lip of the crevasse."

"I don't think you need to. The rope's anchored just fine."

"It's my call, Brad," she yelled, before taking a deep breath. Shouting into the wind is tiring at sea level, but it's exhausting at this altitude. "The lip axe will help the pastor climb out. That is, if he can. We haven't even assessed his situation. Which I'm about to do."

Keeping her center of gravity low, she inched toward the crevasse. She had to move slowly and carefully, as though disarming a bomb, because there was no guarantee that another hidden crevasse wouldn't claim her next. She belly-crawled to within a couple of feet of the edge.

"Lynn! I'm slipping!" Nick called out from behind. She turned, and he pulled his goggles off and aimed his big brown eyes right at her. Snow was already accumulating on his lashes. "I'm slipping, Lynn!"

"Jesus, Nick," Will shouted. "Shut up."

"Lynn!"

"Nick, for Christ's sake, you're not slipping." She was still lying on her stomach, twisting back to look at him. "You're not going anywhere. But self-arrest if you need to. Slam that damn axe in as hard as you can. At the angle we showed you. Remember? And put those goggles back on."

Lynn moved forward just a few more inches and set the lip axe. She peered into the crevasse.

"Pastor?" Lynn shouted.

Ryan looked up.

"Hey, buddy," she said. Her goggles covered most of her face, and the rest of her face was now consumed by a big smile. "How're you doing down there?"

He gave her a thumbs-up.

She lifted herself up and nodded to Brad, still alone on the other side of the crevasse. "He's okay," she called. "He's only about ten, maybe twelve, feet down. You okay over there?"

Brad was still in self-arrest, facing the crevasse, but he had driven a picket into the ground beside him, and wrapped his rope around it, for extra support. "Just hurry."

She saluted.

Because Ryan's pack and sled were heavy, it would be difficult for them to haul him out with the pack still on his back. Lynn had obviously figured that out already, and as she had moved closer to the crevasse and set the pulleys in place, she'd adjusted the rope system accordingly. Now she lowered a rope to Ryan, explained how the sled would come out first, and told him how to climb out of his pack and attach it to the second rope. It wouldn't be an easy thing to do. Already dangling on one rope, Ryan had to find a way to do this while not creating too much pull on the first rope, the one to which his harness was attached.

Lynn talked him through the process and then gave the command for Will and Nick to haul the sled out, followed by the pack.

You'd think they were fighting a dragon, the way they had to work to get the sled and pack out, and I wondered, if it was that hard for the gear, how it would work for a nearly 200-pound man. They both pulled the rope hand over hand through the pulley system, until the pack finally appeared at the edge. Lynn helped it over onto solid ground, but as she did the rope chipped away at the icy edge of the crevasse. Ryan's rope grew perilously taut, but the lip axe still held.

"Well done," she called back to Will and Nick. She secured the pack, swung the rescue rope back down to Ryan, then shouted back to them again. "When I give the signal, you both need to pull. Got it?"

Lynn had her faults, for sure, but I couldn't imagine a more competent person being in charge of Ryan's rescue. She was a cold woman, her heart encased in ice half the time. But an attitude like hers sure came in handy. By staying calm, she kept everyone else—including me—calm. She gave orders with confidence, knowing exactly what had to be done. She didn't yell at anyone, didn't assign blame, didn't ridicule anyone for being afraid. She just got down to business as though she did this every day of the week, nine to five.

What bothered me, aside from the obvious peril Ryan was

still in, of course, was the way Will was looking at Lynn at that moment. It wasn't the least bit lustful anymore; quite the opposite, it was more a look of anger. Maybe even rage, as though something had snapped for him.

"Ready, Pastor?" she called. She gave Will and Nick another thumbs-up and swung the rope like a cowboy swinging a lasso. The end of the rope with the carabiner disappeared below the surface.

"When I say pull, pull like you mean it," she called back to Will and Nick. "Just like you did with the pack. Like your own life depends on it. Got it?"

"Wait!" Brad shouted.

Lynn stopped and looked over at him, clearly annoyed by the interruption.

"I'm still roped to Ryan! When you pull him out, you're going to pull me down into the crevasse!"

I could not tell from the look on her face whether she was dumbfounded or exasperated. She and Brad called back and forth to one another about what to do. Chances were good there was enough slack in the rope that Brad wouldn't be pulled down, but, even so, he'd have to unclip at some point during the process. He had already driven a picket and an ice axe into the ground, so he wouldn't slide anywhere. But there was still a danger that he was sitting atop another hidden crevasse. Once he unclipped, he wouldn't be roped to anything, or anyone. She and Brad stared at one another until he ended the staring contest, gave her the universal A-OK signal, and a nod. He was ready.

"Pull! God damn it, pull!" she shouted, so fiercely I

thought she was going to burst a blood vessel in her head. Nick and Will pulled, drawing the rope in, hand over hand. The wind was so strong by then it threatened to knock them over, and Lynn too. But they fought the dragon again. It took ten minutes of continuous grunting, coiling, bracing, and leaning, as snow blew into their mouths and swept up their nostrils and sweat dripped from their brows. But finally Ryan's hood appeared at the top of the crevasse, then his face, and finally his shoulders. He grabbed hold of the lip axe, hoisted a knee, and climbed out as the edge broke away beneath him.

"Keep pulling," Lynn said, and they kept pulling, and Ryan stumbled to the ground, and the ropes dragged him further away from the yawning gap until he was level with Lynn.

He rolled onto his back, and wheezed, and then began to laugh maniacally again. His lip and forehead were bleeding, his goggles cracked. He'd lost a glove. But he lay there laughing, with Lynn hovering over him, until he began to weep. He reached up and pulled her on top of him, and hugged her so tight I thought he might break one of her ribs. I felt the old familiar tingle of tears at the tip of my nose, as though I, too, were about to cry in relief. When he finally released her, he left a stain of blood on the shoulder of her jacket.

"I am so sorry," she said, still hovering over him. A lone tear slipped down her cheek.

"Sorry? That you rescued me?"

"No, I don't know. Sorry it took so long. Sorry it happened in the first place. I don't know. Just sorry." She lay down beside him, and they both panted in unison as though they'd just had sex.

"Hey! Hello? What about me?" Brad called from the other side of the crevasse.

Lynn sat up and called back. "Hold on! We're coming!"

The team quickly collected the rescue pulleys and other gear and roped up again. Lynn took the lead probing for a stable snow bridge to get to Brad. Soon she was clipping a rope to him.

"Well done," he said to her. The two guides stared at each other through goggles. A truce. They granted each other a nod, then a lingering smile, interrupted when Ryan asked if they could move on.

"Can we please get going? I'm so hungry I could eat my own boot!"

Once at Camp 3, Lynn and Ryan worked together on making dinner for the team. He cooked up the last of the ground chicken while she prepared vegetarian burritos. I noticed Will kept watching them, and later in the evening, he watched as she went into Ryan's tent with her journal and zipped the tent shut, from the inside.

If Will felt a tinge of jealousy, he wasn't alone.

The blossoming friendship between Ryan and Lynn didn't surprise me. Ryan had been through an ordeal and Lynn had saved him, and it's human nature for a survivor to want to bond with his rescuer. But the connection forming between them seemed awfully strong so soon, and I admit it made me uncomfortable. I wasn't sure I wanted to find out what might happen between them, but then again, I couldn't turn away. I had to find out.

They started talking about safe subjects, like politics; she was a staunch Democrat, he was a Republican—even though he supported gun control. They talked education: he had a master's degree and she never finished college. They talked about their geographical backgrounds: Ryan had grown up in the West but spent much of his adult life in Chicago. Lynn grew up in Chicago, and then moved to Portland. Eventually the conversation gravitated toward friends and family. Ryan mentioned Jack and Cece, who were also native Chicagoans; he told her about Jack's candy business and how Cece was once a dress designer, and then for some reason he told her about their struggles with infertility, then Raina, then Frankie. But he didn't mention our infertility, or me, and she didn't talk of her daughter. Not yet. Things like that don't come up easily.

After a couple of hours, Ryan's eyes grew heavy. "I'm sorry, but I'm exhausted," he told her. "I think I'll need to take a rain check on the rest of this conversation."

"I understand. It's been an incredible day. I'm sorry I'm so wired and wide-awake. It's just..."

"Just what?"

"Well, sometime I'd like to ask you more about your faith, and your life as a pastor. I confess I'm intrigued. You're not what I expected."

There were those crinkles around his eyes. He was never what I expected either. "Anything in particular?"

She shook her head no. Nothing in particular. He smiled

again.

It was nice to see Ryan smiling like that. Most people come away from near-death experiences changed, often more solemn or somber as they realize how precious life is. But he already knew about that, and he came out of the crevasse as if he'd left his worries and sorrows down in that chasm. It was what I'd been wanting for him—a fresh taste of happiness—so long as it didn't mean he stopped missing, or loving, me.

Lynn reached for her jacket and journal.

"You're welcome to stay here," he said, unexpectedly. "Nick's staying in Brad's tent tonight because of his condition. So you can stay here as long as you let me sleep." He started to unzip his sleeping bag. "In fact, I think I'd like it if you stayed here until I fall asleep." The zipper stuck, and as he tried to work it, it kept swallowing more of the nylon fabric.

She laughed. "I'm not going to save you anymore. I think, instead, I'll just sit here and watch you work things out with that zipper as I write in my journal for a while, if that's all right with you. I'll go back to my own bag, once you're asleep. Back to my own tent."

He thanked her and said to make herself comfortable. After wrestling for a few more minutes with the zipper that, by now, had gnawed several inches of nylon, he wedged himself down into the sleeping bag and let out a long sigh.

She lay on her stomach beside him, notebook propped on her mittens. She kicked her lower legs into the air and crossed them at the ankle, like a teenager, and I felt a rush of heat to my face along with a tensing between my imaginary shoulders and a clenching of my jaw. I was jealous. Who would have thought you could still be jealous after you're dead?

"One more thing," she said.

"Hmm?"

"I'm still not so sure about all this God stuff, but I have the feeling I've been missing something. I was wondering if, if it's all right with you, Ryan, if—when we're all done here—if you'd teach me something. About God. About how to find faith. Maybe even how to pray."

She might as well have asked him to teach her how to have an orgasm. Prayer is a very personal thing, and even after all those years with Ryan, I hadn't been able to believe in prayer. I hadn't been able to feel God inside me. Sure, I wanted the two to have some sort of friendship, but not an intimate one. And certainly not one where Lynn was able to achieve something with Ryan that I never had. I wanted to hear Ryan say no.

It was a long time before he replied, and I couldn't help but wonder if he could sense my concerns. And then he said yes, it was a deal, and for the first time ever I felt as though he were cheating on me.

He rolled away from Lynn, and she opened her journal.

Dear Sunny~

Already, he was snoring.

What a day! First an avalanche. And then—you recall that I wrote about Ryan, the pastor? The man who promised to bring you my letters if anything should happen to me? Well, today he fell into a crevasse! I orchestrated his rescue, and as Ryan crawled over the lip of that crevasse, I was overcome with something. I don't know what it was. I suppose it could have been some sort of adrenaline release.

But something inside me tells me it was love.

I felt a flush, an accelerated pulse, and I was ready to jump at her, all teeth and claws.

Not romantic or sensual love. Basic human love.

And then a sigh of relief. I was being foolish. After all, she was living and I was not. And I was the one who set them up together on this climb. Not to mention the fact that, if she could love Ryan, then that meant there *was* a heart buried beneath all that down and polypropylene.

Only one other time in my life have I experienced the same intensity of emotion; that was the day you were born. And today it felt the same way. I cried after I rescued him. There was something about me giving him life, as I gave it to you, while knowing I couldn't stick around in his life, as I couldn't in yours. It was like another gift that, for some reason, I wasn't meant to keep.

I know that, in his grief, he has no romantic designs on me, and I should leave well enough alone because love is dangerous. The more you love, the more you stand to lose.

An hour later, someone was humming outside. Lynn had fallen asleep, and now she put on her boots and jacket and went outside. It was still light out, and she found Ryan packing down the snow wall.

"Morning," Ryan said.

"Morning?" She checked her watch. Technically, it was morning. It was after midnight.

"I hope I didn't wake you," Ryan said. "I couldn't sleep."

"No problem. Was that you humming?"

He nodded.

She tilted her head, smiled in uncertainty. "Okay. That's good, I guess. But shouldn't you be roped up to something out here, with all this wind?"

"Probably, but I'm done out here. I'll head inside and try to sleep again."

She said she was going back to her own tent for the rest of the night, and they said goodnight to each other. As she crawled into her sleeping bag, Will opened an eye.

She slept for a short while before again being awakened by sounds outside: crunching snow, a hissing stove, and voices. She poked her head out of the tent. The wind had calmed, and gentle snow was falling. Brad was outside.

"What's going on? What time is it?" she asked.

"Time to move on," Brad said. "Care to join us?"

"Are you serious? We're supposed to stay here for at least a couple of days. We're not ready to go on. The next climb is a 3,000 vertical rise and nearly two miles. And besides, what about breakfast?"

"You missed it," Nick said, now standing next to Brad. His skin was nearly gray in the dim light, and the circles beneath his eyes were purple. He reached into a pocket and pulled out a smashed energy bar. "Here."

"Brad? What's really going on?"

22 Chapter Twenty-Two

14,200' Elevation

Lynn pulled on her fleece layer and climbed out of the tent. She yawned as Brad tapped at his watch and told her he had checked in with Marisa.

"The caribou are moving. And the eagles are flying low. Means bad weather soon."

"Ancient Athabaskan meteorology?"

"More like ancient Auntie's superstitions from who knows where. But the national weather service has confirmed more problems are coming, including thunderstorms."

"I bet Auntie has something to say about that too. The thunderstorms, I mean."

"You don't even want to know. The point is we need to advance while we can."

Nick looked terrible, but said his headache was better.

Brad reminded them the Dex was ready if they needed it. He also said they were bringing all their gear, not just a supply cache, just in case they decided to camp higher up. This time Lynn didn't argue.

She got dressed quickly, attached her shovel and other gear to her pack, and put her headlamp on over her balaclava. It wasn't dark, but sometimes a light helps in the early morning shadows. She stashed her sled with the others. From here on, everything would have to be carried.

This time she was roped to Ryan, while the other three were on a separate rope. Before they set out, she asked Brad if he had checked with the ranger stationed at their camp about the forecast.

"Never saw him," he said. "I'm not sure where he, or his volunteer assistants, are. Probably rescuing someone somewhere."

"Hopefully not Mark."

"You hope they don't rescue him?"

"No, I mean I hope he doesn't need to be rescued."

"I didn't know you cared about him."

"I don't. But I do care about what's happening higher up on the mountain. Did you learn anything else from Marisa?"

"Two teams started to retreat last night," Brad said. "There are two other teams, that they know of, somewhere on the mountain waiting to make a decision."

"Sounds like we could be all alone up at High Camp," Ryan said. "If the others retreat, too."

"Hopefully not completely," she said. "Hopefully there will at least be a ranger there. That's what we're paying our taxes for."

"Oh, by the way," Brad said. "Marisa did say your friend Greg called again. Maybe you should call him on the sat phone. But not now. We need to get moving."

I was surprised Lynn didn't ask any more about it.

"So this is it," Ryan said during one of the team's now frequent breaks. The snow was knee deep, and hiking in crampons is hard work. Each step was even harder than the day before because of the way air thins your blood at higher elevations. They had to rest often.

"Yes, this is it. With any luck we'll be at the summit in a few days," Lynn said.

"Maybe we'll set a record."

She laughed. "Hardly. I think the fastest ascent, so far, was around fourteen hours."

"Whoever did that must have been crazy."

"Actually, I knew him. He's a pretty great guy. The sad thing is his wife died in a climbing accident a few years later. She was awesome. It was a real tragedy. But he kept on climbing."

Ryan looked out at the horizon. "I'm not sure how you do that, keep on going after you lose your wife."

"*You're* here, aren't you?" She touched the sleeve of his jacket. He shrugged, but she was right. In fact, he seemed to have snapped out of his depression the minute he arrived in Talkeetna.

"You just keep your eyes on the prize." She reached her mitten up to her neck, and he watched as she did.

"Your necklace?"

She nodded. "How did you know?"

"I just notice things," Ryan said. "So tell me about it."

She shook her head. "Never mind, it would sound stupid to you."

"Try me." Brad, Will, and Nick were just catching up and would need to rest as well. "We've got time."

She took a deep breath as though ready to dive into a deep swimming pool. But I wasn't sure I was ready for her to take the plunge. I needed her to share her history with Ryan so they would eventually discover the truth about Frankie. But once they did everything would change. Forever.

"Okay, here goes," Lynn said. "Long ago, thirty years ago, I gave up my daughter. She was a newborn, an infant. She wasn't planned. Her father was a climber, and he was teaching me to climb. We were going to travel the world. Climb the Seven Summits. She didn't fit into our plans. So I gave her up for adoption."

"Just like that?"

She lowered her head and shook it, a little at first and then more emphatically. "No, not just like that. It was the hardest thing I've ever done. I didn't want to. But I was young. So terribly young, not quite twenty. Too young to know myself. So against my intuition, I gave her up."

"And the father?"

"He left me after the baby. Went back home. To Iran."

I imagined Ryan raising his eyebrows at that news but couldn't tell with his goggles on. "And the agate?"

"That's the really stupid part. As if giving up a child you

love isn't stupid enough. Before she was born, her father gave me a necklace with seven agates, representing each of the Seven Summits we were going to climb. Each time I summit one of those peaks, I leave one of the rocks there for her. This is the last one."

"I see," he said.

"What do you mean by that?"

"I see why this summit is so important to you. You believe that to fail would...dishonor her, diminish your love for her."

"Yes. I guess so. I don't know. It's hard to explain, hard to find the words to describe how it feels."

I was starting to see Lynn differently now. I knew what she meant, how love is so overwhelming that there's no way to express how you feel sometimes. And the same for grief, and regret, too. I knew this better now than I ever did when I was alive. These feelings rumble up in your heart and they need to come out, somehow, like magma needing to explode from a volcano.

At the next break, Ryan told her he didn't think there was anything stupid about her agates. "It's a beautiful gesture," he said.

And at the next stop, he asked her if she'd like to hear about my ponytail.

I was mad enough when Ryan told Tom about it, but now I was furious that Ryan opened up to her this way. It was *my* dream, *my* wish. It was between us. Our secret, something that had nothing to do with Frankie. Now he was sharing it with her as though they were best friends. I knew exactly how this sort of thing worked. Once you start revealing your secrets, or the secrets of your dead wife, to another woman, the attraction escalates. You're a wounded puppy, and the other woman has to nurse you back to health. I'd seen this happen time and again to widowers in our church.

Sure enough, after he told her, she reached out and touched his sleeve with her mitten. "That's beautiful. You must have loved her very much."

Loved! Past tense!

But Ryan came to my rescue. "I still do," he said.

"So we have that in common," she said. "I mean, these keepsakes we carry, like soldiers carrying photos of their loved ones."

"I guess we're all soldiers," he said.

When they reached the Headwall, the most technical part of the climb, they all stopped and looked up in awe.

"The slope is roughly 50 percent vertical but feels even steeper than that," Lynn said. "This is where a lot of traffic jams occur."

"Not much traffic today," Brad said. "It's a good thing too, because this is also where you have to watch out for bergschrund icefalls and slab avalanches."

"More crevasses, too," Lynn said.

Ryan groaned when she said that. "Are those the infamous fixed ropes?" He pointed.

Brad nodded. "One is for teams ascending and the other is for those coming down. But they're not maintained by the Park rangers. And they make it look like it's an easy climb so long as you're attached to them, but they're deceiving. You clip into them with mechanical devices, but you need to detach and re-attach at each anchor, which is sometimes a tricky proposition. A lot of climbers freak out when they have to do that."

"Another technique we should have practiced," Lynn said.

"The weather over Mt. Foraker's looking a bit ominous," Brad said, avoiding Lynn's glare. "We'd better get moving."

His team took the lead. Lynn and Ryan followed, and another team of climbers followed them.

The snow was thick. As Brad located the first anchor, he gestured back to Nick and Will to be sure they saw it too. Nick's legs were shaking so badly when it came time to unclip that it was a wonder he could stand up at all.

"Be careful," Brad said. "One wrong move could be very, very bad, not just for you but for anyone behind you."

Nick froze.

"Oh, don't mind Brad," Lynn said to Nick from behind. "You'll be fine. Just relax and take your time."

She and Ryan both cheered him on. Eventually Will joined the cheering squad too, as well as the other climbers behind them. Nick successfully maneuvered around each anchor, but the Headwall was grueling and taking its toll, not only because of the deep snow, the slow pace, and the emotional tension, but also because there was less and less oxygen the higher they climbed. And with the sleds now stored back at Camp 3, they were hauling all their gear on their backs. Even Lynn was practically staggering when she finally surfaced at the top of the wall.

They should have cached their supply gear there and

retreated back to Camp 3 to rest. But Brad had already made it clear he didn't plan to climb the Headwall twice. They needed to keep going for the summit, he said. I knew from personal experience that this was exactly the type of mistake some teams make. They rush past the acclimatization and rest periods, especially if they think weather is a factor, and then someone gets too sick or too tired to think straight, and accidents happen. One team, a few years back, lost a member who'd become confused and forgotten to clip into the rope; she slipped off a ridge. Another climber I'd met a long time ago had apparently gone up to Denali after recovering from a bout of flu. I heard through the grapevine that he couldn't keep up with the pace. He said he'd follow his team's tracks and catch up, but he never showed up, and his body was found buried in a poorly constructed snow cave by another team the next day. In both cases, the teams hadn't cached and retreated, as most do. In the second case, it was one of many grave errors the guide service had made, and that was why there was an opening at Denali for a new guide service—and Brad took that slot.

Now Brad was falling prey to the temptation to rush up the mountain, and he wasn't making sense in his other choices either. Besides the new baby, his strained relationship with Marisa, and his fledgling guide business, I was becoming convinced there might still be psychological remnants from his accident in the Andes. Even with Lynn on the team, I feared I'd made a mistake choosing Brad's guide service for Ryan. Being pushed up a deadly mountain by a stressed out climbing guide seemed the equivalent of being operated on by a nervous surgeon.

For once, though, Lynn wasn't playing the devil's advocate with Brad. Now that she was this close, she was likely being drawn in by the mountain's emotional pull, too. She could get that necklace up there, and the faster she did, the quicker she could be free of all that guilt she'd lugged around for thirty years. Brad had his agenda, and she had hers.

I guess everyone on the mountain had an agenda, including me.

The compromise they reached was to set up an intermediate camp just above 16,000 feet, rather than going all the way to High Camp at 17,200. Most climbers don't stop at this point—Ridge Camp—because it's infamous for furious winds and steep, slick slopes. Also, there's no Park ranger there. It's another foreboding, post-apocalyptic site, a place you'd think no one had seen for eons.

The team immediately set up a fixed line and remained clipped into it as they created a campsite from scratch. They built extra-thick snow walls and set up wands around safety zones. Will, Ryan, and Brad worked like slaves digging the walls, and Lynn and Nick were in charge of setting up tents. She tied the tents down with anchored rope, and as soon as the first one was ready, she told Nick to get inside and lie down. When the rest of the tents were secure, she set her pack in Ryan's and began to melt snow on the camp stoves so the men could feast on soup and instant coffee, hot cocoa, or tea. She then crawled into Ryan's tent and fell asleep.

Ryan crawled in later, discovered her there, and gently shook her shoulder.

"I was just so tired," she said. "I couldn't stay awake any longer. And I'm really uncomfortable now with Will, the way he was watching me at the last camp. And the last few days. Well, the whole trip, actually."

Ryan nodded and patted her on the arm. "You're more than welcome to stay with me. I'll just make sure it's okay that Nick stays with Brad."

Brad was fine with the new arrangement, as he wanted to keep a closer eye on his nephew anyway. I watched Lynn and Ryan cozy up to one another in the tent, with more than a growing sense of unease as I recalled doing the same thing with him. I remembered how good it felt to crawl into my sleeping bag and scoot over toward his. How we'd lie side by side waiting for our breath to calm and join, like two rivers flowing together. We would listen to the wind and dream about the thrill of the climb and the magnificence of the scenery. It was way better than sex.

When Ryan asked about her journal, Lynn said she was too tired to write in it, and then she said she felt awfully tense around her neck and shoulders. It was inevitable. He placed his strong hands on her skin, and I imagined how his beard prickled against her as she inched back toward him. I saw his frosty breath mingle with hers, and just when I thought I couldn't stand to watch anymore, he stopped. He pulled away, positioned himself in his sleeping bag, and said good night.

Lynn woke up at dusk. She put on several layers and began to search the tent for something, scratching and digging the way a dog looks for its bone in the backyard. At last she reached into her jacket pocket and pulled out her fleece gloves, shaking her head. When she went outside, the campsite smelled of bacon, but the only person out there was Will, coming back from the latrine. She clipped onto the camp's perimeter rope, and he came toward her with his arms opened wide.

"Hey, baby."

"God, it's cold out here," she said. She walked directly into his embrace, which given the temperature wasn't all that absurd. There were times on expeditions I would have walked right into Satan's arms, I think, just for a little warmth. Will tightened his hold around her, and she looked fragile in his shelter.

"Hungry? You missed dinner."

She nodded.

"I've got some snacks in my tent. I'll boil up some tea if you'd like. Come on." He let go of her and led her by the elbow back to his tent.

She should have known not to go. But she followed him to his tent anyway, seduced no doubt by the idea of warm tea and comfort. It's the type of thing so many women do: ignore their intuition, give undue benefit of the doubt to the guy, and head blindly down the wrong path, all in the name of love or security or warmth. Or even food. Exhausted climbers aren't much different. So when she bent down to crawl into Will's tent and didn't flinch when he set his hands on her hips, as he'd done once before, I wasn't surprised.

He handed her a Ziploc bag of small, frozen chocolates—the ultimate temptation, of course—and, knowing her well by now, a small bottle of hand sanitizer. She cleaned her hands and nibbled on a chocolate as he set a pot of snow to boil in the tent's vestibule. When he pulled back into the tent, he asked what was going on with the pastor.

"Ryan? Nothing." She put her gloves back on.

He sat beside her and unzipped her jacket, slowly. "Hell, Lynn." He touched a single finger to her throat. "Don't give me that. Something's going on. You know what I'm saying."

"No, I don't." She pushed his hand away. "What *do* you mean?"

"You and the grieving widower getting it on. That's what I mean." I was incensed that he thought Ryan would do that especially so soon after...well, after I died.

"You're imagining things," she said. "We're just friends."

He shook some tea leaves from a pouch into two camp mugs. Then he pulled her glove from one hand slowly, finger by finger, and their eyes met. She was cold, tired, hungry. She was a lonely woman, too.

I didn't particularly like Will, but I thought maybe his attraction for her would keep her at arm's length from Ryan. I sure wasn't ready to let Ryan go.

He asked if she and Ryan were *good* friends.

"Not really."

"Mm-hmm."

"Really."

He pulled her other glove off slowly. "Mm-hmm."

"What are you doing?"

"Just making you comfortable."

As he pulled the last glove finger from her hand, he kissed

her fingertip. "Wait right here, baby."

He left the tent, and she rubbed her arms and looked around as though she'd never been in his tent before, as though she was looking for something. He came back in with steaming mugs that smelled of apricot and ginger. Lynn blew on her fingers, then took a mug from him and began to drink the tea.

"Do you have anything else to eat?" she asked.

He handed her a tin of crackers. She ate one, and then two more, and then finished her tea. He fed another cracker to her, and when she bit into it and crumbs fell from her mouth, he caught them in his palm and licked them off his skin.

"Will."

He reached into the bag of chocolates and fed one of them to her, licking his fingers again after they'd been touched by her lips.

"Will, what are you doing?

He cupped his hand behind her neck and pulled her closer. "I'm doing exactly what you want me to do, baby. I'm keeping you warm."

She pushed him away. "No, that's not what I want you to do. I want you to wash your hands."

He laughed. He poured more water into her mug. "Have some more."

When he leaned closer, she suggested they change the subject. "How's your daughter?"

"Let's not," he said. He brushed her hair away from her eyes. She drank the second cup of tea.

Her eyelids became heavy.

"God, I'm tired," she said. "I can barely focus my eyes."

He piled some of his clothes into the corner of the tent; their musky scent wafted all the way up to me. "Here, lean back. You've had a couple of rough days. You need rest." He poured water into her mug one more time and placed the mug between her hands, gently folding her fingers around it and letting his own rest over hers. "You warm enough now?"

She drank, closed her eyes, and smiled. He pulled her back into sitting position; she was limp and it seemed like her spine had turned to mush. He slipped her jacket off, and then her fleece shirt. Her eyes were still closed, a stupid grin now spread across her face. She tugged on her silk undershirt's neckline. "I feel like I'm on fire."

"Mm-hmm." He kissed her cheek.

"Is the tent spinning?"

"Mm-mmm." He licked her neck.

"I feel guilty, Will. I've never been this way before." She giggled. He kissed the tip of her nose, then brushed his mouth against hers.

"You're lonely," he said. He trailed his tongue from her hairline, around her ear and down to her jaw, then to her shoulder and then to her breast. He repeated that move on the other side of her face and body, dampening her undershirt when he licked her nipples. She tried to sit up to pull the undershirt over her head; he helped her and then she flopped back in just her bra as the wind whirred outside. Goose bumps rose on her skin. Her nipples poked at the bra's cups.

"Shhh." He stroked her hair.

"I've got to go," she said, her words slurred, but she didn't try to sit up or move. Didn't even try.

"No you don't." He lifted first her left arm, and then her right, over her head and she lay there, letting him do it. "I won't let you leave me, baby."

He may not have wanted her to leave, but I had to. I couldn't bear to stay and watch anymore. Besides, I needed to check on Frankie.

23 Chapter Twenty-Three

Frankie was still confined to Retreat, sitting in the dirt, as Erma Lou or one of her helpers sat planted on the cabin porch to watch. Although Erma Lou had told Frankie that most kids only spend three days there before graduating to the Lodge, which was two miles away, Frankie had violated the rules by singing aloud and by sneaking into the cabin without permission. The cost of those infractions: three more days in Retreat.

On Friday night, after she'd been brought inside from her circle of dirt to sleep on her hard cot, and after the night counselor finally fell asleep on the cabin sofa, Frankie got up and crept out into the main room, barefoot. She reached under the counselor's pillow for the key ring, freezing when the counselor stopped breathing mid-snore. When the exhalation finally came, Frankie snatched the keys and unlocked the front door.

She ran down the dirt road, barely letting her feet touch the ground, all the way to the iron gate. A dog barked in the distance as she climbed over. From there, she ran past pastures to the highway and headed west, in the opposite direction from the terrifying hogback.

Sandstone cliffs, illuminated by the slivered moon and a spattering of stars, flanked the white lines on the edge of the road. After a short while, an old pick-up truck's engine rumbled toward her, and Frankie darted into the desert to crouch behind a rock. It was Erma Lou's truck, with a dog in the open bed, barking. Once the truck passed, Frankie ran up the road again, hiding when the truck came back toward her. Erma Lou drove up and down the road for the next several hours, with a spotlight roaming from one side of the road to the other, and each time she approached, Frankie hid behind a rock or scraggly bush. By dawn, Frankie had made it about four miles. Once again Erma Lou's truck was coming her way, and as she waited for it to pass, something rattled. There, in the middle of the highway, was a coiled rattlesnake.

Erma Lou slammed on the brakes, stopping five feet from the snake and not more than ten from Frankie, who was hidden behind a stand of sagebrush. The woman swung the driver's door open, and her dog jumped out of the truck's bed, tail wagging.

"Sit! Stay!"

The dog did as it was told, panting, looking back and forth from the snake to Frankie's hiding place. In one smooth motion, Erma Lou grabbed a rifle from the truck's gun rack, aimed, and shot the reptile dead. As the woman walked over to the carcass in her black work boots, Frankie drew in her breath and held her hands over her mouth. The dog barked. Erma Lou picked up the carcass with the rifle and flung it into the back of the truck, then pointed to the cab's interior. The dog hesitated, then jumped in. I wasn't sure if I should be grateful the snake had distracted Erma Lou from the dog's attentions or if it would have been better for Frankie to be found.

That was the last trip Erma Lou made along the road, and Frankie made her way into the town of Cottage just as the sun brightened the red rock and black sky gave way to blue. Rather than going into the all-night café, where Erma Lou would surely have given everyone a heads-up about the runaway, Frankie headed straight for the dusty parking lot. There she found an old trucker dressed in a flannel shirt and overalls, climbing into his cab.

"Which way you heading?" she asked.

He looked her over and adjusted the bill of his Caterpillar cap. "North and west. To Seattle."

"Good enough. I need a ride."

She slept most of the day in the truck's cab, leaning against the passenger window with a pillow and blanket on loan from the driver. Late that afternoon, they pulled into a truck stop in Twin Falls. The driver handed her a twenty-dollar bill and told her to buy herself a shower, some food, and something for her poor, dirty feet. She looked at the money and asked what she had to give him in return.

The old man laughed. "Darlin', at my age you don't need

to gimme nothing. I just hate to see a girl lookin' like that. What would your mama think?"

She eyed him, then took the money. "Thanks."

After using a coin-operated shower, she bought another pair of flip-flops, stole a pack of gum, and wolfed down a hamburger. Then she told the trucker she was actually trying to get to Bend and asked if it was on his way to Seattle. He shook his head.

"Nope, sorry to say it isn't. But see that guy over there?" He pointed to another trucker. "That's Ray. He goes back and forth between Billings and Burns all week long. Depending on whether he's coming or going, he might be able to take you as far as Burns, God willing."

"Insha'Allah," Frankie mumbled.

"What's that you say?" He stuck his finger in his ear.

"Never mind. Thank you for the ride." She held out the change from his twenty, but he waved it off and told her it was his pleasure to help such a pretty girl. His gaze lingered on her face, and I attributed his hesitation to her complexion, a skin tone that would surely stand out in the middle of the Great Basin.

Frankie slept in Ray's cab at the truck stop that night and most of the way to Burns the following day. He had a kind face; I wasn't worried for her. When they drove into Burns, he asked where she'd like to go and she told him she didn't know anything about the town.

"Anywhere is fine, I guess."

So he delivered her to the city park and wished her good luck. She climbed out of the truck and watched it drive off.

A group of small, squealing children played near a swing set at the other end of the park. A jogger ran on a path. A couple of women walked their dogs, and two old men sat opposite one another at a cement table, playing dominos.

The sun was shining, but it was probably no more than 45 °F, and Frankie was still dressed only in her Retreat clothes. She sat on a park bench with green, peeling paint and wrapped her arms around her legs, shivering.

After a couple of hours, a woman with a single, gray braid strolled toward Frankie's bench. She had a stocky build and was dressed in a black fringed jacket, a jean skirt, and knee-high black boots. She wore a purple knit beret and matching gloves. Frankie looked the other way when she saw the woman coming.

"Mind if I sit here?" the woman asked.

Frankie shrugged and wrapped her arms more tightly around herself. By now her teeth were chattering. She buried her face into her arms.

After a few minutes, the woman introduced herself as Mrs. Farley. Her voice was gentle, her face kind—she was the opposite of Erma Lou—and she intrigued me with her appearance.

"Are you new in town? I'm a retired school teacher and I don't recognize you."

Frankie shook her head without lifting it.

"You look cold," Mrs. Farley said. "I'd bet you're hungry, too. Come on, let me buy you something to eat."

"No thanks. You don't have to," Frankie said.

"I know I don't have to. I want to."

Frankie looked at the woman sideways, then got up and followed her into town. The woman led her directly to an old-fashioned diner with chrome tables and vinyl booths straight out of the 1950s. When the door opened, a medley of sugar and grease wafted out into the street. I immediately started thinking about banana cream pie.

Frankie ordered a BLT with fries, and Mrs. Farley ordered a slice of apple pie a la mode, which would have been fine with me too. She took two bites and offered the rest to Frankie, who devoured the pie once the sandwich and fries were gone. I wished I could tell her to slow down and savor it more as I imagined the taste and texture: the buttery, flaky crust; the brown sugar blended into soft baked apples; the cold vanilla ice cream melting on my tongue.

Neither spoke until all the food had disappeared, and then Mrs. Farley, who must have been dying to barrage Frankie with a million questions, asked only a single one.

"What are you looking for, darlin'?"

She was so kind, and I was in such a daze from the pie, that I imagined it was I who was sitting across from her and thought about how I would answer. What was I looking for? The ability to rest in peace? A way to let go of my life? Assurance that those I loved would be safe and happy? An answer to where I was and what my eternal future might bring? Something to believe in? But Frankie was more pragmatic.

"A ride to Bend."

The woman wiped her mouth with a paper napkin. "Why

not?"

"Why not what?"

"Just talking to myself, honey. Why not go for a little drive? I haven't seen my granddaughter for a while, and I don't have anything else to do. She lives just outside Bend, you know. As long as you don't mind the girls riding with us."

For the first time in a long time I saw Frankie's smile.

Mrs. Farley, now acting as though she'd known Frankie her entire life, led her down the street to a pickup truck. Unlike Erma Lou's rusty, redneck ride, this truck was a brand spanking new Cadillac Escalade EXT. I knew it because Ryan had wanted a truck like that.

The girls Mrs. Farley had referred to turned out to be dogs, a standard German shepherd and an orange mutt with a curly fleece coat. They were sprawled across the front seat of the pickup. "Meet Peta and Alice," Mrs. Farley said as she opened the driver's side door. The dogs lifted their eyes toward her and yawned. She ordered them out of the truck and lowered the rear gate for them to ride in the back. "Don't mind them," she said. "They think they rule the world."

After a brief stop at Mrs. Farley's quaint bungalow, they were on the road headed west. First the old woman chatted about ordinary things, like her childhood, the local school, and her favorite recipe for venison stew. Then she told Frankie about the Rajneesh clan that had lived in Antelope in the 1980s, and the current debate between the dam supporters and environmentalists up in the Columbia River basin, and about her volunteer job at Planned Parenthood. Finally, when it was clear the conversation would remain one-sided, she turned on some hip-hop music. She was not at all what I expected.

When they drove into Bend, the navigation system directed them to head south. Mrs. Farley asked if it would be all right if they stopped at the Christian bookstore before heading out of town. Frankie shrugged and said she'd wait in the car. When the old woman came back to the car, she had a small bag.

"Here, this is for you."

Frankie reached into the bag and pulled out a pocket-sized Bible. She looked at its front cover and back cover, then gently put it back in the bag. "Thank you."

Mrs. Farley started the car.

"You're not a believer, are you?"

"My grandmother and grandfather are. Were. Not my mother, though. She didn't believe anything, really."

I had something in common with Raina after all.

"But I found an old Koran in her room. So I'd been reading that lately. Until it was taken from me." Her Koran, and her silver necklace, were back in Utah.

I figured this would be where Mrs. Farley would show her true colors; a small town old Christian woman wouldn't have a clue what to do with this piece of information about Islam. But I was dead wrong. She smiled, just as kindly as before.

"That's good. I have an idea."

She drove south on Third Street and pulled into the Wal-Mart parking lot. Again Frankie waited in the car, and this time Mrs. Farley came out with two bags of groceries. She put them in the cab behind her seat, then pulled out a bottle of

Coke, a package of Sour Punch candy, and a Koran. She handed all three to Frankie, whose face brightened like sunshine on a diamond.

"You sure this is the place?"

Thirty minutes later, the truck's tires crunched up the gravel driveway of a lonely property outside Bend's city limits. Home sweet home! My heart skipped like a girl playing jump rope.

"It looks all closed down," Mrs. Farley said. "Look, the shades are drawn, the lights off. There's nary a garden tool left outside. If you asked me, I'd say it looked dead around here."

She was right. I'd never seen our little cabin look so desolate and lonely. So abandoned.

"No, pretty sure this is the right place. You can just drop me off anywhere here. He'll be home soon."

"Well, all right then," Mrs. Farley said, pulling into the turnaround by our front porch. "Now here's my phone number." She handed Frankie a small card. "Call me if you have any problems. I'll be staying out in Alfalfa for a while with my daughter and her family."

As Frankie opened the passenger door, Mrs. Farley told her to wait a minute. She reached behind the seat for a bag of cookies. "Just so you don't get hungry while you're waiting."

After the truck drove away, Frankie sat down on our front porch and opened the package. The fragrance of sunshine and childhood filled the air. She hungrily gulped down a half-dozen cookies as I watched like a jealous dog. Licking chocolate from her fingertips, she looked up at the sky. It was early evening by then and perfectly clear, with a cool breeze. Behind her, our two green Adirondack rockers were swaying back and forth as though two ghosts were rocking side by side.

She walked around back. There was the large deck I sat on nearly every morning we lived there. There was my river—the Deschutes—and all those enormous ponderosa pines, their dried needles and cones blanketing the ground. There was even a bald eagle soaring overhead. The evening sun's rays filtered down through the trees, and Frankie closed her eyes as she tilted her head back and inhaled. It smelled of pine. It smelled like heaven.

She tried to peer into each window, but Ryan had indeed closed all the window shades. She jiggled the doorknobs and window latches, and even tried to get into our detached garage. But Ryan had done a good job locking everything down, which would have pleased Tom. If only Frankie had known we hid the secret key in the flower box on the backside of the garage.

She went back to the front porch again and sat down sideways on the swing, slinging her long legs over the armrest. Only a few cars passed during the next hour. One or two slowed down as they drove past, and Frankie watched them. But no one turned into the driveway until Mrs. Farley's Escalade returned.

"Still no luck?" she said when she got out of the car, earbuds wrapped around her neck.

Frankie shook her head.

"I had a hunch about that. Well then, I think you should come with me for the night. You can meet my granddaughter Chloe and the rest of the family and get a good night's rest. Then we'll figure out what to do."

They crossed town and headed east to a sprawling ranch with cattle, horses, and alfalfa fields. Mrs. Farley led Frankie through the back door into the kitchen, where a woman and man were plucking and dressing a chicken. Something in the air smelled of spice. Peta and Alice raced past Frankie.

"Hello everyone!" Mrs. Farley said. The couple turned but held their contaminated hands midair over the bird. Mrs. Farley introduced her daughter, Jessie, and her son-in-law, Dalton, to Frankie. Jessie, with a long blonde braid the same length as her mother's, smiled warmly and said hello. Dalton nodded, then quickly returned to the chicken work.

"And this little thing is Chloe," Mrs. Farley said, pointing to the little girl who had just run into the kitchen. Frankie's face lit up, and in a matter of minutes Chloe had taken her by the hand and was leading her out of the kitchen to show her around. When they returned to the kitchen, Mrs. Farley told Frankie to wash up.

"We've already eaten," Dalton said, "at a normal supper hour."

"But we'll still sit here with you and talk," Jessie said.

The conversation at the table was joyful and polite, the way a family meal should be, and Frankie couldn't stop smiling between bites. Mrs. Farley insisted, at least three times, that Frankie smear more butter on her cornbread. "We need to fatten you up like those calves out there," she said.

Frankie finished off two enchiladas and was about to ask for another one when Dalton asked her what kind of trouble she was in.

She wiped her mouth with a floral cloth napkin. “Excuse me?”

“I figure a girl your age traveling alone must be in some kind of trouble.” His eyes skimmed her t-shirt and sweatpants. “Especially one traveling so light.”

“Not in trouble. Just came to visit a friend.”

Dalton and Jessie exchanged looks, and Jessie shook her head as she reached over and placed her hand atop her husband’s.

“Well, I’m sorry but I’m telling you that’s a little hard to believe,” Dalton said. “Hitchhiking throughout the state of Oregon without any money, or belongings, or proper shoes. I just think I have a right to know, as the head of this household, whether I’m harboring some sort of criminal.”

“Dalton.”

“It’s okay,” Frankie said. “If running away is a crime, then I’m a criminal. But I’m really just trying to find a safe place to go. Don’t have a mother or father and my grandmother just died.” She looked at Mrs. Farley. “And my grandfather’s too busy for me. We had some old friends who moved out to Bend, a pastor and his wife. Only she’s dead now, too. Died of cancer, like my grandmother. Thought maybe I could stay with him a while.” She licked her fork and then let it clang down onto her plate. “Sorry. Can leave if you don’t want me here.” She pushed her chair back and stood abruptly, but Mrs. Farley reached out and took her hand.

"Nonsense, you are most welcome here. Am I right Jessie?"

Jessie nodded. "Of course you are. And Dalton, I'd like you to see what you can do to help find that friend of hers. You've got connections."

He stabbed the last enchilada on the serving platter with a fork.

"All right then. But I'd like to have a little chat with you." He pointed a forkful of enchilada at Frankie. "While the women are cleaning up."

"And I'll make up the sofa for you," Jessie said. "If you don't mind sleeping on a sofa that is."

"Thank you," Frankie said. Little did Jessie know that was the best bed Frankie had seen in a while.

Frankie and Dalton strolled around the dark yard. She laughed when the chickens scurried past her, and scratched behind Peta's ears when the dog came near. Dalton grabbed a rake that was leaning against the house and smoothed out the dirt in the garden beds beneath the kitchen window. Then he started to ask her questions: where did she come from, where Ryan might be, whether anyone knew she was here.

She offered him little information. She told him she was from Iowa, but most of her other answers were simple, and honest, don't-knows.

"Look, if you're not going to cooperate, then you might just have to find another family to mooch off."

His sharp tone seemed to catch Frankie off guard after all the kindness that Mrs. Farley had poured on her. Her shoulders sank, and I caught her stealing a glance at the road. For heaven's sake, Frankie, please don't run again.

"For crying out loud," Jessie said as she opened the screen door. She held a stack of thick, fluffy towels, a clean cotton nightgown, and a pair of fresh cotton socks in her arms. "The girl's exhausted. Can't you see that, Dalt? I think you'd best hold off till tomorrow." She suggested Frankie go upstairs for a hot bath and told her there were plenty of new toothbrushes and toothpaste in the cabinet. "Help yourself to anything you like."

By the way Frankie smiled, you might have thought she was being offered a million dollars.

The bathtub was so clean you could practically perform surgery in it. As the warm water filled the tub, Frankie sprinkled a few drops of Chloe's bubble bath in and watched the bubbles accumulate. Then she looked through the cabinets. Lotions, sunscreens, shampoos. New toothbrushes, toothpaste, and dental floss. Extra towels. Tampons and sanitary napkins. And fresh packages of nail clippers, tweezers, and cuticle scissors. It would have been a fair guess to say she'd never seen a house so stocked with supplies, not even Cece's.

Frankie opened the scissors and set them on the edge of the tub. She eased herself into the water, wincing as her dirty wounds met the bubbles, and slowly sank deeper until she was completely immersed.

24 Chapter Twenty-Four

16,200' Elevation

A shriek pierced the thin air. Ryan rolled over, squinted one eye open in the muted morning light, and lifted his head. His hair was slightly tousled, and he had that same early morning fragrance of musk as always. He propped himself on an elbow, and I had an insatiable urge to lean into him, let him wrap his arms around me, and protect me from the frost. Instead I watched him reach for Lynn's journal, which was lying open atop her empty sleeping bag.

Ryan was a good man but not without temptation. He flipped through the pages to the last entry. Rubbing his beard, he read about the day before, about her feelings of love and all that. He looked amused. Then he set his index finger on the final words when there was another cry, or maybe a gasp, and he quickly pulled on his boots and a jacket and went outside into the virgin snow.

Sounds of swishing nylon came from Will's tent. Ryan walked over and called out.

"Lynn? Are you in there?"

After a moment, Ryan unzipped the tent flap and poked his head inside.

Lynn was lying on her side under a fleece blanket. A bra was strewn across a sleeping bag. She looked like she was in pain.

"Everyone...okay?" Ryan asked. Lynn did not look at him; she looked past him and out the tent door. Snow blew in from behind his head and swirled in a miniature vortex inside the tent.

"Everyone's just fine," Will said. "What say we meet up outside for breakfast in a few minutes? Give us a chance to...get dressed."

"Lynn?"

She nodded, and Ryan pulled himself back outside.

"Wait!"

Her voice was elevated—not the voice that had calmly commanded the team in the crevasse rescue. I heard the sounds of a slap, a rustling, and a zipper.

"Ryan, wait!" She crawled out of the tent wearing only a thin silk undershirt, long johns, and socks. Setting her feet in the wells of Ryan's footfalls, one after the other, she hurried toward him. He waited for her to catch up, embraced her, and then hurried her toward his tent. They crawled inside.

She crawled into her sleeping bag after tossing her journal aside. I noticed a spot of blood on her long johns as she did, and I think Ryan did too. But he said nothing and instead sat opposite her on his bag and waited. I thought she had fallen asleep, but then she finally sat up and began to rub her arms with her hands, shivering. He threw his jacket around her. She kept rubbing her arms, big strokes up and down as though trying to wipe something away. Her face was pale, her eyes bloodshot. She avoided eye contact with him.

"What's going on?" he finally asked.

"I don't know," she replied, glancing at him for just an instant. "All I know is that I feel like crap. And that something happened last night. I don't know what. Or how or why. I don't remember much of anything. But something happened."

"What do you mean, something?"

She said she remembered going to Will's tent for tea. She remembered his eyes black and shiny, and his laugh deep and melodious. She had some strange and exotic dreams, she thought, but she couldn't say exactly what they were about. And then she woke up this morning, dizzy and nauseated, and when she sat up, she felt it.

"It?"

"Oh God, Ryan. I've done something awful."

He waited.

"I woke up and felt it. That sticky feeling between my legs. Oh God. This is so embarrassing. I need to go to the latrine. I need to clean myself."

"I'll take you."

He helped her slip into his parka and zipped it up for her like a father helping a child. Then he slipped his snow boots onto her feet. He helped her with her harness and put his on, too. Once outside, they clipped to the safety rope, and he led the way in his regular trekking boots, with her following in his footprints again. When she dropped one of his mittens and it blew away, Ryan did not go after it.

She stopped as they approached Will's tent.

"Keep going. Come on," he said.

The team had designated a latrine area with a single, two-foot-high snow wall for privacy. She stepped behind it and squatted. Ryan looked the other direction as the wind ripped across his back. When she was done, she told him she was sorry and fell to her knees in the snow.

He set his hand on top of her head. "Get up. Get up, Lynn. Get up now." He was wearing only a fleece jacket and was trembling.

She shook her head.

"Yes, now. Do we need to talk to Brad?"

"Brad? What's he got to do with this? No, no. This is between Will and me. We need to leave everyone else out. This is embarrassing enough already."

"You've already got me involved. Besides, I don't like what I'm thinking."

You could never get anything past Ryan. Not that I tried much, maybe a little in our early days together. But he had the ability to sniff things out that not even psychics, nor police-trained canines, could, I swear. Teens, addicts, liars. I still—to this day—don't know how he did it. But somehow he could see right through people. He used to say it was God's gift to him.

"What do you mean?" Lynn said.

"Something's not making sense to me. So we're going to talk to Brad. Now get up."

She stood. "Just give me a little more time, please. I need some more time to think."

Cece told me she used to hear that line from Raina every time she got into trouble, and I had heard it once or twice from Frankie, too. For them, needing time to think meant they needed time to get their stories straight.

"What's there to think about?"

"What happened. I can't remember what happened. I just don't know what came over me. I guess I seduced him, although I certainly hadn't planned to. Or he seduced me. I don't know. I'd been feeling uncomfortable around him, remember? All I remember is being incredibly tired. You must think I'm a lonely old slut." She sniffed and wiped her nose with the back of her bare hand.

"Come on, let's get back in the tent and warm up."

Once inside, Ryan asked if maybe it was possible she wasn't responsible for whatever happened.

"Well, of course I was responsible. You don't mean—?"

He nodded. "Yes, that's exactly what I mean. Look, I don't know you very well, or Will, but what I know about you so far doesn't add up with the notion of you coming on to him, at least not at 16,000 feet. That doesn't sync with who you are. And take a look at those wrists." They were slightly bruised. "I don't want to plant ideas in your head. I'm just wondering." He extended his hands, palms open. She placed her hands in his and he rubbed the bruises with his thumbs.

"Ryan, I doubt he'd take advantage of me like that. I'm old. And, besides, he's married. I just bruise easily. Who knows what might have caused those."

"You're not old. And you're beautiful."

Another twinge of jealousy went through my veins.

"Now let's go over what you can remember," he said.

She recounted the same sequence of events she had told him before, but this time he stopped her when she mentioned the tea. He asked her what it tasted like, and how much she had, and when she began to feel sleepy.

"Why? It was just tea."

"Ever heard of date rape? Rophies?"

Her eyes widened.

"You said you had tea. You said you feel like crap. It all adds up."

"Could be the altitude."

"Could be. But think of this: if you're already having trouble breathing, and having other AMS symptoms, and then you get a drug like that loaded into your body. Well, it could be nasty, Lynn. Could be deadly."

"I have been feeling a little short of breath today. But why?" She lowered her voice to a whisper. "Why would anyone want to do that to me? Especially here on the mountain?

"I don't know. Rape is a complicated thing," he said.

Ryan and I used to worry about Frankie's safety, with all that exposure to Raina's clients. But why Will? A man who seemed well educated and successful, who ostensibly had a family. A man who climbed mountains. He had certainly been forward with Lynn, but she had also admitted an attraction to him. She'd flirted with him on the dance floor and let him sleep in her room. As far as I could tell, she'd been a willing participant in whatever had happened.

"Maybe you're right," she said. "Maybe he did force himself on me. Then everything makes more sense."

"If that's the case, we have a difficult, maybe even dangerous, situation here. We need to tell Brad." He started to get up, then turned to her. "I'm sorry, Lynn. I'm so sorry this happened to you."

"I need to go back to my tent," Lynn said.

"No, you don't. You stay right here and pull yourself together. I'll go and get whatever you need."

"I need my clothes. And my dignity, if you can find it."

Ryan went to see Brad first.

"Shit. This is just what we need," Brad said. He held a paperback book, which now he threw across his tent. "God damn it! We need to have a meeting. If she's going to accuse him of rape, we need to all process this together. We might need to call in a ranger."

"And what will they do about it at 16,000 feet?"

"Haven't a clue. This is a first for me. But there are rangers on the mountain—at least there are supposed to be—for a reason. I can call them right now and they can be on their way to us at a moment's notice, and then it's up to them to decide what happens next."

The meeting was held outside Brad's tent. A lenticular

cloud shadowed the campsite, and the temperature hovered around 0 °F, but at least it wasn't snowing. Lynn wedged herself between Ryan and Nick on the ground, each of whom held a cup of tea. Although Ryan made it, Lynn said she couldn't possibly drink any tea, maybe not ever again. Nick shivered, and his teeth chattered. When Will arrived, he reached toward Lynn and asked if she was feeling better. She knocked his hand away.

"Don't you ever come near me again." She spoke through gritted teeth. He pulled his arm back and held his palms up, looking confused.

"Let's get right to the point here, Will," Brad said. "There's been an accusation and I need to ask you some questions about last night."

"An accusation? Go right ahead. I've got nothing to hide." He started to flash his gorgeous smile but then stopped at half-smile when he saw the way everyone was staring at him.

"Did you invite Lynn to your tent last night?"

"You mean our tent? Yes, of course I did. She was wandering around cold and hungry. I told her to come in and have some snacks and tea."

"How much did she drink?"

"Two or three cups. I guess she liked it." He winked at her. She scowled.

"And then what happened?" Brad asked.

"Then we talked. She told me things, mostly about her past. About a guy named Farid."

Lynn bit her lip.

"And then?"

"And then," he looked down at his hands. "Well, she put the moves on me."

Lynn, who had been sitting cross-legged, lurched forward. "I did not, you asshole."

I was confused about the severity of her reaction, given that only an hour earlier she'd been telling Ryan she was responsible for her own actions.

"Hey, baby, don't go all princess on me now," Will said. "Not after last night. Not after what you said to me."

"Hold on, everyone," Brad shouted, arms outstretched like a referee. "Settle down. Lynn, you'll have your chance to talk. Let's let Will finish."

Will adjusted his jacket and wiped something invisible off the left sleeve. "No offense, but you're a little old for me. Still, you asked for it, darling. You wanted it more than I did. You know it. Don't deny it. You even told me so back at Base Camp."

Brad, Ryan, and Nick looked at her. Obviously none of them knew about her alleged whispers to Will in the middle of the night. Now it was her word against his, and nobody knew whom to believe, including me. I'd seen him putting the moves on her; he wasn't as innocent as he sounded. Was she making up the rape accusation? Or was Will in fact some sort of sociopath? It was possible he had drugged her. All I knew for sure was that at least one of them was acting. When she responded to his comment by looking down into her lap, I figured she was silently affirming what he'd said.

"So, Lynn," Brad said, "how do you remember it?"

"I remember somebody rubbing my neck and shoulders."

"That was *me*," Ryan said. Brad and Nick looked at him.

"I remember someone kissing me."

Brad and Nick looked at Ryan again.

"That wasn't me. Honest."

"I remember the tea," she said. "It smelled divine, like apricots and spice. And then nothing after that. It's blank. But I know I didn't consent to having sex with Will."

Ryan was now pressing his hands together and bouncing them against his lips. He had to know something was wrong with her testimony; it was a weak accusation so far. Everyone had seen Lynn flirt with Will, and vice versa, early in the expedition, even way back at Talkeetna. Everyone knew that she was single and lonely, and that she was also the type of person who would stop at nothing to get what she wanted. So was a consensual hookup all that unlikely? A fling on the mountain, with few—if any—witnesses? No wife, no proof. Why not? On the other hand, there are a lot of reasons a woman might not want to admit to herself, or anyone, that she was raped.

If only I'd stayed that night. But I hadn't; once things had started getting intimate, I was uncomfortable. Dead or not, I didn't want to be a voyeur.

What bothered me was the idea that Lynn—the woman I'd hoped would save Ryan from loneliness and Frankie from Raina's life of vice—appeared increasingly complex and selfish, and promiscuous. And now I feared she was an outright liar who would unjustly accuse a man of a horrible crime like rape.

"You believe me, don't you?" Lynn said to the group. And

when nobody answered, tears welled in her eyes, although it could have just been the cold air causing them. "I never wanted this to happen. None of it. Trust me."

"Will? Anything else you have to add?" Brad said.

"I confess to letting her seduce me. And I'm sorry that I cheated on my family." He was convincing, until he lowered his head and wiped a glove against one eye. There was no way that man would shed a sincere tear. "All I ask is that this stays within our group, our little secret."

Their two performances were worthy of Oscar nominations. If only I knew which of them wasn't acting.

"So you're saying you didn't rape her," Brad said.

"Absolutely not. If you were there, you'd know what I mean."

"And you didn't put anything in her tea?" Ryan asked.

"Like what?"

"You know damn well what I mean. Like Rophies, or Liquid Dream, or something like that. A drug. A date rape drug."

Will fiddled with the metal tab of his jacket zipper. "I most certainly did not."

"Will, we've heard your side. You can go back to your tent. We need to speak privately with Lynn now," Brad said.

After Will left, Brad turned to Lynn. "There's no way for us to know who to believe, Lynn. I don't think we have a strong enough reason to call in the ranger. And I admit I was pretty damn concerned about your flirtatious behavior with him earlier in the climb. It wasn't professional, and we talked about that, and then I let it go. I guess I shouldn't have. My recommendation is that we finish the climb and move on, but that you also stay clear of him." He looked at Ryan, then back at Lynn. "And anyone else you're attracted to. If need be, I'll have you stay in my tent with me."

Lynn's face and neck flushed. "That won't be necessary."

"I don't think it's that easy," Ryan said. "I believe her. I think he raped her."

I was shocked to hear him say it. He hadn't piped up when she'd asked if anyone believed her, and besides I was pretty sure she was lying.

"And if we really have a rapist in our midst," Ryan said, "then we have bigger problems than someone with an overactive imagination. Especially if he really did use some sort of drug. Who's to say he doesn't drug the rest of us?"

"You're saying he could rape us too?" Nick said. He shuddered. "Shit."

"No, but I am saying those drugs are dangerous, at any level, and especially at high altitude. You should know this, Brad."

"How do you know so much about this, may I ask?" Lynn said.

"Part of the old job, I guess," Ryan said. "I always stayed close to my youth groups. But let's not get off track."

"So your point is?" Brad asked.

"My point is this: I think Will probably did drug and rape Lynn. Drugs are the only logical explanation for how she feels now. He probably has more drugs in his pack. I think we need to inspect his things and then call the rangers and see what they can do."

"I'll admit I haven't felt good about this guy since the first day," Brad said. "I should have done more due diligence before I accepted him on the team."

I interpreted the silence that followed to be the team's agreement.

"What if he doesn't even really have a family?" Nick added. "What if he's a total fraud, an imposter? A serial killer?"

"Let's not get carried away," Brad said. "But you're right about one thing, when you think about it. We've all gotten a few messages from friends or family through Marisa—all of us except for him—and wouldn't you think his wife would be trying to reach him? I haven't once seen him try to contact anyone on the outside."

"So now what do we do?"

"I just want to go back to bed," Lynn said. "To my own sleeping bag, to hibernate. Forever."

"Sounds good to me," Nick said. His words were slow and thick, his eyes glassy.

"No," Ryan said. "You don't want to go to bed, Lynn. You want to finish the summit. We all do."

I didn't often disagree with my husband, but this was one instance when I did. Finishing the climb was not a good idea for her, and not for Nick, and maybe for anyone. They needed to turn back. This was the final straw.

"And what about the Park rangers or the police or someone? I mean, we can't just keep climbing and ignore what happened," Nick said, shivering worse now. "Shouldn't Lynn press charges or something?"

"Maybe I don't want to press charges," Lynn said.

This was further evidence she was lying, I decided. Of course she wouldn't press charges if she knew the crime never occurred.

"But if Will really did rape you," Brad said, "you can't let a crime like that go unreported. If word got out there was a rape on my watch, my business would be finished. In fact the whole climbing community would be impacted."

"It's *my* body," she said.

"It's *my* expedition," Brad said. "So I say we call the Park rangers, without telling Will, right after we summit. In the meantime, we'll keep a close eye on him, and make sure Lynn's not alone with him, until the rangers can come and get him, probably when we get back down to High Camp." He pointed toward the tent door. "In fact, the weather's good now. We can start hauling gear up there right away."

"But I can't do it," Nick said. "I'm sorry. I just can't."

The others turned, stunned expressions on their faces.

"What did you just say, Nick?" Lynn asked.

"I can't make it," Nick repeated.

"You're right to speak up for yourself," Ryan said. "We've been pushing too hard too fast—especially with all the symptoms you've been showing, and we've been wrong to rush you."

He was right. Brad should have been paying a lot more attention to Nick than he had been, and he probably should have forced Nick to retreat by now. At a minimum, Brad should have granted Nick more time to acclimatize at each rise in elevation. In fact, given what the whole team had been through, I thought they all should have retreated for rest and acclimatization.

After a heated debate, Brad finally said the answer was simple. Again reminding them that he was in charge, he said they were going to summit.

"Nick stays here to rest today...no ifs, ands, or buts...or else we'll have more problems to deal with. The rest of us carry gear to High Camp, cache it for the night, and tomorrow when Nick's feeling healthier we all move on. Once we've gained the summit, hopefully within a couple days, we call the rangers. And Lynn, you are never alone from here on out. Got that?" He tucked a fleece blanket around Nick—the first sign of uncle-like attention since the beginning of the climb—and began gathering supplies.

When Lynn and Ryan returned to their tent, she asked if he really believed that Will had drugged and raped her.

He scraped his front teeth against his lower lip. "Yes."

Ryan had never lied during our entire time together. But now he was lying. I knew it. I just didn't know why.

While preparing the High Camp cache, Ryan and Brad searched for the drugs. Will didn't resist when they asked to inspect his gear, and he even offered his tea stash to Brad. Although they didn't find anything they could identify as a date-rape drug, I wasn't convinced; there are so many little zippers and hidden pockets in modern mountain wear and gear, and I thought it quite possible Will could still have had something tucked away.

Once the cache was prepared, Lynn said she was still

feeling dizzy from the alleged drugs and volunteered to stay back with Nick. Brad looked at her suspiciously but said it would be fine if she stayed back. He gave her the satellite phone.

"You don't think you'll need this?"

"No, it'll be a quick up and back. We'll be fine."

Brad, Ryan, and Will roped up and set off for High Camp, at 17,200 feet, to cache a three-day supply of fuel and food. Although the weather now was a temptress—perfectly gorgeous other than the wind—it was also notorious for changing its mind in a matter of hours. A southwestern flow of the jet stream could generate moist air and huge amounts of fresh snow. Colliding high and low pressure systems could suck frigid air down into the Alaskan Interior. Or the dry Chinook winds could rake across the mountain range and *raise* the temperatures dramatically, provoking more avalanches.

They stopped several times along the narrow ridge leading to High Camp, huddling alongside rocky outcroppings for protection from the wind. Will pulled a candy bar or some other snack from his pocket each time. He ate slowly, as a chef might savor his culinary masterpiece, indifferent to the strong winds that whirred around them from all directions. Brad toed him with his crampons at each stop, urging him on, yet even once they started up again, Will's pace was painfully sluggish. Whether it was the altitude or his attitude was unclear. What should have taken two hours took nearly four.

Once at the site, the wind kicked ferociously. They put on

their parkas, balaclavas, and another layer of gloves, and Will and Ryan dug a shallow pit for the supplies, marking it with orange wands. Brad walked over to the only other team up there, a group of Koreans with an English guide. Although a couple of them were feeling ill, they were still planning to attempt the summit the next day, the guide reported. He pointed at the sky, a brilliant blue, not the type of sky that normally gives you a reason to worry. But there were faint clouds, or ghosts of clouds, whisking off the ridgelines. "Not much time before the next storm," he warned. Brad asked where the High Camp ranger or volunteer staff were. "We haven't seen anyone. Probably just out on a routine patrol," the guide said.

When they got back down to the Ridge Camp, Lynn was pacing back and forth in front of Brad's tent. Nick's condition had worsened again.

"You're kidding," Brad said. "I thought he was improving."

"I did too," she said. "But something's changed. He's dizzy now and doesn't seem right. We should have gone back down to Camp 3 for at least another night. We were foolish. I need to take him down."

"We didn't leave supplies at Camp 3, besides the sleds. You'd have to haul gear too," Brad reminded her.

"You were the one that rushed us out of there. Are you telling me you didn't even leave an emergency cache of any sort?"

"I don't usually cache there."

"Well, everyone else does. Maybe this would have been a good time for you to start too," she said.

"What's done is done. I'm telling you it would be too hard to down-climb so late in the day, especially on the fixed ropes. It would be downright treacherous for the two of you with all your gear and with Nick in that condition."

"So you're saying he should stay here? What, so you can wake us up and rush the mountain in the morning once again? And how do you know this isn't more severe than AMS? You weren't watching him today. I was. I think he might be developing HACE."

"Edema?" Ryan said.

She nodded. "High altitude cerebral edema."

"That's it then, I'll go too," Ryan said. "Brad, you can stay here with Will."

Brad was willing to accept Ryan's offer, but Lynn wasn't. It didn't make sense, she said, for the lead guide to stay at camp with the rapist while the others descended with his nephew.

"All right then, we'll all go down for another day. But I'm not happy about that."

"You make it sound like it's Nick's fault," Lynn said. "Or mine."

Brad sighed heavily. "No, I know it's not. But this is ridiculous. How many more obstacles do we have to encounter?"

They loaded up their tents, sleeping bags, fuel, and remaining food as quickly as possible, leaving a cache of supplies they wouldn't need for a day or two. They all traveled as one rope team, with Will in the lead for the descent so Brad could keep an eye on him. When they got to the Headwall, Will ignored Brad's directions and began to descend down the fixed rope meant for climbers heading *up* the wall. When he refused to climb back up, the four had to either unclip from him or follow.

"Let's cut him loose," Ryan, of all people, proposed. "He's getting on my nerves."

But they didn't. They followed Will and fortunately didn't encounter any climbers coming up the rope. Nick slipped several times on the way down, and almost lost his balance at one of the unclip points. It was slow going until they reached the base of the Headwall, when Lynn took the lead and led the group off course—without even stopping to debate the matter with Brad.

"We need to let him rest. Now." She probed the ice until she located a hidden cave perched on a ledge, nestled into the rock between two couloirs.

"I never saw this here before," Brad said. "I'm impressed."

"It's been here all along. You just have to know where to look."

Brad approached the cave with the enthusiasm of a Cub Scout but remarked, after a quick inspection, that it looked awfully small for all five of them. Lynn matter-of-factly told him that he and Will would have to locate their tent elsewhere. They found a platform about a hundred yards away for Will and Brad, although Brad worried aloud that it would be ravaged by wind, and was in an avalanche zone to boot.

"One night only," Lynn countered. "You only have to stay there one night."

"See you at the West Rib," Will said. Lynn gave him a puzzled look, then led Ryan back to the cave for the rest of the night.

Ryan watched Lynn boil water for tea, waving the smoke away from Nick when it blew his direction. He watched her wipe Nick's hands and face, help him drink the tea, and even massage his blistered feet.

"You're amazing," Ryan said later, after Nick had fallen asleep. The two of them were huddled together in the cave, away from the wind. "The way you take care of him so selflessly, even after what you've been through. I didn't know you had it in you."

She looked offended.

"Sorry, I mean it as a compliment. In the right setting, you seem to have natural maternal feelings."

Ouch. That hurt. There was nothing wrong with her being maternal; it's just that Ryan used to tell me the same thing, when we were trying so hard to make a baby, and now he used the same gentle, affectionate tone with Lynn that he'd used with me.

Her eyes filled with tears.

"Did I say something wrong?" he asked.

She shook her head. "To think that I had that opportunity—the opportunity of a lifetime, you might say—to have a daughter, to care for her, dry her tears, bandage her elbows, braid her hair... I had that opportunity and I threw it away. I didn't know I had any maternal instincts back then."

She looked out at the sky. "I look back now and wonder how I could have done such a thing."

I wondered, too. And it angered me—angered me to think of how she could give up such a blessing. And as much as I loved Cece and Jack, my dear friends, I wondered how Raina, and Frankie, might have turned out if Raina had been allowed to live with her biological mother. That separation can be so traumatic, even for an infant, that it can last a lifetime.

"You did it for love. It was a supreme sacrifice, to give up your daughter."

She shook her head. "I did it because I loved her father and couldn't have him. It wasn't me that made the sacrifice, it was Sunny. She didn't even have a say in the matter."

"Was your family, and the father's family, supportive of your decision?"

"Supportive? My parents basically forced me to give her up. Not just because I was young and unmarried, but also—mostly—because Farid was Iranian. His family was just as bad. They told him he had to marry a Muslim.

"But it was really Farid who influenced my decision the most. He had once told me we would climb the world together. Then the baby came along and everything changed. It was around the time of the revolution, and he decided to go back and fight for the Iranian people's rights. I could've gone with him. I almost did. Until I learned I'd have to wear those black chadors and a headscarf whenever I went out. And until he started reading the Koran fervently. And started to try to control my every move.

"I could have kept her after he left. But my family was

still pressuring me. They said there was no way I could keep an Iranian baby. Bigotry runs in my family..." She looked at Ryan, "like red hair and green eyes apparently run in yours.

"Besides, I was still determined to climb the world's mountains, even without Farid. Maybe even to show him, to make him regret what he left behind. I couldn't do that with a baby in tow. So I gave her up. How selfish is that? To give up a baby so I could see the world? Sometimes I think I should have kept her, gotten a job in an office, been a single mother. Sometimes I think I should have gone with him to Iran; maybe Sunny would have had a better life there."

I thought about Raina growing up in Iran, and whether she would have survived. Would she have been an obedient, law-abiding young woman draped in black? Or would she have wound up as a prostitute anyway, perhaps even being rounded up and stoned to death by now?

"In either case," Lynn said, "she could have been raised around one of her birth families. Instead, she was cast off to a family with whom she had no ancestral connection."

Ryan stroked his beard and looked out over the snowy peaks, the amethyst sky, the accumulating clouds. "You gave her up to follow a dream."

Lynn gazed out at the view alongside Ryan. "At times it feels more like an obsession than a dream."

He nodded. "And you're climbing the Seven Summits in search of redemption, too."

She rested her gloved hand on top of his.

"But what I don't get," he said, "is what this thing with Will is all about. What does that have to do with your dream, or your redemption? What were you trying to prove with him?"

She pulled her hand away. "I don't know. Maybe he was just damned attractive. Maybe I'm just drawn to trouble. Or I'm weak."

"Nonsense. You're one of the strongest women I've ever met."

"I hope you're right about that. Although I don't think of myself as strong when I think about that decision I made about my daughter."

"You have to believe she had a better life than you could have provided."

"I do. I have to believe it in order to get out of bed every day. But I can't help wondering. From what I hear, there's still a stigma of being adopted. And I'm sure it's painful knowing that your mother chose not to keep you, for whatever the reason. Here I've been feeling sorry for myself all these years, and I'm only now beginning to wonder how much pain I may have caused her too."

I wondered if Ryan had any clue that Sunny could actually be Raina. I wasn't ready for him to figure that out yet. He pulled Lynn closer and rubbed between her shoulders, the way he did with me during those long years of infertility, and later too, when I was sick. If only you could rub away guilt and sorrow.

25 Chapter Twenty-Five

15,000' Elevation

It had snowed overnight, and now on the twelfth day since first arriving at Base Camp, Lynn looked out from the cave. Pristine slopes rose on the opposite side of the basin against a crisp blue sky, and long wisps of snow streamed into the wind from the ridgeline. She tied one end of a rope to her harness and the other end around a cragged boulder, picked up the satellite phone, and lowered herself from the mouth of the cave to an exposed ledge. She tried to make a call, but the phone wouldn't work. She tapped it and shook it and tried again. She was so focused on her task that she startled when Brad tapped her on the shoulder.

After an exchange of pleasantries, he asked about Nick. She said he hadn't awakened yet and asked where Will was.

"He's back at our tent."

"You came up here alone? Brad, you know not to do that. Here." She clipped her rope to his harness.

"I've got a bad feeling about the weather," Brad said. "I came down for the sat phone."

"Take it. I can't get it to work." She handed the phone to him. "Worried?"

"I've been thinking about what the Koreans said yesterday—the ones we met at High Camp. They thought bad weather was coming even though it looked clear." They both turned and inspected the sky, but you couldn't see any heavy, dark clouds yet, anywhere. In fact, it looked like paradise.

"There was that other group behind us on the Headwall. They were still climbing up."

"As of Thursday. We don't know where they are now."

He fiddled with the phone. "You're right. It's dead. I don't understand; I just charged it. Anyway, I'll get the solar charger from my tent in a few minutes. Let's see how Nick's doing first."

They woke him, and he still complained of a headache. When he stood, he staggered. Brad helped him put on his harness and, roped together, took him out of the cave to find a suitable place to pee. Afterward, Brad tossed a Hacky Sack to Nick, who was so slow in reacting it hit him in the head.

"His eyes are swollen," Lynn whispered to Brad. "He needs to go farther down. I'll go. You head for the summit with Will and Ryan."

Brad thought about it for a minute, then kicked at the icy floor beneath the cave's overhang. "No, I'll take him down."

"No, I should. You said it yourself; I've got the most AMS

experience. Besides, you were willing to let me go with him yesterday."

"But I've reconsidered. As the head of this expedition, and as his uncle, I need to see that he makes it safely and file an incident report if necessary."

"You don't trust me?"

"It's not that."

Before she had a chance to reply, Ryan woke up.

"What's up?" he yawned and stretched.

"Nothing new," Lynn said. "Just concerns about Nick and the weather."

"The weather? Again? Damn, it's tricky."

"Yes," Brad said. "It is. I didn't want to worry you about it yesterday, but when I talked with the Koreans at High Camp, they said it's going to be another bad one, and it's coming quick. They were going for the summit today and then heading down as fast as they could. I also didn't tell you they'd heard on their sat phone that someone found a body."

"No," Lynn said.

"On Cassin Ridge. A solo climber."

She squeezed her eyes shut.

"I don't know," Brad said. "I don't know if it was him or not." Even though he and Mark had been at each other since the beginning, no climber wants to hear of another one's death—especially someone they know. The same could be said for cancer patients; I made a lot of friends during my last year, and I lost a lot of them, too.

They stood huddled in their little circle.

"I'm glad you didn't go with him," Brad said to Lynn.

"Perhaps I should have. Perhaps he'd still be alive then. And perhaps..."

"Stop." Ryan said. "No need to wonder about what might have been, or what might not have happened." He used to always say things like that. One of his favorite lines was, 'Don't worry today about what might not happen tomorrow.' And sometimes he'd add that it's all in God's hands anyway, so why bother worrying? "We never know whether we're making the right choices. We just do the best we can. Besides, it might not be Mark." He started up the camp stove.

"Speaking of which," Lynn said, "I'm taking Nick down."

Ryan studied Nick, whose breath was labored.

"I really think I should take him," Brad said. "But I doubt Will would agree to descend with me. I don't want to leave him with you and Lynn, but I don't want us all to have to go down just because of Nick."

They debated their options over breakfast—black coffee and a few spoonfuls of plain instant oatmeal. It was finally decided that Brad would descend with Nick. Lynn would go on to the summit with Will and Ryan, who promised to protect Lynn from Will if necessary, although it was clear to everyone there—even me—that Will could easily overpower Ryan.

Ryan and Lynn collected their gear, and the three left Nick for a short time to return to Brad's tent, which had been nestled behind a hastily built snow wall. From there, Ryan and Lynn would leave with Will to re-climb the Headwall, make it to High Camp for a few hours of rest, and early the next morning, go for the summit, God willing. Insha'allah, as

Frankie would say. But when they approached the place where Brad had pitched his tent, it was gone, along with much of his gear. The snow wall had held, but it now protected only a few scattered items. The solar charger and the family service radio were not among the things left behind.

"Holy shit," Brad said. "Jesus Christ. Not again. Where's my tent?"

"And where's Will?" Ryan asked.

The three looked at each other.

"The motherfucker stole my stuff. I can't lose my tent and gear twice in one climb. I give up." Brad kicked hard at the snow wall.

Lynn pointed to footprints leading away, toward the Headwall. "Great. And now our felon has escaped." I found it interesting she called him a felon now.

"Christ," Brad said. "I'm calling the Park Service now. I know you don't want to be called back down the mountain, Lynn, to report that rape, so you'd better take off before I make the call."

"The sat phone isn't working," she said. "Remember?"

"Fucking A. God damn it!" Brad sat on the snow wall ledge and dropped his head into his hands. "This can't be happening."

Ryan placed his hand on Brad's shoulder. "We'll go after him. We'll either find him or a Park ranger, or both. Then, if the weather's good, we'll make a quick pitch for the summit. If not, we'll just head back down. You just worry about getting Nick down. Maybe you'll find the ranger back down at Camp 3, and you can tell him about Will if you do."

Brad nodded his head in resignation.

"It'll be okay," Ryan said. He sounded like he knew this to be true.x

The three returned to the cave to tell Nick the plan.

"You're finally going down," Lynn said, smoothing Nick's long hair away from his face. "You'll be all right."

Nick lay there shivering, his eyes glassy and unfocused. How awful, I thought, to be in such a phenomenal place and not be able to see and appreciate it. Ryan told Nick he was proud of how far he'd made it, and Lynn said she'd see him again back in Talkeetna. She stood, but Ryan remained in kneeling position for an extra moment beside Nick, as though he were kneeling before an altar. My heart skipped a beat; I was elated that he might be praying again—while I also worried he might be doing so because he sensed something was wrong.

He stood up and gathered his gear. Brad gave both Ryan and Lynn a cursory hug. "See you both back in town."

There was no sign of Will at the Headwall's fixed ropes. They ascended it more rapidly this time; in fact I worried they climbed too fast. We all have a tendency to want to rush unpleasant things, like boring workouts or chemo treatments, but my father, also a climber, always said haste makes waste. I wished Ryan would heed his advice now.

Lynn led as they hiked along the knife-edge ridge after the Headwall—one slow, careful step in front of the next, head down, wind battering from all directions. The surface was slick, blue ice, and steep drop-offs threatened from both sides.

I figured they would have caught up with Will by now; they were both more experienced than he, and there was little opportunity for him to hide, especially in those neon green pants. He was somewhere; they just didn't know where.

"I wonder how many other women are on the mountain," Lynn said at one point when they stopped for a brief rest. "I mean, since we haven't found Will. I hope no one else is in danger." Once again she was confusing me, probably Ryan too. If she had lied about the rape, why go on about it?

"My guess is the other climbers up here are all right. My guess is that it was you he wanted."

They moved on, connected by rope and, maybe, by thoughts too.

"Maybe he slipped off the ridge," she said out of the blue. On one side of the ridge, the slope was primarily slick ice and, on the other, there was more exposed rock. Either way there would be little indication of someone having slipped, unless you could see the broken body down below.

"Am I detecting a hint of hope in your voice? Or is it despair?" Ryan asked. I wondered whether there was much difference between the two emotions.

She shrugged. "You said you thought it was only me he wanted. But did you realize I wasn't the only one he was flirting with?"

"Who else?"

"Marisa. He had her blushing at the airport. What if, instead of climbing toward the summit, he's heading down? What if he gets to her before Brad does?"

"From what I've seen so far, Marisa can handle herself

just fine. If anyone needs to be afraid, it's probably the other way around. Will should watch out for her. She's a tough one, that Marisa. I really doubt he's a serial rapist, Lynn. But we can try to get a message to her through the ranger's radio when we get to the next camp."

Denali Pass loomed over them as they worked their way along the sun-splashed ridge. Lynn's breathing was becoming more labored each minute, and Ryan was out of breath after every step. He was drenched with sweat, and now they stopped every couple of minutes to rest, both of them panting hard.

"You okay?" she said.

He nodded. "Yeah, but it seems worse than yesterday. Harder."

"It's hot today. We're hiking in Gore-Tex saunas. Let's stay here for a little while."

"No," he shook his head as he bent over and rested his hands on his thighs. "Let's push on."

Their crampons bit into the ice with each methodical step as Lynn and Ryan moved in sync like a well-oiled machine. But when they next stopped, Ryan bent over again, panting more heavily, and I found myself holding my breath, waiting for him to get enough oxygen.

"You never climbed this high before, did you," she said, a statement rather than a question.

It was a couple of minutes before he could muster the energy to reply. "Nope."

She spoke slowly, her words now slightly slurred too. "You

know, some people say Denali is as challenging as Everest. The elevation may be lower, but the vertical gain is greater. And we're 2,000 miles or so further north than Everest. You're doing really well."

"I don't know. I think I've got to rest some more after all."

She tried to lure him on to the next camp, only a quarter-mile away, but he insisted on staying a bit longer on the windswept ridge. Meanwhile a helicopter circled nearly three thousand feet below them, near Camp 3, and then swept away toward the West Rib and Cassin Ridge routes.

"Would you like to hear what Greg has to say about golf?" Lynn asked after the helicopter had disappeared. They should have been hiking again, I fretted. The body needs to keep moving at that altitude, especially in the blasting arctic wind. And yet here they both sat. Maybe Lynn was starting to lose her faculties, the probable fatal consequence of cerebral edema.

Ryan sipped from his water bottle.

"Greg wouldn't believe it if he heard me repeating this, but here's the advice he gave me. Mind you, he never climbed. But he is a damn good golfer and a lot smarter than I ever gave him credit for. Like you said, golfers are smarter than you think. He said climbing is a lot like golf. It's mind over matter." Lynn pointed her gloved index finger to her head. "'Think about the next shot,' he'd say. 'Not the hole you've just finished. Not the hole yet to come. Not the score. Just this shot, and this shot alone.'"

She started to lie back, then sat upright again and wiped

her nose on her glove. "I guess he was right, it's good advice for climbing, too. Just think about the next step. You inhale, you exhale, you step, and you do it again and again...all the while keeping your ice axe ready for the big slide." She hoisted herself up and extended a hand out to Ryan. "You don't think about the drop-offs on either side of the ridge; you don't panic when you realize how starved for oxygen you feel. You listen for your heartbeat; you listen to your lungs. You inhale, exhale, step. Like he said, you've just got to keep your focus."

"I think I'd like Greg."

When they finally made it to High Camp, Ryan was wheezing and coughing badly. There were no other climbers there. No Mark. No Will. And no sign, once again, of a Park ranger. The ranger's tent was there, but it was eerily vacant. There were, however, a few decrepit snow walls left behind by previous campers. Ryan helped Lynn set up the tent but then immediately crawled inside and into his sleeping bag. He was clearly exhausted.

She fortified the snow wall around the tent, placed safety wands, and melted snow for water. She moved slowly now too, as though moving through sludge. Thick clouds accumulated in the distance like troops ready to attack. She sat in the snow, with my Ryan lying inside, the two of them together near the top of the world, without me, and yet in a way I felt like they were closer to me than they had been for the entire climb; I felt I could almost reach down and touch them.

But when Lynn offered Ryan some chicken broth, he refused to drink it. And later, he began to remove his jacket and inner layers.

"What are you doing?" she said.

"I'm hot," he said.

"Yes, today was warm. But I wouldn't say hot." She felt his forehead. "You're okay. Your body's just confused. You need to hydrate." She held his water bottle to his lips, but most of the water dribbled down his chin. It froze in his beard immediately.

He reached into his backpack, took out my thick, brunette ponytail, and hugged it to his chest as he curled into fetal position, like a child hugging a teddy bear.

"So that's it. Her ponytail."

He didn't answer her, which meant one of two things. Either he was getting sick, or he was becoming depressed again. I tried to think of what might have triggered depression. Being up there without me, probably. If only I could let him know I *was* there.

He coughed. It was sharp, phlegmy. "I need to sleep."

Lynn covered him with an extra jacket and pulled the sleeping bag up tight around his shoulders. She watched him for a while, then took a sip of his broth, cupping the mug with both hands. As a vegetarian, she would normally not drink chicken broth. But in times like this, your body takes control of your mind. She took a few small sips, then greedily gulped the rest of the soup, holding the mug over her open mouth, catching the last drops on her tongue. She picked up her journal and a pen.

My Dear Sunny~

We are here, at High Camp. But it's getting hard. To

write, to climb, to think.

- *Ryan not doing well—I've got a headache and chills now too. Can't tell him.*
- *We're close to summit—but I am afraid. Nothing has gone right.*
- *Am I not meant to climb Denali? Who's in charge here? Is it God? The Wolf Spirit? Or the Mountain's Spirit, or Mother Nature? Maybe it's Fate. Or your father's Allah. Whatever or whoever, it seems to be telling me I'm not meant to be here.*

Have you ever found yourself in a place and wondered why—Why you're there? Why things happen the way they do? Is it all really coincidence? Is there a grander plan?

It's probably the altitude, confusing me. We came up too fast. Way too fast. Oh, I sound silly. The oxygen is thinning in my blood, and my mind wanders.

She scratched out most of what she'd written, then tucked the notebook into her sleeping bag, and crawled in after it. She tossed about, seemed restless and fitful for a long time, and then fell into such a deep sleep she looked as though she were dead.

26 Chapter Twenty-Six

The family ranch must have seemed like heaven to Frankie. Breakfast was a feast with buckwheat pancakes, ranch eggs, and pork sausage, along with organic berries and fresh-squeezed juice. Lunch was an array of meats, served with sourdough bread straight from the oven and fat tomatoes grown right there in the solar greenhouse. Supper was a family event. Everyone took part in the preparation—chopping, seasoning, and sautéing—and then they all held hands to say grace before eating. Totally *Little House on the Prairie.*

On Frankie's first morning, Jessie loaned her some work clothes and boots, handed her a pair of gloves, and sent her outside. Frankie pulled weeds and swept the back porch, then wandered through the old red barn with Peta and Alice following right behind. It smelled of dried hay, horses, and old manure.

She studied a big spider web, ran her hands along the edge

of the workbench, and picked up several tools. She ran her fingers down a set of reins and traced a horseshoe nailed to the wall in a U-shape. She unhooked the flap of a small saddlebag hanging on the tack wall and sniffed the earthy leather.

"What are you doing?" Dalton stood in the barn doorway, chewing a short stalk of alfalfa.

"Nothing. Just looking around is all."

"Come on. I'll show you how to saddle a horse."

Her eyes widened. "Really?"

She followed him to the corral. Two horses stood ready, with reins and bridle on. He went to the Appaloosa first. Her main body was chocolate, head and hindquarters white with dark brown spots.

"She's gorgeous," Frankie said. "What's her name?"

"Speck."

He showed her the saddling process, helped her mount, and then swatted the horse's flank with his hand. Speck took off trotting around the corral; Frankie held the horn with both hands, one foot flopping out of the stirrup. Dalton laughed. He whistled, and the horse came back to him and stopped. "Ever rode one before?"

She shook her head, but she was beaming.

"Come on then. I'll teach you." He fixed her stirrup, mounted the other horse, and led out the rear gate onto a path lined on each side by a white fence.

"Hang on," he called back to her. He kicked his horse into a canter and then a gallop, and Speck followed. Frankie struggled to stay on as they darted across a pasture, and I was angry that he'd do this without a single word of instruction. Then, at the far edge of the ranch, Dalton coursed down into a ravine.

"Whoa," Frankie said. She reined in her horse to take the trail more slowly, and Speck obeyed. At the bottom, there was a dry creek and a stand of gnarled juniper trees. The horse nibbled at something on the ground. Frankie looked around, and Dalton was nowhere in sight. By then I was furious with Dalton; I might have panicked, being lost in a strange place on an unfamiliar horse in the middle of absolute nowhere. But panic wasn't Frankie's style.

"Oh well," she said. She patted the horse's neck and combed her fingers through its mane. "I guess it's just you and me now. Which is probably for the best." She clucked, and Speck climbed up the other side of the ravine and trotted straight home.

That evening, and the next several after that, Frankie did chores after dinner. She loaded the dishwasher, helped with the dirty laundry, and taste-tested whatever treats Mrs. Farley was baking for the next morning: jalapeno biscuits, coconut madeleines, chutney-coconut scones. She read a bedtime story to Chloe, put on her borrowed nightgown, and waited in the living room for her temporary bed—the sofa—to become available. Mrs. Farley usually worked on a sewing project and listened to an NPR podcast in the evenings; Jessie read the Bible or *Anna Karenina*; while Dalton sprawled on the sofa watching reality TV shows about unsolved crimes with his hand immodestly shoved into his jeans. Mrs. Farley's dogs lay on the floor dozing, and Frankie sat at a corner desk, surfing the net on the family computer.

One night, she asked Jessie to read her a passage from the Bible, and after Jessie read the story of Lazarus, Frankie told Jessie about the story in the Koran where Jesus blows life into a bird of clay. Dalton scoffed and said that was a bunch of drivel, and Frankie didn't say anything the rest of the night.

The next night, Dalton walked up behind Frankie at the computer and asked why she was looking at maps of Iran and Sudan.

"Just curious," she said. Dalton didn't look convinced.

Jessie asked Dalton if he'd had any luck locating Ryan.

"I'm working as hard as I can on it, Jess. I think I might have a few leads. But nothing definite yet." He gulped a tall glass of Squirt that, I suspected, might have been laced with gin. There was something about this family that made me think they weren't so perfect, but I couldn't put my finger on just what. "You know I have a ranch to run. I don't have all day to play private eye. As it is, I'm spending too much time being her babysitter."

"Dalton, you're working that poor girl half to death," Jessie said. "And she's helping you a great deal. So I don't know how you can say that." Frankie had been riding along with him since the first day to help check fence lines, attend new calves, and perform other daily tasks. She'd done everything he'd asked, but understandably, she'd also dawdled at nearly every stop because everything was so new and exciting for her, and he'd scolded her a number of times.

Jessie asked Frankie if she felt comfortable staying there with them.

"Yes, ma'am," Frankie said. She smiled at Jessie and Mrs. Farley, but did not look at Dalton, and when he walked away she deleted the Internet history.

"Well, you let us know if you need anything," Dalton said, once again sprawled out on the sofa. "Anything at all."

After Chloe's bedtime story the next evening, Frankie wandered down the hall to the sewing room, where Mrs. Farley had been staying. A quilt with colorful suns, crescent moons, and stars was draped over the end of the day bed. Scraps and squares of fabric lay on top of it, and loose threads hung from the corners. Frankie sat on the bed, ran her fingers over the quilt, and picked up several scraps, sniffing them and rubbing them across her cheek. When she shifted, her foot knocked over Mrs. Farley's purse. It was unzipped, and a wallet toppled out. Frankie crossed one leg over the other and swung her foot as she scrutinized the floral stencils on the wall. Then she reached for the wallet.

Inside were several twenty-dollar bills and some smaller denominations; she took the bills out, fanned them apart. She sniffed the paper and folded the wad into her pocket. But then she took the wad back out and stuffed the money back into the wallet, slid the wallet back into the purse, and zipped the purse closed.

When Frankie went downstairs, she stood at the end of the sofa and wrapped her arms around herself. Jessie noticed her and suggested they all turn in early, so Frankie could have some privacy and get a good night's sleep. "You look exhausted, sweetheart."

But Dalton said she could wait a little while longer. "A man needs his time to relax. You go on upstairs, Jess. I'll come up when the excitement is over." He nodded at the TV, but then winked at Frankie.

Frankie sat on the floor beside Peta and scratched behind her ears. It was another half hour before his television show was over. When a Viagra commercial came on, Dalton powered off the TV.

"You're a quiet little lady, aren't you?" he said.

She shrugged.

"You been warm enough down here?"

She nodded.

He tugged his jeans higher on his hips when he stood. "Would you like to join me outside for a few minutes?"

She told him no thank you.

"Well, all right then. And like I've been saying all along, you let us know if there's anything you need."

She nodded and started to make up the sofa bed as Dalton went out the back door. She sat upright on the sofa in the dark, waiting, and sure enough he returned ten minutes later, smelling the way he had every night since Frankie's arrival. She knew that smell. Marijuana. At first I found myself revolted that he'd asked her to join him, but then I decided it may have just been his way of being hospitable. You never know.

Later, after he went upstairs and the master bedroom door clicked shut, she slid the cuticle scissors and Koran out from under the sofa cushions. She called the dogs over; Alice jumped up and rested her head on Frankie's legs, and Peta lay on the floor alongside the sofa. Frankie curled up under a quilt and fell asleep quickly, as desert sage wafted through the window to mingle with the interior fragrances of warm butter, sugar, and soap.

It comforted me to see her feel so safe.

And even when a windstorm swept over the high desert during the night, rattling the house and tossing a juniper branch against the window, Frankie did not seem shaken. She got up from the sofa and walked to the window, the wood floors creaking beneath her bare feet. She stood there for a long time, looking out toward the mountains, her face lit up by the moon.

27 Chapter Twenty-Seven

17,200' Elevation

The wind wailed—tearing at the tent from every direction, rocking it hard, threatening to yank it from the stakes and hurl it into the nearest abyss.

Ryan woke up shivering. The temperature had plummeted since their climb into High Camp; the thermometer on his watch registered -28 °F—without factoring in wind chill. He pulled his feet from the sleeping bag and took off his socks. He used his fingers to manually wiggle his toes.

Lynn was still sleeping.

Ryan tried to take a deep breath, but coughed instead. He coughed again, rolled Lynn onto her side, and slid as much of his body into her bag as he could. The effort made him sweat and cough. The wind chastised him with a moan; the tent rocked again. After fifteen or twenty minutes, he shook her shoulder.

"Lynn, wake up." He shook her shoulder again, and yet again, and I was convinced she'd lost consciousness until at last she nodded her head slightly.

"We need to check the tent stakes," he said. He coughed hard, a spell that lasted an eternal minute, the kind that brings a racking pain not only in your ribs and lungs and diaphragm but also in your heart and your brain, the kind that feels like something is ripping inside your body. "Listen...to...the wind."

It wooshed and whirred as if on command.

"Listen to the wind? Listen to you, Ryan. You sound awful." Her voice was gravelly, and she also coughed as she turned toward him. "But you're right, we need to check the wall...and the guylines...and the stakes."

They lay pressed together, until another gust shook the tent. "We'll have to rope up," she said. "But if we both leave this tent, it'll be airborne as soon as we're out the door. She began to scoot out from the sleeping bag. "You stay here, I'll go out." I wondered if one person's bodyweight would be enough to hold the tent down in that wind. It all depended on the guylines.

"No, you stay," Ryan said. He started to sit upright and got caught in yet another coughing attack.

"Rock paper scissors?" She held her hand out in a fist. Her words were slow, stifled, slurred.

"You sound like you're high," he said.

She laughed. "How would you know?"

"My wife. Medical marijuana."

Really—is there no privacy for the deceased?

"I see."

Lynn counted to three, and Ryan covered her fist with his hand. He won the game. Or did he lose it, being the one who'd have to face the tempest? It took him fifteen minutes to get his boots, jacket, goggles, and gloves on, moving as slowly as an astronaut in zero gravity. He shoved my ponytail into a pocket and then started to tie the rope around his waist, but Lynn shook her head and handed him a harness, like a mother handing a hat and scarf to a child. "You've got to put this on first," she said.

They double-checked each other's knots as he was now roped to her. I checked them as well. It's easy to make mistakes when you're this short of oxygen, and when you're practically as cold as a corpse. She zipped up his jacket and snapped his hood shut. When she switched on her headlamp, it illuminated his pale skin and lips, and the dark circles under his eyes. The smile crinkles at the corners of his eyes—that I so loved—were gone, along with his smile.

He held one hand up in a stiff wave, then unzipped the tent and pushed out. I thought about those stories of disoriented climbers who crawl out of their tents only to wander in the wrong direction and slip off a ridge to their deaths. I wanted to call out to him, to tell him to wait and go back, to let me check the tent for him. I wanted to tie myself to him so that if anyone were to save him, it would be me.

The guyline knots were frozen, the stakes secure. The snow wall wasn't nearly as big or strong as it should have been, not only because they'd been so exhausted when they built it but because the snow was so hard to cut. Ryan pulled the shovel out from under the tent, where Lynn had set it earlier, and tried to fortify the wall. The wind, like an angry child, had knocked part of it down. It was agonizing to watch him dig out small bits of ice and pack them onto the wall, coughing constantly. When he finally crawled back into the tent, shovel still in hand, he collapsed on top of his sleeping bag with all his snow-packed clothes still on. Lynn zipped the tent shut and began to undress him, as he sweat and shivered and coughed and, I feared, began to die.

Until then, I had been concerned for Ryan the way you're concerned about tornado watches on a Midwestern summer day. We had a lot of them when we lived near Chicago, and we didn't worry that much. You go about your day, not paying much attention to the real risks because you know everything will be all right. It always is—until the village siren blares over the rooftops and playgrounds, and the reports crawl along the bottom of your television screen of funnel cloud sightings. It's both exhilarating and frightening to see the upside-down triangles dotting the meteorologist's map so close to your town, and even moreso when you look out the window to see the green sky and hear the freight train coming—even though there are no tracks for miles.

And now his freight train was coming up that mountain, and the village siren was blaring, and it wasn't me lying in the tent, tethered to him, waiting for the storm to either take us or give us grace, and it made me mad. It was Lynn who was now his till-death-do-us-part partner, Lynn who was taking care of him and tending to his needs. It was Lynn doing my job, and I started to believe it was her fault he was suffering—not mine—that if it weren't for her he would have stayed with Nick or retreated. If it weren't for her and whatever happened with Will, Ryan wouldn't have been so compelled to minister to her, which is of course what he had been doing until now.

Sure, I had made him promise he'd climb Denali. I'd been the one to set Brad's brochure in the basket next to the couch, so he'd select this particular journey. We'd climbed enough mountains in our past that I was certain he could do it if he trained hard enough and went with experienced partners. And, yes, I thought Lynn would be the perfect partner. But I hadn't expected this. I hadn't expected them to become so personal, so intimate. While I wasn't so naïve as to think Denali would be easy, I couldn't have possibly predicted all the troubles this team would encounter. The more I thought about it the angrier I became, thinking about him risking his life to help Lynn, a woman he barely knew, achieve a stupid goal.

But then again, he was also helping me achieve mine.

It was I who was most culpable in all this, wasn't it? I made that damn ponytail request. I insisted he go back to climbing. I got cancer and died. It was I who sat alone here in hell's balcony, unwilling to let go, like watching a tearjerker movie over and over again. And the more I thought about it, the more I wondered what I really wanted from him—whether it really was all about the ponytail, about finding new purpose and connecting Lynn with Frankie. Or was there something more, something far deeper and darker than I, the minister's wife, dared to see? What was it that had driven me to this? Nightmares? Demons? Did I deserve to be in hell?

Ryan coughed several more times as Lynn removed his boots, his gloves, his outer layer, and at first she turned her head away whenever he coughed. But as she kept removing more layers of clothes, and he kept coughing, she no longer turned away. She helped him into his sleeping bag, then stripped off her clothes and slid in beside him. Her naked breasts pressed against his bare back, her skin warming his, and it stabbed me in my heart. I knew what she was doing: offering her body warmth to stave off hypothermia. I knew I had no choice but to let it happen, to let her do what I should have been there to do. He rolled onto his back, and she set her head on his chest, and her bangs fluttered every time he exhaled.

The weather did not relent, but worsened, dumping another foot of snow. They were confined to High Camp for two more days, the same way they had been confined to Base Camp at the beginning of the expedition, but this time they were all alone, without any way to communicate with the outside world. Will had taken the charger for the satellite phone, and the radio batteries were dead. Lynn roped up several times to work on the snow walls and look for the Park ranger, who was nowhere to be found.

Their intimacy intensified. When Ryan needed to pee, she held a Ziploc bag for him so his urine could be saved as a heat pack. When her unexpected period stained her clothes, he helped scrub the fabric with snow. He even told her that my periods frequently became irregular when we climbed. Why did he need to tell her that?

On the morning of the second day, when thick clouds hung over the camp despite the wind, and when so much snow filled the air you couldn't see the end of your outstretched arm, it was obvious they still couldn't go anywhere. Ryan said he was feeling better, but when he roped up to reinforce the snow wall, his blood splattered the snow when he coughed. He studied the red splotches as though they were Rorschach inkblots. Later, Lynn went out to look for the food cache that Ryan had delivered to High Camp with Brad and Will, and she came back empty-handed.

"I can't find it," she said, stiff with cold and covered in snow. "There aren't any wands."

"Of course there are. I set the wands myself," Ryan said, lying flat on his back. "I'll look." Again they went through the tedious procedure of dressing him and roping up and checking each other's knots and harnesses, and once more they ventured out together, leaving the tent unoccupied. They set new wands with every other step as they searched for the old ones to help find their way back in the whiteout. After fifteen minutes, they gave up and threw themselves back into the tent just as it billowed and threatened to fly away.

"I don't get it," Ryan said, each word interrupted by coughing. "I know where we left the cache. It's just not there."

"Maybe you're confused," she said, and then she laughed weakly. "And it was me that everyone thought was too senile to be in charge of the cache." But Ryan didn't laugh in reply.

I'd seen where he'd hidden the supplies, and he was right. They'd looked in the right spot. "Or maybe it was the Koreans you met when you were up here. Maybe they took our extra food."

"I doubt it," he said. "But Will might have."

She wrapped her arms around her stomach and rocked forward. "I'm so hungry I almost feel sick."

"Maybe when the weather clears. Maybe then we'll find it."

"If it ever does."

They both coughed as they resettled in the tent, but Ryan's cough was now so ragged and deep it seemed his lungs would burst. Again, she helped him out of his clothes, and again they crawled back into the sleeping bag, skin to skin.

"Read to me," he said to her after a while. He used to ask me to read to him; sometimes I read the Bible, sometimes a trashy novel, but what he most loved was my journal. I never shared it with anyone else, and of course I only read the parts I wanted him to hear. He'd laugh when I read about children acting up in the church nursery, and he'd shake his head when I read about the feuds among the ladies' circles. But he was absolutely silent when I'd read my most private concerns and fears and disappointments. The last time I remember reading to him was the last entry I'd written about not being a mother. I knew by then the chemo hadn't worked, and my time was limited. I'd written that my only regret was never hearing a high-pitched voice call me Mommy. I read, and he listened, and we cried, and then we made love for the last time.

"Read to you?" she said. "You mean from my journal?"

"Yes. If you don't mind."

The wind shook the tent.

"Okay, I guess." They both coughed, a harmonious release of phlegm like a secret language between them. She flipped through the pages, scanning the words, commenting that one passage sounded stupid, and then another and another.

"No, nothing's stupid," he said. "Just read."

"Okay. This letter was about some of my feelings about giving her up for adoption. I'll skip to the core.

"They're interconnected, no make that locked, together, these three: guilt, grief, relief. One begets the other, but which comes first? Surely grief, I would think, must come first. Then relief? And then guilt over feeling relief? Or does guilt come first, for whatever you may have done that caused your grief? Can you even have relief without guilt/grief?"

His eyes were closed, but she kept reading.

"I confuse myself the more I think about this, and then I imagine a Scrabble board, and how many different ways these three words fit together. Guilt. Grief. Relief. And the more I think about them the more I wonder who, and what, I'm grieving. In any case, I have concluded that these three words, no these three emotions, are like the three musketeers. All for one and one for all. Hopelessly inseparable."

"Keep going," he said, eyes still closed. "I like the way you think. And I agree with you. About guilt and grief, and relief, that is."

Was he saying he was getting relief from grief now?

She read from another letter, and then set her journal down. "Have you ever asked why me?"

He chewed on the cracked pale skin of his lower lip. "What do you mean?"

"Why me?" she said. "You know, why do bad things happen to me? In your case, why you lost your wife?"

Ryan and I used to lie in bed at night, early in our time together, and wonder why it seemed only *good* things happened to us. But then along came the infertility, and the basal temperature charts, and timed interludes, and buttock injections, and doctor appointments. And the depression that wore us down month after month. I began to wonder the opposite, why two people who adored children were prevented from having them, whether maybe we had some hidden flaws. Ryan said it was all part of God's plan, that someday the reason would become clear.

I had asked him about Cece and Jack, our two wonderful friends who also couldn't have their own children. "What was God thinking about then?" God had given them Raina, a beautiful daughter who turned into an endless worry for them, nearly tearing them apart as she grew. "Was he angry with them for circumventing his plans when he made them infertile?" Ryan assured me that God was benevolent, not vindictive, and that His plan for them had merit too; we humans just couldn't see what it was.

Then came my cancer. That's when he stopped talking about God's plan.

So, yes, we sure as hell wondered why bad things happened to us. But I didn't want Ryan to tell her this. I didn't want him to share any more about our private lives with her.

"No, not really," he said. He lied. Lied for me.

They lay together for a while longer coughing, shivering, listening to the wind.

"Have you ever thought about trying to find her?" he said.

"Find who?"

"Sunny."

She didn't reply.

Ryan reached his arms behind him and rested his head on intertwined fingers. "Lynn?"

"No," she said. "I haven't. Guess I'm too lazy."

"Lazy? Really?"

She didn't reply.

"Do you ever wonder how things turned out for her?"

After another long pause, she said she thought about that all the time. "It frightens me. What if things didn't work out for her? My whole life of climbing would have been in vain. I would have given her up for something meaningless, and doomed her to a horrible life along the way."

This was exactly how I was starting to feel about Frankie. What if this plan of mine didn't come together? With Cece and me both gone, Frankie might also be doomed.

"If I knew she had a rotten life, I don't know if I could go on living. I guess it's not just that I'm too lazy to find her. I'm too scared."

"Are they really all that different?" Ryan said. "Laziness and fear? The two great inhibitors of action?"

They woke to silence on the third day. Hoar frost lined the

interior walls of the tent, and miniature ice columns hung down from the tent seams like stalactites. It was Wednesday, two weeks since they'd left Base Camp. Ryan inspected the tent seams and located the rips where the ice column formed, the rips he should have found the day Tom was at our cabin. He dressed slowly and looked outside. The skies were clear, for now anyway, and the winds relatively calm given the altitude.

"We can do this," Ryan said, starting to pack his daypack. "We can summit."

Those were not the words I expected from him, but I welcomed his attitude.

When Lynn said the only thing they'd be doing was climbing *down* the mountain to get him medical help, Ryan dismissed her.

"It's now or never," he said. "We're going to summit. I'll be fine. Honest, I feel better. We'll be fine." Although he still had that cough, he did seem stronger, and his speech was more distinct. But now she looked worse. "We came here to do this," he said. "So let's do it."

She shook her head and rubbed her eyes. "Now I don't know if I can. Besides, we have no food."

"Of course you can. It's not like you're doing this alone. We're in this together. And as for food, we'll probably find someone out there, or an emergency cache at least, along the way."

He looked up toward the tent ceiling, or maybe he looked through it, as the old Ryan would have done, praying to God to be with them, too.

They checked the conditions outside, studying the sky and the snow wisping off the ridgelines.

"Okay. We'll try," she said. I feared her judgment might be off, the way a drunk thinks he's capable of driving.

They checked the security of their campsite and prepared a couple of small packs. They were coughing and panting as they worked, and they hadn't even begun climbing yet. He stumbled once or twice. As they prepared to leave camp, they exchanged knowing looks that reminded me of the expression I saw on Ryan's face the day the doctor gave us my last test result: a weak smile with the pretense that everything would be okay.

After only a few yards, Ryan spotted something ahead in the distance: a person descending the deadly Denali Pass traverse, a silhouette against the snow. "Look!" Ryan pointed, and as the silhouette drew closer, I saw the red jacket and silver stripes. The climber veered first to the left, and then to the right, before he stumbled to the ground.

"Hey!" Lynn called. She and Ryan hurried through the fresh snow, as fast as they could in their state, like two children running a three-legged race in quicksand. When they reached the figure, he was face down in the snow, and Ryan rolled him over.

Yes, it was Mark.

His face looked like one big, waxy blister, and the tip of his nose was black. He was nearly stiff as ice and barely conscious.

They helped him back to the tent. Ryan struggled to remove Mark's frozen outer clothing and boots; his fingertips were blistered and blackened. When Ryan took off Mark's socks, the stench was vile, the toes black.

Lynn stripped off her own jacket and began to examine Mark as a doctor would a patient, with a pair of latex gloves just as she had done when first examining Nick. His breathing was shallow. His pulse was weak.

"He obviously needs to be kept warm," she said, "and we need to get him to drink. But if his frozen fingers and toes completely thaw, he'll be in even more agony. He needs medical help now. He needs to be flown out."

"Fat chance of that," Ryan said. "No radio, no ranger. Unless Mark has a radio."

Although he was barely able to move or speak, Mark was able to shake his head once to each side. He didn't have one either.

"No, of course not. Shit," Lynn said.

They worked together to wrap his frostbitten extremities with gauze and layer him in dry, loose clothes. They gave him a mug of warm broth with a dissolved ibuprofen tablet. After monitoring him for the next several hours, they noticed his color improved, but he was still shivering and occasionally groaning. The work was exhausting. They rearranged the two-man tent so they could lie down as well.

It was late morning when they woke up. Mark's eyes were open.

"You're awake," Ryan said. "And alive. Thank the Lord."

"Barely," Mark said, his voice no stronger than a single feather. "I feel like shit." His words were slurred, and he, like Ryan, coughed badly.

Lynn asked if Mark had made the summit.

He shook his head and struggled to get more words out. "Couldn't. I was a dead man. Had to come back down."

"See anyone else up there?" Ryan said.

"Yeah. Will."

"Will?"

Mark's face grimaced with the next round of coughing. "Yeah, On the Football Field."

"The Football Field?" Ryan asked. Lynn started to explain about the gentle bowl where a number of routes converge just beneath the summit.

"Yes, I know what it is," Ryan interrupted. "I just can't believe Mark saw Will there. Now there's someone who was hauling ass."

"Tell us what else you know," Ryan said.

"Not much. He was heading for Muldrow Glacier."

"By himself?"

Mark nodded.

"But he seemed okay?" Lynn said. Her voice was tinged more with concern than contempt. Ryan seemed puzzled.

Mark finished his tea and fell asleep. Ryan slurped the last of his tea and asked Lynn what she thought they should do next. They debated taking Mark down, but both worried they wouldn't be able to manage.

"He probably needs another day of rest," Lynn said.

Ryan grinned.

"What?"

"Are you thinking what I'm thinking?" Ryan asked, his eyes more alive now than they had been in days, his smile filled with mischief.

"What? You're not still thinking about the summit are you?" Lynn asked.

He nodded. "I know it sounds crazy, but if he's just going to rest for the day…" Yes, I wanted to say. It did sound crazy.

She returned his grin. "We couldn't ask for better weather. It's probably our last chance." She started to cough, and he did too, as though coughing were contagious.

"But, on second thought, you're the guide. You probably shouldn't leave him."

"I'm not *his* guide. I'm yours. I can't leave you. Which means if someone went for help, we'd both have to go and leave him alone anyway."

They went outside and took in the view as though they were on a simple camping trip.

"What I want to know is where the damn rangers are," she said.

"Maybe government cuts forced them out."

"They wouldn't just pull out and leave climbers on the mountain," Lynn said. "Not after being here for twenty or thirty years. More likely they were called away to emergencies, and with all the bad weather, couldn't get back up here. It's probably just a fluke we haven't run into them. But I hope for everyone's sake they get back here soon."

Her grin returned. "We'd have it all to ourselves. No one else up there."

I understood the draw of having the summit to yourself, but I was not one bit pleased about the two of them going up there in their weakened conditions. Or having it alone, together, for that matter, without me.

"So what do you say?" he asked. "Are we going?"

No, I wanted to say. I hoped Lynn would come to her senses and say no. The summit was a bad idea. The fact that they were feeling temporarily revived was just a minor adrenaline rush. It happens all the time, as Lynn should well know. It's that final rush you need to make the summit and get back down. But in this case, they needed the rush not for the summit but simply to make it down—alive. She had to know that. She had to know their renewed energy was just a mountain mirage, a delusional imbalance fueled by the desire for closure. You're not thinking clearly, I wanted to tell them. The hell with pendants and ponytails, take care of yourselves. Take care of Mark. Retreat now. But neither heard me.

"Yes," she said. "Let's do it."

At first Ryan could go for ten or fifteen minutes without coughing, but soon he had to slow down to clear his lungs every minute or two. At one point, they stopped to rest, and when he'd regained control of his body after another coughing fit, he lifted his eyes toward Denali Pass: 18,200 feet. The place on the route where many climbers turn around and give up after all their hard work, and where some don't—but should have. Where the weather is always the worst. Where more deaths happen than anywhere else on the route. Ryan studied the pass the same way he used to study the wooden cross above the altar right before communion, his lips moving slightly. I wondered if he was praying again.

Lynn told him, her speech slightly slurred, what had

happened on her last Denali attempt, how she and her two partners had stopped at Denali Pass to debate whether to go on. How she insisted they'd be fine, and how one of the climbers insisted they turn back, and how the tiebreaker, a man who'd fallen in love with her, agreed to go on. It was two against one, but all three kept climbing. Then the very same man who was supporting her desires slipped off the Summit Ridge, a quarter-mile, knife-edged trail, only a couple of feet wide and sharp slopes on each side. It happened so fast, she said; no one knew what really happened. It seemed that he wasn't roped to them properly—perhaps a knot wasn't right—and he hadn't leashed his ice axe to his wrist, so he couldn't self-arrest. The axe dug in and was secure, but it was left behind as his body slid, like an out-of-control sled, down the right-hand side of the ridge. The axe Lynn now used was his.

"So his name was listed on the climber's memorial at the cemetery?"

"No, it wasn't. His parents insisted his name be left off because they refused to believe he was dead. Of course they never spoke to me directly, but I heard they waited day after day for him to come home. They lit candles in their windows every night."

"For how long?"

She shrugged. "For all I know they're still doing it. All these years later."

She complained her peripheral vision was thinning, but they started climbing the pass anyway, and she was panting and coughing more than Ryan now. She stopped to clean and adjust her goggles, and Ryan wind-milled his arms and kicked his legs to keep the blood flowing. When they reached the pass—the saddle between the north and south peaks—they shared a granola bar they'd taken from Mark's pack. Chewing slowly, their eyes were fixed only on one another through ice-crusted and scratched goggles. I wished so badly I could ask Ryan what he was feeling right then. About whom he was thinking.

From there it was another long ridge hike to Archdeacon's Tower, with each step more grueling than the last, each stop more frigid despite the sun, each cough sharper and more lethal.

Lynn pointed to a broad plateau ahead of them. "There's the Football Field. Last chance to catch your breath and say your prayers if you're so inclined. Last chance to remember why you're torturing yourself in the first place, before your final ascent."

Beyond the plateau was the ascent to the summit. And also the routes leading off to the right and the left, including the Muldrow Glacier.

"Come on." Ryan tugged on the rope to get her attention. They'd been climbing for nearly eight hours. "Let's get this thing done. I'm exhausted."

She hesitated, and he tugged on the rope again.

"It's just that I'm trying to figure something out," she said.

"Figure what out?"

"Figure out which way he really went."

Ryan turned to her and cocked his head. "He who?" And then he scowled. "Don't tell me you're thinking about Will now."

"I can't help it."

He stamped down the snow where he stood. He was running on empty, I could tell.

"Forget about him, please," he said. "Now's not the time to worry about him. We need to finish what we set out to do."

28 Chapter Twenty-Eight

19,500' Elevation

Lynn dropped to her knees and pressed her mittens against her temples.

"You okay?" Ryan bent over her, touching his hand to the back of her head. "Headache? Dizzy?"

She shook her head.

"Is it your vision? Are you nauseated?"

"No."

"Then what, in God's name, is it?"

"I don't know. I don't know what to do."

Confusion is a classic symptom of altitude sickness. I wanted them to descend, not climb higher. And soon. But then Lynn ripped off her goggles and threw them on the ground, and did the same with each of her mittens, like a temperamental child. I remembered her hissy fit in her hotel room and thought now she was going to lose it again. She would disintegrate before our very eyes like an ice sculpture melting in the sun, and Ryan would be left there on his own with only remnants of the great Lynn Van Swol. She tore her balaclava off, threw it on the ground too, sank down onto her butt, and then lay flat on her back. I almost expected her to start making snow angels in her juvenile breakdown. But instead she lay still, as though dead, until a coughing fit forced her to sit up again. Blood spattered on Ryan's boot.

"I'm exhausted, Ryan. I'm tired. So tired."

He kicked the toe of his boot into the snow.

"But all I know is that right now I feel like I have to find Will, even at the cost of losing the summit."

Ryan picked at frozen spittle in his beard. "So that's why you wanted to keep climbing," he said. "Why you were willing to leave Mark behind and alone. Not for the summit. Not for Sunny. Not for Beth or me. But for Will."

"No. It's not that simple. Don't be angry with me, all right?"

Ryan didn't say anything, and I wanted to answer for him. No, Lynn, I *am* mad at you, I wanted to say. First you claim this lofty goal you're willing to die for—the daughter you gave up—and you're willing to risk who knows how many lives to attain it. Then you get involved with Will instead of focusing on this climb, and then you accuse him of raping you. Now you've done a complete turnaround again, willing to sacrifice everything for him even though he was never part of the original deal. Sorry, Lynn, but I *am* mad at you because you're risking Ryan's life. And because you're out of your mind.

"You're giving up an awful lot for him," Ryan said.

"It's not that it's for him," she said. "It's more like a climber's oath." She slapped her mittens against her legs. "Or at least it's my oath. I can't let someone die up here. No matter what."

Well, that was comforting, except that those words, she later learned, would haunt her.

Ryan had been waiting patiently, but the weather had not. Although the sky was cloudless when they'd left camp, the wind had been building, and another lenticular cloud was forming directly above the south summit. I knew Denali makes its own weather sometimes, and a blizzard could descend at any time at that altitude. The shadows behind Ryan and Lynn were thinning, and still he waited.

"If I left him here to die, I'd probably rot in hell, wouldn't I?" she asked.

The wind drummed harder, and snow tornadoes danced around the two of them like frantic vortexes ready to attack. Like demons. She slammed her ice axe into the ground.

He sat down beside her. They were still roped together, and part of me wanted him to unclip from her, if for no other reason than a symbolic one.

"What?" she said.

"Why don't you tell me the truth?"

"What truth?"

He waited. The eagle feather dangling from her goggles flapped in the wind.

"You know what I mean." I hoped she did, because I did

not.

Lynn had another coughing fit, then threw her arms up in the air. "What the hell. Here's the truth. Will *did* come on to me that night, in the tent. I let him. And I don't remember much after that. But I don't really believe he drugged me. I honestly think it was the fatigue and the altitude that got to me, although I was unwilling to admit it at the time."

"It wasn't rape?"

She shook her head. "I don't think so. I think he started it, and I think I let it happen."

"So why lie about it? Why accuse of him of such a heinous act?"

Good question, Ryan.

She dropped her head into her hands. "I was so embarrassed. About the whole thing. I couldn't believe I'd let myself do that. So when you first proposed the rape theory, I latched onto it. To save face. But I didn't want to report it to the authorities. I wanted to give him an out. He's not a criminal. He's just a man. I never meant it to come to this. This was an unintended consequence."

Ryan sat quietly as she spoke and as the wind drummed around them. When she finished, he stood up and said it was time to go.

"That's it? That's all you have to say?"

"What else is there to say?" That was Ryan. He was never one to rub guilt over anyone. If it were me, I would have laid into her—about the false accusation, her selfishness, the endangering of more than one life. About the way she'd manipulated all of them. This was the woman I wanted to take care of Frankie? Oh, dear Lord. She wasn't the only one making grave and costly mistakes. I wanted to reverse all the wheels I'd set in motion.

"And now you've got to make a choice," Ryan said. "The summit, for your own victory and redemption. Return to High Camp to save Mark and the rest of us. Or gamble on which route Will might have taken from here and try to find him, for your own inner peace, but at great risk to all of us."

She looked at the sky, then up Pig Hill leading to the summit, and back at Ryan, who was holding my ponytail in the wind. Rubber bands were tightly bound around each end, and the gold chain and cross he'd given to me our first Christmas together dangled from one of them. Marisa's eagle feather fluttered on the other end.

"I'm sorry," she said. She got up, turned her back on him, and headed across the Football Field.

"Is this the way to Muldrow Glacier?" Ryan asked.

"Nope, that's over there," Lynn pointed.

"And the summit's up there," he said, pointing in yet another direction. "So where are we heading?"

"Toward the West Rib and Cassin Ridge."

"But why are we heading this way? Mark said he thought Will was headed for Muldrow." His question was valid. Also, I knew there was no way Will could have escaped down the West Rib or Cassin Ridge and still be alive—he didn't have the skills.

Lynn didn't answer. She trudged on, coughing. Ryan kept coughing too as he tried to keep up with her. He reminded me of an old dog following his master.

"Lynn? Where are we going?"

She stopped. "That evening when we got to the cave. Before Will and Brad set up their own tent. He said something to me. I didn't understand what he meant. Something about seeing me at the West Rib."

She took off her goggles and wiped them with a cloth.

"I thought he meant the West Rib Pub. But now I don't think that was it."

She hiked on, and in less than an hour, after they'd descended below an elevated edge of the field, and before they'd reached the steep decline, Lynn led Ryan toward several orange wands surrounding a partially collapsed snow cave.

Ryan picked at the hardened crust of the cave with his axe while Lynn began to dig first with her shovel and then with her mittens. In a matter of minutes, they found his bright green pants.

Will was on his back, his hat and gloves removed. His boots were set to one side and he wore only socks on his feet. The beautiful sheen of his skin was gone and his face was now crusty and nearly unrecognizable. Lynn and Ryan pulled him out from the cave and kneeled beside him. She placed her gloved hand on his chest and lowered her ear close to his mouth.

"He's still breathing."

His breaths were wet, weak, and shallow; his lungs were obviously clogged with fluid. He did not open his eyes. His arms were stiff. She started chest compressions.

"Did you bring any Dex?" Ryan asked. He rifled through

her pack. She hadn't.

"No camp stove either?"

She shook her head. "I'm sorry. I guess I was trying to make our load light. And I thought Mark might need the stove. I should have known better."

"Water then," Ryan said, and he held his CamelBak to Will's mouth. Most of it just drizzled down the side of Will's face.

The wind, now stronger than before, pummeled their backs. The lenticular cloud had grown, and it shadowed the area like a giant spaceship. It was a Hollywood cinematographer's heaven, I thought from my balcony seat, with the three small figures crowded at the mouth of a collapsed snow cave, perched above a precipice and beneath a charcoal-hued cloud looming overhead. All around, the colors of snow and sky and rock muted together into vast and forbidding shades of gray.

"May I have a moment with him?" Lynn asked. Ryan took her pack, stepped to the side, and set out supplies to build a makeshift gurney: telescoping trekking poles, an emergency blanket, duct tape, ropes. Meanwhile, Lynn knelt down beside Will, pressed her hands together, and bowed her head.

"I'm sorry," she whispered. She gently stroked his head. "I'm sorry, Will. For everything. For coming on to you. Hanging you out to dry. And now this. I am so, so terribly sorry."

It sounded trite even if it was sincere, and I almost felt sorry for her. How do you apologize to someone when you've literally ruined his life?

They loaded Will on the gurney and roped themselves to it, and to each other. Lynn took the lead. They half-lifted and half-dragged Will, breaking a new trail because their footprints from a short while ago were already covered by blowing snow. When they got back onto the Football Field, she stopped for a moment, as though listening to the summit's siren call.

It looked like such a quick jaunt to the top from where they stood. Just a short climb for her agate. For my ponytail. But the scale is deceiving there. On a good day, they might have been able to make it to the summit and back to Will in an hour, hour-and-a-half tops. I could see how tempting it would be: they could set Will's heavy gurney down, brace themselves against the exposure on the Summit Ridge, staying to the left on the way out, where everyone says it feels safer. They could stand at the top of North America and let the wind wipe them clean of their sorrows and regrets and mistakes. They could stand up there and smile. But this was not a good day. And an hour of summit time could have meant the difference between life and death for each of them.

"You can always come back another time," Ryan said.

She yanked on the gurney with her rope and moved down toward High Camp without replying, and Ryan watched the route to the summit pass him by, too.

The descent to High Camp was steep and icy, slow and strenuous. They dug their axes in with nearly every step. They stopped often to rest, cough, and breathe, and to scrape ice from their goggles. Ryan checked on Will whenever they stopped, and I wondered what they would do if he stopped breathing, whether they would drag his body back to camp or all the way down the mountain, taking on additional risk, or just leave him there to save themselves and hope that sooner or later a ranger would claim the body. I wondered what I would do. It would be so much easier, just then, to untie him and let him go, watch the gurney skid down the slope hundreds of feet and tumble over an edge.

Nobody else would ever know.

But they didn't, and by the time they got to High Camp—several hours after they should have been back, and soaking in sweat—it was long after midnight. Pellets of ice had rained down on them for the last two hours, and their clothes were heavy, drenched, and frozen. They had not eaten for hours, but neither of them mentioned food. Mark woke up as Lynn dragged Will into the tiny tent, but no one said a thing.

A few hours later, Lynn woke up. Aside from her shivering body, it was so still in the tent that I wondered if anyone else was alive. Finally I saw Ryan shivering, too. The wind thrashed the tent while the ice pounded it. It was torture to watch them, held hostage in a tent that stank of unwashed bodies, unbrushed teeth, flatulence, and rotting skin—a tent that stank of death itself.

Lynn checked to see if Will was breathing and then searched through his pockets. She found a crumpled Ziploc bag with some beef jerky and a handful of dried cranberries. She ate a few cranberries, and when Ryan and Mark awoke, she passed it to them. "Sorry, no more hand sanitizer." They ate their meager meal voraciously, then slept and woke intermittently through the rest of that day.

During the night, Ryan shook her by the shoulders. "Wake up," he whispered.

"Is it Will?" she asked.

"No. Here, drink this." He held out a cup of tea, and she sat up and took it just as he started to cough again. But then she shook her head. "No tea for me."

"Drink it." The dark circles under his eyes matched hers.

She took the mug.

"I'm beginning to think it wasn't worth all this," she said, her teeth chattering. "I'm beginning to think we're not going to make it."

Ryan's hands shook, and his teeth chattered in between the last sips of his tea. "We just need to get down the mountain as soon as we can."

"How can we? With Mark, and Will?" she said.

"Mark can do it."

"And Will?"

"I don't have much hope for him."

They both glanced in Will's direction, and Lynn lowered her voice to a whisper. "Are you suggesting we just...leave him here...to die?"

"First of all, we aren't going anywhere yet. And second, it's not in my hands, Lynn." He pointed his index finger skyward, which was the first time I'd seen him refer to his God in a long time. I hoped that maybe his faith was returning, almost as much as I hoped for his health, because I was sure his faith would be like a shot of Dex for him. "Will hasn't moved since we got him back here. We can't take him down the Headwall on that gurney. We're practically out of food; we don't have a working radio. We don't have any medicine."

"Did we forget to get the solar charger from his pack?"

"I looked," Ryan said. "I didn't see it."

"So what are you saying?"

"What I'm saying is that we don't have a radio, and he needs more help than we can offer. We might have to leave him to get the help he needs."

"We can try to warm him up," she said. She began to undress.

"You don't have to do that."

"Yes, I do."

Ryan watched as she stripped down to her bra and underpants, and also as she gagged when she lay her emaciated body next to Will's body, half-devoured by the elements. He covered them both with her sleeping bag. "Just think about that shower you'll be in soon," he said. "A nice hot shower with lavender soap."

Her stare was blank. "I can't think of that yet. I just need to focus on staying alive."

On Friday morning, Lynn woke to the sound of digging. She looked around; she was the only one in the tent. The ceiling sagged with the weight of accumulated snow, and a small drift had formed in one corner. The ice columns had grown even bigger and were straining the tent's seams. She dressed and went out, squinting at the bright snow. The wind had finally died.

Ryan sat on the ground, twenty feet away, shovel in hand. He wore a bandana around his face. He dug at the snow, chipping away small chunks at a time, as unproductive as a toddler digging in the sand. After two or three digs, he sat still, breathing hard. Then he dug a couple more times and rested again. She watched him for a few minutes before moving toward him but then stopped when she saw Will, lying on the ground just past Ryan, a tarp pulled over his face. She reached her hand out as if to steady herself, even though there was nothing there for support.

She sat next to Ryan. "You look awful." She was right; he did. "How long have you been at this?"

"Forever."

"And where's Mark?"

Ryan shrugged. "Don't know. He was gone when I woke up. His jacket, boots, pack. Everything about him was gone. I wondered for a second if I'd imagined the whole thing."

"Seriously?"

He nodded. "I don't know why I didn't hear him leave. I didn't think I was even sleeping. I thought I heard thunder, though."

"I didn't hear any; you must have been dreaming." She dug for a minute, then stopped. "I wonder why he'd decide to climb down without us? After we rescued him. What an ass."

"I guess that's just who he is," Ryan said. "Selfish. A lone wolf. An outcast."

"Well, all I have to say is that he's going to have quite a time of it getting down on his own, with those frostbitten toes." She leaned around Ryan to look at the shape beneath the tarp and held her mittened hand to her mouth.

"By the way, I am sorry," she said.

"Are you apologizing to me or to Will?"

"I don't really know."

They took turns chipping away at the grave with the shovel. Finally, Ryan dragged Will's body to it, staggering and nearly falling into it himself.

"It's not deep enough," she said.

Ryan ripped off his goggles and looked at her with cold eyes. "It'll have to do. We'll cover him with snow and rocks. I can't dig anymore."

She lifted the tarp and reached into one of Will's pockets, fishing out the picture of his wife and daughter. Then she walked away, leaving Ryan to deal with the mess.

"We need to go down now," she said when Ryan came back to the tent. She handed him a lukewarm mug of weak tea, made with the last used teabag. She was right, they had to go down, and the break in bad weather was like a gift from heaven. "I should have insisted on it days ago. I'm sorry. I'm sorry for everything." And from my perspective she should have been sorry. But Ryan didn't say anything. He just sat and slowly sipped the tea.

"You'll have to go by yourself," he finally said, surprising both Lynn and me. She placed her hand on her chest exactly where I felt a stabbing pain myself.

"Don't be silly. We need to stay together."

Yes, I wanted to say. The three of us need to stay together.

"I can't. I can't do it."

"What do you mean? You just dug another man's grave, not your own! You can do this, Ryan. Of course you can. You just need some time to rest. Take your time, get some sleep. We'll do this, you'll see. Remember how you said, before we found Mark, that we were in this together? Well, that hasn't changed one bit. We still are. Besides, you're just a young whippersnapper. If I can do it, so can you."

Although he looked more like a sullen old man, I appreciated Lynn's effort and encouragement. She pulled his travel Bible from his open pack—the one I'd bought for him after we moved back to Oregon. I'd left it for him in the basket with Brad's brochure, with the hope he'd pack it for this trip. I was thankful he did, especially because it had a picture of Frankie and me tucked inside. She opened the Bible.

"If you're going to read that," he said, "then hand me your journal. Fair trade."

She reached into her pack for the notebook, and gave it to Ryan. "Keep in mind this is just one of my many journals."

They silently skimmed and read a few passages and flipped through each other's pages. I guessed it was like reading foreign literature; Lynn—from what I knew—was no expert on God, and Ryan was reading the intimate thoughts of a woman he'd only recently met. Once in a while he would stop and look up at her, and they would exchange a raised brow or a weak smile, but only for a moment. Then, Ryan came to the blank pages at the back of her notebook.

"It isn't finished," he said. His words, once again, were slow and slurred.

She put her finger on a page in the Bible to hold her place

and studied his face before answering. "No, you're right. It's not."

"What...else...are you planning to write?" Suddenly, every word now required an enormous effort, and I noticed his voice was huskier and his breath wheezier than before. He panted after each short question. "What else...do you want to tell Sunny?"

She held his Bible to her chest, her finger still marking the page. "I don't know anymore. I was going to write about this climb, about my final accomplishment, about the last agate for her. But now I'm not so sure." She touched the pendant. "Now I think I should write about failure."

He did not look directly at her but rather let his gaze wander around the tent. It was an old trick he used to get someone to talk, almost like a cat who's only nominally paying attention to you. Ryan used to say that eye contact sometimes shut people down, whereas a leisurely study of the surroundings tended to invite confession. But maybe I was being obsessively hopeful; there was the other possibility that his gaze wandered because his mind was drifting off and his brain shutting down.

"I would write first, I think," she said, "about my failure to climb the Seven Summits. My failure to keep the one promise I made to her. And the fear behind my failure."

He lay down on his side, his head propped in his hand. "Surely you don't blame yourself for not achieving the summit? Or maybe you do. Maybe you're even more afraid of success."

"I don't know what you mean."

"That's why you went to look for Will, instead of going for the summit, isn't it? It wasn't really about him. You were afraid to complete your goal, afraid of where that might lead. You're more comfortable with failure."

"No, I told you why I wanted to find Will. And I don't know how you can say I'm more comfortable with failure. I've succeeded on many mountains."

"You only told me part of the truth." He coughed. Blood dripped from his mouth into his hand. "The part you knew. You don't know the other part, about yourself. And those successes, if that's what you want to call them, were a long time ago."

"What do you mean the part I don't know about myself? Christ, I even confessed to you that I'm lazy and afraid."

"Self-sabotage."

She looked stunned, and I admit I was too. She dropped the Bible and squinted at him. "You have some nerve. Are you suggesting I never wanted to reach the summit?"

"The thought has crossed my mind. Maybe you didn't. The summit was always an obstacle that kept you from having to face Sunny. Once that obstacle is removed, then what?"

I hadn't thought about it that way, but his theory held some validity. And then I turned it on myself. Had I somehow set this whole climbing debacle in motion so that I couldn't rest in peace? Had I sabotaged my life-after-death by devising a scheme that allowed me to stay connected to the living?

"So let me get this straight," Lynn said. "You think I don't really want to succeed because if I do, I'd then *have* to find

Sunny? You think I'm afraid of seeing her?"

And *I* don't want to succeed for the opposite reason. I don't want to let go.

"Something like that."

I could tell she was thinking it over. "Oh, I see. You think I'm afraid to see her because I'd have to face up to my adoption decision. And whether or not it was a good one. Well, I'm sorry. You're wrong. You're way off base. I am not afraid of success." She stopped and sucked in a deep breath as though she'd been running for miles. "Maybe it's you who's afraid. Maybe you're the self-saboteur, afraid of facing your miserable life alone—if you do succeed and make it back down." She reached out and snatched her notebook back from Ryan, and he looked at her like a downtrodden old man whose only possession has been stolen away.

She started to put her boots on.

"And then—switching back to the original topic," she said, "—then I'd write a letter to Greg. Damn, I never did call him back. I wonder why he kept calling. Anyway, I screwed that one up too, didn't I? Is that what you're thinking? He was another great guy who loved me and I never appreciated him for what he had to offer? Well, I suppose you're right. I focused more on our differences, especially the irritating ones; I focused on hanging on to control."

As did I.

Ryan shifted, now like an old dog searching for a comfortable spot. Lynn kicked a boot, wrapped her arms around her knees, and dropped her forehead to her arms.

"I have some other things to write about too," she said

after a gaping silence. "It's not all doom and gloom. Just in case you're wondering."

He raised his eyebrows, and for the first time since they left for the summit, I saw the green sparkle in his eyes.

"There's trust. And forgiveness. And survival, too."

"You've probably tempted survival many times on your expeditions."

"Yes, I have, and I don't know why I have survived—impossible terrain, suffocating jungles, even Maoist guerillas one year. Why did I make it through all those things when others didn't? I don't think it's skill, and I certainly am no more eligible for luck than anyone else. Maybe it has more to do with determination." She reached out to him. "The desire to survive, I mean."

He wrapped his gloved fingers around her mitten. "I had a friend tell me he didn't think I had a desire to live anymore. He said I didn't care what happened to me."

"Do you?"

"I'm not sure. He may have been right. Maybe I don't." With this he went into another violent coughing spasm that seemed like it would never end.

Dear Lord, this was not what I needed to hear, this apathy. I'd wanted him to climb Denali to rekindle his faith, to regain his joie de vivre—not to lose his interest in living. And even though I was starting to see in myself a shadow of resentment that he was alive and I wasn't, or an unbecoming need for control, or even a darker desire that he join me here on this balcony, I didn't *really* want him to give up on life, to lose all hope, to not care. To stop caring, I decided, must be an even deeper level of hell. Worse than being ripped away from loved ones, or discovering your mistakes, or not being able to correct them. Worse than being mired in madness. Worse than not feeling physical pain. Apathy must be the sixth level of hell, and thankfully I wasn't there yet.

"I need to go outside," he said. He started to put his jacket on upside down, and she helped him get it right.

"And I'd write more about love," she said. Ryan did not respond. "Not love for anyone in particular, not romantic love. Just love."

He kept dressing, and she kept talking.

"It took me nearly fifty years to figure out the importance of love. How pathetic is that? But it's true. I didn't know how to grow love. Imagine someone destined to be a gardener who wasn't able to grow flowers. Or someone who loves children, who can't have babies." Now of course he stopped and looked at her from the corner of his eye. "I've wanted to love but haven't known how to show it, or maybe it's been there all along, but I thought there was no one to give it to."

Ryan now had his goggles, jacket, and hat on but no pants other than his long johns, and he started to take off his socks instead of putting on his boots. The toes on his left foot were starting to look like Mark's. Lynn didn't say anything, she simply reached over and stretched his sock back over his foot and pushed the boots on his feet, one by one.

"And then you came along," she said. "You."

He raised his goggles and I saw a ghost of those crinkles at the corners of his eyes. "Me?"

"Yes, you."

Holy shit, she was either manipulating him once again or falling in love with my husband. Not good, either way. Not good at all. I was feeling sick the way you feel when you're on a roller coaster that goes not only up and down but also jerks you sideways and spins you around.

"At first, I admit, I didn't like you very much, or at least you frightened me," she said. "I haven't been this close to a pastor since I was baptized as a baby. But when you climbed out of that crevasse, something switched on inside me."

Finally dressed, he crawled toward the tent door, listing to one side and then the other, like a man on the deck of a boat being tossed in the waves.

"Ryan, I'm trying to tell you something. I think I love you."

He stopped, one arm outstretched for the tent door's zipper. He started to cough. "Say again?" He coughed again, and again, and I needed him to stop so I could listen to what she was about to say. She loved Ryan?

"Yes, I do. I think I do. You did something to me, you changed me. I do believe I love you and everyone here all of a sudden."

He looked around. "I don't see anyone but you and me."

"I know, not right now. But the team. And everyone else on the mountain. And people not on the mountain, too. All of a sudden, there it is, this warm feeling about everyone in the world. I think it must be love." He was struggling with the tent zipper. She reached over to help him. "Corny?"

"Yeah." He wheezed. "Delusional too. Maybe I...should be the one worrying about you. But right now, I've got to go."

He dove through the tent door.

She lay back in her bag, reading his Bible and smiling, and it reminded me of how I used to lie in bed and read his old Bible after we'd made love. It was marked up all over the place with his pencil and ink marks and my occasional spilled wine. Ryan would underline and highlight passages that he wanted to incorporate into a sermon, and I'd even circle the ones that spoke to me. Some nights we'd fall asleep reading to one another, and we'd wake in the morning, the Bible nestled between us where we'd hoped someday a child might lie.

But I still didn't trust her. She didn't even notice that Ryan hadn't roped himself to her or the tent.

After a while, his voice wafted into the tent, and she turned the Bible over on the floor and listened. It started as a whisper, a hissing whisper that an angry person might use in a middle-of- the-night argument. But then his voice strengthened; he was definitely in a heated conversation with someone. She sat up, pulled on her jacket and boots, and crawled out of the tent.

29 Chapter Twenty-Nine

When Frankie came into the kitchen Friday morning, there was a visitor at the table biting into a slice of Mrs. Farley's pumpernickel bread. It was Jack.

"Good morning, Kitten."

Frankie stood in the doorway, tugging at the cuffs of her long-sleeved shirt. She glanced at Dalton and Jessie.

"You don't look too happy to see me," Jack said. "But I must say, I'm relieved to see you. You have no idea how worried I've been." He stared into his coffee, then told her she looked pretty good. "Better than the last time I saw you. Maybe this ranch life is good for you."

She did have a healthy glow to her skin from all that fresh air and hard work in the high desert sun. Or maybe from living in what had seemed to be a happy, nourishing home.

"How did you find me?" Frankie asked. She pulled a chair up to the table and Mrs. Farley stood behind her, with her hands placed on the back of the chair.

"It was a team effort," Jack said. "The Utah program called to tell us you'd run away, and they reported you missing to the state police. We alerted the authorities in Illinois and Iowa, while at the same time Dalton, unbeknownst to us, had contacted the County sheriff here. Funny thing, though, none of the state police talked to one another at first. Finally it was Beatrice who put two and two together, after your escapades at O'Hare, and we figured you were probably trying to get to Oregon again. So the Illinois police contacted Oregon, and here I am. But not for long. You and I have a flight out in a few hours."

"So soon?" Mrs. Farley said. "Why don't you stay a while? Frankie could show you how she's learned to ride a horse."

"That's kind of you," Jack said to her. "But I've spent more time this week looking for Frankie than tending to my business. And there are still some things regarding her mother that need attention."

Everyone turned to look at Frankie.

"You have a mother?" Jessie said.

"Of course she does," Jack said.

Dalton scowled. "That's not what you told us."

"Long story," Frankie said. "But I can't leave yet, Papa. I still want to see Ryan."

Jack took a deep breath. "Well, we've done some searching for him too. I feel like a private investigator these days."

"I know what you mean," Dalton said.

"We think he's in Alaska," said Jack.

"Climbing Denali?" Her face brightened.

"I don't know. Did he tell you that?"

"No, but Beth talked about Alaska a lot, about how she always wanted to climb Denali with Ryan. Why else would he go up there?"

"Well, you may have solved one of the pieces of our little puzzle. We—Beatrice and I—were able to get a hold of a friend of Ryan's out here, a man named Tom Marquardt, who happened to be on Cece's old Christmas card list. Cece was my wife," he explained to Dalton's family. "Anyway, we wound up exchanging emails and he said Ryan left for Alaska about three weeks ago, but he didn't say why or where. That's as far as we got. But the good news now is that we know where to look for him. But not today. I need to get back to work."

Frankie bit into a big strawberry. The juice dripped down her chin, and she wiped it with the back of her hand. "Can't we just stay here a little longer? All you do is work, work, work. Can't we stay at least until Ryan comes home?"

"She's welcome to stay with us," Jessie said.

Jack denied Frankie's request to stay on, but he did let her convince him to drive out to our cabin before packing up to go home. It was another sunny day in Central Oregon, and red-tailed hawks circled against the blue sky. Horses stopped grazing and lifted their heads as Frankie and Jack drove past, and she asked him if he'd ever seen any place so beautiful.

"I'm not sure if I have," he said. He looked awestruck.

A branch had fallen across the mouth of our driveway, its twigs reaching for the car's tires like fingers. Frankie jumped out of the car, dragged the branch to the side, and raced Jack and the rental car to the house.

The doors were still locked, of course, and the blinds still drawn. Nothing had changed since Frankie's last visit other than more ponderosa needles on the ground and a fallen bird nest on the porch. Frankie led Jack, with Jessie's picnic basket, around the property. They stopped at the riverbank to watch the water ripple past, and Jack tried to get her to talk about why she'd run away from Utah. She refused to answer any of his questions. Finally, frustrated, he raised his voice. "Talk to me, Frankie!"

"Fine. You want me to talk? Okay, I'll talk. I'll tell you I'm not going back to Chicago."

"That's not an option."

"But what if I don't want to? What if I want to stay here? What are you going to do, hire those snatchers again?" She waved her arms wide. "Look at this place. It's heaven. Listen to the river, to the squirrels sassing in the trees." She picked up a pine cone. "Here, take this. Smell it. Feel the prickles. See what I mean?"

Jack sniffed at the pine cone. "Yes, of course Kitten, I see what you mean. In fact, this little pine cone reminds me of you. Small and perfect, but with a dangerous edge."

"I'm not joking, Papa. I don't want to leave."

"It's beautiful here, I agree. But you're too young to decide where to live. You need to come home with me. Besides, doesn't family count for something?"

"I have a family here."

"Dalton's?"

"No. Ryan."

"He's not your real family," he said. Although accurate, his comment stung. We were as close to family as she could get without a blood connection or legal adoption papers. "What about me? And your mother?" He checked his watch.

"Raina's not a real mother."

She ran up to the deck and walked its perimeter, running her fingers along the cedar railing that Ryan had built only months earlier. Jack was still down by the river.

"She's working on it, Frankie," he called up to her. "She's doing well in rehab. I've visited her a couple of times. It's a nice facility. And she's asked about you."

She rested her elbows on the railing. "She has?"

He approached the deck and set the picnic basket down at the base of the wooden stairs. "Yes, she has. She loves you, you know. She's worried about you."

Frankie threw a few pine cones over the railing. "Come on, please. You know she won't really change. How long is she in for this time, a month? You expect her to change after only thirty days of not using? Besides, she's probably already found a way to sneak alcohol and drugs in there, or she's turning tricks, or something. She's been trouble since the day she could walk and talk, Papa, and you know it. You've basically told me that yourself."

"I know I have. But I still think she's trying. I still think she loves you. I'm sorry, I don't know what else to say."

"That's because there isn't anything to say." Her back was still turned to him. "Maybe now you understand why I don't want to talk."

He thought for a while. What do you say to a teen like Frankie—a stubborn, chronic runaway? That you're going to send her away again? That she can live with you, where she doesn't want to be, knowing full well you can't shackle her to the bed?

"So you'd just leave me like that?" he asked. "To stay here?"

She turned. "Please don't lay that guilt thing on me." She ran back down to the river's edge, took off Jessie's work boots and socks, and dipped her toes into the cold water. How I wished I could have stood beside her then, feeling the slippery rocks beneath my feet, the rushing water massaging my toes and ankles. She squatted down, collected a pool of water in her hands, and splashed it on her face, and I remembered how I'd loved to do the same thing. There is nothing more invigorating than a splash of cool water, not from a metal pipe, but direct from the earth, replete with the scent of soil and minerals and life itself. She came back barefoot across the bed of pine needles and sat down at our picnic table.

"There's nothing like this in Chicago," she said. "I can see why Ryan and Beth moved back here."

She reached into the picnic basket and ripped off a piece of bread. "And I'd have Ryan. I'm sure he'd let me stay with him. I know he would. I bet he'd even teach me to climb a mountain. Just a small one. What if we just stay here until he gets back so we can ask him?" She pointed at the cabin's back door, and I longed to be standing there welcoming her. "You and me, just stay here, the two of us?"

"And how do you suggest we get in?" I was surprised he

didn't bring up his work obligations; even Jack seemed to be falling under the spell of the high desert.

She grinned.

"No, we are not breaking in, Kitten. Absolutely not. That's against the law."

"Only if Ryan pressed charges, which he wouldn't do. Come on, Papa. Lighten up."

She was right about that, Ryan wouldn't press charges. He would love nothing more than to come home and find Frankie there, dressed in some of my old clothes, her long legs sprawled atop the old pine coffee table, a novel in her hands, a mug of hot chocolate at her side. If he had known it was even a remote possibility—even with all her quirks and issues—maybe he would have been more motivated to come down from Denali. If only I had a way to tell him.

"Now where's that Swiss army knife of yours?" she said.

Jack sighed. "Hold on."

He called Tom and told him he was now out in Oregon to retrieve Frankie. He also asked if he'd heard any more about Ryan. When Tom told Jack he hadn't heard a thing, Jack said Frankie was hoping to stay at our cabin until Ryan got home.

"What did he say?" Frankie asked.

"He said hell, yes. He's on his way out here with the spare key right now."

After Tom got there, Frankie raced through the cabin, touching every doorjamb and countertop, and I hadn't seen Jack smile like that since long before Cece died. He made some phone calls to cancel meetings in Chicago, and then called the airline to cancel their tickets.

Meanwhile, Frankie stretched out on our bed. She pulled book after book down from my shelves, reading random lines here and there—I take full credit for bestowing upon her a love of literature—and she even glanced through my Bible, a book about Zen scriptures, and my copies of the Vedas, the Tanakh and the Koran. I had always been curious about different religions, right up until my death when I wondered what the afterlife was really like, if there was one at all. I had never argued with Ryan about whether Christianity was the correct religion or whether Jesus was the one true Savior; somehow he honored my right to be curious and I honored his right to believe as he chose. Of course, the parishioners never knew this about us.

Frankie's explorations continued through our closets, dresser drawers, and kitchen cupboards, and she even inspected under the bed. If anyone else had done this, I would have been appalled and offended, but this was my dear Frankie. When she went outside to the back deck, where Jack had set out the picnic lunch that Jessie had packed for them, she wolfed the food down and then dozed off in the warm sun on a chaise lounge.

Later that afternoon, they drove back to the ranch. Dalton greeted them on the front porch, along with Peta and Alice. Dalton held the door open for Frankie, who went directly to the kitchen where a plate of peanut butter cookies sat on the table.

"I've been doing some thinking," Dalton said as he leaned

against the kitchen counter. "After learning you lied to us about being an orphan, I did some digging, and I think your grandfather should know some things. Come on in and have a seat, Jack."

Jack looked confused as he sat across from Frankie.

"First off, I know you stole some money from us," Dalton said. "From her purse." He pointed his finger at Mrs. Farley, just then walking into the kitchen, as if somehow she was complicit in the alleged thefts.

"Did not," Frankie said.

"I know for a fact you did," Dalton said. "Because I set a trap. I had a hunch about you right from the beginning. Anyway, I left her purse zipper open one night," he pointed again at Mrs. Farley, "and later on the zipper was closed. You were the only one upstairs at the time. There's proof right there you took something."

"All it proves is that I was nosey, and there's no damn crime about that now is there?"

"Frankie, watch your language," Jack said.

"But that's not all." He set Frankie's Koran on the table. "I found this under the sofa cushion. This explains why you've been spending so much time on the Internet looking at all those Arab countries."

"Arab countries?" Jack said.

"I've been looking at maps and stories about Iran, Papa."

Dalton ignored her. "And all I can say is that, with you running away all over the country, it got me to thinking about whether you're involved in some sort of terrorist cell. You hear about these things all the time on the news nowadays, with wayward teenagers getting caught up in all sorts of trouble."

"Hold on a minute," Jack said. "Are you accusing Frankie of being a terrorist?"

"Dalton!" said Mrs. Farley.

"Well, just look at her. She certainly doesn't look like a normal American girl."

Frankie flushed as everyone looked at her.

"Are you referring to her complexion?" Jack asked. He stood up so fast that his chair knocked over backward onto the floor. "I've never been so insulted in my entire life. Come on, Frankie."

Frankie did not move, no doubt trying to understand what had just happened. This ideal family was not ideal after all. I wished Jessie had been in the room at the time; she may have been able to talk Dalton down.

"You heard your grandfather," Dalton said to Frankie. "You need to get going. Go pack up your things and get out of here. Before I call the FBI."

Mrs. Farley rested her hands on Frankie's shoulders. "She didn't do anything to hurt us, Dalton. If anything, she's been a blessing here."

"We don't know that, now do we? We don't know what that lying little Muslim might have done. She's probably brainwashed our little Chloe."

Silence hung in the room the way death hangs in a mortuary. Frankie straightened and got up from her chair, holding her chin high.

"You asked me to let you know if I needed anything here,"

she said. "But I've just now realized you don't have what I need. And you never will."

An image of Frankie bouncing on the back of one of Dalton's horses, the wind blowing her hair and her laughter lingering in her wake, suddenly loomed in front of me. And the image of her sitting on a railing behind the barn, watching Dalton smoke his joints and laughing at his jokes. And her reading to Chloe and playing fetch with the dogs and helping Mrs. Farley fold the laundry. All that joy and freedom, that carefree childhood delight, that dream of a perfect family, had yet again been yanked away from her. It had been an illusion all along.

"And by the way," she said as she now stood at the back door, "Iran's not an Arab country. You obviously don't know shit."

30 Chapter Thirty

17,200' Elevation

Ryan walked in circles, stumbling and ranting, periodically stopping to point one finger to the sky, now bright and sunlit, having changed drastically once again. He cocked his head to the side, listening to the air, or to voices from somewhere else. He shook his head and walked again and talked again and ranted again, sometimes with words I didn't recognize, words that sounded like they were from another place far away. And he coughed.

It was not the first time he had paced and talked to his God, and there certainly was plenty to pray about. Lynn had just told him she loved him. He had just buried a teammate. They were on the verge of death. But as soon as Lynn stepped out of the tent and saw him, she went for a rope and her medical kit, and I saw what she'd seen. This was HACE, a fast-acting villain.

Ryan dropped to his knees and covered his face with his gloved hands. He started to shake and then heave and convulse, all the while coughing and sputtering words indecipherable to the human ear. He tore off his goggles and pressed his forehead, nose, and palms into the bitter snow, like utter submission. I tried to shout to him, tried to tell him to pull it together, to no avail.

I was in my balcony behind what may as well have been soundproof glass. I could not get his attention. I could not do anything but watch the slow-motion self-destruction of the one person I loved more than any other, more than life itself. This was worse than hell, far worse than demons with pitchforks and fiery pits. I had yet to figure out what I'd done to deserve this torture, although it was starting to become clear, like a lone figure coming toward you through dense fog.

He pulled himself back to his knees and dropped his hands to his sides and let his head flop back. With closed eyes and tears streaming down both cheeks, he whispered Tom's name, Lynn's name, Frankie's name. And then he called out one more name, putting what seemed to be every ounce of his strength into it, the sound of which reverberated against the surrounding peaks and bounced back to him again and again. It was not God's name he bellowed, but mine.

"Beth!"

Lynn ran to him as fast as she could, and kneeled beside him, wrapping her arms around him, the hypodermic needle in her hand. When she released him, he leaned away from her and fell sideways, as though he'd been shot, then landed in a loose fetal position, slamming his head against the frozen ground. She bent down and listened for his breath.

"Fine, then," he said, his voice less than a scraping whisper. "All right, fine."

She did not give him the injection, and instead tried to coax him up. But every time she lifted him, he fell back over. After several tries, she cupped her arms under his armpits and dragged him back toward the tent, stopping three times along the way to catch her own breath. His eyes were open but unfocused. He was limp deadweight as she hauled him across the flimsy nylon threshold and onto his sleeping bag. She peeled off her parka and wiped sweat from her forehead and upper lip.

She turned his head so that his dazed eyes faced hers. "Ryan!"

He lay silent and stiff, nearly unconscious. It was clear to me that they had waited too long to descend. She should never have let him rest. She had made another bad decision.

Or was it I who made the bad decision? I had been the one to send him to this mountain. I had been the one to sacrifice him for a purpose I'd inadvertently deemed greater than his life. How ironic that I was criticizing those who sacrifice their loved ones when I had done that very thing. This was why I'd been sentenced to hell.

Where were the angels now, the ones Ryan used to preach about? The ones who were supposed to watch over you? If only there really were angels who could lift him up on gossamer wings and float him back down to Base Camp. If only I could have been his angel, but I could not, for I was not a believer in anything.

"Lynn."

"Ryan? You're all right, yes! You're all right." She brushed his hair, now filthy and matted, from his forehead and told him she had medicine for him. She told him he would be all right.

He closed his eyes and shook his head. "I don't need the Dex."

"Of course you do." She turned her head to cough into her hand. There was blood on her palm when she finished.

"No. You might need it. On your way down."

"What are you saying?"

"I'm saying it's time for you to go. You have to leave me behind."

No, no, no. That wasn't the right answer. My heart was pumping erratically now, the heart I didn't even have. She could not leave him behind. He would die. Alone. I could not bear to watch that.

But it wasn't as simple as being afraid of him dying. Something was niggling in my gut, in my brain. A chorus of sneering voices. And something else. The putrid smell of unadulterated joy.

I was afraid of my own thoughts and intentions.

My subconscious mind was thinking reprehensible thoughts, ideas I couldn't believe were coming from inside me. Those what-if sorts of thoughts, like what if he were to join me? Here? Or even better, in heaven, wherever that was? I could escape this lonely hell. Or if I couldn't escape it, then I could at least be with him again. I cursed myself for those wicked notions. I was no better than Lynn lying about Will because, on a ghoulishly selfish level, there was a part of me now hoping my own husband would die. I was making myself sick.

I didn't know why Ryan had called out my name, whether for help or forgiveness. Maybe he thought he was letting me down. It didn't matter, though. If anyone should have been asking for forgiveness, it was me.

Lynn spat into her hands, rubbed them together, and wiped the blood from her palms onto her pants. "You're out of your mind."

"It's your blood, not mine," he said, his voice now raspy. "If you leave, that doesn't mean you'll have my blood on your hands. You know that, right?" His body writhed as he coughed, and I now saw as he shifted that his nose had started to blacken and that spots of blood caked his beard. "You aren't responsible for me."

"You once told me I didn't care about anyone, including myself," she said, after a moment's pause. Her eyes were brimming with tears. "But the fact is I do care. And I can't leave you here."

"Then you'll die here, with me, proof that you don't care about yourself." He struggled with each word. "You'll die, and I don't think you're ready for that. You have more to do."

"Like what, face the stark void of retirement from climbing? By myself? And what about you? Are you saying you don't have more to do?" When he didn't answer, she held her hands to his cheeks. "You're cold. But the rangers will be here soon now that the weather's clear. We just have to hang on a little longer." She lay down beside him and threw an arm over his chest.

"We don't know that."

"You have to have faith."

He laughed. It was a weak one, but a laugh nevertheless. "So now you're preaching to me? About faith?" He inhaled a shallow breath and exhaled a gurgling moan. "You go. You can get them up here faster, guide them to me."

"I don't know if I can do it by myself." She hugged him, tightly, until her squeeze made him cough yet again. When she pulled back, I saw how their tears had flowed together on his cheek and had run down to his neck, where I used to bury my face and breathe in his scent.

I felt more helpless than I had felt lying in my hospital bed hooked up to all those tubes and monitors.

Ryan shivered. "You know how I heard thunder? There's an old Welsh superstition," he whispered. "About winter thunderstorms."

She sat up. "Brad said Auntie had a superstition about thunder too. He said I wouldn't want to know what it was. I have a feeling I don't want to hear yours either."

"A winter thunderstorm means death."

"Will's."

"No. Not just any man's death."

She waited. "Then whose?"

"The death of the most important man in the parish."

"The priest? Or pastor?"

"Likely yes, he would be the one." His eyes were closed as he said this, but he nodded as though affirming his own statement.

She sat up again, wiped a single tear from the corner of his eye, and then from her own cheek. "What do the Welsh say about tears?"

He chewed on his blue lip. With great effort, he answered her. "Some say if you cry for a dying person it will hinder his peaceful journey to the next world."

Ryan had cried for me.

She wiped the rest of her tears and her runny nose and asked what she could do for him.

"Read to me."

She sat up. She reached for her journal and started to read from a random page in the middle. He shook his head.

"The Bible."

Thank the Lord. He had not abandoned his God after all. I now wished I'd been more convinced of what God had to offer.

She picked up his Bible and placed it on her lap. "Can I ask you a question?"

"Shoot."

"What do you know about the Koran?"

For a while I thought he had fallen asleep, or worse. Then he whispered, "There are many paths to God."

"Is it ever too late? I mean, to find your path?"

Her question brought a smile to his face. "No. Never too late."

Perhaps that meant there was hope for me, too.

She started to read from Genesis.

"No, Psalms."

She flipped through the Bible until she found it. “Are you sure you don’t want the Dex? I’ve got it right here ready for you. But once you take the shot, you’ve got to promise me you’ll descend.”

“Just read.”

She blinked away tears. “ ‘Blessed is the man who does not walk in the counsel of the wicked’?”

“Psalm 59, toward the end. The dogs.” He tried to take a deep breath, but he couldn’t. It sounded like someone blowing through a straw into a drink. He closed his eyes.

She frantically started flipping through Psalms. “I don’t understand,” she said. Her voice was elevated, panicked, the way she’d been in her hotel room before the climb. “You were fine yesterday, Ryan. Even this morning. How could this happen so quickly? Don’t do this to me.”

He groaned as he turned away from her. “You know it happens. Please, just read.”

She took a deep breath when she found the page.

“*They return at evening,*
snarling like dogs,
and prowl about the city.
They wander about for food
and howl if not satisfied.”

She set the Bible on her lap. “Who prowls and howls? Who are they talking about here?”

“Keep reading.”

“*But I will sing of your strength*
In the morning. I will sing of your
love;

for you are my fortress,

my refuge in times of trouble."

"That's so, incredibly beautiful. But what does it mean? Does this mean you'll be stronger in the morning? Tell me it does."

He opened his mouth as if to speak but was immediately out of breath. "Go. Psalm 23."

She turned the pages and read the first few lines. "No, I know that one. We're not going there."

His lungs rattled as he took in and let out another breath. "Okay, then 147. Read it to yourself." He stopped to inhale as deeply as he could. "Until you get...to the part...about unfailing...love." She did as he asked.

"*The Lord delights in those who fear*

him

who put their hope in his

unfailing love."

I had heard that Psalm countless times but only now did it ignite a sense of dread in me. All those years I spent questioning God's existence. If he were here somewhere, he was certainly not delighted in me. I had neither feared him nor put my hope in him.

Ryan lay there, flushed. "Now skip ahead. To 148. The second half. Praise...the...Lord."

She flipped back and forth until finding the right page, hurriedly, practically tearing the pages as she did. She skimmed with her finger to the part he requested.

"*Praise the Lord from the earth, you great sea creatures and all ocean depths,*

lightning and hail, snow and clouds,

stormy winds that do his bidding,

you mountains and all hills."

"Stop there." He slipped his hand into one of his pockets and fumbled around. First he pulled out my ponytail, with the cross and feather, and handed it to Lynn. His weak laugh opened up a fit of hacking and phlegm that made his back arch unnaturally.

She asked if there was anything she could do for him, and he said he'd like a glass of wine.

"I want...to take...communion," he said.

"I guess water will have to do." She gave him a sip from her canister.

He closed his eyes. His lips moved without sound. When he was done, he fished around in his pocket again and pulled out a folded and creased picture of Frankie with me. It had been shot in my rose garden. She took it from him.

"Is this Beth?"

He nodded.

"And who's the girl?" She peered closely into the photograph.

"Frankie. Jack and Cece's granddaughter. I told you about her."

She knitted her eyebrows together, then looked up at Ryan. "They—your friends—were the ones that adopted a daughter, right?"

He nodded. "Raina."

"And this is their adopted daughter's daughter?"

He nodded again. It was a barely visible nod, but it was there.

"It's the eyes," she said. "I know those eyes."

He groaned and coughed. "I know what you're thinking," he finally said. "I don't know...the answer. Only God knows. And...maybe Beth. Now go."

She set the Bible on his stomach and helped him place his hands upon it. She told him he never taught her how to pray.

"You know. It's in your heart."

"Hold on, Ryan. Please hold on. Someone will be here soon, God willing."

I couldn't quite hear what he said next. It may have been *Insha'Allah*, as though he were preparing Lynn for Frankie's spiritual quest. Then he took in a long but shallow breath, and when he exhaled, it sounded like a baby's rattle.

31 Chapter Thirty-One

17,200' Elevation

Now Lynn had no choice. The early afternoon sky was clear of clouds and the winds had died; it was eerily quiet, as quiet as a tomb, and if Lynn didn't hurry the tent would become just that. She folded herself into lotus position and chanted that me-mantra of hers for about a minute while I nervously sat at the edge of my seat waiting, willing her to just go already. Finally, she melted snow for her water bottle, stuffed her daypack with minimal gear, and unclasped her necklace with the final agate. She looped it around Ryan's finger. In exchange, she slipped my ponytail, with its cross, into her pocket.

She kissed him on the mouth and left.

Unfortunately, the view from my godforsaken balcony wasn't an omnipresent one, and I had to make a choice. I could have stayed there with Ryan, hoping that somehow my presence would give him strength. Or I could have watched Lynn downclimb. I needed to know that she made it safely and would do everything in her power to send rescuers up to him. She was his only hope. So I went with her, perhaps another poor choice on my part.

I followed her along the ridge, across the football field, down the Headwall, and into Camp 3. The ranger's tent was still empty, which made sense if the rescue team had descended and not been able to make it back up yet. She searched for a cache at the camp, the way Frankie had searched through garbage cans in the park in Burns for something, anything, to eat. She pushed into the wind at Windy Corner, and then stopped abruptly at a panoramic lookout facing the Northwest Buttress and a wall known as Father and Son's Face. She nodded, as though someone were talking to her. Then she moved on again, and I watched from a distance as she descended Motorcycle Hill, one small figure staggering against a vast and white open terrain with the whirr of frozen air streaming across the snow, until she collapsed.

I looked around, but there was no one as far as I could see. No climbers coming up the slopes. No helicopters searching for Ryan, Lynn, or Will. The storms had been so horrific that everything on Denali seemed to have frozen in time. Once again, I had the urge to run, to shout, to get help. To yell at her to get up, God damn it! Get up! But there was nothing I could do for her, and nothing I could do for Ryan. I felt like a poor soul hammering on the inside of her coffin lid.

Then Lynn sat up as abruptly as she'd collapsed. She looked pale and shaken as she shifted to her knees and lifted her head up. Toward me? Toward God? Toward Ryan at High Camp?

And then I knew. Ryan was dead.

32 Chapter Thirty-Two

11,000' Elevation

I was struck with a blizzard of emotions unlike anything I'd experienced while alive. Pain, shock, sorrow, anger, regret, frustration—all of those, yes, but something else too. Something that reeked of curiosity—and elation. As a dog anticipates her master coming home, I felt a pulsing in my heart, a sensation that Ryan might be nearby. It sounds monstrous, I know, but I couldn't squelch those feelings of hope that he was near, that he would soon find me. We would be together again. I tried to force those thoughts out of my head like a mother trying to push a demonic baby out of her womb, with all my might and then some. And at the same time I tried to shift my view, my vantage point, away from Lynn, to find Ryan. But I couldn't; it was as though the channel he was on had gone off the air.

And then came a gnawing feeling in my gut, a sort of mimicry. Dear Lord, I thought. Was this the deepest level of hell, the seventh level? A bitter, jealous, eternal loneliness where you see how you've been set aside? You see that others who have died are in a different place? It had struck me as odd that I hadn't found my friend Cece here. And now it seemed Ryan had joined me in death, but he was not here with me, not here in hell. If only I had found something to believe in before I'd died, perhaps then I wouldn't be in this wretched place. Here I was, a minister's wife, doomed. I wondered if it was too late now.

Lynn's snowshoes crunched on top of the crusty ground. She kept going, steadily and quickly. The descent usually takes a couple of days with rest periods; but at this pace, she would be back in Base Camp in record time. She had climbed through the night, and it was now early morning. All those years of self-discipline were paying off.

Whereas Camp 3 had been empty, with only a few ravens digging in the snow for scraps of food, Camp 2 now hosted several climbing teams. Lynn approached a Brazilian team that was just setting out from camp. The Brazilians, however, either spoke little English or cared little about what she had to say. Just behind them was an American team. She frantically explained what had happened, and they let her use their satellite phone. She called Marisa.

Words tumbled from her mouth and tears poured from her eyes. She told Marisa about Ryan, and about Mark and Will too. She asked how long until a helicopter could reach Ryan, and she told Marisa she planned to keep descending on her own to Base Camp.

As the Americans listened, they reached into their packs for food and offered a water bottle to Lynn, too. She nodded and took their gifts.

"By the way, Marisa, I'm sorry I never thanked you for everything you do. It means a lot to me." Her voice was at least an octave too high and almost squeaky; her tears and nose were running uncontrollably, and she didn't even try to wipe them. This was not the Lynn Van Swol of three weeks ago.

"And thank you for the eagle feathers." She still had the feather Marisa had given her, and she also had Ryan's—attached to my ponytail. She had two feathers, and he had none. She was alive. He was not.

When Lynn got to Camp 1, two rangers were waiting for her. She asked if they knew anything about Ryan; they said no news yet. They gave her clean, dry socks and gloves and a bottle of Gatorade, and they offered to let her rest a while before they escorted her down to Base Camp, but she insisted on continuing her descent.

Marisa was waiting for Lynn with her uncle's Beaver. Several climbers and the Base Camp manager wanted to ask her questions, but one of the rangers shook his head and led Lynn past them. He climbed into the back seat of the Beaver and left the co-pilot's seat for Lynn. The plane hopped a few times upon takeoff.

"I suspect you're not ready to talk about anything," Marisa said from the pilot's seat. "But be forewarned. There's a throng of people waiting at the airfield, probably more at The Roadhouse. And tonight there will be even more curious gossipmongers at The Fairview. They're well meaning. It's just that in a town this size, when word gets out about missing climbers and other troubles, everyone comes out like grizzlies in the spring."

Lynn leaned her head against the plane's side window most of the way back to Talkeetna. She kept her eyes closed, missing the views of the glaciers and the forests and the braided silty rivers. Only when the plane landed, smoothly, did she open her eyes and sit up straight. A small crowd milled around the plane as soon as Marisa parked.

Lynn scanned the faces, and I did too. I didn't see anyone I knew. Marisa and the ranger broke through the crowd and headed directly for the shuttle van with Lynn's small bit of gear. Lynn followed behind and the throng followed her. I would have expected the great Lynn Van Swol to ignore them and climb into the van with her arrogance intact. But she turned to face them.

Immediately, she was bombarded with questions. How long was she stranded? How bad were the conditions? Is it true there were multiple casualties?

She held up her hands for the crowd to quiet.

"Casualties? How do you define casualties? High altitude climbing almost guarantees casualties of some sort. Frostbite and lost digits. Anguish and despair. Broken relationships, broken equipment, broken souls. And sometimes death."

"So there were deaths?" someone asked.

Lynn glanced at the ranger, who said no deaths had yet

been confirmed.

Somebody asked if she'd made the summit. She straightened and stared with her icy blue eyes.

"No, I didn't reach the summit."

It would have been an easy lie. There was no one there to prove she hadn't made it—but a true climber would never lie.

"Ms. Van Swol," the local reporter said, "I've heard this was your third attempt on the mountain. To what do you attribute your failures on Denali?"

Marisa, having by now climbed into the driver's seat, turned on the ignition and revved the engine. Lynn looked toward the mountain, although it wasn't visible from where she stood. She reached to her bare neck where the necklace had hung for thirty years, and then reached into the pocket where she kept Marisa's eagle feathers and my ponytail and cross.

"I didn't reach the summit. But I wouldn't call this expedition a complete failure. Not from my perspective, anyway."

Strangely, I think Ryan would have agreed.

Nick was outside The Antlers Hotel, juggling his Hacky Sack, when the van pulled up. Mark sat on a rocking chair on the veranda with bandages covering his nose and fingers. Brad opened the van's side door.

Lynn hugged Brad and Nick, then glared at Mark. "You asshole. You could have waited, after what we did for you. Or at least sent someone up to help us."

"I was going to," he said. "But the weather changed

again."

"Bullshit."

The desk clerk handed her a set of room keys. "The second floor corner room. The one you like, Ma'am. Your street clothes are already there, waiting for you." He handed her a stack of messages.

Lynn took a long, hot shower, moisturized her skin, and brushed her teeth. She put on clean flannel pajamas and sat down at the small desk.

Dear Sunny~or should I call you Raina?

I told Ryan I would write about trust and forgiveness. But I don't know where to begin. I do not deserve to be trusted or forgiven.

She set the pen down and picked up the stack of messages. All were from Greg. She cranked the thermostat up to 80 ºF and crawled into the old, sagging bed. She slept until the following morning.

33 Chapter Thirty-Three

Lynn got to The Roadhouse early. It was a balmy day in Talkeetna, already in the mid-70s, and she had slowly strolled down Main Street in her red tank top and tight jeans, looking in shop windows. She walked in through the restaurant's front door and perused the bulletin board. Cabins for rent. Yurts for sale. Poetry and yoga workshops. Birch sap wanted.

She peered into the case of pastries, filled with cinnamon rolls, berry turnovers, bear claws, and muffins, before sitting down at a table with a purple vinyl tablecloth. She was absentmindedly stirring the apple butter on the table when Brad walked in with Marisa and Aashka, followed by Nick and Mark.

"What are you doing here?" Lynn said to Mark.

"I invited him," Nick said. He looked sheepish, but Lynn said that if it was okay with Nick, then it was okay with her.

The waiter seemed to remember her from before the climb.

"Your usual? Fresh fruit, hot oatmeal with honey, and English muffins with huckleberry jam?"

She shook her head. "No sir. I'd like the full order of eggs and reindeer sausage along with your fabulous potatoes, thick-sliced homemade toast, and a hot cup of coffee."

"Lynn?" Brad said. "Do you realize the eggs and sausage are real? They're not made with Tofurky or something like that?"

"Yes, I do."

"And do you have any idea how large that order is? I mean Marisa and I can barely get through a half-order usually."

"Yes, I do. And that's what I'd like to order. And a cinnamon roll too, please," she added.

As they waited for their food, Lynn asked Nick how he was doing collecting money from his friends.

"The bet? But I didn't summit."

"Doesn't matter. You said the bet was for a successful climb, didn't you? I'd say that's open to interpretation. I'd say it was successful for you because you gave it your best shot and you made it down alive."

"I wouldn't think you'd see it that way."

"I wouldn't have thought so either until now."

She burned her tongue on the coffee and ate the food ravenously. Only when their stomachs were full could the inevitable questions no longer be ignored. But Lynn shook her head. "I'm not ready to talk about what happened up there. Someday I will, I promise. But not now, other than what you need, Brad, for your incident reports. And I would like to know what you found out about the missing rangers."

Brad had aged ten years in the past three weeks. His forehead was creased, his brows seemed to be permanently protruding, and there were now flecks of gray in his new and sparse goatee. I imagined Brad would not only be filing incident reports, but he'd also likely be facing an early review by the NPS given what happened on this expedition. A climb like this with all the errors, injuries, and fatalities—due at least in part to negligence—had the potential to reflect poorly on the mountain and the climbing community as a whole unless someone was held accountable.

"It was a series of unfortunate incidents, they said." Brad spooned baby food into Aashka's mouth. "It's been a crazy season up here, already one of the most deadly. They're blaming it on the weather of course. But they had fewer volunteers than usual to help the Park service on the mountain, and more climbers than usual. They had one rescue call after another, and although they didn't want to leave their posts on the mountain, it was unavoidable. Once they left to rescue climbers, they couldn't get back to their stations because of the weather. Eventually they had to descend too, which meant even the rangers had to acclimatize all over again on the way back up. They were starting to head back up as you were coming down. And that was the first break they had in the weather to send out a chopper once we realized you were likely in trouble. We tried, Lynn. Believe me, we tried."

"Nobody's saying it's your fault," Marisa said to Brad, taking the spoon from him and feeding Aashka herself.

They dwelled more on the weather, with the past two

weeks of record snow and savage winds and now the near-tropical conditions the latest climbers were seeing. They gossiped about other teams. Marisa said Aashka was coming down with a sore throat, which Auntie had predicted when she heard the raven croaking before dawn.

"Well, I didn't hear any birds this morning so I guess I'm healthy now," Nick said. "In fact, maybe I'll head back up the mountain. You up for it, Uncle Brad?"

Brad threw his wadded napkin at Nick.

"But in all seriousness," Nick said to Lynn, "I really appreciate everything you did for me. I'm sorry I was so sick." He reached over to her plate and tore off a chunk of what was left of the cinnamon roll.

"Hey, thief!" she said. "Speaking of which, we never found that cache you left at High Camp, Brad. I hate to think it was stolen."

"Doubt it," Marisa said, now spooning applesauce into Aashka's perfectly round mouth. "I'm guessing the only thieves out on the mountain this past week were the ravens."

Lynn tapped herself on the forehead with the heel of her hand. "Of course," she said. "It must have been those damned ravens. I knew it couldn't have been the Koreans, but I couldn't see who else it might have been. It all makes sense now, especially now that I remember Ryan said it was a shallow pit he'd dug."

The conversation stopped immediately when she mentioned Ryan's name. The waiter brought the check and refilled their mugs. Aashka slapped her hands on the table to a melody only she could hear.

"They found his body, you know," Brad said.

"I didn't know," she said. Of course, neither Lynn nor I needed confirmation. We'd known it all along, but still when I heard Brad say the words out loud, I again felt that stabbing pain, and I went into a freefall. Someone remarked that at least Ryan died doing what he loved—as if they had a clue what he loved—and someone else said at least he'd be with his wife now—as if they knew a thing about the afterlife. It was all just clichéd, irritating chatter about my Ryan, the way you talk about something you've read about in the newspaper. Lynn, though, was silent.

When the waiter came back and saw nobody had bothered to pay yet, the conversation about Ryan ended, and they began to squabble about who owed how much.

"Oh, for Christ's sake," Lynn said. She took all of the cash from her wallet and tossed it on the table. "Take it. Who the hell cares how much we have to pay? Ryan's dead. He's gone. Forever. Think about what *he* just paid. The price he paid to climb a mountain he didn't even want to climb, wasn't in any shape to climb, with a dysfunctional team." She glared first at Brad, then at Mark. "The price he paid so you could be a big-shot and climb solo. The price he paid so Brad could come down with Nick. The price he paid so I could get to the top. The price he paid to try to save Will who, by the way, was not the demon I made him out to be, and for that I should forever be damned. He did not rape me. I am the monster in that drama."

"What?" Mark apparently had not heard the story of her allegation or of Will's attempted escape.

But Lynn ignored him and went on. “And then there was the price Ryan paid to throw a damn ponytail into the Athabaskan winds for his dead wife. Just take the damn money and figure it out. Or better yet, leave him,” she tilted her head toward the waiter “a big tip. For Ryan.” She pushed back from the table and stormed out of the restaurant, branding the image of those six tattooed mountain peaks on her back, and the blank space for the seventh, on my memory forever.

She was right. Ryan never wanted to climb Denali, but he did it anyway, for me. He sacrificed his life for me and my stupid, selfish, horrible ponytail and my deceptive plan to introduce Frankie to Lynn. I was certainly not in heaven now, and I’d probably never get there after this. I had sealed my fate.

Back in her room, Lynn packed the remains of her gear. Some things had been left on the mountain with Ryan, and some things were so ragged and wet, she threw them away. What she kept she now stashed into duffels and packs without bothering to fold anything. No more precise military creases and crisp corners, no more organizing by outer or inner layer. It was all jumbled together. She slipped her ID and travel documents into the front pocket of her daypack, and she put her journal and a ballpoint pen from the hotel in the second pocket. At first she’d tucked Auntie’s feathers and my ponytail inside the pack along with her phone, laptop, and extra socks, but then she took them back out. She tied the feathers to the outside of the pack and threw my ponytail and cross into the trash. She had figured out where they really belonged.

She waited in her room, alone, until Marisa called.

"The van's here," Marisa said. "Need help bringing your stuff down?"

Lynn said she had everything under control. But when she got down to the lobby, her expression revealed nothing like self-control. It was as though she were seeing a ghost.

Greg was there. Her ex-lover, a non-climber and another person she'd ruined a relationship with, was there for her.

He was dressed in a bright yellow and green golf shirt, a Palm Springs visor, his khaki shorts, and boat shoes. He was holding a large Styrofoam cup in one hand and a tote bag full of books in the other. He couldn't have looked more out of place if he'd tried.

"Not bad for an old geezer," he said, that same boyish grin accompanying his words.

Lynn shrugged and kept her distance.

"Sorry. I guess it was a bad joke," he said. "Anyway, I heard about the storms. I was worried. And you never returned my messages." He held the cup out to her. "Decaffeinated green tea, blended with hibiscus herbal? No strings attached."

It could have been a scene straight out of a romance movie, but I knew Lynn wasn't ready for it. She smiled a little, nodded her head, and thanked him for the cup of tea.

"We'll have to talk. But not yet," she said.

"I understand."

Mark and Nick charged through the front door and carried

Lynn's gear out to the van. Greg held out the tote bag like a peace offering.

"I brought you some books. Figured you were having reading withdrawals up here. Or at least you could use them as backpack weights. When you're training for your next climb."

"My next climb? Seriously? You've got to be kidding."

Brad hugged her outside. "You'll be getting your check in a couple of weeks," he said. "The full amount."

She nodded.

"Aside from everything that happened, it's been an honor climbing with you, Lynn. Please let me know if you need anything else."

She thanked him for making arrangements to send Ryan's body back to Tom. His body, alone in a box. I got stuck on the image and missed some of the goodbyes. I did see, however, when Marisa took both of Lynn's hands in hers.

"I was worried about you, but Auntie said the Great Wolf Spirit was watching over you. And when the first eaglets were hatched, she knew you would be calling me for rescue."

Lynn raised her eyebrows. "She did? We've never even met."

"I know. But Auntie has a special feeling about people sometimes. This time it was you. She said something about new horizons and eaglets flying high. She said they follow their hearts." She touched her hand to her chest. "That's what Auntie says about you, that you, too, will fly high. Someday." I was glad to hear this, on Lynn's behalf. She'd been through a lot, and although a part of me blamed her for Ryan's death and hated her for the relationship that had blossomed, another part of me loved her for being with him and trying to help him in the end. She'd been through her own version of hell and needed some good news. Despite all my flaws, I could see this much.

"Good old Auntie," Lynn said. "And what about the wolf spirit?"

"Not sure about that. I'll have to ask her."

Nick and Mark said their goodbyes to Brad as Marisa dialed a number on her phone.

"I'm sorry," Mark said. "About everything." Brad simply nodded and shook his hand. But Lynn stepped forward and put one arm around Mark's shoulders.

"I'm not saying I forgive you, not yet anyway. I'm still quite angry with you. But we all have to move on, weave these past few weeks into our lives, and learn from them, as long as we don't forget. We can't forget."

Lynn hesitated as she climbed into the van, looking at the row where she and Will had sat on the way from Anchorage to Talkeetna. This time, she chose the very back row. Nick climbed into the middle row, followed by Mark. Greg hesitated, then climbed into the passenger seat next to Marisa. I guess he figured Lynn wasn't ready for him.

Marisa got in last, and as she pulled away she said she'd just been talking to Auntie on the phone. "She says wolf is a teacher, a pathfinder. And she says the wolf family—or pack—is the highest priority for wolf, except for food of course. Wolves are not meant to be alone. I don't know...does that mean anything to you?"

"Yes," Lynn said. "Stop the van. I forgot something."

She wriggled out, ran back into the hotel, took the key back from the desk clerk, and ran up the stairs two at a time. The wastebasket had not yet been emptied. She retrieved my ponytail and cross.

For the first few minutes, Lynn flipped through the old *Time* magazine that she'd brought to Talkeetna. Again she studied the picture of the young climber on the cover and the other pictures in the story. She re-read the sidebar that mentioned her. She looked at the cover one more time, then threw the magazine to the floor and started to cry softly.

The van rumbled past birch forests, and Marisa talked about an Iditarod musher from the area who'd gone missing recently, and still Lynn cried. Greg turned around only once; by then she was leaning against the window with her eyes closed, clutching her journal and my ponytail in her hands.

The Chugach and Talkeetna Ranges came into view as the van approached Anchorage. Lynn was awake by then, and she opened up her journal—now stained and warped—to the final blank page.

Dear Raina~

It's time for confessions.

I've killed three men.

A man who loved me. A man I pretended to love. A man I did love. I killed them all on Denali. The first fell from me, the second ran from me. The third trusted me.

What more can I say?

I once thought I could ask for forgiveness. I once thought I could find redemption. I now know the truth.

My heart sank as I read her opening line, to think this was the woman I'd been tracking all along. The woman I hoped could take care of Frankie, who in fact was a killer. And yet, I was no better. I had killed Ryan, my own husband, right alongside her. We were co-conspirators in crime.

I had more in common with Lynn than I had originally thought, and more in common with Raina and Frankie than I had ever known. I had wondered, when Frankie was back at O'Hare, whether there was something in her blood that made her who she was, that compelled her to lie and steal and manipulate. Raina certainly didn't abide by society's mores. And in her own way, Lynn didn't either.

No matter how you looked at it, despite our apparent differences, I was like these three women—willing to do whatever it took to get what we wanted, to get what we believed in. For Lynn, it was redemption. For Frankie, it was freedom and security. For Raina, I think it was a way to fill the hole in her heart from having been given up as an infant so many years ago. For me, my erroneous belief was that I had the power and ability to create security and comfort for those I loved, that by my hand Frankie and Ryan would be all right—whatever and wherever that might be—after my death, they would find a place to call home. I was wrong. I believed in myself as the answer to their needs, a lowly minister's wife with no spiritual foundation, when I should have believed in something, or someone, else.

But just as Seamus had said to Frankie, we are neither all

good nor all bad, we all did the best we could, even if you could argue the end didn't justify the means. The good news was that, although Lynn had made some monstrously tragic errors, and she would likely never find total redemption, she was at least starting to look in the mirror. There was hope, then, for the other two—Raina and Frankie—as time was on their side.

I did not know if there was still hope for me.

Lynn reached into the back pocket of her jeans and unfolded the photo of Frankie and me. I didn't know she'd taken it from Ryan and at first I was incensed that she had. But I watched her touch Frankie in the photo gently, lovingly, and I quickly changed my mind.

I am going to find your daughter, Raina. And then Insha'Allah, I will find you. These long, thirty years are over.

With more love than you will ever know,

Mom

She slipped the journal and my ponytail back into her backpack, blew her nose, and asked what could have been a rhetorical question to anyone or everyone.

"Have you ever felt you were saying goodbye to the only thing that mattered in your life? And that you're about to take a giant leap of faith into the unknown, not knowing where you're going or how you'll make it?"

Mark and Nick shook their heads. Greg did not turn around. But Marisa looked in the rearview mirror and laughed. It was a hearty laugh, the kind that warms you like a cup of hot chocolate. The kind that makes you feel like there really are new horizons in your future.

"You've never been a mother," Marisa said. "Have you!"

34 Chapter Thirty-Four

Frankie lay stretched out beneath the sun on our back deck, bundled against the cold desert morning in one of my sweatshirts, my sweatpants, and a knit ski cap. Mrs. Farley had given Frankie the quilt she'd finished sewing, and Frankie had it wrapped around herself. Jack sat on the deck too, drinking coffee and working on his laptop. The gravel on the driveway crunched beneath approaching tires.

Tom came around the corner of the deck. "Good morning," he said, but his expression didn't suggest anything was good. The two men shook hands, and Jack offered Tom a cup of coffee, but he declined.

He walked over to Frankie and sat cross-legged on the deck beside her. She tightened the quilt around her body. He placed his hand on her shoulder.

"Hi, Frankie." He waited for a reply from her, but she offered nothing. "We got some news. About Ryan."

Frankie sat up, shook her head, and covered her ears with her hands the way a toddler would. Then she stood quickly and threw off the quilt and started to run down the back steps toward the river. "No! I know what you're going to say and I don't want to hear it. You're going to say he's dead, but you're wrong."

She ran into the river, fully clothed and in her stocking feet. The sun reflected off the water's ripples, and she stood still as a boulder, the knee-high river dividing its course around her legs. Jack and Tom called and ran after her, warning her to get out of the water before it swept her away.

She ignored them, and began to walk downstream, slipping on the uneven, rocky bottom. The men yelled at her again. As she turned around, she lost her balance and fell into the river. I tried to shout at her too. All I could see was her face under the water and the river carrying her body away.

But she regained her footing and stood up, drenched. She picked her way over to the bank. Once there, she kept on walking downstream for ten, maybe fifteen, minutes through sage and scrub brush.

At last she crouched down beside a fallen branch, broke off some small twigs, and tossed them, one by one, into the water. They floated downstream. She broke off more twigs and repeated the process, then a clump of pine needles, then a larger branch. Next she threw a fistful of pebbles, each toss becoming more forceful, until she found a rock the size of her head, which she struggled to lift and which created a big splash. She kept going, finding larger and larger rocks, until they were too big to lift. She rolled a couple into the water, practically falling in after them, and then sat down on a bed of needles and cried.

Tom and Jack stood at a healthy distance watching her.

She spent over an hour in that spot, hardly moving. When a spider crawled onto her hand, she brushed it off. When a squirrel came closer to investigate, she ignored it. Whenever Jack or Tom called her name, she looked away. The river curved about fifty yards ahead, and from there you couldn't see where it went, like life itself, but you could hear the thunder of an unseen waterfall, a rush that could either agitate or calm you, depending on your state of mind.

I could not tell what the waterfall was doing for her. I couldn't save her from her own private hell any more than I could make the river change directions. I thought back to Lynn's question of Ryan, about whether he ever wondered why bad things happened to him, and I couldn't help but wonder why Frankie, at her young age, had been forced to face so much ugliness and death. I also thought back to John Muir's quote in Talkeetna, and still couldn't quite understand how he thought that, by walking with nature, children could find death stingless and beautiful. Frankie was weighted by anything *but* beauty.

It was not long until she began to shiver uncontrollably. She stood and turned toward the men. Jack took this as a sign of welcome, and he rushed along the riverbank to wrap the quilt around her. The three slowly walked back to our cabin together.

"I never got to say good-bye to Beth," she said. "And now

I haven't said good-bye to Ryan."

"I never said good-bye to Ryan, either," Tom said. "And I don't know how I'll ever forgive myself for that. But look at me, Frankie."

She stopped and turned.

"We both need to forgive ourselves. And, in time, we need to let go."

That evening, after taking a hot shower and a long nap, and after the sun had slipped below the horizon and the mountains were bathed in a pinkish gray dusk, Frankie stepped into some of Jessie's clothes and, holding my Koran to her chest, followed the scent of tomatoes and cayenne into the kitchen. A pot of chili simmered on the stove, releasing steamy comfort into the air. She picked up a small knife from the cutting board and put it in her back pocket. Then she opened our squeaky screen door and went outside.

"There you are, Kitten." Tom and Jack were standing on the driveway in the dark. "I'm glad you woke up before Tom left."

She nodded, shrugged, looked at her bare feet.

"There's a bit of good news for you," Tom said. I could see a tentative smile on his face now in the dim light, which triggered an anticipatory smile on her face, a look of curiosity. It had been three and a half long weeks since Frankie had flown to Portland, and since Lynn and Ryan had flown to Anchorage, and Frankie was finally about to hear what I'd been waiting for all this time.

"There's a climber who wants to meet you. Someone who

was with Ryan. Her name's Lynn, and she'll be contacting you soon."

It gave me goose bumps. The good kind.

"Meet me? Why me?"

"I don't know the details. All I know is she said Ryan told her all about you. She has a keepsake for you, something from Beth, she said. And she thinks the two of you may have some things in common."

"Oh." Frankie nodded and shrugged again. "Okay."

I tried to imagine what that meeting might look like. I tried to imagine the expression on Lynn's face—sorrowful, but kind. And on Frankie's—uncertain and hopeful.

After Tom left, Jack went inside to finish making dinner. Frankie stayed outside, pulling the knife from her back pocket when she heard the screen door slam. She looked up at the sky.

One summer a few years back, when Ryan and I still lived in the Chicago suburbs and Raina was in trouble with the law, Frankie spent a lot of time with us. We'd eat ice cream cones and catch lightning bugs, and sometimes we'd go camping up in Wisconsin and stay up late to watch the stars move across the sky. I told her my theory that each star represented the soul of a dead person, and that it twinkled to communicate with loved ones back on earth. The more twinkling you saw, the more people in heaven there were who loved you. We sat on the shore of a northern lake counting all the twinkling stars.

The high desert in Oregon is one of the best places to study the night sky: crisp air, high altitude, no big city lights.

It was one of the reasons I needed to move back there when I knew the cancer had won. The closer death came, the more I wondered about heaven, and at one point I decided I'd better find heaven on earth just in case there wasn't really one in the afterlife. For me, the high desert sky was at least one level of heaven, maybe the closest I'd ever get.

Frankie stood on the driveway beneath the stars, feet planted like the roots of a young ponderosa. She held the tip of the knife to her neck. I sat on my balcony watching her, now too overcome with fatigue and remorse to worry. I pictured her scratching the knife along her neck: long, thin vertical strokes parallel to one another and evenly spaced—thirteen of them, one for every year of her life thus far—reminding me of an Elizabethan collar. I envisioned the blood surfacing as she threw her head back, the bloodlines stretching down the skin of her neck where a silver locket had once hung, and where my gold cross would soon hang. The blood would be a clear indication that she was still very much alive.

But she did not cut herself. She withdrew the knife without making a single pinprick of blood. Tom had said they both needed to forgive and let go; perhaps she was ready for that now, ready to push through to a new life like a crocus slowly pushing through the spring soil.

I watched the constellations and star clusters and lonely, single stars overhead with Frankie, and oddly I no longer felt so alone. Or as desperate as I had felt for the past several months.

I no longer felt like I was in hell; maybe it was because my hope for her future had been renewed. Or maybe I had reached bottom, had learned the lessons I needed to learn in my afterlife journey. Just as I'd lain in a blackened purgatory after my death until I gave in and admitted defeat, I now no longer felt the need to follow Frankie. I could finally surrender. I could finally let her go.

And while I didn't know for sure, I somehow felt a sort of faith blossoming—faith in something I couldn't even name, and also faith that I'd be reunited with Ryan. I felt the way I used to feel at the movies with him, sitting in the dark and watching the scenes unfold and knowing everything would work out in the end because, in Hollywood, it always did.

Frankie put the knife into her back pocket and inhaled the clear mountain air as the fragrance of chili and the tinkling sounds of silverware emanated from inside the cabin. She closed her eyes and lifted her lovely, exotic face to the sky, and I hoped when she opened her eyes she would see that a brand new star was twinkling for her.

Acknowledgements

It may sound cliché, but writing a novel and sending it out into the world is a lot like climbing a mountain. It requires research and planning, training, fortitude and commitment, strong support from family and friends as well as technical experts, an unanticipated amount of introspection, and a good deal of luck. It's also dependent upon your motive for the adventure in the first place, your ability to forge a path to the top, your willingness to get up every time you fall and slide backward, keen awareness of the risks you're undertaking, and your innate ability to answer the question *What Next?* once your project is completed, whether or not it was successful—however you choose to define success.

Regarding my sherpas and other support team members, I'll start by saying I'm deeply thankful to the readers who have affirmed, questioned, and critiqued me throughout this long, arduous hike: Jo Ann Heydron, Bharti Kirchner, Chris Mason, Sue Moseley, Barbara Pettersen, Jack Spiese, and Sheri

Weisenberg. Many thanks, from a larger perspective, to those in the writing community who have supported me in many ways: Kim Barnes, Claire Davis, Tammy Dietz, Jack Driscoll, Molly Gloss, Kake Huck, Craig Lesley, David Long, Linda Weiford, Kirsteen Wolf. I'm also grateful to Ingrid Emerick, Collene Funk and Glenys Loewen-Thomas for their editing prowess, Laura Paslay for her cover art, and Gerri Russell and her team at Visual Quill for all their technical production assistance.

Special appreciation goes out to those who helped with the technical components of this climb: Beckie Elgin, Joe Horiskey, Phil Klahn, John Lyle, Andy Saxby, Missy Smothers, and Jago Trasler.

And finally, loving gratitude to all those friends and family members who saw my dream alongside me, listened to me whine and worry, and cheered me through the adventure—especially to John, Dylan, Forrest, and Harrison, who've inspired me in countless ways.

ABOUT THE AUTHOR

G. Elizabeth Kretchmer holds an MFA in Writing from Pacific University. Her short fiction, essays, and freelance work has appeared in The New York Times, High Desert Journal, Silk Road Review, and other publications. She has three adopted sons and lives in the heavenly Pacific Northwest with her husband. You can visit her website at www.gekretchmer.com.

CPSIA information can be obtained
at www.ICGtesting.com
Printed in the USA
FSOW01n1018250914
3153FS